DANCE WITH DESTINY BOOGIE TO OBLIVION

Dance with Destiny, Boogie to Oblivion

Published by: Melis Publishing Company LLC
Delray Beach, FL 33484
E-mail: mamamelisiandme8151@gmail.com
Website: www.mamamelisiandme.com

ISBN 978-0-9897157-1-3 (paperback)
978-0-9897157-2-0 (ebook)

Printed in the United States of America.

Book & cover design by Darlene and Dan Swanson of Van-garde Imagery, Inc.

DANCE WITH DESTINY BOOGIE TO OBLIVION

By Charles Hardy Kelley

For Audrey, my patient muse.

Thank you, Jackie, for bringing this book to print.

I could not have done this writing
so happily without my lap-cat,
Amy to encourage me.

Prologue

Ted paused at the crest of the pass to scan the threatening sky. Storms develop quickly at this altitude in the Himalayas, even in late spring. He was more than halfway from the base camp to the nomadic settlement he was studying for his sociology fieldwork. John Tobin, his study partner, developed the severe fatigue and nausea of altitude sickness early on the trail. Tshering, their Bhutanese yak-herder guide, assured him that it was a short run on a clear trail from the crest to the settlement. Tshering then supported John on the trip down to the base.

Ted took another look at the sky, shrugged, and resumed his hike at a faster pace, until the trail branched. Tshering had not mentioned this. Ted selected the gentler incline as the probable common pathway. It veered to the left and divided again. The clouds darkened. A light rain spattered his face. He trotted. It rained in earnest, limiting his view, just as the trail filled with runoff that branched into numerous rivulets. A chill wind shifted to the northeast, off the glacier-laden peaks. The temperature dropped precipitously and the rain became large wet flakes. Shelter became imperative.

As the trail disappeared beneath the snow, he turned uphill, aiming for a rocky escarpment. Despite the exertion, he shivered in his wet clothes. The force of the wind diminished, revealing a bluff that loomed out of the thickening snow. He paralleled its face and searched for a haven. Fissure after fissure, overhang after overhang proved too shallow or drifted with snow. The cold was intense, the snow like cornflakes. His hands and feet lost feeling. The cold seeped into his bones. Another cleft, this one deeper and dry. Two bends and it opened into a larger chamber indistinct in the gloom. He shrugged his backpack to the floor, clumsily retrieved his flashlight and illuminated a cave. His hand could not reach the roof. The tunnel angled again a dozen feet back. Perfect. He unrolled his sleeping bag and used a ground cloth to cover the entrance and block the wind. He fixed the tarp with stones and packed snow. The wind blocked, he relaxed his frantic efforts and turned back to the cave. Suddenly, he couldn't move. His head throbbed. Without words, he sensed a desperate message.

"Help!" Ted pulled the tarp aside and stood at the entrance. A beacon in his mind blazed toward the right. He could not resist. He walked into the whiteout with his right hand grazing the wall for reassurance. It was a suicidal illusion but he could not stop. He stumbled over a soft ridge in the snow. The throbbing ceased. He reached into the drift and straining with both arms pulled out an inert body. Caught between sweating and freezing, he dragged the body, following the wall for guidance. Time lost meaning. Had he passed the cave? Was he headed right? Should he be touching with right hand or left? He paused to suppress his panic.

He stepped on the tarp. Ted pulled the body inside and replaced the tarp with fumbling hands. He took the flashlight from his pocket. A dim red glow told him he had left it on and drained the batteries. He half carried the heavy form back to the sleeping bag. A frightening thought struck him. Was this person dead? He could not hear a breath. He took a wrist but felt no pulse. He pulled up the sodden parka and under tunic to feel for a heartbeat.

It was a woman!

He put his ear to her chest and heard a faint lub-dub. She lived. Ted removed her wet clothing and rolled her into the sleeping bag. His numbed hands fumbled with his boots. He removed all his clothing, found dry long johns in his pack and donned them. Exhausted and shivering, he climbed into the sleeping bag and gradually worked the zipper closed. The woman was ice cold. Her undoubted hypothermia threatened her life and perhaps his as well. He wrapped her in his arms and held her close. Her cold flesh worsened his shivering but gradually they warmed each other. He slept.

Her struggles awakened him. The woman tried to exit the neck hole, climbing on him and pushing down on his shoulders. Despite her small stature and recent hypothermia, Ted had to exert a major effort to subdue her. She ceased struggling and disengaged herself. He moved apart several inches.

"I am Ted. Who are you?"

Silence. "Me Ted."

"*Kto eto*?" Russian! He placed her hand on his chest. "*Yah* Ted." She understood his rudimentary introduction. She placed his hand on her chest. "Brisa." Brisa took both his hands and held them. Minutes passed. He waited, idly recalling his hike in rain and snow, sensing her plea for help, finding her and bringing her to the cave. He could feel her panic subsiding. She turned over, snuggled close, pulled his arm across her shoulder and slept again. Feeling protective and warm, he also slept.

Ted awoke warm, refreshed and hungry. He reached an arm out to his pack and retrieved his emergency rations. Brisa stirred. They sat up in dim light and shared rice, cheese and onions. Ted unzipped the bag, groped his way to the entrance and opened a flap of the tarp at the top. Snow had drifted more than halfway over the entrance. Heavy flakes still swirled in the air. Brisa stood beside him in the near dark. Her head was below his chin level. Her hair did not reach her shoulders. He could not make out her features in the dim light.

The woman walked farther back in the cave and relieved herself, then reentered the sleeping bag. He groped his way to the back and followed her example. He shivered as he struggled to close the zipper. She spoke in a warm tone and pulled him nearer. Muttering softly, she unbuttoned his long johns, removed them and snuggled up. Her warmth enveloped him. A flood of passion surged through him. She responded and held him tighter, their passions merging.

They made love with a fire that he had never known and with a profound sharing that made him feel he knew the depths of her soul. Furthermore, he felt the grandeur of the mountains; the boundless expanse of the plains; the sharp, clean bite of the winter wind; and the fresh smell of the luxuriant springtime grasses. He felt the camaraderie of close-knit herders, the laughter of simple pleasures at festive times. He saw these ways stretching back through time. He saw her parents and felt the pangs of loss. He saw young people playing and knew that she was young. There was no other lover in her memories.

He knew that she, in turn, saw his memories of this expedition to the mountains. Their streams of consciousness were one.

They lay together sharing tenderness, joy, satisfaction and renewed desire. They walked through each other's memories in a misty dream that shrouded details but let their love blaze through and weld their bonds.

They dozed and woke and loved again and dozed.

Rough hairy hands tore Ted from the sleeping bag and flung him against the wall. A strong musky odor filled the cave. He saw a huge stooping figure fill the cave mouth and exit with Brisa in the sleeping bag.

Ted struggled to the entrance on hands and knees, then out into the still falling snow. A broad path of huge, widely-spaced footprints led down the hill. He broke through the deep snow between the footprints for fifty feet before the bitter cold told him that he could not follow. He returned to the cave, shivering and raging.

He pulled on his long johns, dry socks, still wet outer clothing and boots. Ramming the tarp into his pack, he ran after the kidnapper, laboring through drifts, falling frequently. Over and over he screamed, "Brisa!" There was no answer. The snow deadened all sound, blinded him and covered the trail.

His furious pace at this altitude told on him. His breathing became gasping. He fell more often and took longer to rise. A jarring collision with a rock ended his pursuit. He lay sobbing, "Brisa," unable to rise. The cold penetrated his rage. He pulled the tarpaulin about himself, put his feet in the pack and gave in to unconsciousness. The snow banked over him.

Refuge

Two pairs of footprints, one set large and one set small, traversed the desert landscape. Brandon followed his mother's tracks across the dry wash, nimbly skipping over tumbled rocks and brush into the secure footsteps she had made. He shared Brisa's excitement as she strode briskly up the slope and across the sandstone bench to its terminus in a small bluff. There she sat on her heels, gazing out across the rugged desert vista with its rocky foothills carved by twisting gulches and jagged outcroppings. In the distance the foothills stair-stepped to bare brown mountains that turned to green only at the higher elevations. As Brandon approached, he felt the aura of excitement about her and shared the electric tensions in her body that said this was the place. After weeks of wandering and searching, they would settle here.

To six-year-old Brandon it had started as an adventure when his mother awakened him early one morning at the secluded home in the forested hills and said that they must leave quickly. Sorting their possessions and packing the truck took little time for they had a Spartan lifestyle. Brandon sensed his mother's final goodbye to a home they had come to love because it was so rich and vibrant with life. Their quick flight brought them to this sere and desolate land. Beneath its harsh appearance, Brandon could feel a more patient pulse of life – the speculative gaze of eyes watching from the shade; the slow circling of a bird of prey; the occasional darting of a small rodent between shelters; and the plodding passage of a tortoise. He was a non-threatening transient in their realm, not a factor in their daily lives. The boy absorbed his surroundings with their kaleidoscope of new sensations while dutifully following his mother's quest.

Brandon approached his mother and squatted beside her, next to the backpack she had set on the ground. Her hand touched his arm as her gaze scanned the area for washes, trails, and a possible access road for their four-wheel drive pickup. He knew from the light touch on his arm, her relaxed figure, and the satisfied expression on her face that this spot met her criteria. Leaning his head against Brisa's arm, her son could sense her vision for this austere forbidding site, a vision transforming it into their own friendly and comfortable home.

The next few weeks entailed almost daily trips to Claymore to determine ownership, arrange terms for a lease through the local agent for the distant owner, and then stock up on supplies for their homestead. Brandon kept close to his mother's side saying nothing, but soaking up the myriad new sensations and variety of human expressions on his first real visit to a town. The people they met were very vocal using long convoluted sentences with words that were new to him. Often their facial expressions, gestures and body postures were completely at variance with their physical clues: their muscle tensions snapped spasmodically so that Brandon could read nothing at all. After his mother had finished a long conversation about business or supplies, he found himself asking, "Mommy, what did that person mean when he said, 'You're getting a good deal on this, ma'am,' but the rest of his expression said you weren't?"

"Later," she would say, "when we're alone."

There seemed to be grudging admiration all around at his mother's competence when she procured her supplies and loaded the truck. Brisa was below medium height, compact and sturdy. She selected quality tools, shouldered them effortlessly, and packed them securely. She was polite, but knowledgeable and definite. As the days wore on, Brandon noticed that words and expressions of the townspeople began to complement one another. Pretense was wasted on his matter-of-fact mother. People were not openly inquisitive in Claymore and they soon accepted that Brisa would do whatever she did competently. Desert rats were not uncommon. She was just a new variation.

They met several of the others and Brandon liked them immediately. They had few words and no subtleties. Hap was a Vietnam veteran, mired in the sadness of some repressed remorse. He lived in a cave about five miles out of town, his life reduced to bare essentials. After a few waves as they drove past, he signaled them to stop one evening.

"Dinner?" he invited.

"Thank you," Brisa responded without hesitation.

They entered his cave silently. The smell of beans and salt pork was in the air. Hap put several tortillas in a Dutch oven by the fire. Carved sandstone formed their table and benches. Primitive carvings adorned the walls – a coyote, a roadrunner, a snake, and an eagle. He served their meal in tin plates with hot tortillas in the middle of the table. They ate in a companionable silence, sharing the food and the mood of their new acquaintance.

Hap broke the silence. "Lonely out there and barren. Can't hide from others. Can't hide from yourself." It was obvious that he had tried to hide and failed. He wanted to share what he had learned.

Brisa replied, "We do not hide. We will become part of this land, seen but not noticed. We wish to be among friends, but never discussed except among friends. We do not disturb the land or its dwellers. We share. We help. We do not intrude."

Hap nodded affirmatively at her terse statement, but did not speak.

They ate in silence again. A sense of calm and family enveloped them. Hap served refreshments in front of the cave and they sipped quietly as the constellations emerged above. Brandon traced the familiar patterns that his mother had shown him.

"We shall have water," said Brisa. "Come visit soon."

"I'll keep it in mind," said Hap. He collected the tin cups, went into the cave and extinguished his light. The visit was over.

Brisa drove back carefully to their camp, defining the road by one more passage through the ruts.

Brisa took her pick and scribed the dimensions of an entrance on the face of the sandstone butte, thirty feet above the base. Sculpted steps soon led up the face and forceful blows of her mattock quickly hollowed the entrance. Brandon enjoyed these days as his indefatigable mother tunneled deeper into the sandstone, carving a chamber while the boy gathered the debris and carried it into the wash below. He could dimly see her vision of a tunnel to a large cave with a well inside and reflected light providing luminance to this cool and moist refuge from the desert sun… but it was slow and tedious work.

Daybreak in the desert was Brandon's favorite time. He would awaken expectantly in the hush before dawn anticipating the excitement soon to come. At first light he would head for the vantage point on top of the bluff. The soft light and cool air encouraged the nocturnal animals to scurry about for their last activity before sheltering from the heat of the day. Diurnal life started noisily and exuberantly with birds stirring, vocalizing and taking to wing. Soon the reptiles would seek the sunlight to warm and animate them.

This time of day aroused ambivalent feelings in Brandon. There was joy at the start of a new day; pleasure in the cool air, growing light, and the sun rising over the distant hills; and a sense of stirrings, beginnings, and quickening to face the next round of challenges. There was also an oppressive sense of the coming excess of those qualities now quickening life – light, heat, and the warm breeze.

Of all the things his mother taught him, Brandon liked best the merging of his self with that of other creatures about him. Through them, he could experience heightened awareness of the senses he had – seeing, touch, smell, hearing, taste, electrical tensions – and even be aware of sensations for which he had no name. His favorite spot was atop a small prominence near the edge of the bluff. He would sit cross-legged, close his eyes, relax and retreat to his inner self by cutting off all external stimuli. Then slowly his inner self would expand and pick up faint murmurings of sensation all about him – the rustle of the grasses in the wind, the heightened awareness of a potential small meal in the offing, the rattle of sand particles across a rock surface, the slow intake and exhale of breath of a resting creature, the light tensions in a soaring bird.

Focusing on muscle tensions of the bird, Brandon gradually felt an increasing awareness of the exhilaration of soaring, the wind rushing across his feathers, the imperceptible trimming of wings to the wind to guide the flight path. Soon he could see the panorama of sand, rock and washes flowing past his gaze. A tension in his being told him that he was waiting for a signal. It came – a flash of movement against the stationary background. Immediately his soaring configuration put him into a steep glide and then a dive. With talons outstretched he flashed across at ground level, but shrill cries had his prey dive into a hole. Unsuccessful this time, the hawk rose swiftly to the heights again to resume his patrol. Brandon felt the quick flash of disappointment fade as the hunting vigil was resumed. After several minutes of enjoyment of the sensations of flight, the complexity of his domain, and the emotions of the bird of prey, Brandon withdrew his inner self to his body on the promontory. Gradually, the sensations of his body became dominant.

He opened his eyes and to his surprise saw a weathered coppery face not five feet away. Sitting on crossed legs, features composed, eyes closed and back erect was a gray-headed man. A white band circled his head. His hair hung below his shoulders in a thick braid. A loose-fitting white shirt, belted at the waist, hung over a pair of white cotton trousers. Handmade moccasins shod his feet. His entirely relaxed posture conveyed the impression of patient attendance and proffered companionship.

The Indian's eyes opened slowly. He looked at Brandon, pointed a finger at his own chest and said, "Cristo Lopez: Dreams with Manitou."

Brandon could perceive Cristo's pale blue aura of serenity that corresponded with his gentleness, curiosity and a deep undercurrent of sadness. After a few silent minutes the Indian spoke. "I am shaman, keeper of tribal lore. Welcome to my world."

"Thank you," said Brandon. He gestured toward the cave. "I live here with Mother. We will grow flowers. I watch animals." People other than his mother require some words to understand thoughts. They apparently had difficulty in reading body language.

Cristo listened to the words attentively and nodded. Cristo's speech became sparser and his body language became almost grotesque in emphasis. Brandon absorbed Cristo's meaning through all of his senses, combining words, postures, gestures, aura and electrical fields into a totally comprehensible picture. Cristo's story was this: "My people have long been here, tilling the land, grazing livestock and hunting. There is one spirit that pervades all things. We are part of this world, imbued with the same spirit. Each part of the world has a role to play and must play it in harmony with all others or disaster results. Each part feels what other parts feel. Each gains or loses as the sum total gains or loses. The tribal shaman carries this message, that we are alone in Manitou. The message is carried in songs and stories, taught to the children and repeated by adults in ceremonies. We cannot destroy any part of our world without sacrificing some part of ourselves."

"Yet the old faith is losing. Bit by bit we see the land destroyed by others for mines, farms and pasture. The animals are shot for sport or exterminated as pests. And our children learn these ways in government schools – then sell themselves, the land and all living creatures on it for television sets and automobiles. No wonder we are dying as a people when we trade our birthright, our very souls, for trinkets.

"The voice of Manitou is fainter in the land and soon may cease. Yet now I hear him through you and my faith is reviving. Who are you to listen to Manitou and bring his voice clearer to me? Who are you to make my spirit soar yet bring my heart to grieve for my people, for all people, for all that Manitou imbues with being? Alas, you are too young to know. But we shall wait here, carrying a new hope in our hearts. I shall prepare my people for your message. In a time of need but call my name 'Dreams With Manitou,' I will respond."

Brandon murmured the name "Dreams With Manitou" and envisioned the shaman as the man of vision who made dreams into reality – a steadfast warrior who gathered the strands of timeworn ancient lore of his people into a net, which he could cast into the future to capture their dream. The boy placed his hands into those of the shaman and said, "I shall not forget you, 'Dreams With Manitou.' You know my world also. If you call, I will come."

They sat in silence seeing the shaman's dream of the world in harmony; all life respecting the role of others; all nature contributing to the rhythm and harmony derived from their mutual source in creation. The broader concepts were new to Brandon, but he could understand the sense of pulsation and life in all of nature that he felt. In this time of reverie, the visions of 'Dreams With Manitou' became part of Brandon's vision, although he could not yet comprehend its entirety.

They became aware that Brandon's mother Brisa was standing there. She spoke to the shaman. "He is too young, shaman. Let him grow in harmony with nature. You could bring danger to him." The shaman gave her an understanding look for her maternal concern. He replied earnestly, "He is part of my world. No one outside shall know or harm him. He has reawakened in me my people's past in full harmony with all life. Perhaps he will be the instrument to restore our song in time to come. My faith is revived. I am a soul reborn in ways that are old and derided, yet forever true. Through your son one soul at least is saved. I shall bring this Word to my people. We shall not let it be forgotten again."

Brandon gradually reawakened to his surroundings and the unexpected company discussing him. He spoke. "I have sensed this man before, Mother. He is a friend."

She nodded. "We cannot survive without friends. You are welcome, shaman."

He arose, nodded, and quietly said, "Adios," and walked down the trail into the wash and out of sight.

Brandon felt the warmth of recognition of a new friend in his small world of acquaintances; a friend could spell danger to their refuge. They needed friends now. The long-term dangers would have to wait their time.

Desert Home

Brandon stood at the mouth of the cave and gazed across the wash to the distant mountains. The setting sun lighted the brown higher slopes while evening purple hazed the lower slopes and desert. All was quiet at this transition time from the day's heat to the evening's comparative coolness. He shifted the large basket of sandstone to his outer shoulder and walked easily down the path they had improved to steps on the face of the butte. Crossing the wash, he unburdened himself into a deep trench cut into the floor of the wash by cloudburst waters. His mother wished to minimize their impact on the environment and hide any evidence of the extent of their excavations. Later they would add boulders and sand from the bed of the wash to cover the excavated sandstone. Rid of his last load for the day, Brandon skipped nimbly up the path to meet his mother at the cave mouth.

Brisa had removed her work clothes, facemask, goggles and hat. With washcloth and water from a pail, she was removing the heavy layer of dust from face and body. She was tired and enjoying the cooling effect of her minimal bath. Brandon stripped off his clothes and began to bathe himself. Obviously proud of her sturdy son who was such a willing and cheerful helper, Brisa looked lovingly at him and smiled.

"This is far enough, Brandon. Tomorrow we dig down to our water level. With water we can work wonders."

Brandon sat next to Brisa and let the desert air dry him as he joined her vision of a cave with its own water supply from a small aquifer; a shaft to the butte top for sunlight and air; and a small pool for bathing and fish. Hazily pictured were other plants and flowers along the walls, on the floor and hanging from ceiling hooks. A sense of humidity accompanied her vision, and a sense of cool dampness absent from the desert environs. It felt like a glade in their old forest home, a transplanted cool retreat. The vision faded as his mother rose to dry herself. Brandon sat there, holding on to this evanescent vision, willing it to be real someday soon. Brisa called him in to sleep, for another day of arduous tunneling lay before them.

The next morning Brisa took Brandon to the top of the butte for a more accurate survey of their proposed water supply. The shaman, Dreams With Manitou, was there as usual at Brandon's favorite promontory, waiting for their customary commune with life about them. They nodded silent greetings. Brisa beckoned them to follow her. She had them sit in a close circle holding hands. All three relaxed, diminishing most internal and external sensory inputs but holding on to one, which seemed gently to stretch the body from the soles of the feet to the top of the head. All the tissues, muscles and bones participated in this stretching, generating internal electrical fields as the body resisted the elongation.

Releasing one of Brandon's hands, Brisa walked the trio slowly across the flat top of the butte. They could feel the reactive field increasing until it seemed almost a compressive force holding their bodies together against this unknown expansive power. Brisa walked in a purposeful pattern until finally she stopped at the point of peak intensity.

"This is the apex of our reservoir," she stated. She released their hands and the intensity diminished until the force was almost reduced to a memory. She bent down and gathered several stones into a marker. Walking alone now she erected markers of various sizes in an acute triangular pattern, which had its wide end towards the mountains. "This is the pool. These rocks show depths. There is enough water. Now we must dig down and drill over to it."

Under her direction Brandon and the shaman established markers at the edge of the bluff and dropped weighted lines down the face. The length of each line was determined by the size of its corresponding stone marker. In this way she laid out a three-dimensional outline of the aquifer.

Taking their hands again, Brisa started at each marker and walked five paces directly away from the reservoir. Her companions realized that they were sensing the decrease in the force filed. Brandon and the shaman walked back in the direction of the aquifer boundary markers. Now Brandon could associate the increasing compressive stress in his body with his approach to the water supply. The shaman obviously felt nothing. Brandon took his hand and immediately the man's expression changed. He said to Brandon, "You are water dowsers. Once my people were, the legends say. Now all is forgotten. I must learn from you." Holding hands they walked erratically like children laughing softly as they traced the irregularities of the reservoir boundary. A new sense had been awakened in them. It was a new bond with the land that talks to all who will listen. When their light-headedness passed, they noticed that Brisa had gone back to the cave to continue the excavation. Brandon dropped the shaman's hand and ran over to the path down the butte face. When he looked back, he could see the shaman walking back and forth across the aquifer boundary, a look of intense concentration on his face. He wanted the old ways to return, to be reunited with his land and with the ways of his forefathers.

Brisa had laid out lines and arrows on the tunnel walls, floor and ceiling to guide her further excavations. Brandon was a little confused by the shifting alternatives in her mind as she considered the water supply relative location, her possible room dimensions and the need for an airshaft and water flow. Satisfied at last, she put on work clothes, took up her pick mattock and began to widen the tunnel. Once more Brandon gathered the debris, loaded his basket and carried the debris out to the wash. The loads seemed to grow lighter as the room took shape.

They extended the entrance passage seven feet and then widened it another four feet to the left to make it eight feet wide. This stone face, eight feet wide by six feet high, Brisa now extended forward. Brandon carried endless baskets of debris. As days blended into weeks, the enormity of the project became evident to him when he compared their progress of the vision of the cave that his mother had given him. Sometimes in the evenings he felt like crying for weariness and dread of the long job ahead. But he didn't cry, because he could sense his mother's greater exhaustion and knew that she was building this home for him.

One morning he awoke feeling the same weariness that he had carried to bed. He lay there next to his mother, not wanting to rise, not wanting to wake her, not wanting the day to start. His mother stirred. Brandon lay perfectly still, hoping that she would slip into sleep again. Instead she rolled over, smiled at him and said, "Brandon. Wake up. No work today. Let's have some fun."

Her sudden lightheartedness flooded over him. He hugged her to him as hard as he could. "Oh, mama! Could we? I just want to run around and see everything and smell everything and let the whole world talk to me. I'm so tired of—" He caught himself and looked apologetically at her, for she so wanted to finish their house and enjoy flowers about her.

Brisa understood and hugged him back. "I have been too anxious to dig in and hide. We must enjoy life, too. We will slow down to have fun now. I cannot tie you up in my anxieties. Let us relax."

Brandon felt closer than usual to his mother as they ate a leisurely breakfast, cleaned up and then walked to the top of the butte. The fall weather was beautiful with just a slight nip to the air. The morning sun was stirring all the creatures. Brandon flew with the hawks, ran with the rabbits and hopped with the kangaroo rats. His mother was with him every bit of the way, sharing his feelings as well as those of the birds and animals. At last they rose and skipped up the path like two kids on holiday. They explored new paths, climbed new hills and gazed across their land from the summits. Physically tired and hungry but refreshed, they headed back towards home.

A lone figure walked on their butte tracing out the boundaries of their aquifer. It was the shaman trying to awaken in himself the dowsing power that he had experienced with Brisa and Brandon. "I cannot," he said when they approached. "The lore of the elders is only words to me now. I cannot feel what they felt. I cannot become one with the land."

They shared his sense of loss at being cut off from the circle of the spirit that once guided the lives of his forebears. The brief glimpse of what should be, shared briefly with these two newcomers, only heightened his feeling of loss because what had only been words from the past were now sensations he could not call forth again. They took his hands between them and trod the boundaries again, overlapping his unconscious rejection to let him feel the water in the depths of the earth. Tears coursed down his face. "I cry," he said at last, "for what my people used to be and what we might have been. But now we have accepted the role thrust upon us, outcasts in our own land. We sell our land for waste dumps and mines. We think ourselves wily when we pander to lonely gamblers in our reservation bingo clubs, taking their meager paychecks while the government takes our manhood. I cry for myself that I cannot call my people back to their birthright, to be again brothers of all life and not poor imitations of despoilers who subjugate us."

Brisa grasped his arm for emphasis. "You have not lost your ability to sense water, shaman. You have merely forgotten the way. Now you know what to seek. Open your spirit to the world about you and you will rejoin the circle again. If we can help you, we will."

He searched her face with his moist eyes, looking for confirmation for his new hope. "Perhaps you can help me. There are several men of my tribe who listen to my words, who want to hope, but there are no deeds to match my tales and so they despair. We need a more abundant water supply. Will you help us find it?"

Brisa was moved by the shaman's words, his expression and his posture of dejection. She was also concerned about any notoriety that help to him could bring, notoriety that would negate their attempt to be inconspicuous. She weighed their needs and their danger, then responded, "We will help. You must also help us. Others must not hear of what we do."

"I say it. No one will know. My people may have lost their way. They have not lost their pride. We keep our word."

The next day the shaman was waiting on the butte top when they came up. He was sitting quietly, watching the desert awaken. Without forcing himself, he was letting the spirit of the land seep into his soul. He did not know what it would mean, but he no longer wanted to be a stranger in his own land. They could feel the peace in his body as they approached.

Dreams With Manitou said, "Last night I sat on a hilltop and smoked the seed of dreams. As though a dam had burst, I felt all impurities and all doubts wash from my soul. A great voice spoke to me, but I heard no words. I saw the desert bloom. I saw my brothers, the deer, the wolves, the cougars, the eagles, in great numbers. They looked at me with hope in their eyes; hope that their roles in life would return, that they would live their destinies. I felt my soul expand to encompass the world. Then it contracted to a point again and the desert stared at me with blank and lifeless eyes. Last night I dreamed with Manitou. Today my soul is small and frightened. I am the desert plant at the first raindrop. I want to bloom and seed the world, but I am afraid that I will merely open wide to be seared by the noonday sun. Yet I must trust the first raindrop, for that is my destiny. If I do not trust, I shall wither and die in my self-doubts. You have given me that first raindrop. There is no turning back. That is my destiny."

The shaman led them across the rugged land to a small mesa. On it was a collection of adobe houses surrounded by small garden plots struggling to survive in this harsh climate. Several goats nibbled at the sparse vegetation. A dog looked up incuriously. No people were evident. Dreams With Manitou explained, "Saturday they go to town. Sell a few rugs, maybe some jewelry. Shop a little. Buy a few drinks. Come back tonight."

He walked them to a small building and opened the door. Inside was a wellhead with a small gasoline pump beside it. A faucet with a hose attached was on the top. A hand pump was also there for emergency use. "This is our water supply. Sometimes it's good. Sometimes we have to haul water. You can see our fields. They have given up the same as our people have. Is there any water that we can depend on?"

Brisa took his left hand and motioned Brandon to his other side. "Let us sit awhile, shaman, until we are one with the land. Then we will walk and hope for the best."

They sat in silence while the land filled their spirits. The shaman began to feel the faint sensation of water near him, the water of the well. Still they sat and now he felt his spirit expanding but the water sensation stayed at the same faint level. At last Brisa rose to her feet and pulled the others up.

"We must walk now. There is little water here," she said.

The trio walked while the shaman strained to sense water. Their walk seemed aimless to him. They could not help. It was just a trick they were playing on him.

"Stop it!" said Brisa. "You are blocking us with all your doubts. Don't listen to yourself. Listen to your spirit."

She had them sit again and once more let their spirits merge with that of the land. They arose and resumed their walk in a widening circle, waiting for the faintest sensation of water to guide their path. At last the sign came and Brisa headed them northward off the mesa. The signal became stronger and seemed to compress their bodies. On a small ridge she stopped the group. "Here is the water. Not a great amount, but it is flowing slowly. It is fed from the hills, I think. The flow is an overflow seeping into the sand. It will help you in time of need. I do not think it will fail."

Dreams With Manitou accepted her words. He, too, had felt the water. "Show me the best way to get the water. I will follow your advice."

"You do not need a pump," she said. "Dig a well on the side of this ridge near the base, this side of that rock. Dig down twenty-five feet. Water will slowly fill the well almost to the level of that rock."

"Thank you," said the shaman. "I will do as you say."

Brisa and Brandon decided to stay on holiday for a week. The cool weather was welcome, although it meant jumping into their clothes in the chilly mornings. They compensated for this with the luxury of sleeping later and lingering over breakfast. Long walks made them better acquainted with the local desert. Brandon delighted in introducing his mother to all the desert life with which he had been in rapport, explaining their lifestyles in infinite detail. Brisa patiently listened more about her son than about nature. The respite from work brought them even closer together.

During one day's walk they saw a makeshift campsite below them in a small box canyon. Several Washingtonian palms grew in a cluster in the center of the canyon, attesting to the trapping of occasional rainwater. Palm fronds, canvas, wood and rope had been used to provide shelter from the sun. Table, chairs and kitchen equipment indicated the semi-permanent nature of the site. A rutted trail indicated the inhabitants drove a vehicle to the camp. No one was visible, but Brisa led Brandon away cautiously.

"These are transients," she told him. "They might carry word of us to the outside if we became known to them."

The boy nodded his understanding. There did not seem to be much interest to him at the camp.

The end of their week came much too soon and they were up early again to continue their excavation on the large room. When Brandon went up to the top of the butte for his morning relaxation, he found the shaman sitting waiting for him. They nodded greetings and then sat cross-legged on the ground to relax and prepare for rapport with the wildlife. Soon they were soaring high on thermals with the red-tailed hawk and watching the ground below for signs of prey. At times the hawk's eyes focused on a tiny patch of grass and magnified the scene where ground squirrels and kangaroo rats might feast. At other times a broader view held steady while the predator waited for a telltale sign of motion against the fixed background. At last the hawk fixed on his prey and dove at a frightening speed, then soared again when his prey vanished. The washes and buttes went by in dizzying fashion as their flight path turned upward. They withdrew to their proper bodies and rested there from the exhilaration of the flight.

The shaman spoke, almost as from a reverie. "The earth and rain bring forth grass which offers itself to the grazing animals. These animals – the rat, the rabbit, and the deer – must go out to the patch of grass to eat and grow and multiply. At the same time they offer themselves to the higher predators – the fox, the coyote, the owl and the hawk. The higher predators in turn may fall to the cougar. One day the cougar himself dies and offers himself to the earth and its scavenging creatures great and small. The sun, the wind and the rain nurture all creatures and yet at death they turn all the creatures back to the earth. Tying all together in this circle is the spirit that never dies. We as individual creatures are manifestations of one spirit. We are bound together in the spirit. We take to sustain our lives. We must give to sustain other life. In this sense we never die, but are transformed into other manifestations of one spirit. We are bound together in the spirit. That is our nation's belief. It sustained us through the times we were masters of this land. In times of trouble and defeat we lost faith and had nothing to sustain us. As a nation, as individuals, we deteriorated to wasted shadows of our former selves."

His voice trailed off and his thoughts turned inward. Unconsciously, Brandon was drawn into the confused vortex of his memories of defeat. At first the memories were sweet, as he learned tribal lore from the old shaman who recounted stories of countless herds of game animals, a sky filled with birds, the danger of cougars and bears, and the joy of riding the open range on a horse as fast as the wind. Tribal ceremonies retold tales of creation, of spirit manifestations in every aspect of life, and the bonds that tied all together in a constant renewal and celebration of life.

The tales also told of the white man's coming, his devastation of the land and his slaughter of the animals. They told, too, of the warriors such as Geronimo, Sitting Bull and Crazy Horse who fought against great odds to protect the land and maintain their way of life. These tales inspired the youth who would become a shaman himself and preserve tribal lore for generations to come.

Suddenly the joy faded from the reverie. The youth had grown up and was now a shaman himself. But there were no admiring groups of youths paying rapt attention to the tales of paradise lost and long departed heroes. His ceremonies were unattended and unnoted. The beautiful girl who was entranced by his tales and his vision of glory regained soon became a disenchanted shrew whose verbal abuse about his pitiful dreaming soon drove them apart in a violent fight. His remorse and lowered self-esteem only contributed to the complete loss of respect from his community. His attempts to communicate the tribal lore through ceremonies and discussions at tribal meetings generated only hoots of derision. There was no past. There was no future but the white man's way.

The rapport ended abruptly. The shaman suddenly realized that Brandon was sharing his self-demeaning reverie. He jumped to his feet and glared at the boy with angry, accusing eyes. "You saw! You entered my mind! You betrayed my confidence! You are an evil witch... no friend of mine! You and your mother are just white people laughing at the stupid Indian. I'll tell everyone who you are. You'll never live here. Never!" His face was livid as he stood over the boy, shouting his indignation at this invasion of his mental privacy.

Brandon was speechless. He could sense the loathing in the shaman's mind and hear the words of rejection from his best friend. "I didn't mean it," he stammered. "You just drew me in with your stories. I never did this before except with my mother when she invited me. I thought you were my friend. I'll never do it again. I promise. I promise."

The apologies were to no avail. The shaman stalked off in a rage. Brandon, devastated, ran back to the cave to find his mother waiting for him. He flew into her arms and cried in gulping sobs on her shoulder. She comforted him and brought him into the cave to cry himself out. At last he told her the story of his rejection by his friend for going into rapport with him unintentionally. Brisa talked long and earnestly to help him understand that people consider thoughts and emotions to be very private. He must avoid being drawn too deeply into people's feelings because most people are afraid or ashamed to be understood too well.

Brandon awakened the next morning with a feeling of emptiness instead of expectation. He could not bring himself to go to the promontory. He knew he no longer had a friend to share his experiences. Work became a heavy burden for he felt that this could no longer be his home. His mother also frowned frequently in deep thought and lagged at her work. Brandon knew that it was his fault that they would be homeless again.

On the third morning he dragged to the cave entrance to see the now leaden sky dully lighted by the rising sun. Glancing downward he saw a small object in the opening. Picking it up he recognized it as an Indian doll that the shaman had shown him before, one that symbolized friendship and remembrance. He jumped to his feet and ran up the path the promontory. The shaman was sitting there cross-legged, looking expectantly towards the trail. Brandon ran over and threw himself on the shaman, sobbing his happiness at seeing him again.

Dreams With Manitou sat the boy down in front of him and said, "It is I who am sorry, my friend. You did no wrong. It was I who wanted you to see me as more important than I really am. When you saw the shabby side of me, I was ashamed. I could not bear to have you take your friendship from me, so I threw it away. Look into my soul again, son, and see all my fears and self-doubts. If you can take me back as your friend, then I shall be honored."

The shaman opened his feelings to Brandon and did not try to hide his weaknesses and mistakes. Brandon could see none of them, only that the shaman's soul was filled with the glow of love. Brandon opened his eyes and leaned over to embrace his friend. They cried softly together for a moment. Dreams With Manitou disengaged himself, drew his knife and lightly cut his right wrist. Then he took Brandon's right arm and scratched his wrist. Pressing the two wrists together, he told the wondering Brandon, "Our blood has mingled and now flows in both our veins. We are brothers. Nothing will ever come between us. You are my people, I am of yours."

Brandon brought the shaman back to the cave entrance. Brisa was there in the opening. Brandon showed his mother their wrists. "We are brothers, mama. Friends forever. Nothing will part us."

The shaman nodded gravely. "I will be a good brother."

Brisa put a teakettle on her propane stove. She then invited him in to see the progress of their work. Brandon held close to his arm as they walked back through the passage to the expanding room. Her flashlight made their shadows dance along the narrow tunnel while Dreams With Manitou commented approvingly on their efforts. At the end she turned on the electric lights to illuminate the extent of the large room they had been excavating. The shaman stopped his polite remarks and a look of incredulity came over his face. The hand tools and baskets attested to the primitive tunneling method. The eight-feet-wide by six-feet-high face had been extended back twelve feet, an excavation of over twenty-three cubic yards. This is a small hole for modern drag lines with their cubic yard buckets, but a large achievement for hand tools and baskets.

"You have accomplished much for a woman and child in this short time. I am your brother. Let me help."

Brisa looked at the old man's slight frame and demurred, "No, shaman. It is our work. We will continue."

The shaman understood her concern about his age and physical condition. He smiled quietly. "Not I alone. A few younger brothers, sworn to secrecy, would help. Let me do this for you."

Again, Brisa was torn between her desire for concealment and her realization that even she could not burden her son with tasks beyond his capacity. "Two men," she said at last, "No more."

They went back to the mouth of the cave and drank their tea in companionable small talk. The shaman recounted tales of the good life his ancestors had lived when game was plentiful, water was adequate and the range provided sustenance through wild plants. Whether it was true or merely a Garden of Eden myth could not be determined from current conditions, but Dreams With Manitou wanted that vision to be realized for his people. Tea was finished and the shaman strode off to his village.

Brandon told his mother of his rapport with the shaman during which his failures, doubts and fears were revealed. Brisa wondered whether tomorrow would mark the end of their attempt to build a new home and whether she should plan for another quick move. At the thought of these laborious weeks wasted even her strong will wavered. Was all this running worth it? Brandon's question echoed in her mind, "Why are we running?" She suppressed her impulse to respond: time enough to know when he is older.

The next morning they were wakened by the sound of a truck laboring up the wash to their site. They rushed to the cave mouth and saw a three-quarter ton parked next to their pickup. Two large men alighted and stared at them. A moment later the shaman clambered out and waved.

"Brisa! These are my brothers. We come to help!"

They ran down the path to the wash and greeted the newcomers. The shaman introduced them. "Brisa. Brandon. My tribal brothers, Quiet Wolf and Lonely Eyes. Call them Wolf and Joe. They will help. They know you found our new water supply. They believe in the old ways. They believe in me. They will not talk."

The two Indians dropped the tailgate of their truck and began unloading equipment. Air hammers, hoses and couplings came out, revealing a motor-compressor in the back. Shouldering the jackhammers, they followed Brisa up the path to the cave where they deposited the equipment. They then walked with Brisa down the tunnel to the new room.

"Jesus!" exclaimed Joe. "Didn't really believe the Dreamer. You two did all this? Jesus!"

Wolf said nothing. He merely measured the excavation with his eyes and estimated the size of the task. Turning, they all went back for the hoses, fittings and remainder of the equipment and protective clothing.

The next week was a deafening nightmare to Brisa and Brandon as the two miners methodically cut away the sandstone, while she, Brandon and the shaman hauled away baskets of rubble. The room materialized before their eyes. It first went back twenty-five feet. The miners then turned their air hammers to the side and shaped out the first three pillars. A second aisle was begun before the day ended. The crew was astounded at their own progress when Brisa called them for a dinner of hot vegetable soup and home baked bread. They headed for home with a promise to return the next day. Brandon and Brisa fell into bed that night and not even the excitement of the day's progress could keep them awake.

By the end of the week the twenty-five feet by forty feet room with its six pillars supporting the roof was completely excavated. The floor level had been dropped three feet to give a ceiling height of nine feet. The pillars measured two feet by three feet at the base and mushroomed at the top to spread the load. There were two rows of three columns. The electric lights casting shadows of the pillars down the aisles gave the feeling of a wine cellar extending far beneath a castle where ancient secrets might be hidden.

Joe Lonely Eyes said of the room, "It gives me the creeps."

On Saturday morning they all sat down to discuss the further progress of the work. They agreed that the room was getting depressing and unanimously adopted the suggestion of Quiet Wolf that they start on the light and ventilation features before digging further. First they used four-by-four braces to support the ceiling where the shafts would enter the room. They enthusiastically hauled their equipment to the top of the butte and laid out the markings for the upper ends of the two shafts. The air hammers made quick work through the sandstone and they dropped their platforms foot by foot on opposite sides of the shafts as they dug. At nine feet they drove a bit down the center of each shaft to make sure of the remaining depth to the room and accuracy of their dig. The shaft would come out very close to the planned location. From the bottom, now, they squared out the edges of the shaft so that the hole would not break through in ragged fashion. Back to the top they went and deepened the hole until less than a foot of excavating remained. They then broke through the center of the shaft and worked out a foot to within the edges. The rest of the shaft they carefully cut out from the bottom. With laughter and hugging they celebrated the first shaft.

Confident now, they followed the same technique for the second shaft. All were covered with dust and weary as they neared the bottom. Respecting Brandon's unflagging efforts, the crew decided to give him the honors of making the second breakthrough. Helping him with the air hammer, they steadied and weighted the tool while he added his own strength to the job. He greeted with a shout the first breakthrough and then the subsequent chunks of rock that dropped through the opening. At last Wolf took the air hammer from Brandon and carried it down to the room below. Again, they carefully shaped the ceiling opening and returned above for the final stone removal.

They clambered out of the hole at the end, tired but satisfied. There waiting for them was Brisa, clean and neat now, carrying a bucket of cold orange juice. They had almost forgotten that she was a small attractive woman because of the amount of hard labor she had performed with them.

"Quench your thirst, cool off and wash up. I have supper cooking. We will eat and rest now that the shafts are dug. I do not know if we could have done them alone," she said.

Wolf laughed. "I have seen your work, Brisa. Nothing is beyond you. Together we could move mountains."

After bathing, they all went back into the room to review their handiwork. The dust had almost settled and now the light from the shafts gave a dusky brightness to the room. The effect was now more like the somber lighting of a medieval church than a shadowy wine cellar. They stood quietly immersed in their own thoughts of a new home, of past glories, of the changes wrought by this new partnership. Then all went out to eat.

They sat at the front of the cave polishing off the remains of the barbequed chicken, corn and beans. Dusk was descending over the desert. The heat of the day had given way to the comparative cool of the evening. Joe brought a guitar up from his truck and played some soft Spanish songs. Occasionally, Wolf would join him in singing them. A warm bond of shared accomplishment gave them a feeling of family. The guitar drifted into silence and they sat quietly for a while letting the bonds strengthen.

At last Joe spoke up. "The shafts cannot be left unfinished. I think that a frame with mirrored shutters and maybe some reflectors underneath would catch the sunlight and diffuse it around the room. I have seen that done in buildings before. It works pretty well. Tomorrow Wolf and I will go over to Bakersfield and look around. It would be worth the effort."

After the trio of helpers had left, Brisa and Brandon sat at the cave adit and watched the desert stars. "We are fortunate to have such friends," she said to her son. "What I feared was our doom has proved to be our salvation."

Brandon nodded sleepily. "They are like you, mama. I love them."

Brisa and Brandon worked alone for the following week. They cleaned out the debris and dug a pool area five feet wide by fifteen feet long and three feet deep at the end nearer the aquifer. This was a relatively easy job using the air hammer that the crew had left behind. Brisa was not as adept as the two construction workers, but she had ample strength to manage the bucking hammer. They were working at an easy pace now, waiting for the men to return with the fixtures for the shafts.

Their trips to town had become routine, hardly noticed by the people there. Foodstuffs and supplies varied little until this trip when Brisa asked for drilling supplies at the hardware store. Water was a subject of interest in the desert.

"Going to drill for water, are you? Not much been found out that way in the past."

"Have the Indians shown you an old waterhole? Rumor says there used to be some, but the Indians filled them in when they were pushed back to the reservation."

Dick Swain has a drill rig in Alberville. Maybe you should see him before you wear yourself out putting in dry holes."

Brisa calmly put aside all the questions with noncommittal responses. "The rains will come in the winter. Maybe I can dam part of the wash and store some. I don't need much anyway."

The questions died down and they left with two-inch and four-inch drills, a length of well casing, some pipe fittings, cement, and a drill stand. She also rented an electric drill and a gasoline-driven generator to power it. The storeowner was hesitant about renting the equipment at first, but her knowledge about what she wanted and the ease with which she lifted the heavy equipment into the truck impressed him.

"No hurry, ma'am," he said. "Not much drilling going on around here. Won't be either, unless you have some success, I guess."

Brisa thanked him and drove off to the cave with Brandon for this most important stage of their excavation.

They carried the drilling equipment up the stairs, through the cave entrance and back thirty feet to the main room. The truck generator supplied electrical power for the drill and a water tank with pump provided for cooling and lubrication of the drill. The first bore that she had planned was the drain from the pool to the outside wall above the wash. This would be cut entirely through sandstone. She mounted the drill stand in the pool and adjusted the mount to bore at a downward slant of forty degrees. The four-inch bit cut rapidly through the sandstone.

She had added forty feet of extension to the drill before she heard Brandon's excited call, "It's through, mama, it's through!" With that she withdrew the drill and fed the plastic liner through the bore. At the top she attached the "Y" fitting for floor and upper drains. All was now ready for tapping the aquifer.

Brisa had cut an alcove into the sandstone wall nearest to the aquifer. It went back six feet through the sandstone until it exposed the granite face of the rock that formed the water basin. At this point she had to bore through four feet of the hard rock to reach the aquifer. She anchored the drill stand to the floor and mounted the drill against the wall. This time she used a smaller two and one-half inch drill. The well casing pipe was driven in as the bore progressed. In three-quarters of an hour the first evidence of the water supply trickled through the pipe in augmentation of the drill supply. Brisa checked the casing head and gate valve to be ready for the main flow. She backed out the drill and immediately a full stream shot out from the pipe. They shouted and danced in the water for a few moments, and then Brisa closed the gate valve and shut down the flow.

Brisa's next concern was one of comfort. She had bought a shower enclosure, and with Brandon's help, carried it up to stand above the end of the pool near the drain. She quickly made temporary connections to the water supply and the drain. A turn of the valve had the shower running immediately. She and Brandon jumped into the shower and danced about in the joy of washing off the dust with relatively cool aquifer water. Life was beginning to look much brighter.

The next day the two Indians returned with the skylight, mirrors and diffuser for the ceiling shaft. They carved out a seat at the top of the shaft and placed the top fixture at ground level. The lower light diffuser was supported from the top fixture and braced against the sidewalls of the shaft. The manual control mechanism was operated from the bottom. Not only did they have shaft components, but they also thought of a set of convex mirrors for the sidewalls to spread the light to all corners of the room. The gloom completely disappeared.

When Wolf and Joe saw the progress she and Brandon had made on the pool and water supply, they brought up bags of waterproof cement to seal the pool and shower. They also suggested drainage channels in the floor to take care of any runoff from her plants. They decided to install the commode in an alcove cut into the sandstone near the pool outlet and to bury the septic tank down in the wash. Each suggestion was followed by work and the whole system quickly took shape. Each afternoon the shower brought the day to a pleasant close. Within the week heavy labor was completed. Wolf and Joe packed their truck and prepared to leave.

Joe Lonely Eyes locked the gate of the truck and turned to Brisa and Brandon. "You are building a beautiful place here. You have helped us with water, and more than that, have revived our faith in ourselves and in the ways of our fathers. You are part of our people now. We shall watch out for you as our own."

Wolf took out the guitar and sang a song of parting for them that promised they would be held in his heart. The shaman stood quietly by, but joined in the hugs that preceded their departure.

Brisa decided that they should work outside for a while and take on a garden as their project. Brandon happily agreed with this. The drainage pipe exited the bluff just at the level of a small terrace above the wash. This was an area that would require only minimal effort to turn into a garden plot. It could not be seen from any distance up or down the wash and only from the edges of the buttes on either side of the wash. The task became a fun project as they designed a small well for the spring using rocks from the wash and some of the remaining waterproof cement. She decided to run a small diameter pipe inside the drainpipe so that clean water could be used in the well while the drain water was diverted for the garden or to a dry hole where it would sink into the sand.

From the shaman they received seeds for varieties of corn, beans and melons that would thrive in this area. A lemon tree was Brandon's suggestion for its continual flowering, sweet odor and shade when it grew tall and lemonade all year long. Colorful flowers were Brisa's choice – geraniums, petunias and sweet Williams. They happily anticipated this outdoor phase of their home. Having revived their enthusiasm with the outdoor work, they were now ready to finish the inside of the large cave using extra supplies that had been dropped off by Joe on one of his visits.

The sandstone floor was finished with a thin coat of the cement to keep down the dust and to permit runoff into the drainage channels in the floor. The plastic piping system extended to service the entire room. Valves were installed to permit flexible watering. Drip fittings were also connected to enable nearly carefree watering for extended periods. Brisa also laid out a system of wall shelves, tables and plant containers to hold the varieties of plants that she intended to cultivate.

Once in place, the containers were filled with potting soil appropriate for the plants she intended to grow. They had to be relatively expensive, yet marketable within a reasonable distance of their home. Quiet Wolf and Lonely Eyes had volunteered to bring her plants to market in Bakersfield whenever they made a trip. This suited her desire for anonymity better than selling in Claymore, so she accepted their offer. In return, she offered to help them set up a similar nursery in adobe buildings near their new water supply if the venture proved profitable. Long-term stability seemed a possibility in this new home.

The garden outside was doing well with a drip irrigation system that she and Brandon had installed. The flowers were up and blooming. The vegetables were growing apace. Two young lemon trees were now beginning to blossom. The outside of their abode was becoming homelike. Their cave nursery was a refuge from the dry heat of the desert and a sensory delight of color and odor. This was their desert paradise.

The heavy work of excavation and construction was behind them. The pace of their daily activities slowed so that they could sit and talk, smell the flowers, explore the desert, visit friends, trace the paths of the stars at night, and learn through rapport with the desert life. Brandon entered a new phase of growing and learning.

Origins

Brandon enjoyed his leisure with all of the new aspects of life, nature and friends that were opening to him. Mornings found him on the promontory for his rapport sessions with desert life. Now there were three friends with him – Dreams With Manitou, Quiet Wolf and Lonely Eyes. Their bonds with nature were strengthened through him and respect for their ancestral lore deepened. Brandon was careful not to intrude on their personal thoughts after the reaction of the shaman. They in turn shared their knowledge with him. Sometimes in the evenings they would share with him the tribal lore of the creation of the world, the spirits that dwelt in all things, the Spirit Circle that tied together all the cycles of life in nature, the close relationship among all animate and inanimate beings and their responsibilities to each other in maintaining these relationships that ensured the continuity of life on earth.

These stories were not entirely verbal, but were intertwined with dance, music and chant that better expressed the intricacies of their stories than words alone could do. Brandon's eidetic memory, powers of mimicry and love for dancing enabled him to learn the many tales they recounted.

Brisa often joined them, playing the drum and taking female roles they would assign her. She, too, repaid them with further instruction in the art of dowsing. She also helped them to remember details of their tribal lore and rituals that had grown indistinct and garbled from long neglect. She taught them techniques of relaxation and concentration that enhanced their own memories. With their consent, she also used rapport with them to guide, merge and firm their thoughts as they worked in concert to reassemble the near-forgotten lore. Deep bonds were formed through these shared experiences and memories.

Brisa sat with her son at the cave entrance sharing the quiet companionship as the constellations progressed slowly across the night sky. She put her arm about his shoulders and pulled him closer. "You are growing older, my love," she said, "and it is time that you learned more about who you are, who we are and why we are hiding here."

"Who we are? Don't we know that, mama?"

"I mean what kind of people we are, Brandon, not our names. You have found out already that other people talk and act and think differently from the way that you and I do. In some ways they are much the same, in other ways very different. They speak more but say less with their bodies. They do not sense life about them. They have great difficulty feeling what others feel. They sense nothing of the message from the earth itself. They feel themselves apart from and greater than all nature rather than an integral part of nature, sharing in all life. These differences set us apart. Nature, no matter what they think, binds us all together. You must learn all of this and the role that destiny has shaped for you, for I feel that in your lifetime all that we have on earth may be threatened."

Brandon stared at her with furrowed brow. "Mother," he said, "How can I understand all this?"

"I'm sorry, my love," she responded. "I feel so pressured with all that's going on about us. There's no time, and I want you to grow up so fast to help me – but I want you to stay young and be my little man, too." She hugged him more tightly and kissed him on the top of his head. "Tomorrow we'll begin. Tonight we watch the stars that guide our way."

The next day after their gardening chores Brisa brought Brandon to the corner of the room near the pool. There a small sparkling waterfall splashed down the rough wall, chattering in bright half-heard phrases as if about a carefree gambol. This sprightly chatter brought a relaxed atmosphere to the corner of the room. It formed a barrier to intrusions from the outside world. Here only the local present mattered.

Brisa began. "First I must tell you that we are humans and are a part of all nature on this earth. We are the elder people who were here before those who call themselves humans came to be. We coexisted with all creatures and the earth itself for many generations. Long ago, a hundred thousand years ago perhaps, the first of these new people appeared upon the earth. They multiply rapidly. They work in large groups. They make tools and weapons that give them control over everything. They must dominate everything about them or destroy it. Our people, whom they now call Neanderthals, are not like that. We live in small family groups. We know that we are related to the world about us: animals, plants, and earth alike. We know that we can only live if all other things live and share our lives. We wanted to live with the new people, too. They would not let us live. Every one who looked different from them they killed or drove away. We could not fight back effectively, so most of our people died."

"Some of us were not killed because we looked something like the new people. Eventually, as with weeds in the garden that have evolved by such selection to look like the plants being cultivated, we look on the outside like the new humans. Inside, we know that we are not the same. So for tens of thousands of years we have lived among them without them realizing that we are here.

"We have been content with our share of the world. But in the last two hundred years the new people have started to destroy the earth – our earth, not just their earth. This has started a struggle among our people. Some of us want to reveal ourselves and make the new people realize that we must work together to save our world. They feel that we should now trust them not to exterminate us as they attempted in the past. Others of our people want to interfere actively with their works so that the world will revert back to what it was. The majority is fearful of any action that might call attention to us. They are content to let the present trend continue and hope that we will survive and the others will pollute their way to extinction. Today we are a people quarreling ineffectively among ourselves rather than fighting for our world.

"I am one who believes that we can work together with the new people to save the world for all. The fearful ones and the active obstructionists combined to detain me until they can agree on a safe course. They want only delay while the world dies... so I fled. I want you to grow up free and help me seek a way to save us all. For this reason we are fugitives."

Brandon voiced his central concern, one that he rarely spoke of. "Mama, where is my father?"

"I don't know," replied his mother. "We met in the mountains of Asia and were parted before you were born. I have not seen your father since. Soon after, I left the Himalayas and made my way to Mount Shasta in North America."

"Is father alive?"

Brisa hesitated. "Yes, he is alive. I would sense if he died."

"I shall find him some day, mama. I shall find him for both of us," said her son in a determined voice.

She regarded him with a strange sad look but said no more. They sat quietly, listening to the splashing of the waterfall. Brandon formed hazy images of their future together as a family.

Brisa broke the silence. "All of our thoughts become part of us, Brandon, physical parts of these bodies we inhabit. Our experiences, our dreams, all the thoughts we hold tightly become part of us. Because they are part of us, we can pass them on to our children and our children's children. In this way memories can be passed down to instruct our descendants in how to live. Also, our visions of the future become part of our beings, they can be passed on and become reality for our children. The desire for our people to resemble the new people became reality and we were saved as a people. Holding the right thoughts can change an individual, his descendants and the world. I tell you this because I want you to learn how to listen to your ancestors and to learn from them."

"Come into rapport with me," invited his mother, "and we will begin this communication with our ancestors. Just follow my lead, and when you understand how it is done, you can do it yourself at any time."

They sat side by side with Brandon holding his mother's left hand and listening to her with his mind. They rested comfortably, their thoughts stilled, and their spirits settled into a serene interior portion of her being. The sense of time disappeared. A feeling of communion filled their space as though they were in the midst of a large family with whom they share one spirit. Brisa quested for someone familiar to her, found him and merged with him. They moved then out of the serene place of the large family and along branching pathways to a volume occupied by this one identity alone. The volume was separated into compartments, into one of which Brisa brought Brandon. Immediately Brandon felt himself to be walking in a dry land, his throat and nostrils dry, and a hot wind blowing in his face. He was suppressing those sensations and anxiously waiting for a sensation inside himself. The unknown ancestor at last felt the awaited sensation. Brandon felt it also. It was the compression he felt when his mother had shared with him the search for water. This entity had found water somewhere in a dry land. They left the compartment as the entity dug a hole with his spear to reach the underground water. They passed through the starting serene place and Brandon was again conscious of sitting next to his mother.

"Mama," he exclaimed, "that man was dowsing for water just like the way we did."

"Yes," his mother smiled at him. "That was one of our ancestors named Quarg whose thoughts I have contacted many times. From him I learned dowsing and other things. You must search through your store of memories to find ancestral thoughts of value. What is important to them became fixed in their bodies and then in their heritage so that future generations might share and benefit. All that we are, and think we are, may pass on to our children and our children's children. We must be careful to save for them that which is good."

"Can we do it again, mama? I want to learn more and to know more of my family. I felt warm and good with them."

"Of course we can. But this time you must try to lead the way and I will help you if you need it. Let's relax and try it."

They explored Brandon's memories at random since he had no guideposts to help them. There were burned fingers, hunting accidents, storms, volcanoes and scenes of beauty in a kaleidoscope of experiences. At last Brisa brought him back to the outside world.

Brandon's face was excited, his eyes full of wonder. "Mama, mama. Who were all those people? Why are there so many different memories?"

Brisa laughed. "Those are thoughts that your ancestors felt were important at the time. The thoughts are valuable so they were remembered and kept for future generations. Fire burns fingers. Falls can hurt. Animals bite. Volcanoes burn and cover forests and homes. There are thoughts you have not found yet. Animals and people can be sensed. Earthquakes send warnings before they occur. Lightning can be felt farther than it can be seen. Landmarks can be remembered that lead to special places. Medicines may be made from plants and trees. You must explore your memories to find knowledge that was important to your ancestors and adapt it to your life today. You must be your own guide to this knowledge. You will become familiar with some who have much to give you. You must ignore some who were misguided in what they deemed worth storing."

"Why can't I remember my father, mama?"

"Some memories are painful and we hide them from ourselves until we are ready to confront them. You will find him there when you are ready."

She rose. "Now we must go. Our nursery needs attention."

The Desert Years

Brandon loved hiking in the desert to explore the canyons and bluffs; to collect rocks of all types for decoration of their home and garden; to gaze at the scenery which ever revealed new aspects according to vantage point and lighting; and to familiarize himself with all the plant and animal life of the seemingly barren desert. His innate sense of direction and knowledge of the positions of sun and stars kept him from ever being lost. His growing familiarity with details of the topography fixed the local map clearly in his memory. He learned the terrain and its inhabitants for ten miles around his home, including many of the human inhabitants who came to know and accept him.

Brandon became a frequent visitor to the campsite of a family named Costain. Doug and Joy had made a comfortable home in a protected spot in the desert. A collection of tents and tarps shielded the area from the sun and potential rain, and divided the area into several separate rooms for family and private use. The kitchen included a propane stove and barbecue; a painted pantry cabinet; a water tank and sink; and a food storage chest. Two ice chests served for short-term cold storage. Several Coleman gas lanterns provided good lighting. The curtained sleeping areas contained a queen-sized bed for the parents and two hammocks for the children. An unpainted student desk accompanied each hammock. Books and writing materials spread on the desks attested to their studies. The family room had a battery-operated television set and VCR for watching the video recordings stored underneath the set. Outside there was a portable shower. They were obviously experienced campers with a taste for the comforts of home.

Doug and Joy were warm and friendly people who were concerned about maintaining a close knit family life and assuring the welfare of their children. Both of them played thc guitar and sang a widc varicty of songs from hymns to country western, to popular and semi-classical. The children joined in with the singing and played a few pieces on the guitar. Brandon soon learned to sing along with them and felt like one of the family.

Brisa heard so much about the Costains and Brandon went there so often that she went with him to meet them. When Brandon introduced Brisa to the Costains, Joy said, "I'm so glad to meet you at last, Brisa. Brandon has spoken of you so much. I'm surprised, though. You don't look anything like I expected."

"No? What did you expect?"

"Well, we thought that you were an Indian."

"No," Brisa, smiled, "We live near the reservation and have friends there, but we are like you, just visitors."

"You must stay and eat," invited Joy. "We'd like to hear how you manage in the desert, especially in the summer."

Brisa lowered her pack to the ground and opened it. "I was hoping you'd invite us," she replied. From the pack she extracted corn, tomatoes, potatoes, pinto beans, onions and several herbs. "We grow some of our own food and we would like to share this with you."

"Grow? You have water? I wish we could have found a place with water, but everything is as dry as a bone around here. How far away are you located?" asked Doug.

"Only about three miles on foot," Brisa replied. "By car you would have to go back to the main road through Claymore and then west to the range road."

"Too bad," said Doug. "I was hoping for a closer water supply. Hauling water is one of our biggest chores. Come, sit down. We'll make tea and talk a while before dinner."

Time passed quickly with talk, dinner, songs and more talk while the children played. Brisa learned that Doug had been a construction worker. He had been injured on the job and was unable to find other work in Los Angeles that paid enough to support his family adequately. Joy was asthmatic and unable to hold steady work. After two years of enduring boring jobs, subsistence living, dangerous neighborhoods and schools, pollution, drugs and the social services bureaucracy, he and Joy decided to move to the open country. They loaded their pickup and drove about, seeking work with no success. To their surprise, they found themselves living better on Doug's disability pension and enjoying life more than they had in the city. They became more of a family and studying with the children made them all appreciate and enjoy education. They then looked seriously for a place to stay permanently and found it in Claymore. The local people were not overly inquisitive. The children were accepted in school. Joy's asthma improved considerably. Their campsite was heaven compared with Los Angeles. They had been here for a year now and hoped to stay permanently. There were inconveniences, but the desert life made up for them.

The couple did not press Brisa for details of her home. For her part, Brisa's natural reluctance to publicize her whereabouts initially kept her from making all but the most general comments about her place. As time passed she became more drawn to the couple. Blond Joy was near Brisa's height and weight but did not have her sturdy muscular build. She effortlessly kept everyone in food and refreshments while keeping up her end of the conversation. Doug was medium height and strongly built. Both had positive dispositions – she was quick-witted, bright and sunny; he was more deliberate with an underlying droll humor. Brisa soon realized that they were completely forthright and honest with no hidden agenda. They were coping with life and their situation in the best way they could for their children. Brisa gradually spoke more openly to them about the home and life that she and Brandon were carving for themselves in the desert. When she and Brandon were leaving, Brisa told the family that Brandon would lead them to the cave home whenever they wished to visit.

Brandon and the Costain children played many games together. They introduced him to recreational games they played in the schoolyard and educational games they played in the classroom. Brandon showed them games he played with his Native American friends when hiking and exploring the desert. He taught them about the environment and animals. He showed them proper climbing techniques and helped them over the rough places. Meanwhile, to Brisa's surprise, Brandon slapped palms with Dan and both shouted, "All right!" His social graces were expanding.

Schoolwork took precedence over games for Dan and Emily. Their mother made certain that all reading was completed and all written homework neatly finished before they ran off with Brandon. He would wait patiently while Dan labored with his reading and then helped Emily with hers.

Brandon opened the book on American history and became engrossed immediately. He sat turning the pages quickly while scanning the contents. When Dan turned to him again, Brandon had put the book down and was leaning back against the desk.

"Dull stuff, isn't it?" commented Dan. "It puts me to sleep."

"No," responded Brandon. "It's exciting to learn how this country grew from a few explorers to so many people in cities. But why did they fight with the Native Americans? And where did all the Native Americans go?"

"C'mon, Brandon. You didn't read past the first page."

"I read it all," replied Brandon, "but I'm not sure that I understand it all."

Dan picked up the book and opened to the middle. "Who gave the Gettysburg Address?" he challenged.

Brandon answered, "President Abraham Lincoln made this address at the dedication of the National Cemetery on the battlefield of Gettysburg, Pennsylvania on the 19th of November in 1863. He said, 'Four score and seven years ago—.'"

"Hold it! Hold it! You peeked." Opening to another page, Dan asked, "How do you do that? Can you read upside down?"

"I just remember the pages and I can see them whenever I want. You are on page 243. The top left corner is folded down. Six names are underlined. Robert E. Lee on line 6; Ulysses S. Grant on line 9; and—"

"Okay, okay," Dan halted him. "You must be a genius."

"No," said Brandon thoughtfully. "I suppose anybody could do it. Pictures are easy to remember. I just see something that I want to remember and picture it in my mind. Then I can see it again whenever I want to."

"I wish I could do that," sighed Dan, "then we wouldn't have to wait so long to play."

"I think I could show you how," responded Brandon slowly." I can't tell you how, but I think I could show you."

"When?"

"Finish your lessons, Dan. Then we can go up on the mesa and try."

"Emily, too? Otherwise we'll have to wait for her."

"I guess so."

Ten minutes later the trio climbed the back wall of the box canyon up the mesa carrying two copies of a primer from which Emily was studying.

The three children sat cross-legged in the shelter of a rock overhang with Brandon. He held one book on his lap and Dan shared the other with Emily.

"Your body has to be relaxed to do this and you have to concentrate on the page you want to remember. As soon as you see it clearly, you have to snap it into your memory just like taking a picture with a camera," instructed Brandon.

The other children nodded but not very confidently.

"Turn to the first page, rest the book on your knees and let your whole being relax. Everything must relax – your whole body, your whole mind and all your feelings." He was repeating what his mother had told him long ago. "You have to be like a clear, calm pool of water without a ripple. That way, everything you see can come right into the depths of your being. When the picture is clear, you just snap your mental shutter and you have the picture forever."

Brandon looked up smiling. "See how easy it is! Now it's yours forever."

Doug appeared puzzled. "I don't see a thing."

Emily seemed unsure. "I see it a little but it's fading away. And now it's all gone."

They both looked at Brandon with disappointed expressions.

"Try it again," directed Brandon, "but this time I'll watch you to see how you do it."

Again they relaxed and tried to fix the pages in their minds. Brandon grabbed Dan lightly by the throat. "That's it!" he exclaimed. He touched Emily lightly on her throat also. "You're reading out loud, but under your breath! I can almost hear you talking, Dan. Emily is just barely whispering. Put your fingers here on your throat," he said, demonstrating on his own, "and feel the vibrations while you read the page. You want video, not audio, when you fix the page in your mind. If you stop reading out loud you can see the story happen when you video read."

"Once more," he directed. This time he watched Emily closely. Her eyes were obviously moving across the page in painfully small increments, fixing on each part of each word in turn. "Just see big parts of the page," he told her sternly, "Don't look at each letter."

Emily's eyes began to tear as she tried harder to please him. Dan appeared to be choking off his sub-vocalization by tightening his grip. They couldn't grasp his directions. The class was about to collapse.

Brandon was crestfallen. "But it's so easy." In his eagerness to teach his friends, he forgot his reticence about showing his abilities to others. He moved closer to the others and took their hands in his. "Let's relax again and this time we'll all form one big calm pool of water together."

They grudgingly composed themselves and sat quietly again, relaxing themselves completely. Brandon attuned himself to the other two and felt their spirits calm. He then expanded his aura so that it overlapped theirs and brought them all into rapport. He scanned the page without vocalizing the symbols and brought it into his being, telling them to do the same. Feeling what he did, it was natural for the children to accept the reality of the page entering within them. He held the image of the page motionless for a moment. "Now!" he told them forcefully, "Start at the bottom of your mind and snap it right over the page to hold it tight." He guided the others to their brain stems where he started a pulse of energy that intensified the image of the page for a moment and then subsided. The page itself stayed fixed where each child held it in his mind.

"I have it! I have it!" shouted Dan.

"So do I! So do I!" piped Emily.

"Again," said Brandon, and led them through the process a dozen times, diminishing his role until they were doing it alone. The two children kept turning the pages, repeating the process and then looking away to recall the image of each page. They were ecstatic about this new way to read. Each repetition shortened the time it took to fix a page.

Emily jumped to her feet. "Let's go show Mommy! Let's go now!" She started for the path down.

Brandon was alarmed. He, too, jumped up. "No, Emily. No! You can't do that! You mustn't let anyone know that I taught you to read fast. It has to be a secret. My mother might not let us play together anymore."

The children looked puzzled, but their own training in concealing their campsite from others made it seem rational. "Okay," said Dan holding his sister's arm. "We'll keep quiet. We wouldn't want to get you in trouble with your mother. We'll just say we learned it by ourselves." Turning to his sister, he said sternly, "Right, Emily?"

She stood there puzzled, but agreed. "I promise, Brandon. I'll never tell." They both crossed their hearts. The shared secret forged another link in the strong bond growing among them.

Brisa finished trimming and cultivating the last row of plants in the cavern greenhouse and stood for a moment in the slight breeze at the opening of the corridor to the bluff face. She wiped the perspiration from her eyes with the back of her forearm. Rivulets of perspiration from her neck and shoulders ran down her nude body. Dust, mud and sweat formed a myriad of tiny streams that crisscrossed and coalesced as her breathing changed their pathways. Deeming her work enough for the day, she stepped over to the shallow pool and slipped down into the cool water. The grime and sweat washed away and with them the fatigue of the day's efforts. She lay in the water with her head resting on the side and let herself relax completely. The little waterfalls she had carved into the wall tinkled out their soothing music. The dim light and damp earthy odor gave the semblance of a secluded forest glen.

Her mind went back to her childhood in the Urals. Storyevo, isolated by rugged mountains and deep winter snows, came to life in the spring. Snow still blocked the roads to the outside world. The party officials and production supervisors sat in Moscow waiting for summer to vacation under the guise of re-indoctrination for their rural cadres. The snow pack on the southern slopes welcomed the lengthening days with thousands of tiny streams singing their jubilant notes of freedom at the release from winter's crystalline prison. Her childhood friends became part of nature's springtime joy. They tiptoed across the icy streams. They walked hand in hand under the burgeoning canopy of the trees. They watched and listened to the courtship rituals of the forest creatures; lolled in quiet glades and joined in nature's songs; and merged their beings in love for Mother Nature and knew Her every secret. The world was born anew.

This sylvan paradise disappeared the year that she was twelve. Clear-cutting removed every tree and shrub and evidence of animal life from the land. The sullen spring freshets gorged themselves on the red dirt; they uttered hoarse oaths as they toiled their burdens down the slopes and left ugly gullies in their wake. The despoilers traded a small ripple in the economy for a scar on the landscape that would last for ages. The barren vista etched an image in her soul that would endure in her descendants for eons. This defloration of Mother Earth by *Homo sapiens* personalized the environmental struggle for her by this, her paradise lost.

The people of Storyevo had no place in the work force at the new missile center. They were sent to remote areas in the Altai, the Pamir Mountains of Tajikistan and Kamchatka in the Far East. Brisa's parents joined a work team at the secret Dushanbe site. She was sent by them to live with a nomadic group who traveled along the borders with Afghanistan and Pakistan. The bitter expatriates organized ecology movements among their own Neanderthal people and even among the outsiders, *Homo sapiens*. The alarmed conservatives among their own people resisted this overt activism as a threat to their very survival. The agents of the establishment were already investigating the movement. A committee of elders counseled limitations on the activists, including restriction to their own Neanderthal neighborhoods. Brisa continued her activities through contacts with small villages along the nomadic trail. The fate of the world could not be entrusted to the endless debate of conservative committees.

The train of memories slowly faded and Brisa was once again conscious of the murmuring of the waterfall, the faint breeze from the entrance and the damp odors of her greenhouse. She rose from the pool and walked slowly to the cave entrance. She sat there and let the warm air dry her skin and hair. Faint doubts returned whether she had taken the right course when she opted for activism. Brandon was growing without contact and guidance of his own kind. The earth was being despoiled at an increasing pace. The science-deniers were in control of national environmental policy. Should she have found her own paradise and let *Homo sapiens* dance onward to their foreordained self-destruction, a dead end on the tree of evolution? Or would this mean oblivion for both kinds of people? She knew that she could not leave that legacy to her descendants. She couldn't leave that memory of herself to her descendants through untold generations to come.

Brisa became aware of Brandon's approach not far up the trail. His aura was mingled with others whom she gradually recognized to be the Costain family. They were accepting her invitation to visit. Brisa arose and shook her hair, which fell into place at shoulder length. She went inside and donned a loosely fitting sleeveless shirt and denim jumper. Her feet she left bare. She busied herself making lemonade with the cool water from the pipe in the cave while waiting for their arrival.

The children were the first to reach the cave entrance in a final dash to announce their parent's arrival. Emily stood at the entrance breathlessly forming the words. All at once they shouted, "Surprise! We came to visit." Brisa picked Emily up for a hug and then bent over to hug the boys. They immediately ran in to see the wonders of the cave. In a few moments their parents arrived, walking slowly as they took in the view of the garden outside, the steps up the bluff and the cave entrance high on the rock wall.

"Oh, Brisa!" exclaimed Joy, "How beautiful you have made this little oasis. I'd love to have a garden like this. Just the smell, and the feel of the dirt, and the dampness when you water – I would just love a garden of my own."

She walked through the garden touching the plants, smelling the blossoms, and crushing several herbs under nose to savor the spicy odor. Doug Costain admired the irrigation tiles and traced them back to the water outlet at the bluff in the back of the garden. There was no water flowing, but it was the obvious source. "Where does the water come from? And how?" he asked. "I wish we had found a spring like this."

"Come," invited Brisa. "I'll show you our greenhouse. You will see everything."

She led the way up to the adit. When their eyes became accustomed to the shade, they walked through the tunnel to the nursery cavern. Their wonder grew at every step and turned to awe as they saw the dimensions of the main cavern, the skylights, the rows of plants and finally the water system. The pool was a vision of heaven to Joy when she saw the three children in the pool splashing each other exuberantly.

"I wish I could do that," she sighed wistfully. "A daily soak is what I miss most out here in the desert."

"But you can," encouraged Brisa. "Just jump in. I was bathing before you came."

"I can't go in like this," she said, looking down at her clothes, "but I suppose I could dangle my feet over the edge."

Brisa unselfconsciously dropped her shirt and jumper to the floor and splashed in among the children. Emily saw Brisa's action so she immediately threw her shirt and pants out on the floor. The boys quickly followed suit.

"Come on in, Mama," called Emily. "The water is so cool." She turned bottom up in a short dive and called again impatiently, "Come in!"

Joy hesitated but then removed her shoes and outer clothes. She gave her husband a quick embarrassed look, removed her underclothes and joined the others in the pool. They all looked up at Doug and laughingly called, "Last one in is a rotten egg."

He was visibly more embarrassed than his wife at this unexpected nude bathing scene. He started to undress slowly, then quickly stripped down and jumped into the other end of the pool. After the kids gave him a rousing water fight all the timidity disappeared and they all enjoyed the bliss of a cool soak after their hot desert hike.

The adults were out first and toured the cavern while drying off. Self-consciousness about their nudity had disappeared. It had vanished in the spontaneity of their water frolic. The Costains were now captivated by the marvels of this underground nursery.

"Did you dig all this yourself?" asked Doug. "How did you know that you'd find water? And where does the water come from? Or shouldn't I be asking all this?" He paused for breath and looked at Brisa with amazement on his face.

"Come outside," said Brisa. "Let me pour some lemonade for everyone and we can talk about it." She picked up her clothes and donned them as she walked through the tunnel towards the entrance. She decided along the way that she would confide everything to the Costains except, of course, that she and Brandon were Neanderthals and a different species from *Homo sapiens*. The adults settled down near the entrance while the children returned to the pool.

Brisa started discussing her background. "I'm a botanist. I lived up north on a small ranch and raised plants for florists. Also organic fruits and vegetables for our own consumption. It was a simple life, but it suited our lifestyle. Northern California has many people who are concerned with living in harmony with nature more than they are concerned with material success. Naturally, we were concerned with our local environment and did our best to preserve it. However, there is no purely local environment on Earth. The Earth is one and what happens in one locale affects the whole Earth to some degree."

She looked down in her lap as the memories flooded in, and began talking in a quieter, more reminiscent tone. "I saw that pollution, poaching, mining and indiscriminate logging were destroying animal and plant life. I could smell and feel the changes in the air caused by the atmospheric pollution. Sickness in the animals and global warming. Each new threat to the environment alarmed me more. Eventually I realized that all life on the planet was being threatened, not just the lives of the polluters and environmental rapists. I became an ecological activist because there was no alternative."

"I thought it would be enough just to inform people of the danger of mounting ecological disasters. Most people would be concerned and respond favorably. A few people might be ecological vandals and resent what we said. We were wrong. Only a few people cared deeply, encouraged us and worked with us. Most people were apathetic, barely reacted to our message and forgot it moments later. Our opponents reacted most strongly. Some worried about lost jobs. Some resented curtailment of their sporting activities. Some feared lost property values. We felt that we could withstand their heckling and threats and overcome their arguments."

"Our first surprise was that our own friends and neighbors were against us because they didn't want to be part of the adverse notice that we would draw. This was more frustrating than our interference of our direct opponents."

"Our second surprise was a strong covert opposition. Some powerful interests with global scope worked against us wherever we went.

They seemed to have government and business contacts that worked together to stymie our efforts at every turn. Their attempts to identify and locate all the environmental activists made us fear that at some future time they would try to crush us, perhaps violently. That made our friends and neighbors more adamant that we should stop our activism. They did not want to become involved in a struggle of titans." Brisa looked up at her guests as she came back to the present time. They were watching her intently as she relived the story that had shaped her life and made her a lonely fugitive.

"Friends of mine were detained. I was away with Brandon when I heard of this, so I fled. Coming down here was natural because I had explored this area several years ago."

"But this is all background," she continued, "and you are probably more interested in how this home of ours was built. The water was the simplest thing because of my interest in hydrology. Satellite photos showed that the contours of the land from the mountain range to the north down to this area favored underground runoff. A number of possible channels existed and I selected a few with the best potential flows. The runoff would naturally drain away unless there were topological features to trap it. We needed a natural cistern, a dense rock formation that would trap the water and hold it underground safe from evaporation and leakage. The land around here has intrusions of dense rock. I just walked around and searched for one that held water."

"You just walked around and found water?" exclaimed Doug. "I've worn out several pair of boots traipsing over this desert and I haven't seen a damp spot, let alone a lake. How did you do that?"

Brisa smiled at his outburst. "I have an advantage, Doug. I'm a dowser. I can sense water under the ground. I think that Brandon may have inherited this gift, too."

"A dowser!" Doug chortled. "A dowser. No wonder you're at home in the desert. What did you find, one of the Great Lakes?"

"No," responded Brisa, "just a small basalt trap that fills up when there is sufficient runoff. I mapped the shape of the trap by dowsing. After that we just had to dig our tunnel and cavern to take advantage of the water supply. Then we bored a hole low into the trap, put a valve on the end and set up our sprinkler system."

Joy broke in with admiration in her voice. "You have done something here that to me compares with digging the Panama Canal and you try to pass it off as a minor task. This is wonderful, Brisa." Joy leaned over and hugged her friend. "You're the most terrific person I ever met. And the most modest, too."

"I didn't do this all alone," Brisa demurred. "Brandon was a great help and my best morale booster. He never complained. Then we had several of the Native Americans who volunteered to help us. Their power equipment made the dirt fly. They did the skylights for us. It would have been much more difficult without them."

Doug leaned back and looked up at the walls and ceiling of the tunnel. He said admiringly, "So you had some help. I can see how much you and Brandon did by yourselves. And you would have done it all, if you had to. I don't think that the polluters have a chance. You'll never let up on them. You've convinced me that one determined person can make a difference in this world. If I can help you, Brisa…"

"If we can help," interrupted Joy. "We were looking for a better life. You've shown us that we must make a better life, not expect to find it lying around somewhere waiting for us. If we can help you, just ask."

Doug nodded his assent. "Just what I was trying to say, Brisa. I feel that I've come to a church of the Earth and been enlightened. We have closed our souls to the wonders of God's Earth, and in trying to own it completely, we are killing it."

The children came out hungry and all pitched in to gather salad greens and prepare a quick meal. Dusk was on its way, so the families hugged each other warmly when the Costains started their trek home.

"Remember," said Joy, "If ever we can help…" Brisa responded thoughtfully, "Perhaps you can. We'll talk about it soon." As they passed out of sight down the canyon, Brisa and Brandon stood holding hands at the tunnel entrance. She was mulling over the thought that they might work together at the cavern and benefit each other.

On their way home Doug and Joy walked together while their children ran ahead in a game of hide and seek. Joy looked sideways up at her husband and with a little smile on her lips commented, "I was afraid you wouldn't be able to control yourself swimming with not one, but two naked ladies."

Doug gave her a more thoughtful answer than she expected. "When Brisa took off her dress I was shocked. I thought that she might be initiating an orgy. She's pretty attractive, too, much like you, love. But after that first shock there was nothing sexy at all. She might have been one of the guys in the locker room. It puzzles me. She's got it all – looks, body, brains, personality—everything but sexual attraction. I wonder why?"

"You're kidding!" Joy responded unbelievingly. "Any man would go for her."

"No," said her husband, still serious. "I like her. I really do. And she is a real woman, I know that, but when it comes to sexual attraction —nothing. I didn't realize it before, but this nude scene brought it to mind. She just doesn't have appeal. Just a buddy, not a sweetheart."

"If you say so, lover. But I'll keep an eye on your temperature gauge next time we go skinny-dipping."

Doug laughed at that and hugged her to him as they continued home. She knew then that the skinny-dipping hadn't been without physical attraction in her direction. They quickened their homeward pace.

Peyote Dreams

Brandon, Dan and Emily were sitting on the bluff above the box canyon one Saturday morning when their three Native American friends Juan, Manuel and Gabriel came hiking along the crest. They approached the sitting group and stood next to them, eyes searching the box canyon and beyond. There was an expression both furtive and expectant on their faces.

"Folks home?" inquired Juan in an overly casual tone.

Brandon wondered what surprise was in store for he could see that the two younger boys were bursting to reveal something the parents might disapprove. "No," answered Dan. "They're shopping. They'll be gone for hours."

"All right!" exclaimed Gaby. "Let's get..."

Juan's glance silenced him. "We've got a new game for today. We gathered some caterpillars yesterday." He held out his hand proudly showing several furry little objects to his friends.

Emily shrank back.

Dan looked puzzled and observed, "Those aren't caterpillars."

"We call them caterpillars," stated Juan. "This is peyote. It's from a cactus. It's magic. With this we can play medicine man."

"How do you play medicine man?" asked Dan.

"I don't want to play," Emily stated firmly and got up to leave. "Not with dirty old caterpillars from a cactus."

Manuel tried to mitigate the effect of Juan's description. He held out several more buds in his hand. "These aren't caterpillars, Em. Juan was just kidding. These are little fruits from a desert plant."

Emily moved next to Manuel and looked at the peyote more closely. Convinced that it was no bug, she picked up one of the buds and examined it in detail. She sniffed it and then put it back. "It still looks buggy," she concluded emphatically.

The three Native Americans sat down with the others. "It's not buggy," asserted Juan. "This is real medicine used by our tribal elders. They use it in ceremonies and stuff. Old Dreams With Manitou used it. We watched him. It makes you dream and fly and everything just like Brandon." The boys nodded assent and looked Brandon's way.

"Brandon doesn't make us fly," denied Dan. "You can't fly, can you?" he asked him.

Brandon didn't answer. Juan realized he was not supposed to reveal their episode of rapport with birds. "I'm sorry," he said contritely. "It just slipped out. These are friends, anyway."

Brandon remained silent. The Costains took that as agreement.

"I want to fly with Brandon," said Emily. "Even if I have to eat a bug."

"I'm game," joined in Dan.

Juan put the peyote buds on a flat rock, took out a pocketknife and proceeded to trim the buds and cut them into small pieces. "Now we have to prepare ourselves," he told them. He held out his hand and received six strips of red cloth from Gaby. He passed these out to the others. "Tie these on your heads like this." He put one around his own brow and tied it in the back with a square knot. Dan corrected Emily's granny knot into a square. "Now the ceremony begins," he said solemnly. "Manuel, the drum." Manuel took a small drum out of his pack and began a monotonous rhythm. After a few moments, Juan started in with a wordless repetitive chant. Gaby soon joined him. At Juan's signal the other children began to hum along and quickly picked up the wordless syllables that Juan was chanting. This continued for several minutes. Then Juan put a few small fragments of the peyote into his mouth and chewed them as he chanted. He motioned to the others to follow his example. Emily made a wry face as she started chewing the smallest piece she could find. They continued chanting for several more minutes. Emily fidgeted when nothing occurred. Brandon did not chew but relaxed to the chant.

"Ma mouf feers funny," said Emily in a garbled voice, saliva drooling from the corners of her mouth. "I doan wan any more."

Dan looked at her with a flat stare, also drooling and not comprehending her completely.

Juan pushed the buds in her direction and told her, "Keep chewing."

Brandon noted that the faces of the other children had become flaccid, saliva drool was now on all their chins, the chant was ragged and the drumbeat was uneven. Gaby, at Juan's signal, passed a water bottle around so that they could rinse the bitterness out of their mouths. Emily surreptitiously spit out the small piece of peyote that she had been chewing. Dan swallowed some of the water and saliva. Moments later he vomited that liquid off to one side. The three Native Americans tried hard to chew, chant and keep time with the drum. The ceremonial congregation degenerated into a gaggle of tired and slightly sick children. Emily's body swayed gently to the uneven beat of the drum.

Her eyes closed. The boys' eyes were open and occasionally jumping about as though trying to focus on something half seen. Brandon could sense an expectant awareness in the boys. In contrast, Emily seemed to be fading away from the group.

Brandon became concerned about her diminishing presence and decided to go into light rapport with her so as to sense how she felt. He relaxed and retreated into his inner self. He took her right hand in his left. From the other side he felt Gaby's hand slide into his right hand. A feeling of completion told him that all the boys had linked hands when he did. Brandon tentatively expanded his aura to include Emily. Their auras touched lightly and then Brandon felt himself being drawn irresistibly down into the crucible. He sensed himself merging with her so that their feelings were mingling, giving each strange sensations that might havc had their origins in the other or be some blend of both mixing experience and fantasy. The feelings expanded and blurred as Brandon sensed the four boys joining him now, all enveloped in Emily's aura and being merged into one entity in her inner being.

Now their egos and racial memories blended into a single awareness. A cacophony of voices in many tongues that yet were comprehensible echoed in the vast chamber of this new awareness. A kaleidoscope of images flashed and turned and scurried as though seeking their places in a new order. Then all wound slowly to a halt and everything went black. All sounds ceased. They were in a void.

A slow rumbling rotation began. Faster and faster it turned while the rumbling increased to a roar, a whine and then a scream. The darkness lightened and now they perceived themselves in a maelstrom whose whirling funnel shape was striated with bands of differing colors. They were sucked down into the funnel where the pitch of the noise rose above the aural scale but remained as a pressure on the soul, and the colors flashed through the rainbow with every turn as they descended. They passed through the apex of the funnel and through the surface of the Earth into its core. There they merged with all of the elements of the Earth as heat and gravity stirred the huge cauldron that recycled everything on the planet. A tree today, a limestone cliff tomorrow, followed by a flower and a bee and a rock and a cloud. The tenuous thought holding them together asked, "These elements are me for now, but who were they yesterday and who will they be tomorrow?"

The mixing was complete. A jet gathered mass and speed and

headed for the surface. Stirrings of life permeated the jet and it broke through the Earth's crust with a roar, splitting into smaller jets of wriggling life, of swimming life, of crawling life. The jets arced across the surface of the planet subdividing again and again into jets of life that flew and ran and dug and climbed. The planet heaved and brought forth mountains. It convulsed and brought them low. Heat and cold, rain and snow, winds and calm turned the jets into twisting and metamorphosing streams of life. Some terminated, some expanded, but all recycled with the rhythm of the planet's roiling. Life changed, but all life was linked by the change

The pace of change slowed and now they were identified with a single jet of life composed of bipedal figures walking more erectly the farther they forged ahead. They still formed, but one equal jet of life among many. A bolt of lightning struck their jet and split it into multiple streams. One stream split off sharply, roiled and twisted, and then began to swell. Its figures now were fully erect and striding across the globe. No longer was this an equal part of the jet of life, but now it lashed its way across the planet, crushing all in its path as its erect figures proudly strode through their world. Shields grew about them. They no longer merged their auras with all life about them and no longer respected other life. They denied their coexistence with the rest of life.

The other streams of life diminished as this major stream expanded and slashed across the world. Soon all other streams became pale wraiths and fell to earth with their vitality gone. Then the Earth itself dried and cracked beneath that dominant lashing jet. The Earth was conquered at last. But now that stream could not redouble itself at every rebound from the surface of the Earth. The Earth had no more to give. Instead the desiccated Earth drew all life from the stream and it, too, became a lifeless wraith upon a barren surface.

All sound ceased. A burning sun shone pitilessly upon the sere Earth. Nothing moved. The Punic battle against the Earth had succeeded in destroying everything. Total victory was its own antithesis of total defeat.

The group felt itself held in stasis where nothing moved or changed and time had no measure. Then faint rumbles crested to a crashing roar. The surface of the Earth cracked, then broke into huge blocks that pitched and slid over each other, wiping clean its surface in a great catharsis. Once more a whirlwind formed its swirling spectral striations and drew the universal life force down into the core of the Earth. The circle of life would begin again.

This time the entity that was the group was not drawn into the whirlwind. They floated aimlessly above the still barren Earth. Slowly the essence of each withdrew and became an individual again. The vision faded and all was void.

With a growing awareness, Brandon felt himself shaking and heard the growing rumble of an anxious voice. "Brandon, boy. What's going on here? Wake up! Wake up!" Now he felt big hands on his shoulders and recognized the voice. It was Mahmoud shaking him awake. Mahmoud was a new friend of the family, a wandering prospector, another desert rat.

"What are you kids doing with peyote? You could kill yourselves or scramble your brains. Wake up! Walk it off. Get moving. Get moving."

Under Mahmoud's prodding, Brandon was soon on his feet and walking about, breathing deeply and willing himself awake. He had chewed no peyote. He was empathizing with the other children. He breathed more deeply, calmed his emotions and withdrew into himself immediately fully awake and in control of himself.

Mahmoud had Juan and Gaby supporting each other as they staggered about. Brandon went to Emily who was sitting quietly with tears streaming down her cheeks. He shook her gently to no avail. He called to her softly and shook her again without response.

Mahmoud leaned over Brandon's shoulder. "What's the matter

with her? Won't she come out of it? Let me try." Mahmoud cradled her in his arms and crooned wordlessly to her. Now and then he called her name. Emily remained inert and silently tearful.

Brandon reached out for the little girl and sat her in front of him, still holding her hands in his. The others, including her brother Dan, watched quietly and fearfully as Brandon closed his eyes and relaxed into apparent sleep. In a few moments he, too, was crying silently. The others watched silently.

For Brandon it was a journey back to the barren Earth. Emily was holding the final vision of devastation and crying for the vibrant Earth that was no more. She had identified with the glorious fecundity of nature and the sense of unity among all its children. Now her family was gone and she was entirely alone in this barren world.

Slowly Brandon merged his spirit with hers and felt her desolation grow within him until he was nearly overwhelmed. Holding his ancestral thoughts of the fertility of the Earth that was, he brought her to share the tranquility that he was holding firm in his soul. When her desolation lightened, Brandon focused on his mother's vision of the brotherhood among species that she was working to bring to the world. That world would continue the circle of life now threatened by the supreme egocentricity of *Homo sapiens*. Returning them to an awareness of the unity of all things would reform the circle of life and return the Earth to vitality and growth in its natural order.

Emily gradually joined Brandon's vision. Her desolation gave way to a determination to be part of this new direction for the world. Happiness flooded her being and pervaded Brandon's in its overflow. He gently withdrew to his own self, but to his surprise a small a part of his soul was inextricably intertwined with hers. At last that small part of both of them divided into two. Half returned to him and half remained with her. Neither could ever be alone again.

They awoke. Emily opened her eyes and looked at Brandon with an adoring smile on her face. "I love you," she said. She turned her eyes up to the others. "I love you all."

Despite their upset stomachs, headaches and disquietude over the vision, the boys all smiled in relief at her apparent complete recovery. Emily jumped up and hugged each in turn. Mahmoud shook his head in disbelief at her cheerful demeanor. "Little girl," he said, "you must have a stainless steel tummy. I never saw anyone shake off peyote so fast."

Mahmoud walked over to his donkey and fished in a saddlebag. He brought forth an unlabeled bottle and a tin cup. Pouring some brownish liquid in the cup, he handed it to Juan. "Drink." he ordered.

Juan smelled the liquid and handed the cup back. "No thanks." Mahmoud stepped closer and held the cup to the boy's mouth. "Drink." he repeated forcefully.

Juan looked up at the stern face of Mahmoud, grimaced, took the cup and drank it down. For a moment he appeared uncertain as to whether it would stay down.

"Walk." ordered the big man. "The medicine will circulate and you'll feel better in a minute."

The others watched as Juan shuffled off. Soon he picked up his pace and was walking briskly when he returned. With a wan smile on his face, he told them, "Hair of the dog. Tastes bad but does the job."

The three boys followed suit and were soon back almost to normal. Brandon declined. He had not chewed the peyote and was unaffected by the little he had put in his mouth.

"Now tell me," said Mahmoud, "Just what was going on here?"

The children looked at each other guiltily. Juan spoke up. "We were playing medicine man. We gathered the peyote." he replied, indicating Manuel and Gaby. "We wanted to see a vision."

"Did you?" pursued Mahmoud with interest.

There was no answer for a moment. The children silently looked at each other for a response. Juan again became spokesman. "I guess so. It was all weird. Just about animals and earthquakes and storms. Nothing special."

Emily started to speak, but her brother silenced her with a squeeze on her arm. The boys were not ready to bring an adult into their confidence about this marvelous vision they did not understand and had not talked over among themselves. Brandon's normal reticence kept him silent also.

Mahmoud searched their faces and knew that he was being excluded from their adventure. He did not pry. He picked up the remaining peyote buds and pocketed them. "I'm going," he said. "You kids are on your own now. Keep walking. Drink lots of water. Tell your folks about it when you're ready. And stay away from drugs. You may get a lot more than you bargained for. Some people never get their heads on straight again."

He picked up the donkey's lead strap and continued along his trail. The children stood watching his erect figure striding easily along his path to understanding the desert and himself.

The children stood in an uncomfortable group stealing glances at each other. "You all saw what I saw?" Juan half stated and half questioned. "It was like the beginning and end of the world. It was a real vision, just like Dreams With Manitou talks about."

"I'm scared." chipped in Gaby, still holding part of the vision.

"It was like a sci-fi movie." Dan described his reaction. "Was it real or just some doper nightmare?"

Emily's face still shone with the inspiration of her concluding revelation guided by Brandon. "It was a message for us," she explained with little girl gravity. "People are destroying all the animals and plants and land and air. We have to save it."

"What do you know?" railed Juan. "You're just a girl."

"She knows more than all of you put together. I could feel her leading us all in that vision." answered her brother.

"No way." replied Juan. "Anyway, I'm going to ask the shaman. This is Indian magic, not white men's. Our people know more than she does about that."

The three Indian boys arose and walked slowly away. "Don't tell anybody." Juan cautioned. "This is our vision and nobody else's." They picked up their pace towards the reservation.

"Why don't you say anything?" Dan asked Brandon.

"Brandon knows everything." observed Emily, gazing at him with adoration in her eyes. She put her hand on his arm. "He brought me back."

Dan looked intently at them. He knew that there was some secret between them now that he could never know. Resentment welled up in him. No one could share something with Emily that he could not be a part of. "Stop that, Emily. He brought those Indians here. He got us into this. We've got to forget it so that Mom and Dad won't know."

Dan turned to Brandon. "Go home. We don't want you and peyote and visions around here anymore."

Brandon looked back calmly understanding that Dan resented the first break in sharing his young life with his little sister.

"Go on. Beat it!" shouted Dan. "We don't like you anymore."

Brandon stood up to leave, pained at this distressing fallout from Juan's medicine man game.

Emily hugged her brother and spoke with a new maternal tone in her voice. "The vision was real, Danny. We must know what it was. Only Brandon knows. He can tell us what to do."

Dan raised his head and stared into her eyes. He saw something changed there. She was not his dependent little sister any longer. He dropped his head and cried. Her vision had changed his world. His shoulders sagged. The resentment faded from his face. He sobbed to Brandon, "I'm afraid. I don't know what it means. I'm too young to do anything. I want my mother and father. I'm afraid of you. Please go home."

Emily was now the strong and protective one. "Go now. Come back next week. I have to know what to do. That vision was for you and me."

Brandon arose, patted the confused Dan on the shoulder and waved goodbye to Emily. He headed for home after this day that had affected him and his friends so deeply.

Brandon walked slowly to the cave pondering over how to recount to his mother all that had occurred in the peyote ceremony. He knew that he could not hide his upset state from his mother and he did not want to conceal it. He wanted to know what had occurred among them and what it might mean. His friends had betrayed his confidences and pulled him into a situation for which he was not prepared. Fortunately, it was saved from immediate disaster. He hoped that there were no long-term consequences that they could not avert. He needed her help and insight. By the time that he arrived home his thoughts had stopped whirling and the experience was ordered in his mind.

Brisa was preparing dinner but stopped when she sensed his troubled state. She hugged him more warmly than usual, then stepped back to arm's length and asked him, "What happened? What's troubling you?" She pulled him over to sit on a seat beside her. He looked into her eyes and told her how he had been playing with the Costain children when their Indian friends arrived with the peyote. Her eyes widened at mention of the hallucinogenic drug but she did not interrupt. He told her of their attempt to reenact the peyote ceremony to call up visionary powers. He, himself, did not intend to participate in the drug taking and visions, but suddenly he was pulled into the vortex of their vision and became part of it. His tale slowed as he recalled the details of the vision and became immersed in it again. This time Brisa took his hands and helped guide him through the experience. Now he became more aloof from the whirl of emotions and sensual jolts. His mother became a buffer between him and the direct sensations that he previously had.

He could sense that it was Emily who orchestrated the vision, pulling together the ancestral memories of the group, organizing them and becoming the conduit for the allegory that was the vision. Brisa softened the images and sensations and they both withdrew from the grip of the vision to the quiet of the cave.

After a quiet interval, Brisa spoke. "You are fortunate, my son. You have been through a dangerous experience that could yet have permanent consequences. I think because of your ages and the bonds among you that nothing bad will happen. You will all be affected but perhaps only by an increased awareness of the unity of all nature. That will be good. Emily may be most changed and we will have to help her to adjust to her new awareness.

"Women have different spirits from men. We are the family builders, the ones who pull together all the elements of our descendants into a connected group. You felt this force when you were drawn into Emily's vision.

"Women have different memories from men. There are some aspects of inheritance that come only from the mother. Also, some things are inherited only by daughters and not by sons. In particular, these are the characteristics and related memories that continue the family ties from generation to generation, the warm emotions that cement these ties to form a family and perhaps even a species. The woman's memories make sense out of the seemingly chaotic course of evolution. Mother senses the growth of the embryo within her and the growth and destiny of the race outside her.

"Homo sapiens, 'the humans' as they call themselves, have another characteristic. They are organizers. You sensed that Emily organized the ancestral memories that all you boys had inherited. Humans organize their society, their concept of the universe. They feel compelled to organize every other species in the world and perhaps Nature itself. Unfortunately, they do not comprehend that nothing is completely or-

ganized until it is dead. Thus organization has helped them to dominate all other species. It may also condemn all of us to a common death.

"Their success at organizing and dominating has developed a monumental egotism. It is evident in their religions. They see themselves as the designated 'stewards' of all the Earth and its inhabitants. Everything, every animate and inanimate form, is dedicated to their benefit. The destruction they have wrought makes it evident that they are unjust stewards. Up to now there has been no control to curb the excesses of this unjust stewardship. Your vision indicates the probable consequences of this egotistical domination of Earth."

"Your experience shows that humans have inherited capabilities that could relate them to the totality of life in the universe. It is primarily their egotism that prevents communal thought with neighbors as well as with their ancestors and with other species. Can this be changed? I do not know. I have dedicated myself to this task. Today you have had a vision that, if heeded, could change the world. Learn from it. Share it. It may truly be a gift from our maker to reunite humans with the rest of the world."

Brandon listened intently with every sense to absorb the meaning of her discourse and to relate it to his vision. "Do you think then that the vision was real? How could that be when everything moved and grew and changed so fast? And how could we see a future that hasn't happened? And how can we change it if it's real? I don't know what to believe of that vision!" He bowed his head in frustration and gripped his arms tightly across his chest.

"I can't explain everything," replied Brisa. "I know that we all inherit memories from our ancestors. These memories were important to them. They are sometimes important to us for survival. They are small fragments from other lives. We have learned little things like divining water, knowing edible plants, identifying medicines and having rapport with other life forms. Your young friend Emily put all those little memories together into a continuous story for you and then composed an ending from all that went before. Maybe it is the future. Maybe it is not. But it is something we can work to prevent. Perhaps that is the reason for visions of the future. Our people are not good at foreseeing the future. The humans are not good at remembering the lessons of the past. You may have found a bridge that will bring all of our talents together at last. I hope it is so."

"What should I do, mother?"

Brisa considered the question for a few moments, then answered, "Nothing, unless they ask for help. If there is a seed planted in fertile ground, it will grow in its own time. Watch, wait and help when it is necessary. Do not try to force it. We do not know the human potential. They must find it for themselves. If we try to give them our ways, they will suspect our motives, resent us and attack us. It is enough that a door has been opened for them. Do nothing more for now that will make your actions intrusive on their thoughts."

Brandon hugged his mother and went up to the mesa to think over all that he had seen and been told. It was a major concept for a young boy. There was much waiting, watching and thinking to do.

The three Indian boys hiked back to their homes without speaking. Each was assimilating his experience in his own way.

Juan was overwhelmed by his altered concept of his heritage. The game of tribal ceremony had started as a self-demeaning and derisive gesture against the old Indian traditions and those who lived in the past through them. They had been no protection against the order and technology of the European invaders who had taken the Native Americans' food, land, independence and pride. Native peoples did not want to be white and could not be themselves. Their heritage had been stolen. Juan's jest had boomeranged. The ancestral ties had been rebound. The glorious inexorable march of technological civilization contained the seeds of its own destruction in its alienation from the rest of creation. The exile of the tribal peoples to reservations, both imposed and self-chosen, was not entirely destructive. They were insulated to some extent from the technological culture. Like the residents of all ghettoes, they maintained their identity as a people and preserved ways and customs that ensured survival and ancestral continuity. Like ore in a crucible, impurities were burned away and the pure metal remained to be cast into stronger and more enduring forms. Juan decided that he wanted to renew and strengthen his ancestral ties. His ancestors would speak through him to others as they had spoken to him in his vision. He must speak to Dreams With Manitou. He had much to tell and much to learn.

Manuel walked with head up and eyes wide open, but he did not see the desert; he saw the lush and game-filled lands of the early vision. A great joy was in his heart at the sight of green vegetation, healthy animals and confident people who were an integral and respectful part of his life. A great sadness was in his soul that a philosophy of pride and domination was making a barren desert of the living Earth. The memory of brotherhood with all life, respect for all Nature and sharing the blessings of creation among all living things remained with him as a basis for hope. Once more the Earth could flourish if each person renewed the land about him. Manuel's vision of the past segued into a vision of himself turning his own land into a paradise. The sadness of his soul was lightened. His step became brisker with the desire to begin the rebirth of Earth at his own door.

Gabriel walked with a steady mechanical pace. He felt himself carried along by the marching hordes of humanity who strode across the Earth unfeelingly crushing everything in their path. He tried frantically to step carefully, but he was lock-stepped into their march. He tried to divert their path to avoid the helpless life before them. He could not. In desperation he willed himself to grow so that he could see over them; he willed himself to be stronger and pushed himself to their forefront; he willed himself to lead them in more circumspect paths so that life and beauty were spared; he willed himself to break the martial lockstep and to guide them in a more graceful choreography of progress. Gabriel's own steps became lighter and playfully offbeat as he continued homeward. He had much growing to do to be a leader of his people.

Before they reached their settlement Juan called Manuel and Gabriel to him. "Tell nobody nothing," he counseled. "I have to think this over. When I'm ready, maybe I'll tell the old shaman. Maybe it is a real vision and he can tell us what it means."

"I know." said Manuel. It means I have to take care of my own house and land. And I will, too."

"No." contradicted Gaby. "It means that I have to grow up to become a great leader so that I can keep people from trampling everything on Earth. You have to help me."

Juan was surprised at the backtalk from his younger friends.

The vision had changed everyone. Frowning at them, he repeated, "Tell nobody nothing. I have to think."

When they arrived home Doug and Joy Costain were mystified by the strange behavior of their children. Emily was quietly cheerful, responding affectionately to her parents' greeting. After a brief welcome, she sat by herself on her bed and became introspective, apparently content to review her own thoughts. Dan was obviously troubled. He barely suppressed his scowl when greeting his parents. He stepped away from them immediately, fidgeting about and glancing at them sideways, caught between his pledge of secrecy and his need to communicate with his parents to obtain their comfort and support.

Doug pulled his reluctant son to the sofa and sat beside him with an arm about the boy's shoulders. "Tell me about it." he prompted gently. Dan dissolved into uncharacteristic tears. His father held him until the boy quieted and then prompted again. "What happened, Dan?"

Dan spoke through his diminishing sobs. "Juan and the others did it. They gave us caterpillars and beat a drum and sang like medicine men and we all got sick and we had a weird dream about the end of the world and..." He dissolved into sobs again and buried his head against his father's chest.

"Do you feel sick? Do you want to go to bed?"

Joy came over and sat on the other side of him. "Oh, Dan! Let me see you. Let me take your temperature. Let me hold you." Dan responded by falling into her arms and sobbing uncontrollably. The psychological impact of the peyote, the vision and his own inability to control the situation overcame him. The emotional scene persisted for several minutes while the distraught parents tried to calm him and learn the details. Emily sat serenely on her bed and communed with her own thoughts, oblivious to the turmoil about her.

Dan at last quieted and his mother let him lie down on the couch to collect himself. Her thoughts then turned back to Emily. She sat down beside the girl who was so strangely calm and aloof from the emotional storm swirling about her. "What happened, Emily? What has upset Dan so badly?"

Emily returned slowly to the here and now focusing her mind as well as her eyes. "Yes, mama?"

Joy repeated, "What happened today?"

Emily looked up raptly into her mother's eyes. "We had a vision, mama. We saw the whole world being created, and all the animals and people being born, and paradise, and then the world ended. And Brandon was there. And maybe we can make it not end." Her mother was astounded at this matter of fact recital of the dream that had badly shaken Dan. Emily was so serene and convinced that the vision had a beautiful message that it seemed a totally different experience. Joy probed further but could get no clear picture of what her daughter had experienced. One thing seemed certain. It had been an experience of tremendous scope for the children, all six of them, and Brandon was a central figure in the dream for Emily.

Joy probed her further. "Weren't you frightened? Dan says that everyone chewed caterpillars, the Indian boys played medicine man with drums and singing, and he had a weird and scary dream about the end of the world. Did you do all that, too?"

Emily frowned as though trying to remember the details that frightened her brother. "Yes," she said tentatively and then brightened. "Everything was dark and scary. I was all alone and sad. But then Brandon came to find me. He held my hand and we became like one person and I loved him like I do you and daddy and Dan. And then the world became nice again because Brandon and I helped everything become part of one circle of life that never ended. That's what I have to do, mama. I have to make everything in the world from one circle of love. Then the world won't end. And it will all be beautiful again." She gazed entreatingly at her mother. "You see that, mama, don't you? I have to make the world nice again."

Her mother grasped one unsettling aspect. "What do you mean, 'Brandon and I became like one person'? What did he do to you?" she asked anxiously.

"He held my hand and I thought what he thought and we were like the same person, only not really. It was like being inside each other and yet inside myself. Haven't you ever felt like that with Daddy?"

"What do you mean 'inside each other'? Did he touch you anyplace else?" Joy pressed this line of questioning.

Her daughter responded in precise tones to make her understand. "I told you. Brandon held my hand in my vision. We became one person almost. Then the world became nice again. When we separated part of Brandon stayed inside me, right here in my heart. And it's still here," she assented with hand on her breast.

"Then we awoke." she continued. "We were still holding hands. Dan and Juan and Manuel and Gabriel were sitting there watching us. And Mahmoud was there, a big man with a little donkey. He made the boys drink some medicine to feel better, and then he left. Brandon knew him."

This revelation made her mother even more upset. "Let's take a bath now," she ordered, determined to inspect her daughter for any possible molestation. "I think we all need to rest and calm down. Tomorrow we'll go see Brandon and his mother."

To Joy's relief there were no physical signs of molestation, but she had to get to the bottom of this. She told Doug about Emily's story that night after Dan went to sleep between them. They determined to see Brisa and Brandon as soon as possible.

Juan kept to himself the next day, sitting on a rock outcropping while he reviewed the vision and in a way new to him asked his ancestors for guidance. There were no more visions. He heard no voices. Yet the act of asking for guidance brought him closer to his people, to their land, and to the culture that he had been deriding in mimicry of his rebellious teenage friends. There were values he did not understand in his culture. This ignorance had kept the meaning of the vision from him. He needed to talk to the once despised shaman to understand his vision and himself. As the sun descended and hid the landscape from his eyes, the desert shadows illuminated his inner spirit. He could see himself as a mean and self-centered child. He was ashamed of his people and how he had rejected their ways, and because he had accepted the outsiders' view of their lives. He was too lost in this rejection and self-doubt to look for lasting value in his own culture. He was too ignorant about his own culture or that of the outsiders to compare their values. A deep sense of guilt filled his soul. He knew that his Mexican friends confessed to their priests to remove the guilt of their sins. He must confess to Dreams With Manitou and ask for forgiveness for rejecting the old ways. Then he must tell him of the vision and ask for help in understanding it. He could not let ignorance be his shelter any longer. The shadows in his soul faded and were replaced by the hazy outlines of the landscape. Juan was surprised to see that it was dawn.

Juan went first to his adobe where his mother was sitting by the door waiting for him. He walked over to his mother and leaned down to hug and then kiss her with unaccustomed tenderness. She looked up at him in surprise.

"I'm sorry, mama. I'm sorry for all the trouble I've been to you. I'm sorry for ridiculing you and dad and the old ways. I'm sorry I've been a pain in the ass."

She looked at him with an astounded expression but was unable to compose a response.

Her son continued, "I had a vision yesterday, a vision from our grandfathers. It showed me the birth and beauty and ugliness and then the death of the world. The big civilizations are destroying everything. They cannot live in harmony with the Earth as your grandfathers did. Last night I sat on a high rock and thought about this vision. The guilt is on all who have forgotten that they are part of the circle of life. I am one of those. I am sorry and I say this to my ancestors through you and then my father and then the elders of our tribe. Today I must confess this to the shaman. I must rejoin the circle of life before I can understand what the grandfathers want me to do."

The round and stolid face of Gentle Wind softened to reveal the beauty and tenderness of the young wife and mother she had been when Juan was born. She arose to enfold him in her arms and cry softly with her face against his hair. The promise she had once envisioned in her newborn son was now renewed.

Juan stood before the shaman who was sleeping in a chair propped against the front of his house. The shaman's mouth was open and he snored intermittently; a frown creased his brow as unwelcome dreams coursed across his dreamscape. Juan felt pity for this man who had been given a half-formed vision in his youth but was now bedeviled by the dream that never materialized. Juan knew that this might be his own fate, but the knowledge helped him to understand the shaman at last. An unfulfilled dream can be a greater burden than no dream at all. And so Juan stood before the shaman, a boy who had taken the first few steps in the moccasins of his elder.

The pity and sympathy and concern for his own future brought the boy to his knees beside the sleeping shaman. "I am sorry, Dreams With Manitou. I looked at you with the white man's eyes and despised myself. I was wrong. I want to rejoin the circle of life and listen to my grandfathers again. I want to see through your eyes and listen with your heart. I ask for your forgiveness and your help. I want to be one of the people again."

Juan knelt there quietly for a while, remembering the once bountiful Earth and its destruction by the organized marching hordes of civilized man. He must understand his vision and find his own place in the renewal of the Earth or he would grow old in the emptiness of an unfulfilled dream.

At last he raised his head and looked up at the shaman. Dreams With Manitou was no longer asleep. He was smiling down at Juan with fatherly affection in his eyes. "I dreamed," he said, "that I had a son who took me by the hand and led me to the top of the mountain that I have been seeking all my life. When I saw his face, it was you. There is not guilt, my son, only poor teachers. You must lead me, not I you."

"I mocked your ancestral rituals to the white children. I made Manuel and little Gabriel come with me. We used the peyote buds and mimicked your songs. Then we had a vision, Dreams With Manitou, in which we saw the creation of the Earth and its destruction by man. Somewhere I play a part in this vision, but I do not know what it is. I need your help to find my way, but I am ashamed to ask."

The shaman stared at him searchingly for a long moment as though looking for something he had long expected to see. At last he nodded approvingly to himself. He had first felt the germination of the new spirit within himself, then in the three workers at the cave garden, and then in several who had worked on the new water supply doused by

Brisa and himself. He was not surprised that it would be manifest now in the youth.

He told Juan, "The wisdom of our people is shared among us. You must come to the council where we will listen and offer our interpretations. Only you in your heart can tell which is the true meaning. I will call the tribal council meeting for tonight. We will ask the grandfathers to guide us so that we may enrich the circle of life. Our fires have grown dim. Let us hope that our ancestors have not forgotten us as we have forgotten them."

It was the first time that he, Juan – no, not 'Juan' in the council meeting but 'Dust Devil' – had been inside the ceremonial chamber when village elders were present. Of course, he had poked his head inside the entrance to steal a quick glance, but all he had seen was a windowless, dimly lit and barren circular room. The arched ceiling was low with a smoke hole in the center. A small fire pit was in the middle of the floor. There was no furniture. The empty and featureless room was as devoid of life as the bleached and tumbled adobe bricks of long abandoned archaic settlements he had seen in the desert. The emptiness was representative of tribal religious life and lore. It was fitting for the cardboard characters of the elders and their puppet children who performed their ancestors' holiest and most soul stirring rituals for the coin-tossing amusement of tourists.

Now, when Dreams With Manitou stepped inside the room before him, it took on the magical quality of a dream. A small kindling fire in the pit barely lighted the room with its infrared glow. As the fire flickered, shadows and coppery highlights danced across the visages of the elders who were seated in a circle around the pit. Dreams With Manitou joined the circle in a cross-legged position on a rug that he spread on the floor. Juan stood hesitantly inside the door, not knowing whether it would be proper for him to join the circle of elders.

The elders wore their traditional tribal regalia that Juan had rarely seen, not the beads and bells they donned for tourists. They were barefoot and wore fringed buckskin pants. Matching buckskin vests were decorated with traditional symbols among which he recognized the sun, moon, earth, winds, thunder, lightning, water, fire, maize, sky and ocean. Each vest was decorated individually with combinations of these symbols plus the guiding spirit of the wearer. Among the guiding spirits he recognized were the bear, deer, roadrunner and lion. Their hair was worn in a traditional fashion, long, loose and straight or in a single braid. Except for Dreams With Manitou, their headbands bore little decoration. The color of each band was that appropriate to the natural spirit who gave power to the elder – blue of sky, red of fire, white of water, gold of sun and black of thunder cloud. Body paint was on their faces, arms and chests. The patterns and colors were simple, but their meanings were hidden. He knew that they represented to each one the path that his personal vision indicated he must follow to find wisdom and understanding. Perhaps he, too, would try some day to depict the unutterable and indescribable meanings of his own vision in such a fashion.

The solemnity of the meeting changed all the men in Juan's eyes. It was no longer the old and limping George Piñon that he saw, but the stern chieftain Running Buck, who had met Geronimo; it was not the desert drifter Paco, but the canny scout Road Runner who knew every trail and waterhole; it was not the temperamental Banty Bonsera with his long hair and headband, but the seasoned warrior, Crouching Panther, a member of the last resistance against the reservation boundaries imposed by the federal government. The spirit of the people had not died. It had been suppressed and compressed within the souls of a few, but it was waiting to be released when the proper catalyst was found.

Juan saw that each of the elders carried paraphernalia that must be related to his role in the council. Dreams With Manitou had an owl feather in his headband, a necklace of bear claws, and black ankle bands that appeared to be of crow feathers. He held a carved staff that was painted red to signify life and had an owl head on top signifying wisdom. A decorated drum leaned against his knee, ready to accompany the rhythm and power of songs and stories. Running Buck held a ceremonial pipe and willow bark pouch in his lap, ready to send a call to the Great Spirit for counsel. Road Runner held an ancient divining rod that denoted the power of water to bring life to the desert. Crouching Panther held a ceremonial bow and arrow that signified the power over life and death. They took his vision seriously for it was in accordance with the traditions of their people that the spirits sent visions to match the needs of the times and the capabilities of their people.

Juan's sense of guilt deepened as he realized that he had been viewing his people through the eyes of the oppressors. He had seen only the outward trappings of those who had lost a battle and not the unvanquished spirit inside the people. Now the strengths were more evident in their features, the determination more evident in the bearing, the tribal bonds more evident in their dress, the cultural linkages more evident in their speech. Suddenly Juan felt at home, among his own people at last. The estrangement of his rebellious youth was ended. He bowed his head and let the tears of joy run down his cheeks. The elders looked at one another and their eyes, too, became moist. A prodigal son had returned.

Dreams With Manitou beckoned Juan to join the circle. "Come Dust Devil, sit with us and we will talk about visions that the Great Spirit sends to instruct and guide us."

Apprehensively, Dust Devil sat between Dreams With Manitou and Crouching Panther, wondering how to describe the vision whose scenes were bright as day inside his mind, but too chaotic and unassimilated to relate in words. He began to sweat and breathe in shallow gasps as stage fright overcame him.

The elders appeared not to notice his dread. Dreams With Manitou fed the kindling fire. He picked up his drum and started a soft rhythmic beat. Running Buck began to chant in their tribal Kitanemuk dialect. Dust Devil had difficulty following it because of his own rejection of things Indian, including his refusal to converse in his native tongue.

"Hey-ah, Heyah, Heyah, Hey-ah! Great Spirit, Grandfather of our Grandfathers, source of all life and spinner of the sacred web that bonds all creation. You have guided your people in times of trouble with visions that warn us of danger and show us the path of life. Each of us here has received a vision, both a blessing and a burden. Our times of trouble are now generations long. Yet we keep the flame of our faith burning so that our people may survive to join the reborn nation when the Earth shall live again." Running Buck fell silent.

Crouching Panther raised his bow and arrows. "Oh, Great Spirit! I hold the symbols of combat, the power to take life. These have failed us when we sought to preserve life by taking life. May they symbolize for us now the power of the combative spirit to survive and eventually to win our way to the reborn Earth."

Road Runner held aloft the divining rod and cup of water. "Great Spirit, water symbolizes the power to give life. Our Earth has died for us. Our troubles seem insurmountable. Tell us what to do or our people shall be no more."

Juan was now little Dust Devil as his father had called him. His days had been spent in aimless vortices of contention, raising angry dust clouds that obscured the beauty of life. But now he was a frustrated Dust Devil, wondering why he had been given a vision without understanding of its message or the role he was meant to play. He clenched his fists and bowed his head in dejection.

Dreams With Manitou spoke in a fatherly tone. "Dust Devil, my son. Do not be afraid that we are here to question you about your vision and to criticize your every thought. Visions are sacred. They are messages to the people sent through the dreamer. You are blessed to have a vision. You will be burdened all your life with this vision. It will change your life forever.

"We have called this council to ask for guidance from the Great Spirit for all of us and to tell you of your experiences with your own visions. Whether or not you tell us your vision is up to you. We can tell you that visions are chaotic experiences. They are filled with overlapping sights, symbols and emotions. You cannot grasp the vision all at once. You cannot understand the full message in a flash. Only as you grow older will the message become clear. Even then, you may never be able to communicate all you have seen and learned to others. But time does not matter. The vision is yours forever to review and examine. It will not fade. It will not let you be. There is power for you in the vision to help you make it a reality. However, the power of the vision cannot be attained until that vision is performed for others. Some day you will perform your vision for your people. From that day on your power will grow for you will be carrying out the work of the Great Spirit."

He was silent, recalling his own vision. The other elders nodded in agreement with what he said. The shaman played softly on his drum. The others sang occasionally from old tribal songs about the beauty of the Earth, the brotherhood of all life and the sacred duty of man to respect the world in which he was permitted to live.

Dreams With Manitou spoke again. "It is not surprising that you should be gifted with a vision, Dust Devil. You are descended from the great medicine man, Whirlwind Chaser, of the Oglala Sioux tribe in the Dakotas. He was the uncle of Standing Bear and cousin of Black Elk, a very holy man. In 1889 and 1890 there was a man with a vision that he said told him how to rid the Indian lands of the foreign invaders and to bring back the bison so as to create a new Earth. His name was Wovoka, a Paiute from Nevada. Whirlwind Chaser and several others went to Mason Valley, Nevada, in mid-1890 to see this holy man reputed to be the son of the Great Spirit. They were all convinced by this man that the invaders could be made to disappear from our lands."

"While in Nevada, Whirlwind Chaser fell in love with one of our women named Morning Star. He promised to return to her after bringing the message of the Messiah back to the Dakotas. That dream of a new Earth ended in the Massacre at Wounded Knee on December 29, 1890. The tribes were fenced into reservations. We did not see Whirlwind Chaser again. Your great grandfather, Desert Storm, was one of the last rebels against the reservation laws. He, too, followed the vision of Indians free in their own land again. He was killed in 1928 in a protest raid. Your mother, Gentle Wind, has been against violence all her life. Too many of her family have died in lost causes."

"What shall I do?" asked Dust Devil.

"You must wait and pray until you understand your vision better. When it is time and you want to communicate your vision, come again to this council. We can prepare you to perform the vision and to realize your power and your mission. Only you can decide to accept it."

"And what about the others, Manuel and Gaby?" He stopped and then continued apologetically, "I don't remember their Indian names."

"We will speak with them also. The Great Spirit must have much work for us to have three of our people see this vision."

"And three others," added Dust Devil. "And three others."

Running Buck took a coal from the fire and lit the pipe. They sat silently for a long while. The sweet smoke of willow bark carried their thoughts and prayers aloft.

The next Saturday morning Brisa told Brandon, "The Costains are coming to see us. Fetch Dreams With Manitou and your Indian playmates. We must discuss what happened in your vision."

When the Costain family arrived, they found Brisa, the shaman and the four boys sitting in a circle in the garden area. The greetings were solemn and the children merely nodded to one another. Brisa rose and invited them to join the circle. The Costains appeared uncomfortable at finding a larger crowd than they expected for their confrontation about the peyote incident.

"Dreams With Manitou has just started to tell us about the use of peyote in ceremonies to stimulate visions. The children told us about their play-acting ceremony that went awry. The shaman is explaining the significance and the danger in what they did. Please sit down and listen with us."

They sat down reluctantly to one side of the circle because they wanted to talk about what happened to their children. They obviously did not want to endure a long lecture.

Dreams With Manitou put several buttons of peyote in the middle of the circle and began his explanations. "Peyote or mescalito is a small desert cactus that looks like a smooth, round, green rose with some tufts of hair. It contains a drug that induces visions. The drug is not very strong in the plant. Much must be chewed to induce visions. It has a bitter taste and causes a big saliva flow. Indians rinse with water and sometimes with alcohol to get rid of the taste. It makes the mouth numb so that the user may drool. If it is swallowed it makes some people sick to their stomachs. One must want a vision very badly to use peyote. It is not a drug for recreational use."

"How dangerous is it?" asked Doug impatiently.

The shaman responded to his concern. "Used properly in ceremonies, with teachers nearby and for the right purposes, there is no danger. We use peyote in ceremonies to initiate our youth into manhood. We use it in councils to seek visions that may make clear the muddled thoughts in our heads. Holy men use peyote to seek wisdom and understanding through visions. Often these visions relate only to the man and the peyote. Once in a great while the vision may come from the Great Spirit. If that happens, the visionary is given both a gift and a burden.

He is given the gift of insight beyond that of ordinary men. He is given the burden of carrying out the tasks of communicating the message and of bringing it to reality."

"What happened to our kids? They aren't holy men. When will this wear off?" demanded Doug.

Dreams With Manitou responded carefully, "They did not know what they were doing. They used little peyote, not enough to hurt them. Their vision may have been their own fears about the world and about growing up in it. But I never heard before of all the people in a ceremony having the same vision. Perhaps it is a vision from the Great Spirit. Perhaps it is because a girl was included in the ceremony. With us, only men may use peyote in ceremonies."

"Then you don't know anything to help us," grated Doug in exasperation. "Fine."

"Only time will tell," said the shaman. "Dreams fade quickly. A true vision stays sharp and clear for all time."

"What do we do now? These are just kids. We can't stand still to wait for permanent damage to set in. We'll see a doctor and report this." Doug moved to rise.

Brisa halted him with a gesture. "We may be letting hysteria mar our judgment. Remember, these are just children and peyote may have played only a small part. You heard that they chewed little. I think that we can remedy things right here."

"How?" asked Joy. "What do you know?"

"Yes. How?" seconded her truculent husband.

Brisa explained patiently. "Children have very good memories for pictures. Almost perfect memories. Let us have them hold hands again and relive their vision. This time all of us will be in the circle. And Dreams With Manitou, also. The children can tell us what they see and we can reassure them by being here. Where there is no hysteria or guilt all the fear will go away."

Joy and Doug took their children's hands and brought them into the circle. Dreams With Manitou brought out a small drum. He beat it gently to accompany his soft-voiced chant in the Kitanemuk dialect. Brandon recalled the vision and described it in sparse terms. Brisa picked up his vision and gradually shared it with the others, being careful to keep the outlines of vision hazy and its emotional impact soft. She also strengthened Dan's sense of bonding with Emily so that he would not feel threatened by her new intimacy with Brandon.

The children excitedly added their verbal comments as the vision progressed so that it assumed the air of a game in the Costain's minds. When the vision concluded and all eyes were open again, anxiety about the vision and its possible ill effects had dissipated. The Costains were convinced that overactive imaginations had imparted serious overtones to a childish game. Dan had forgotten his jealously of Brandon, even his rejection of his friend. Emily realized that she must downplay the importance of the vision to her when she spoke with her family. The three Indian boys realized that they could return to the vision when they wished to reexamine it and to understand better its meaning. The shaman became convinced that this was indeed a holy vision, one so important and complex that it was shared among the six children. He made silent thanksgiving that through his own vision he had helped maintain the vestiges of the old faith among his people. There remained fertile ground to nurture this new vision that might indeed lead to the rebirth of the people and the Earth.

A sense of ease and intimacy had come over the group. Brisa made lunch for all. After that the children played together while the elders spoke of the future. Brisa suggested that the Costains should move closer to her nursery and help her with the work. If they enjoyed it, then an extension to the cave could provide them quarters at the site and access to the water supply. The relief of the moment, added to their genuine mutual affection, sealed the agreement. The Costains accepted the offer of a partnership in the nursery business and a new home. The children were ecstatic at the news. They ran into the cave to claim worktables and finally jumped into the pool in their excitement.

Dreams With Manitou approved of this development. The keepers of the vision were to be kept together. The Great Spirit was assembling the elements that would bring the vision to reality.

Flight North

The smooth white satiny sheen with a tracing of dark blue veins held Brandon's gaze. His right hand was drawn to touch, then to caress sensuously the soft curving fullness so like his mother's breast but formed of pale moonbeams. An erotic flush suffused his body as he cupped it lightly with his left hand and raised it to his lips. He exhaled gently to let his warm breath swirl across the surface and remove the last traces of desert dust. In his mind's eye he could see the cascading waterfall of their cave glistening and leaving tiny droplets to trace their zigzag courses back to the stream.

A piercing cry shattered Brandon's reverie. He dropped his stream-polished marble back into its place in the small interstice in the rocks. Another sharp telepathic warning from Brisa vibrated in Brandon's brain, startling him into momentary response. Her pursuers had arrived. Their desert idyll had ended: time to flee.

Brandon knew that the momentary resonance of his mind with her alarm had already sent a pulsating beacon to their trackers. He sat on the ground, closed his eyes, and stilled every muscle as she had taught him. Bioelectric emissions must be minimized. Precious minutes passed before his calm became absolute. Rising at last, he walked farther up the canyon. He kept to the rocks and hard ground as his Indian brothers had taught him so as to leave no trail. With studied speed on this long practiced path he quickly reached the narrow red rock gorge entrance that marked the beginning of his escape route. Faint pinging probes at the edge of his consciousness told him that his pursuers were already coursing on his trail, focusing on the single beacon pulse he had emitted. His minimal response now was too faint for detection at their distance.

Entering the gorge through the iron-bearing red rock, he wound his way up the tortuous path and the main canyon was soon lost to view. The probing signals of his pursuers were rapidly attenuated to undetectabilty by the shielding iron.

The walls of the gorge rose several hundred feet above him. He could touch either side with his outstretched hands and often had to turn sideways to pass through narrow slits. His view ahead or back was usually but several feet. Without panic, he worked his way up the gorge so that signs of his passage would have been invisible even to his Native American instructors. Patiently he progressed, knowing that he would have to penetrate far up the trail to outdistance his keen and tireless trackers. Only the multiplicity of gorges and potential escape routes from the main canyon would frustrate the search if he could succeed in hiding his trail. He pressed onward, skirting sandy patches, picking his way up the vertical chimneys, selecting every hand and foothold so that no trace of his passage would be left. He held on to his sense of calm without slackening his pace. Only panic could betray him now.

Brandon pressed ahead as daylight waned and shadows deepened at the bottom of the gorge. His goal, a cave high up on the wall of the gorge where he had cached his backpack and supplies, was just a short distance ahead. The deepening twilight and his care to avoid leaving a trail slowed his progress, but at last he reached his landmark rock formation projecting from the left hand wall into his path. Its water hewn and polished shape resembled a howling coyote squatting on his haunches with sharp pointed muzzle in the air. Just beyond the coyote the gorge narrowed almost to a close at a point above head height. With a hand on either wall he levered himself up to a straight-arm position, then placed a foot next to either hand. The familiar hand and footholds were reassuring as he ascended the forty feet to the small cave mouth and rolled inside to be stopped by the reassuring bulk of his cached backpack. The first leg of his escape was completed.

Secure at last in his iron ore protected retreat far up the narrow gorge, Brandon let down his guard and thought of his mother. She was his only close friend, the only one who knew him to the depth of his being. She had schooled him for years to avoid revealing himself entirely to anyone, even the best of friends, and to avoid notice or show that he differed from others. She had also trained him to set up an escape route that he would follow automatically the instant he heard her telepathic warning that their pursuers had found her. She was sturdy, independent, self-reliant and resolute. She wanted Brandon to grow under her tutelage in a world that they would help change for the better. Meanwhile, she and Brandon would have to be free so as to work through friends near Mount Shasta to keep the spark of change alive. Brandon did not yet understand what was occurring in the broader world beyond their desert home, who and what their pursuers were, nor why he and his mother were caught in the maelstrom of change. He did know the warmth and softness of his mother beneath her resolute exterior, the loneliness she felt at being separated from her people, and their own mutual dependence on the close ties that bound them together as two strangers in a strange land. Now she would be alone in a different way, among her own people but as a captive. Brandon was entirely on his own, traveling a rugged mountain trail to reach sanctuary with friends in Mount Shasta, not knowing when it would be safe to emerge and begin the search for his mother.

Brandon lay there next to his pack feeling completely alone for the first time in his life. His mother and her warm aura of concern had always been close. Other people and animals had been near at hand sending out their unconscious signals of life activity and thoughts. But now this desert gorge was empty of life. The lode of iron shielded him completely from the emanations of more distant life forms. Not a quantum of light penetrated to his cave. He felt sorry for himself and his mother and allowed self-pity to wash over him. Brandon felt the tears well for his mother and himself and their plight. He rolled closer against the pack and gripped it tightly. The tears of a lonely boy adrift in a grown-up world coursed down his face. Where was his mother?

Suddenly his longing quest touched a chord in his memory and she was there. Her arm was about him protectively, their bodies were pressed together spoon fashion for warmth, their hearts beat and the lungs breathed in unison, their body scents mingled into a familiar odor, and their auras merged into one. Brandon could feel her pride in him and the love that was in her heart for him. Her expectations for him were uplifting his spirit. Brandon was no longer alone. Her memories lived on in him and linked him to an unbroken chain of ancestors reaching back to dim antiquity. Here in the quietest of chambers the ancestral memories reassured him that he would never be alone and he also would live forever, in the memories of his descendants, to guide and comfort them in time of need. He was the racial future, the past lived on in him, and his present formed an ephemeral link between the two.

At last he slept, nestled in the warm dreams of his mother. He was puzzled that he could not detect his father somewhere in his memories.

Brandon awoke to the sharp crack of a lightning bolt and the diminishing echoes of thunder expending itself in the absorbent folds and chambers of the gorge. When the echoes died away he could hear the drip of water. In the pitch dark he slid cautiously towards the cave mouth and found its edge with his fingers. Several drops of water splashed the backs of his hands. Extending them beyond the mouth of the cave, he felt only the dampness of mist and occasional raindrops. Elated, he knew that the lightest of rain would conceal any faint trail he might have left. A sudden spatter of rain on his hands turned the elation into concern. A steady rain would send a torrent raging through the gorge and effectively trap him in the cave. His pursuers would have time to gather reinforcements and block a wide expanse of the ridge against any escape. He sat in the darkness, quieting his emotions and listening to the intermittent spatter of raindrops while waiting for the dawn. His uncertain ally, the thunderstorm, playfully interspersed the rattle of distant thunder and the spatter of rain. Brandon could but wait for daylight and a hazardous climb down the wet wall if serious rain held off.

The first faint light gave hazy indication of the rim of the gorge. Dawn, not with rosy fingers but with grey tendrils of mist, stretched down the canyon walls of Brandon's retreat. He damply touched each foothold in turn to make his descent a challenge and at last reached the floor of the gorge to lose himself in the few dark puddles formed by the intermittent rain. He leaned out for a better view and the storm playfully spattered his face with a cold shower. A roll of thunder came high on the ridge. Brandon reached for his pack. He must do it now.

Brandon lowered his pack to the floor of the gorge and dropped the rope after it. Lowering himself to the first foothold, he began his descent. The gorge seemed wider than last night as he stretched his other leg to the far wall. The wet footholds, out of sight beneath him, seemed to be in odd places and at odd angles, and too small for solid footing. The floor of the gorge seemed farther down than when he had lowered the pack. His left foot slipped from the next toehold and Brandon's shoulders scraped down the rough rock face to wedge him between the gorge walls. His muscles stiffened as he locked himself in place. He remained immobile until the momentary panic passed and his pulse slowed. An effort of will unlocked his muscles and he tortuously turned against one wall, until his feet were flat against the other. The security of his solidly braced position calmed him further. Spitting raindrops told him not to tarry.

Inches at a time he lowered himself by sliding his shoulders and feet alternately down the walls. As he gained confidence, he moved more rapidly, although an occasional slip slowed his progress. Nearing the bottom he turned on one shoulder and raised himself spread-eagled between the walls to stand on two opposing footholds. He stepped lightly down the remaining distance and dropped beside the pack. He shouldered it and faced up the trail. Only the first step had been taken.

The rain made the sand mush underfoot and the jumbled rocks poor stepping-stones. The treacherous footing and irregular walls slowed Brandon's pace despite the pressure to outdistance his pursuers. Distant rumbles of thunder and occasional spatters of rain in his face warned him of the imminent danger of a flash flood. Every slip reminded him that an injury in the gorge would immobilize him for capture or to be swept away in the cascading waters. The tension between speed and caution increased the pressure on him as he picked his way forward.

The puddles became more frequent and small rivulets darted to connect them. Was it sweat or rain coursing down his face? Was the thunder louder or was it the growing rumble of a cataract further up the gorge? The rivulets were broader now, coalescing into tiny streams. Soon those, too, were joining into a larger flow. Brandon picked up the pace despite the deteriorating footing and his jarring collisions with the walls. Safety was now more dependent on speed.

Approaching the bend, he saw a ledge twenty feet up the wall on the left on which three rocks were stacked in decreasing order of size. His trail marker! Next side gorge to the left. He slogged forward more rapidly through the deepening water to the opening on the left. To his dismay the water deepened and flowed faster as he rounded the bend. Another bend, a step up onto a flat rock, and the flow ceased. That had been only a split in the main channel. The side gorge had no flow as yet. Taking a few deep breaths, Brandon strode quickly up the side gorge. Potential injury was now a secondary concern. There was more rain in this storm for certain.

Black clouds overhead dimmed the wan light in the gorge. The walls of the gorge were lower, slanting away from the vertical and less steep. The top of the ridge was near. Brandon squeezed through a narrow passage, stepped left to brace himself, and was pinned into his niche by a wild surge of water that rose over his head. He couldn't move or breathe. Holding the scant breath in his lungs against the surging pressure of the water was impossible. He exhaled in a choking cough and felt panic sweep through him. Then the pressure was gone. He gulped fresh air as the water swirled away beneath him. Frantically clawing the rocks he pulled himself forward and up above the rapidly diminishing pool. Now he could see that the transient flood had resulted from collapse of a temporary blockage above him. Ignoring his bruises, Brandon readjusted his pack with a quick shrug and scrambled over the detritus and up the trail. A deafening clap of thunder greeted his exit from the head of the gorge. The rain beat against his face. The trickle at his feet grew to a stream, increasing the anxiety that strained against his control. Another turn and the trail veered from the streambed to climb more quickly to the left toward the ridge.

Despite the slippery going, he outdistanced the rising water. However, he was also leaving the protective shield of the iron ore. Another clap of thunder overrode his concern. The electrical discharges jammed his senses completely. He could not sense his pursuers nor could they sense him in this charged environment.

Brandon reached the ridge tired and bruised, soaked through by the now driving rain. Visibility was limited to a few tens of feet. There was not time to pull out his poncho, nor any use in doing so. He slogged down the slope along his familiar route to higher country. Once across the dale and into the next row of foothills pursuit would be impractical. The rain and lightning had changed from threat to protection. He would be safe in an hour if the storm continued.

He retreated into himself and became a dull automaton plodding across the sodden landscape. His shoulders hunched his pack higher to cover his back. His broad brimmed hat cascaded water to the front when he bowed his head. Weariness set in, but Brandon's pace did not slacken. The lightning was receding and he must reach the hills before the protective curtain of electric static disappeared. The trail at last turned upward, alerting Brandon to the entrance to a canyon. There on the right he could barely make out the rock formation shaped like a clenched fist with the index finger raised. The first anxious leg of his journey was completed. He was moving on to higher ground.

His pace quickened as he followed the trail over hard ground, rocky stretches, and through the growing stream. He wanted to minimize signs of his passage, although the rain would obliterate most. He had come too far to be careless now.

The red walls of the canyon rose about him in a welcoming shield of iron ore. Thunder rolled in the distance now and the lightning was a faint background in his brain. The trail was above the streambed for the most part, only occasionally crossing sides on large stepping-stones. His last crossing was partly on submerged rocks, threatening him with a white-water trip down the canyon on his backpack. Gauging his steps carefully, he reached the left shore and climbed the bank up under a large overhanging rock. Human hands had enlarged the shelter into a cave. He dropped his pack on the floor and leaned against it. A wave of fatigue nearly put him to sleep, but Brandon rose in a few moments and untied his poncho. He unrolled it to reveal a towel, dry clothing and socks. Undressing, he dried himself, donned the dry clothing, rolled up in his poncho and immediately fell asleep. There was nothing to do but wait for the weather to clear and the stream flow to drop so that he could continue on into the mountains.

The next day was an enforced day of rest. The sky began clearing and the air became cooler. The water level dropped quickly at first and then more slowly, gradually losing its muddy color as the force of its current diminished. Brandon's bruises were only dull aches and purple splotches reminding him of his harrowing race up the gorge. He ate some of his cold food, rearranged his bedding and settled into a quiet period of recuperation and concealment from his pursuers. He could not enter into rapport with the birds or ground animals because that would entail projecting his self outwards and thus providing a potentially traceable signal to others of his kind. Instead he retreated inwards to search his ancestral memories for highlights from his racial past.

The tentative explorations of racial memories under his mother's tutelage had not prepared him for this trip. The initial contacts on his path into the past were those he had made before. They were moments with simple emotional impacts of an extraordinary sunset at the shore, a mountain peak rising through the clouds, a startled deer bounding over a fallen tree, and ten thousand geese rising from the wetlands to continue their journey north. Brandon browsed his way along, sorting and cataloguing the memories for future reference. Suddenly panic froze him as he strode, senses blinded by an electrical storm, into a group of hunters armed with spears. One immediately raised his weapon and threw it. Brandon felt the blade crease his side with searing pain. He whirled into the brush and ran in zigzag fashion as shouts and the rattle of spears sounded behind him. The "Others" had once again expanded into the territory of the people and would kill on sight any living thing they encountered. It was time to move farther into unexplored territory. No one was safe near them. No one could reason with them. Brandon was shaken by the remembrance, but regained his emotional stability and continued his memory sorting.

The culled memory experiences covered an emotional kaleidoscope for him. He was hurt in accidents; separated from his loved ones; experienced the thrills of first loves and the agonies of rejection; fled from the pursuit of the Others; found his friends killed by spears; and felt the emptiness of a world from which those of his kind were disappearing. Brandon also felt a determination to protect his children so that they would not be targets for the Others. They would hide, not among the trees and rocks of inhospitable areas, but among the Others themselves. They would mimic the Others in appearance, but yet know their own kind. The pressure of survival would help them do it.

Brandon returned to his outer consciousness at last, shaken by the basic emotions, the bits of violent history and the craving for racial survival and identity that he had experienced. His mother had warned him that there were dangers involved in experiencing the emotions of others, especially for a youth who had not yet fully experienced the range of his own emotions. He was surprised to see the sunlight, to hear the rush of the floodwaters, and to feel the cool breeze on his skin. It was as though he had returned from a strange violent world full of mortal dangers, soaring excitement, deep despair and ecstatic fulfillment. Now he was a young boy trying to understand emotions beyond his experience, emotions that would not be his own for at least another decade. He lay there and thought of his mother and her sheltering love, letting the vicarious experiences of his ancestors retreat to their memory cells. The softening weather outside lulled him to sleep with gentle murmurs and tender caresses. In his dreams his mother's love for him cushioned the violent excursions of the past and present and carried him into a future of gentleness, laughter and love.

He woke to the first light of dawn rimming the canyon walls. From down below he could hear the playful splashing of a stream flowing gently again. The sky was mostly blue with little flocks of sheep-like clouds drifting lazily towards the east. It promised to be a good day for hiking. The first trees were marching singly up the slope to where their taller fellows were gathered in great numbers. Brandon was drawn to join them. Shouldering his pack, he walked beside the creek using its rippling rhythm for his marching cadence. The world was wonderful, the mountains beckoned and he was on his way to Shasta for eventual reunion with his mother.

Beneath the surface enjoyment of the glorious day, Brandon felt a questing ping on his subconscious and then another. His pursuers were drawing near! He hurried over to the side of the canyon and crouched amid a jumble of boulders from where he searched his back trail for signs of them. The pings grew stronger and Brandon drew back into himself to prevent a response. Stronger came the pings but the trail remained empty. Then he heard a humming sound that quickly increased in volume, passed overhead and diminished rapidly. A shadow passed across the canyon floor. Looking up from his cover, he saw a helicopter following the upward course of the canyon. His pursuers were conducting an airborne search. Knowing this, he had to alter his path. Now Brandon kept closer to shelter at all times so that he could hide from overhead view on a moment's notice. He suppressed his appreciation of nature to concentrate on hearing the faintest of interrogating signals from his pursuers. He saw them no more despite hearing the motor and sensing their questing pings. Soon he entered the woods at the top of the canyon and hiked quickly along under their sheltering canopy. Discovery became a faint possibility rather than an immediate threat.

Brandon strode lightly now, enjoying all the new sights and scents and sounds of the forested terrain at this higher elevation. The sharp odors of low desert creosote bush, ocotillo, cholla and palo verde in their sandy terrain were far behind. He had passed through the less familiar levels of yucca, juniper and Joshua trees in the rain-drenched phase of his flight. He had reached the woodland altitude of piñon and scrub oak. Now the lighter mountain air seemed to carry all the sensations to him with an unusual clarity. Each odor was distinct, each sound individual, each panoramic view sharply drawn. When he paused to rest, the memories of his young childhood near Shasta mingled with the current sensory impressions until he expected to see the woodland home close at hand. Tears welled frequently when the sense of mother and home gave way to the reality of loneliness in his present plight. At those times he shouldered his pack, breathed deeply and pushed along on his path to the north.

His trail led upward away from the dry desert floor. Green grass carpeted the open spaces. Scrubby bushes abounded. He could feel more life around him – rodents, rabbits, an occasional deer and burro.

Brandon's route took him into the mountains west of route 58. Occasionally he could see the highway and its traffic. Sometimes there were ranch buildings lower down and the dust clouds of cars on dirt roads. Mostly he absorbed the sights and sounds of the wooded land he traversed. The trail continued upward. The route and symbolic landmarks described to him in detail by his Indian friends were engraved in his memory. They corresponded perfectly with the distances and visible landmarks he encountered. He kept on in the general direction of the three-pronged peak in the distance. At each landmark – the rock shaped like a shambling bear; the small double waterfall; the needle's eye boulder; the junction of three small streams at the base of a granite face – he modified his direction to follow the recommended trail. Centuries of hunting, tracking and seasonal migrations had defined the trail north for the native peoples. Perhaps wandering wolves had pioneered the first trails. The ancient trails now lived mainly in memories and tribal lore. Hunting, trading and seasonal migrations were ended. Travelers drove cars and stayed on the highways below.

The late afternoon cast its deepening shadows on the trail as Brandon descended into a park-like canyon. A small stream rippled through its center. The trees in the grove were well spaced. A little-used dirt road came up the canyon and ended in a flat area that showed signs of occasional use as a campsite. Reflected sunlight from the east wall gave a soft rosy glow to the park. The idyllic setting at this magical sunset moment entranced him. He paused to absorb the scene, the odors, the sounds of stream and birds. To his alarm, he also detected four men who were quietly seated by a cold fireplace, apparently expecting him. He had dropped his guard completely, lulled into false security by his solitary trek into the mountains. The four men stood as he approached.

"Hi, Brandon," said the nearest. "We've been expecting you.

Brandon smiled broadly, relieved that they were Indians and therefore the contacts that had been arranged to speed him on his journey. They introduced themselves as Big Tree, Spotted Owl, Running Hare and Striding Elk. All had the look of rangy toughness that one expects of mountain people.

"Dreams With Manitou relayed the code words to us by telephone as soon as you left. He calls you his brother and names you 'Soars With Eagles,'" said Big Tree. Looking down at the boy, he added, "You're not quite the mystical leader we'd expected to see from his reverent description of you. You're just a kid."

Striding Elk shifted Brandon's pack over towards their own gear. "The boy carries a man-sized load," he observed. The intimations of a spreading fame were more than Brandon expected or wanted.

"Dreams With Manitou is our friend. He is my brother. We have helped each other to understand the world and ourselves. People have taken my mother. They follow me. I must travel to Mount Shasta to meet friends, to carry on my mother's work and to free her."

"The Shaman has told us of this," said Spotted Owl. "Your story is closely held among those of us who remember and venerate the old ways."

"Let's eat before dark," interjected Running Hare. "This is a cold camp for we will not risk a fire."

He opened a pack and brought out large sandwiches of chicken and greens on wheat bread, plus carrots, celery and oranges. They sat in a circle and ate quietly, washing the food down with water from canteens.

Big Tree cut an orange in half and ate one section. He began talking.

"We are going to cover the next stage by truck after dark. It would be long and difficult on foot without access to supplies. After that I think that you can continue better on foot. It is a long journey to Shasta through the Sierras, but a good woodsman can do it at this time of the year."

Striding Elk continued, "We are Yakuts, people of the Sierras. Our grandfathers roamed these mountains on trails that even now are not known to outsiders. We will show you such a route." He spread a large packet on the ground before him, "Here are foods you can gather along the trail at this season to reduce the pack load you must carry."

The trail food was divided into roots, berries, fruit and nuts. Striding Elk pointed to each in turn and described the plant that bore it. "No one gathers these today," he observed, "except for ceremonial and tourist purposes. No one wants to walk miles to gather food when he can drive to the supermarket. But we have not forgotten. For us it is part of what it means to be Indian, to be connected with our grandfathers."

He proffered the food to Brandon. "Taste these. They may be important on your journey."

Brandon did so, committing the description and taste to memory.

Before darkness descended, they helped Brandon to reorganize his pack. A lightweight nylon mountain tent was provided for shelter from winds, rain and possible snow. A pair of hiking boots and several pairs of socks were added because the journey was long. A warmer mountain jacket with zip-out thermal liner replaced his lightweight windbreaker. Thermal underwear was added in the event of a cold snap. A folding pick-mattock was included for digging roots and for trenching the tent in wet weather. Canned rations and a large bag of trail mix provided emergency rations when wild foods were in short supply. His desert-oriented equipment was removed to lighten his load. At last they secured the packs and carried them down the road to their concealed pickup. They then climbed into the king cab to keep warm in the chilling twilight while waiting for nightfall.

They sat quietly watching the pink of the scattered clouds fade to deeper shades of red and purple. Dusk settled into the canyon. Brighter mountain peaks stood out against the sky.

Spotted Owl spoke quietly as though from a reverie. "Many years ago, long before the white man came, the Yakut peopled the big valley to the west and the mountains to the east. These are now called the San Joaquin Valley and the Sierra Nevada Range. We farmed, hunted, and fished. We traded our goods from the Pacific Coast to Nevada and from the San Fernando Valley to Sacramento. This was our home and we prospered. Those times we commemorate and revere in song and dance. Every word, every step and every motion evokes the sacred memories that tie together every living thing with our Mother Earth."

His voice droned on and the tired Brandon drifted off to sleep, followed there by the descriptions of steps and stances, facial expressions, clothing and ornamentation, weapons and ritual objects. He dreamed, and in his dream, he saw wide plains covered by waving grasses; herds of deer and elk; a line of wolves trotting across a field; small animals scampering from cover to cover; a panther lying on a prominent rock; flocks of birds crossing the skies. He surveyed the valley and savored the sights and odors and sounds of a bountiful land. His heart overflowed with thankfulness that the Great Spirit had so blessed his people. Turning his head further he saw three companions near to him – Big Tree, Running Hare and Striding Elk. Their faces were transformed with joy as they beheld this land throbbing with life. They were wearing breechclouts and each carried a bow, arrows and a light spear. A flint knife was in each waistband and arrows and spear were tipped with flint. Brandon then noted that he, too, was similarly clad and armed. His skin was bronze and he was as tall as they.

Striding Elk motioned them forward towards a deer isolated near sheltering brush. Brandon stayed with the group as they stalked their intended prey, drew ever closer behind the covering brush, then loosed their volley of arrows and ran to the side of the fallen buck. Striding Elk offered a short prayer of thanks to the Great Spirit and words of kinship with the deer that was fulfilling his part in the Circle of Life. He reverently slit the throat of the deer. The group butchered the deer and slung it over two poles for packing.

Success in the hunt hastened their steps. Soon the quartet of hunters approached the site where their tribal band was camped. Yells of recognition and cheers at their success signaled that the deer they bore had been seen. An older man in prime health strode to greet them.

Running Hare called out with trembling voice, "Grandfather! Grandfather!"

The hunters quickened their pace to a trot, but they drew no nearer the camp or the elder. They broke into a run and now the camp and people grew smaller and shrank into the distance. The shouts faded to inaudibility.

The quartet stopped. Running Hare fell to his knees and with arms outstretched and pleading whispered, "Grandfather. Grandfather." The lush panorama faded to a drab field fenced with wire. The dust of cultivation hung in the air. Tears cut channels through the dust caked on his face as he knelt in the dirt and sobbed, "Grandfather!"

Brandon awoke to darkness in the truck cab and the sound of tremulous breathing from his companions.

"Time to go," rasped Running Hare in an uneven voice, wiping his face with his forearm. "We have a long way to go over bad roads to reach the Kern River trail above where the Little Kern forks. It will put you in the middle of the range like you wanted. Little chance of campers and hikers on this route."

They drove without lights until they reached a paved road. There they sat patiently until a caravan of four pickup trucks with camper shells passed heading north. Running Hare pulled out onto the road and fell in behind the group, blending with them. Brandon dozed off as their pickup followed the others in the featureless tunnel of night.

Brandon awoke when the truck came to a stop. All was quiet. The pale light of the old moon outlined the spider web of evergreen branches against the sky. The sound of rushing water was a low roar in the background.

"Where are we?" asked Brandon.

"Just north of the Little Kern fork from the Kern River," responded Striding Elk. "Your journey begins here at daybreak in an hour or so. We will go back after the traffic picks up."

All were silent for several minutes, too occupied with their own thoughts to make small-talk. Spotted Owl began to speak in the measured tones of a storyteller. "The wasichus are people who look to exploit others, who are greedy, and organize to take from the first peoples of North America. Wasichus moved steadily into the Indian lands, taking and destroying, bringing starvation, disease and death. They were many. They were organized into governments, armies, and corporations. They were well armed. We fought and sometimes we won, but always there were more Wasichus but fewer Indians. By 1889 all the tribes were despairing as starvation forced them to accept meaningless treaties and barren reservations in exchange for inadequate and spoiled food. Hopelessness settled over our people."

His voice enlivened with hope. "Then great news spread to all the tribes. A sacred man of the Paiutes, Wovoka by name, had talked with the Great Spirit in a vision. Wovoka was shown the desolation of the Indian lands and the death of our people. Then he was shown a whirlwind arising in the west, which raced across the Earth, growing in power, and fury as it swept all the evil from the land into a great swirling cloud that obscured the sky. And the frightened screams of the Wasichus were lost in the deafening roar of the whirlwind in which they were carried aloft. When the Great Winds ceased, all the Earth was clean and empty.

"Then from the west again came a wind, but a clear and gentle breeze. And when this breeze had passed over the barren land it brought forth the streams and the grasses and the trees; then it repopulated the reborn land with all of the fishes and birds and animals large and small that had been destroyed; and finally, the Indian tribes walked the fruitful lands again and were reunited with all their grandfathers who had gone before. This was the Earth that the Great Spirit had intended."

Spotted Owl paused and then resumed in a quieter tone. "The land darkened and Wovoka was alone in a small circle of fire light. Out of the shadows appeared four sacred men. They were clad in buckskin and decorated with strange designs that he somehow knew meant life, healing wisdom and brotherhood. They wore eagle feathers in their hair. They danced around the fire and communicated to the Great Spirit their sorrow that the people had forgotten Him and their desire to be with Him in the Great Circle of Life that includes all of His creation."

"Then the vision faded and was gone."

"Wovoka brought to the people the story of his vision and the dance beseeching the Great Spirit to bring this reborn world to His people. The story of the vision spread across the land. Wovoka was deemed to be the Messiah. The ritual of communication with the Great Spirit became known as the Ghost Dance. Our desperate people grabbed at this hope and roused themselves for a last struggle against the wasichu. Perhaps the dream was false. Perhaps it was misunderstood. Perhaps it was for a time yet to come and in a way not yet disclosed."

His voice grew sad. "The dream ended at Wounded Knee. Our people were shattered and dispersed to reservations that were prisons of hopelessness. Our children follow the Wasichu dream of greed and power, or worse yet, no dream at all."

The first faint light of dawn now disclosed Spotted Owl's sorrowful face. He sat sideways by the steering wheel, shoulders slumped, chin down and eyes moist with the memory of Wounded Knee and a world lost. He straightened and turned his eyes to Brandon. The lines of his face firmed and his gaze was direct.

"You brought a vision to us, one that seems related to this great vision of Wovoka. Perhaps this dream was meant for another time, not Wovoka's time. Perhaps this, too, is a false dream. Whatever, it will make us think together and dream together to see if we can find a way to our promised land. You have brought us closer to the Great Spirit and to each other. Maybe our dream did not die at Wounded Knee, but was only postponed."

Brandon responded thoughtfully to Spotted Owl, "What you experienced was not my vision, but your vision. My visions are of my ancestors. It just seems that people have forgotten how to reach their ancestral memories. Sometimes I seem to be one with good friends. Then their ancestral memories are unlocked. Tonight I was one with you, Spotted Owl. I do not know what it means. I think that your ancestors have wisdom they saved for you. You must discover its meaning."

Spotted Owl drew his knife from its sheath. "Soars With Eagles, you were closer to me tonight than a brother. We have shared our souls. Will you share your blood with me?" He drew the blade lightly across his wrist and extended the arm towards Brandon, offering the blade with his other hand.

His three companions did likewise with their wrists. Brandon's heart surged with love in response to the emotions that emanated from them. He cut his wrist and pressed it to each of theirs in turn. The four clasped hands briefly.

"Our home is your home," said Striding Elk. "If you ever need a brother, come to the Sierras. Mention your name, 'Soars With Eagles,' and any Yakut will help you. This we promise." Brandon's eyes welled with tears for he felt a sense of family and home much stronger than he had ever felt before.

Striding Elk opened his door and stepped outside. "Dawn is breaking. It is time to be on your way. May your grandfathers guide you safely to your destination."

They descended from the cab and stood outside looking to the lightening east. Facing each quarter of the compass in turn, Spotted Owl raised his arms towards the rising sun. Softly he chanted, "Great Spirit, Creator of the World, I send my voice in prayer to the four quarters of the Earth. From The East I ask for healing of my people; from the South I ask for a renewed blooming of our culture; from the West I ask for an end to destruction of our land and the will to live in beauty again; and from the North I ask for a cleansing wind to remove the pollution and the polluters from our land."

Bowing his head, he stood in silent reverence as the sunlight brought his countenance from twilight gray to the copper red of life. "You have shown us this night the beauty of a greening Earth as it was meant to be. Bless us with the power to make it bloom again."

They stood in silence beside the truck, each lost in his own vision. Running Hare moved at last, swinging Brandon's backpack from the truck bed to his side.

"Time to go, brother. The sun now lights your path. Follow the way we showed you. There will be help when you need it."

Brandon swung the pack to his back and shook each man's hand in turn. "I did not dream that my path would be made easy by brothers I had never seen. I will not forget you."

Striding Elk handed Brandon his knife, a medium-length hunting knife with an intricately carved elk horn handle. "Take my knife, Soars With Eagles. It has served me well on many a lonely trail. It was my father's and his father's before him. May it keep us together in spirit when our paths take us far apart."

Brandon started north on the Kern River trail as the sun rose over the horizon.

Through the Sierras

Brandon padded quietly up the Indian trail paralleling the course of the Kern River towards its headwaters. The sounds of civilization fell far behind. Sensations of human life faded from his consciousness as he distanced himself from his four Indian guides and the tent-campers at Quaking Aspen Camp. The morning dampness and the early light hazed the air. The mountains loomed as indistinct masses on the horizon. Tall pines stood thickly along the trail. Their fallen needles cushioned the ground, limiting the growth of underbrush and absorbing all sound. It was not the expansive soaring aura of the dry desert morning but rather the inward-turning solitude of an empty cathedral. The trail was a carpeted aisle leading past ceremonial alcoves.

The rhythm of his steps kept beat with an unvoiced hymn of joy. The trail curved around a granite face and he was engulfed by the sound of a waterfall. He hurried forward to glimpse the water from an overlook. The falls were just a hundred yards away, whitewater cascading down a gray cliff and thundering into a pool below. He stood in awe at the volume of water and the overpowering sound. Then the edge of the morning sunlight crept across the cliff face, turning its somber gray to bright white. When the illumination reached the falls, the waters became luminescent and a rainbow arched above them. The metamorphosis of the falls from stark black and white to this glorious display transfixed him. He dropped his backpack and stood there until the sun rose higher in the sky and softened the rainbow colors to their daytime pastels.

The morning haze evaporated. When he lifted his eyes he could see the tree-clad mountains in the foreground and the loftier peaks rising in the distance. Kern Peak was visible to the northeast and the taller Mt. Florence further into the northwest. He could not see his next major landmark, Mt. Whitney, which would be almost due north. Scanning the range brought him back from enjoyment of the scenery to his arduous journey ahead. Mount Shasta lay 400 straight-line miles to the north-northwest. Lake Tahoe was the halfway point 200 miles ahead. Depending on terrain and weather, he might travel ten to twenty miles per day. Considering the directional changes of the trail to conform to the terrain, the trek would probably take about two months. Taking a last look at the fading colors of the waterfall, Brandon swung the pack to his shoulders, shrugged it into a comfortable position and continued on his way.

The hike settled into a routine that he experienced on several levels. The act of walking was monotonous repetition of footsteps in one sense, a wearying grind that subtracted little from the long journey ahead. Yet the underlying rhythm of the pace awoke in him the responsive sense of an Indian chant. The steady beat persisted for long periods but was then interrupted by a change of timing, alterations in effort, and variations in emphasis. His pace also adjusted to the difficulty of the terrain as he went uphill or down, over rocks or through wet or sandy places. He thought that the Indian sense of rhythm in song and dance was representative of nature's rhythms in this respect. They were basically steady but yet ever changing with subtle variations. Being attuned to nature, the Indians expressed the essence of these rhythms in their own terms and modes. He was beginning to appreciate that these rhythms better expressed the essence of physical reality than did the mathematically based constructs of the music of western culture that he had heard.

Brandon strode along, marching more and more closely in step with these fundamental rhythms until he merged into the rest of nature itself. His heart beat with the pulsing of sap in trees and plants; he swayed with the trees to the unsteady pressure of the fitful breeze; his back muscles and shoulder blades responded to the tingling surge of wings overhead forcing back the winds; the aromas of plants and the pheromones of insects and animals carried their chemical communications of reproduction and continuity among all the living things; the Earth itself resonated to the acoustics of distant quakes and ocean tides. He walked for miles unconscious of the ground underfoot and the scenery to the sides. He had been reabsorbed into the womb of Mother Earth.

The rhythms of nature slowly faded and were replaced by the sensations of his own body – the pressure of the pack against his back; the crunch of gravel underfoot; the warm sunlight on his face; and the growing hunger in his stomach. Hours had passed. The sun was high. Lunchtime was here. He stepped off the trail, dropped his pack, and sat on a fallen log. Fatigue from the long hike set in. He leaned back against an upright limb, closed his eyes, and immediately fell asleep. Even hunger could not overcome his tiredness.

Brandon awakened refreshed and clearheaded after a short nap. The air carried clean evergreen scents. Tall pines shaded him from the bright sun and gave a patchwork view of cloudless blue sky. A ground squirrel stood on the end of the log watching him with curious eyes. In the distance a crow cawed. Otherwise all was silent. The boy saw and heard these things with his own senses, not as part of the total sensory stream of the Earth. He wondered whether he had experienced another dream while he hiked or whether he had actually merged his inner self with the total consciousness of Nature. He sat quietly exploring the sensations he felt, but all were his own. Except – just beyond the limits of perception there seemed to be a faint pulsation that he knew but could not identify, an ever-changing pulsation hinting of myriad lives in one. Perhaps this faint murmur below the sensory threshold was the remnant of the link he had established with the living Earth, a link once made that could never after be broken.

Hunger pangs drew him from his reverie. He rummaged in the side pockets of his pack and found a cheese sandwich, trail mix, and an apple. These he ate quietly while recalling the landmarks his guides had discussed with him only last night. Shouldering the pack again, he headed up the trail, keeping his mind and senses alert to his surroundings rather than listening to the siren song of the heartbeat of the Earth.

The Indian trail was easy going in this stretch with moderate slopes and no hard climbs or barriers. Emerging from the pine forest into an open meadow, Brandon again saw the buttes and craggy mountains stretching into the distance. Due east was Kern Peak, rising above its neighbors. Off to the northwest, several miles more distant, was the taller Mt. Florence. When he crossed a straight line sighted between Kern Peak and Mt. Florence, he would look for the trail markers locating his first camping spot. That would be about three miles ahead, he judged.

The trail cut downhill across the meadow letting him set a brisk pace for this late in the day. The meadow was green and filled with more diverse life than the pine forest. Flowers were not abundant but he recognized purple lupine, scarlet monkey, and yellow lotus. Occasional butterflies fluttered past. A few bees droned by. A flock of small birds rose from the grass ahead of him and settled again a hundred yards to his right. The trail intersected a dirt road, which Brandon took to be the fire road to a bridge across the Kern River. Turning west on the road he reached the river within half a mile. The road dipped down to the bridge that spanned the river. Brandon leaned on the guardrail absorbing the sounds of the river and the sight of the white water coursing over and around the rocks in the streambed. After his years in the desert the wild free-flowing streams in the mountains fascinated him. The sun had dropped nearly to the level of the western peaks so he pressed forward to reach his camp before dark. A cloud of midges had him coughing, sneezing, and flailing his arms as he raced out of their midst and off the end of the bridge.

Another half mile on the road brought him to a large rock shaped like a flat iron standing with its nose in the air. The trail left the road at this point and led to a semicircle of boulders in front of a granite up-thrust. A spring at the base of the granite wall and just outside the boulder semicircle fed a small stream flowing down towards the river. Brandon dropped his pack under an overhang of the granite wall and then knelt beside the stream for a deep drink of its cold water. He arranged his sleeping bag and camping gear in this small alcove. A cold meal of trail mix, dates and an apple was all that he allowed himself in the waning light. Despite having seen no one all day he still was highly cautious about pursuit.

Brandon undressed after eating, cleaned his teeth and refreshed himself with a quick bath from the cold spring. With the sun now down, the air cooled rapidly. He climbed into this sleeping bag and sat against his pack watching the stars come out. The northern constellations were bright and clear around the pole star. He traced in his mind the outlines of Ursa Major, Ursa Minor, Cassiopeia, and Cepheus while recalling the myths told him by his mother and the shaman about the origins of these guideposts in the skies. Tired from the long day, he stretched out on the ground and fell fast asleep.

His dreams brought reassuring memories of the recent past – working with his mother in the cave home; receiving her warning to flee; escaping through the canyons in the thunderstorm; meeting his Indian guides on the trail; and hiking the trail to this campsite.

A threatening stranger entered his dream, a huge shadowy figure approaching the spring for a drink. It paused, becoming aware that

Brandon was nearby. After a few moments of attentive immobility, the intruder drank deeply from the spring and then approached the boy's camp. At first the young fugitive felt a sense of alarm at being discovered and stirred in his sleep to flee, but then a feeling of security and safety flooded through him. He decided then that this was only his dream continuing. The shadowy figure stood in the circle of stone, not menacing now but gravely observing him. The outline of the figure became clearer as it moved into the feeble moonlight. He was very big, both tall and large, the biggest person that Brandon had ever seen. Despite his size, he moved with majestic grace. At first it appeared that he was wearing fringed buckskin clothing, but the better light showed it to be a coarse fur that covered his body. Brandon remembered then – this must be the Sasquatch of Indian ancestral memories that had entered into his dream, perhaps a memory transferred to him through rapport with his Paiute guides.

All apprehension left him and Brandon observed the figure more closely now. He could see that the Sasquatch was speaking to him, not in vocal words, but in the total body language that his mother used.

"Do not be afraid. I bring a warning to you. Your pursuers have not given up. They have moved ahead to the big lake where all trails converge. They have set up surveillance and wait for you. You can continue safely to your next rendezvous with your Indian friends, but you must not follow their trails around the lake. Take the high mountain game trails to the west of the lake and travel warily. This is your most dangerous stage where your pursuers and also many humans are concentrated. You must learn to travel as the Sasquatch do, keeping beyond the fringes of awareness of all other primates. Only thus can you succeed in your escape."

As the Sasquatch communicated the dangers to him, Brandon felt a heightening of all his senses and a triggering of alarm bells along sensory paths that had never been stimulated before. He realized that there were senses and subtle biological links that his own people had forgotten as they blended with the humans in their struggle for survival. Long unused neurological networks became saturated. Noises were sorted and correlated into a complete picture of his surroundings. Every object became brightly illuminated and more sharply delineated. The neurological overload stimulated him to jump and flee in all directions at once. Yet, it paralyzed him to trembling inaction because he had no experiential basis for evaluating the messages to determine the proper response.

The Sasquatch moved back into the shadows and disappeared. The scene of rocks and spring fed stream was empty and still. Brandon found himself sitting erect, gasping and trembling. The unnatural brightness and clarity of vision remained. His alert senses brought in a flood of intense stimulation that his nervous system began to sort and tag. New kinds of data mixed with old to provide a detailed picture of his surroundings and all the life in them.

Brandon realized that he was now fully awake. He explored with all his senses, including those newly awakened, but nowhere could he find a trace of Sasquatch. Had that been a dream? Was it a vision meant to prepare him for the difficulties ahead? Or were there really Sasquatch living just beyond the fringes of perception of all other species? Brandon lay there assimilating his new sensations and concepts in a world more complex and interconnected than he had ever realized before. The moon set, the constellations wheeled in their paths and the night turned slowly to dawn as he adapted to his new awareness of the world.

He arose at the first light, ate a hasty cold meal, packed quickly, and removed all traces of his stay from the campsite. There were no footprints or other signs of his shadowy night visitor. Perhaps it had been only a dream.

The morning was crisp and clear, dew sparkled on the meadow grass and trills of early birds announced the day. He walked back to the fire road and followed it across the meadow parallel to the river. The road turned west so he left it and continued on along the river, swishing through the wet grass while scanning about for a possible game trail that would make the going easier. At last he found an area of flattened grass where deer had bedded down and from there a path following the general direction of the river. He shifted his pack a little higher and walked at a faster pace. The memory of his warning dream sped his footsteps, although his mind told him that he must pace himself and dole out his energy resources for the long journey ahead.

Weariness slowed his pace on a long uphill climb stair-cased with boulders more suited for the deer to jump than for him to surmount with his pack. The late morning sun had him sweating. Insects seemed to have nothing else to bother. His left heel was feeling tender. There was no comfortable position for his pack. The joy of the crisp morning had been replaced by the drudgery of a long uphill climb with eyes fixed on the uneven path. The reality of the arduous distance to Mount Shasta asserted itself.

Brandon toiled over a succession of boulders, rounded a steep hillside and had his first clear view north. Just ten miles to the northeast was the majestic snow capped peak of Mt. Whitney dominating the vista. Due north about twenty miles was the lofty Junction Peak. Six miles beyond rose University Peak. Off to the north-northwest was Table Mountain at the same height. Brandon forgot the toil and weariness as he drank in the beauty of the range he was traversing. He shucked his pack and climbed onto a boulder. There he sat cross-legged and slowly scanned the view to store it in his memory. The peaks stood staunchly holding up the skies. White scarves of clouds were thrown jauntily about their white granite shoulders. Low cut gowns of evergreens draped their flanks and softened the image of strength and power to one of refuge and repose.

A feeling of peace and harmony flowed through his being, washing away his tiredness, his resentment of his pursuers and his frustration at his slow progress towards reunion with his people and freedom for his mother. These mountains were not barriers to his progress but protectors from his pursuers, challenges for his strength and endurance and inspiration for his spirit. He sat there as his tensions eased, relaxed to the core of his being and dreamed of shouldering his burdens as effortlessly as the mountains held up the skies.

After a short nap he awoke and ate. Changing socks gave his feet a fresh feeling. Adjusting the pack straps finally settled it to a comfortable position. The grandeur of the mountains, their overwhelming presence and impact on his spirits faded into the background as he satisfied the immediate physical needs of hunger and comfort. Once more he tackled the uphill trail, but it was no longer a tedious grind. The ever-changing vista of the mountain range lured him onwards for more memories to store in his soul.

Mt. Whitney, its snowy crown reflecting the setting sun, was due east when he made camp for the evening. This time he made a small fire in a rocky shelter and enjoyed a hot vegetable soup with his meal. He turned in early, tired physically but elated spiritually. He was anxious to continue on the trail to drink in its unfolding splendors. The night air was cold at this altitude, but he quickly warmed in his sleeping bag and dropped off to sleep.

The next morning he passed the headwaters of the Kern River and enjoyed a downhill segment of the trail passing west of a magnificent mountain peak, which he correlated with the map in his memory as University Peak. Three miles later he reached a line of boulders resembling a herd of bison proceeding northwest in single file. He turned in that direction as indicated by the Indian trail marker. Five miles further he reached the Kings River, which he now followed north. In a short time he was overtaken by the shadow of Goat Mountain on his left.

He reached a suitable camping spot near the river and gratefully settled down for the night.

Sunrise roused him and Brandon was on the trail to his next rendezvous. He followed the river north for five more miles and then cut west across a pass to the Middle Fork of the Kings River. This he followed north again, passing between the North Palisade and Mt. Goddard. He ate lunch in view of the Palisade Glacier, a stupendous river of ice. It called up racial memories of walls of ice stretching to the horizon. Cold winds dropping off those walls reduced temperatures to numbing depths in seconds. He wondered if this glacier had that same abysmal chill. Shouldering his pack, he soon crossed the Pacific Crest Trail after he had ascertained that there were no hikers in the vicinity. It was not an easy hike to the vicinity of Lake Sabrina where a needle pointed rock indicated his rendezvous. Approaching with care, he sensed only one person there. It was an odd sensing to Brandon for it gave him no information about the person, only the steady pulsation of life force without any indication of activity or thought. It was not concealment of a presence, but the cloaking of any sentient activity. Brandon waited patiently, but no one else appeared and the lone person at the rendezvous did not stir. At last he stepped into the shadow of the rock and walked up to the immobile figure.

An old woman sat cross-legged, hands in her lap. Her white hair, drawn back tightly into a single braid, hung below her shoulders. Her face was serene and expressionless. Fine lines of age and weathering crosshatched her skin. High cheekbones, a generous nose, and a wide mouth with thin lips highlighted her face. Firm muscles and tight skin belied the age indicated by the mosaic of lines. Even in complete repose her expression combined strength and self-confidence. Her body was broad and full, but powerful hands and forearms indicated strength. A knitted vest and sweater covered her long earth-colored dress.

"Hello," he said, somewhat tentatively.

The woman's eyes opened slowly and focused on him. He saw that they were dark brown and gave the impression of endless depth. They radiated intelligence, understanding, and wisdom honed by the positive and negative experiences of a long and active life. The silence lengthened. He descended into the depths of these eyes full of sympathy for his plight. As she awakened from her passive state, she emanated an aura of honesty and forthrightness that invited a relaxation of suspicion and an exchange of confidence.

She spoke in a strong friendly voice accustomed to addressing others of any station as equals. "I am Quiet Fox, a Paiute from the Yerington way. I did not feel you approaching. You must be the one I am waiting for. How are my friends from your home?"

The young fugitive recognized the tests embodied in her greeting. His response revealed only what was necessary. "You are well named yourself, Quiet Fox. Your name is apt as that of my brother, 'Dreams With Manitou.' I am called 'Soars With Eagles' by my friends."

While he was speaking, the old woman nodded her head as she echoed the names he spoke. "I have heard that you may be a holy person, one who has visions that others can see." Her gaze defocused from his face to scenes distant in time. She continued, "I was not yet born when Wovoka, a very sacred man, shared his visions of our land being made free of the Wasichus. Word of his visions spread and other sacred men added to them. For several years the despair of our peoples turned to hope. But it was in vain. The Wasichus kept growing in numbers while we suffered starvation, disease, massacre, and total defeat. Later, when I was a young girl, I knew Wovoka. He was a sorrowful man. He felt that his visions had been misinterpreted, that other false visions and false hopes had distorted their meaning, thus leading to useless warfare and death. He felt that the vision of our people reborn was true. Our lives will be free of the wasichu's yoke. But it will only come true when we dedicate ourselves again to the beliefs and the ways of our grandfathers."

Her gaze returned to the present and held Brandon's eyes. She repeated, "I knew Wovoka." Her figure became more erect as she asserted her own worth. "I, too, had visions. I saw peace and prosperity and our people's ways reborn. I saw oppression, famine, death and desolation of both land and spirit. I do not know what these visions mean. No longer do I want visions. Now I want peace and acceptance of the world as it is."

Her eyes fixed his with a penetrating rejection. "I do not know if you are a fraud, a sacred person or a dupe of your own false visions. I do not care. Go back to your own people and leave us alone. Our own visions have brought us sorrow enough."

Brandon could feel the turmoil of conflicting emotions within Quiet Fox – her childhood adoration of Wovoka; the sorrow she shared with that sacred man; the kaleidoscope of emotions from hope to despair engendered by her own visions; the environment of hopeless resignation in which she was raised; and her rejection of both inner visions and outside influences that led her to erect a barrier between herself and all others.

He started to speak, but the old woman leaned forward and placed a restraining hand on his forearm. Time and motion stopped. As with the little Costain girl when the group had tried peyote, Brandon felt himself drawn into a whirlpool of indefinable sights, sounds, sensations and emotions, each clamoring for attention. Focusing on the stability of his own sympathy for the old woman's internal conflicts, he gradually slowed the motion and separated the elements of her suppressed internal maelstrom.

Like a slowing carousel, each part separated from the blur into a well-defined entity of love, hate, fear and hope. He allowed his own sympathy and love to combine with hers to soften the hard outlines she had frozen into her memories over the years. The events of her life settled into a pattern of growth in wisdom and understanding.

Brandon realized that he was still sitting before her, gazing into the eyes that had lost their angry hostility and were now softer, overflowing with tears. They sat quietly until the fixation of their gazes became an exchange of affection and support.

Quiet Fox said at last, "You are indeed a sacred man, Soars with Eagles. There is a depth to your spirit that brings Wovoka to mind but in a different way. You have made me feel that there is meaning and order and hope in life." Tears pooled in her eyes again and she squeezed his arm forcefully.

"Now I must tell you. Strangers like you came to Yerington. They get inside people the way you did to me. They asked about a hiking boy, about you. They knew the right answers, even if no one spoke. They learned from everyone but me. I closed my eyes and my mind and shut everyone out." She made a tight-lipped smile of satisfaction. "They thought I was crazy. They asked only one question and went away." She chuckled softly, wrinkling her cheeks and the corners of her eyes. "I can make them all go away. Wovoka taught me that."

Brandon stirred uneasily. "Then they know I am here?"

The old woman motioned with her hand for him to remain seated. "They wait to follow the men. I left early to gather herbs." Another self-satisfied grin crinkled her visage. "I took a wide loop around Walker Lake to mislead them. You have several hours head start. You must go completely on your own. All that I have for you is this warning and a small parcel of dried foods."

Quiet Fox reached behind her back and withdrew an old buckskin bag with a rawhide drawstring. "This is my herb satchel. Take it and go. Stay off the main trails. Avoid people. They will give you away. They cannot help it."

Brandon took the bag and stood up. "Thank you for the warning and the food. But how can I make the journey now? I have not covered a quarter of the distance, I have little food and my pursuers would have caught me but for your talent."

The old woman looked at him compassionately for several moments. She then took his hand and pulled him down to be seated again. "All I can give you is my gift from Wovoka, the gift of silence."

She held his two hands and leaned closer to fix his eyes with hers. Again the boy felt himself drawn into her soul, but this time it was down into a well of utter silence. His body cells seemed to realign themselves into the crystalline pattern of the Earth's crusted rocks. Nothing penetrated into his being, nothing emanated. He resonated only with the multi-million year cycle of the tectonic plates. Time and direction meant nothing.

He saw an infinitesimal pinhole of light like a single faint star in his universe of night. Brandon knew that this was his sole portal to the biological world of pulsing clocks and sensory images. He approached the portal and peered through. The eyes of Quiet Fox were regarding him.

"You have Wovoka's hideaway. Your soul, your thoughts, your feelings are yours alone whenever you so desire. No one can find you now if you go into concealment. Leave now."

Brandon arose at her tone of dismissal. "Thank you, Grandmother. I pray that my journey will bring blessings, not sorrow, to you and to your people."

He shouldered his pack and started uphill to his northerly route. When he looked back he could see Quiet Fox smoothing the dirt with a branch as she backed away from their rendezvous and returned to the campground at Lake Sabrina. There would be no trail for his pursuers to follow.

For the next two days he set a punishing pace in his anxiety to distance himself from his pursuers. He stayed within the sheltering tree level as he cut across the slopes of Mount Darwin and on to parallel the South Fork of the San Joaquin River to Florence Lake. He made a cold camp on the slopes above the lake and ate sparingly of his dwindling food supply. He slept fitfully, dreaming of an army of pursuers combing the Sierras for him, listening for his every breath or thought or emotion. In his dreams he used Wovoka's technique to conceal himself from his pursuers by suppressing all biological sensations, reactions and radiations. Then, frighteningly, he lost contact with the comforting memories of his mother and awoke cold, shivering and alone. A quick breakfast and he was on the trail again. He passed Lake Edison and continued on to the junction with the main channel of the San Joaquin River. Here he camped again, another night of fitful sleep and intense loneliness. He was awake before dawn waiting for the light so that he could be on the move to outrun his fears. Now he turned due north on the San Joaquin River, keeping to the north fork when the river branched.

Brandon was tired in the late afternoon when he traversed the slope of Mount Lyell and saw to the east the cylindrical lava extrusions of the Devil's Postpile. Despite his fatigue he strained his eyes to see its wonder, regretting that he dared not go closer to see this natural phenomenon that the Indians had described to him. The trails and campsites would be crowded with hikers seeing the Postpile and nearby Rainbow Falls. He resolved that one day he would return and drink in their wilderness beauty to his heart's content. For now he pressed on to reach the Pacific Crest Trail and make some distance across the Tuolumne Meadows while other hikers were making dinner in their camps. That night he camped in the meadows near Route 120. He saw the lights of an occasional vehicle and wondered if they were his pursuers patrolling for him. The thought had him retreating to another guarded and lonely night followed by a daybreak start on the trail. Near Mount Conness the trail turned west, but Brandon continued due north across less traveled country towards Fales Hot Springs, avoiding forestry roads and their associated campsites.

He camped in misery. He was cold and hungry that night. The food supplies were gone and native food was nonexistent in this area. His original hiking boots had been discarded and buried. The new boots chafed his feet and made every step an uncomfortable reminder of the distance yet to go. His pack was a little lighter, but he could not drop the mountain tent and the cold weather clothing that he would need if the weather turned bad.

In the morning he crossed Route 108 and continued northwest looking for the Carson River. The joy of wilderness hiking had diminished. This time he decided to camp early near the water. Here the river ran through a wide flat bed of jumbled boulders. In some places the water was swift and channeled; in others there were quiet pools hemmed in by piled up rocks. Thick brush lined the shores and made access from land difficult. Traveling upstream on the rocks seemed the best way to go. With his strength and agility he could reach a refuge not accessible to most hikers. Moving through water and on rocks would leave no trail.

Jumping from boulder to boulder, he went more than a hundred yards upstream searching the banks for a suitable campsite. The difficulty in traveling was offset by the beauty of the river. The rocks in the stream had braced themselves against the power of the rushing water, forcing it to turn aside into narrow channels to continue its downhill rush. The gurgling water at each rock face grumbled its protest at this delay. Water backed up into crests at the channels and then rushed through in a sparkling whitewater release to speed heedlessly into the next constriction. It created the atmosphere of a good-natured holiday crowd jostling its noisy way through park attractions, ever on the move yet ever beguiled by distractions along the way. His worries dissipated as he hopscotched over the rocks and succumbed to the lorelei song of the water playground.

He found his site at a spot where two lines of boulders marched down the hillside to the water's edge and created a quiet eddy within the shelter of their locked arms. He scrambled over the rocks and down into the quiet shady grotto. A minute sandy beach graced the shoreline. A flat rock above it was a natural balcony. Brandon put down his pack, removed his boots and sat with his legs dangling over the edge into the water. He drank in all the beauties of his haven and let nature's balm soothe his pains of body and spirit.

The reality of his immediate concerns at last penetrated the euphoria produced by his surroundings. His feet hurt, he was bone weary and he must have food. The Carson River was stocked with brown trout, he had been told, and one of his gifts from the Indians was a fishing line. He rose stiffly to his feet and forced his way up into the brush. In short order he raked up a small supply of grubs and worms and returned to his cove. He took the fishing line from a pocket of the pack and tied a length of it to a pole cut from the brush. A hook was quickly attached and baited. He sat back on his balcony with his feet in the water and began casting his line to sheltered spots where trout might lurk. The cold water was so soothing on his tired feet that he was not anxious to pull in his dinner. That attitude changed as the ache in his feet diminished and the hollowness in his stomach became more insistent. Three small trout rewarded his persistence. He cleaned the fish with the knife that Striding Elk had given him, built a small smokeless fire and broiled them over the embers. His loneliness faded as his belly filled. His perception of the arduous trek ahead eased a little. When at last he rolled in for the night, he slept well for the first time in a week.

The next morning was cold and dreary, signaling an abrupt change in the weather. Brandon ate a little trail mix along with the leftover fish, washed at the water's edge and started downstream. A cold wind blew in fitful gusts that intermittently spattered him with large raindrops. The downhill slope and the cold wind kept him moving at a fast pace. Before noon he crossed Route 4, skirted Silver Creek and continued northwest staying clear of the highway.

The rain became more persistent, so Brandon donned his parka, put up the hood, bowed low against the elements and continued on his path. The advent of cold weather would make his way much more difficult as he moved farther north. The adventure was becoming more of a cold and wearying drudgery. Hunger pangs added to his misery. It was time to seek shelter and plan how to continue. Without the support of his Indian friends, the trip had become much more arduous. Nuts, berries, grubs and fish had sounded like ready sources of emergency rations, but in truth they were scarce and would require a large part of his time spent gathering food rather than covering the miles toward his goal.

The rain created rivulets on the slopes. These spread out beneath the fallen leaves and pine needles to make his footing treacherous. Innumerable slips and falls left him bruised and wet with a pack lopsided from its shifting contents. Visibility was poor, hiding the landmarks that he had committed to memory. Early nightfall limited his options. He judged himself to be in the vicinity of Grover Hot Springs and decided to camp at the first likely spot. Slipping and sliding down a slope, running a little to maintain his balance, he came up short against the side of a small lean-to. Edging around to the front he saw that it was a park trail shelter, dark and unoccupied. He stepped up onto the wooden floor and walked into the lean-to, grateful to be out of the rain for the first time that day.

Brandon dropped his pack in a corner and peeled off his wet clothes. Socks and pants legs were sodden. The parka had kept him dry from mid-thigh up. The damp chill had him shivering as he unrolled his waterproof pack and took out his dry clothes. His old underwear sufficed for toweling off. Fresh dry clothing and a blanket on his shoulders soon armed him. A search of his pack uncovered only a handful of trail mix in a sealed plastic bag. He ate it all. Tomorrow he would worry about replenishing his food supply. He wrung out his wet clothing and hung it on pegs he found on the wall. Wrapping himself in his tarpaulin and ground cloth, he curled up in the corner. For a few moments he warmed himself with thoughts of his mother. He firmed his resolve to make it to Shasta and struggle for her freedom. His fears abated, his stresses relaxed and he fell into an exhausted sleep.

Stomping boots, loud voices and darting lights startled the sleeping boy awake. He opened his eyes to see enormous dancing shadows on the walls and three men shaking off the rain and dropping their packs on the floor. He sensed at once that they were not his pursuers.

"Hot damn!" exclaimed one. "I thought you were lost for sure, Boomer. I'm soaked to the skin."

"You're soaked, Jack? Look at me! I don't need a towel. Just wring me out!"

The second speaker shucked his outer clothes to the floor and rummaged in his pack. "Here we are! A little Wild Turkey hundred proof anti-freeze that I brought to celebrate bagging old Bigfoot with the legendary Boomer Bomano. We need it more now," he said, opening the bottle.

"Give me a drink, Art," demanded Jack, grabbing the bottle. "Bigfoot can wait but I can't."

Boomer methodically arranged the packs and hung the wet clothes on the far wall. He was mid-sized and compact, obviously in control of himself. He made no comments about physical discomfort and did not take a drink. His water repellent hunter's garb had numerous pockets. Weather was no problem to him. It was doubtful that any environment would shake his demeanor.

"Looks like the rain kills this trip, Boomer. It'll wash out any tracks we might have found," observed Jack.

"Yeah. Just another wild goose chase." complained Art. "We might as well kill the bottle and sleep until noon." He upended the Wild Turkey for a long pull.

Boomer rebuked them with an annoyed look. "Nothing's lost. That Indian kid told me that the medicine people have been running the hills secretly for days. Some strangers are quizzing everybody and trailing the medicine man. I can smell Bigfoot in this. Nobody's going to beat me to that hairy ape man."

"So what do we do?" asked Art. "Follow your nose?" He hunched his shoulders and took another drink.

"Lighten up," barked Jack. His tone softened as he added, "There'll be other sightings and other hunts. Today the weather is against us. Let's make the best of it."

"I'll drink to that!" exclaimed Art as he took another swig. He then handed the bottle to Jack who held it near his lips while looking over the bottle for the leader's response.

Boomer became conciliatory. "All right. It's been a miserable day. We can't go out tonight. But I tell you, something is going on and we're in the middle of it. I have an edge on the other guys: I can sense Bigfoot." He produced a zippered leather bag and held it out.

"What's that?" asked Art in a slurred voice.

"Marijuana. When I'm high I sorta 'feel' the people all around me like their arms are touching me and they're trying to talk to me. And a few times, out on a hunt, I felt something else. It was like I surprised something that didn't expect me to sense it, and then it quickly shut down and was gone. I know it wasn't human and maybe it was Bigfoot. I have a hunch it was. I want to listen for him tonight. You can, too, if you want."

They looked at him speculatively.

"Are you saying you're psychic or something?" queried Art.

"I don't know about that. All I know is that I can feel things when I'm high that I don't normally feel. Maybe this gives me an edge on Bigfoot."

"What the hell!" laughed Jack. "I'd rather be high than miserable."

Boomer produced a fluorescent lamp from his pack and switched it on. The lamp illuminated the whole interior of the lean-to. They saw Brandon for the first time. He stared apprehensively at the hunters, wide-eyed and fascinated.

The Sasquatch hunter stepped swiftly over to stare down at him with hostility. "Who the hell are you?"

Brandon forced himself to give his practiced response. "I'm Tommy Seldon from Scout Troop 37 in Carson. I'm on a Wilderness merit badge hike from Silver City to Tahoe, but I got caught here by the storm."

Jack held up the boy's shirt, which had been hanging on the wall. "Must be so. This shirt has a scout emblem and number 37 on the sleeve. And his pants are soaked."

"Stand up!" commanded Boomer. Brandon threw back his blanket and jumped to attention.

"Scouts travel in pairs," stated the man. "Where's your buddy?"

"I'm an Explorer," answered Brandon. "This is a solo hike for my merit badge. The troop is waiting at Tahoe."

Boomer nodded to indicate acceptance of the story but he muttered suspicion. "You look pretty young for a solo trip like this. But I could have done it at your age."

"There's no food in his pack." observed Jack.

"It got lost on the trail," volunteered Brandon quickly. "I slipped a lot in the mud." He knew that his muddy pants would support that claim.

"Yeah. Me, too." spoke up Art. "I sat down in the mud so much that it felt like I shit my pants." He laughed as he held up the mud stained pants to prove his point.

Art's laugh broke the ice and all relaxed.

The leader spoke to Brandon in a confidential tone. "You hear what we're hunting? Bigfoot."

Brandon nodded that he heard.

"Do you believe in Bigfoot?" pressed Boomer.

"Maybe," the boy responded noncommittally.

"Do you think I can find Bigfoot with marijuana?"

"I don't believe in drugs," answered Brandon, standing taller.

"That's right. You're a good scout," smiled the man. "Want to watch us try?"

Brandon felt that he had to respond affirmatively, but he was fearful that the hallucinogenic drug might have unexpected effects as peyote did with the Costain children. He nodded a very tentative assent.

Art took another drink from his bottle and gave a lopsided smile. His face was now flushed. The fat around his waist seemed to have sagged. He brushed back his thinning blond hair and then awkwardly sat down in the middle of the floor.

Jack was more in control. He sipped form the bottle and then sank in one sinuous move to a cross-legged position facing Art. His lean strong face wore a noncommittal expression as he waited for the leader to sit.

Boomer put his lantern between the two men and covered it with a shade to leave only a dim background of light in the lean-to. He motioned Brandon to sit next to the two men. He then sat opposite Brandon and scanned the group. His saturnine face showed a deep but carefully controlled passion. His eyes were direct and penetrating, capable of looking beyond the facades of pretension that people wear. His hair was jet black and cut short in a military style. His nose was aquiline befitting a bird of prey. His lips were thin and mobile, responsive to his every mood. They were not cruel, but rather fiercely determined. His body was lean and hard, made compact by well-conditioned muscle. He was obviously the driving force in the search: mentally, physically and psychologically prepared.

Brandon recognized in him the embodiment of a dangerous and implacable foe for Sasquatch. He feared for that quarry of this determined hunter. He feared for his own safety when they entered the drug-induced state of psychic awareness.

"Relax, everybody," suggested Boomer. "At worst, we'll all get high and have a good time. At best, I'll find Bigfoot out there and we'll be on his tail in the morning." He looked at Brandon. "Sure you won't join us, Tommy? You catch Bigfoot and you'll get a real merit badge."

Brandon shook his head negatively, his thoughts going back to his own dreamlike encounter with the Sasquatch. He wondered if this drug enhanced sensitivity session placed Brandon himself next on the endangered list.

The leader took cigarette papers and marijuana from his pouch and deftly rolled nine joints with his left hand. He passed one each to Art and Jack. They all lit up and took long slow drags. The sweet odor made Brandon vaguely uneasy. Half an hour passed with alternate smoking and drinking. Art overdid both. His expression became slack jawed and vacuous. He tilted slowly to his right side and then crumpled to the floor, breathing torturously, asleep. Jack sat upright, relaxed but alert. He drank occasionally in small sips, savoring the taste a long while before he swallowed. His joint was consumed mainly by idle smoldering. His gaze was a contemplative one fixed mainly on the leader with rare side-glances to Art and the boy. Boomer drank little but smoked with long deep drags, holding and savoring the smoke before letting it drift upward from the nose and mouth. He remained in the lotus position completely at ease. From time to time he chanted a muted mantra. His face was relaxed and unlined. It showed no inner tension or direction but only acceptance of whatever messages the environment would bring to him.

Brandon sat motionless in his place and attempted to follow the techniques of Wovoka taught him by Quiet Fox so that he would provide no emanations for them to detect. The impact of Art's head against his knee broke the youth's concentration momentarily. A frightened glance at the leader's face showed a wave of excitement ripple across the hunter's features. Opposite him, Jack's eyes registered the change in his friend's expression. The boy pulled his awareness inwards again and his sphere of sensory impressions contracted to an infinitesimal region. The Sasquatch hunter's questing psyche was a faint ripple at the edge of Brandon's awareness.

A sudden battering of mental probes rocked Brandon to full consciousness. His eyes flashed open. The leader's gaze was fixed in Brandon's direction but passing right through him. A look of elation was on the man's face. The hunter reached out and grasped the boy's forearm.

"Bigfoot!" Jack was now fully alert and tense, watching the tableau. Boomer held on to Brandon's arm and levered himself erect. The pull on one arm toppled the frightened boy sideways to the floor.

"Bigfoot is here!" cried the hunter, "He's right here!"

Brandon jerked his arm free. Jack scrambled to his feet.

Two dripping wet figures stepped into the lean-to from outer darkness. They grabbed the two hunters. Jack was slammed into the back corner of the shelter. He was easily held down while short cords bound him. Boomer was a surprisingly tough adversary, his every move an attack. Brandon scrambled over to the side wall, dismayed at this sudden overwhelming onslaught by his pursuers. He knew that the hunters were no physical matches for them. The boy grabbed his boots and parka to make a desperate escape run. Boomer's captor dragged the struggling hunter with difficulty towards the boy to prevent his flight. A quick grab netted only a boot as Brandon rolled back against the wall. The other pursuer hauled Jack from the far corner and clamped the boy's ankle in a crushing grip. The arduous escape trek was ended. Brandon's muscles turned flaccid in the despair of surrender.

Shots rang out in the dimly lit shelter. Across the room the forgotten Art was propped on one elbow firing a heavy caliber automatic toward the struggling group. The attackers sheltered themselves behind their captives. Jack yelled, "For God's sake, Art, don't shoot us." Two more rounds thundered out. Art was too disoriented to understand.

Brandon slipped out the front into the driving rain and ran off into the night. Another shot cracked faintly, attenuated by the rain and wind. Brandon did not run blindly but headed steadily uphill in a northwesterly direction. He knew that there were large rock formations about eight miles ahead in which he could seek shelter from the weather and his pursuers. If he could elude them now and take a short rest then he could cover the remaining fifteen miles to Lake Tahoe in daylight tomorrow.

His elation at his escape was quickly dissipated by the cold rain, the rocks and mud under his bare feet, and the concentration he needed to maintain his direction in the dark. Mishaps of sliding, falling and bruising himself were so numerous that he accepted them as part of his flight. He was unconscious of time and distance until the sky lightened almost imperceptibly and dawn slowly illuminated his path. Not far ahead he saw his goal of a mountainside littered with massive blocks of stone in jumbled disarray He headed for an undistinguished mass that offered both shelter and a panoramic view of his back trail. He picked his way across the hillside to avoid leaving any perceptible trail. It was with great relief that he entered a dry crevice sheltered from the wind and stripped off his sodden clothes. He wrung the water out and spread them on the rocks although drying was out of the question. He sat on a rock and gazed out over his back trail as far as he could see through the slackening rain. Nothing moved. No one was visibly following.

The excitement and exertion of his flight abated. The penetrating chill of the damp air set him to shivering. He became aware of the aches and pains of his bruises. Weariness overcame him so that he dozed off immediately only to be awakened by his shivering.

Even in his stupor he realized the danger. He must keep warm. He must remain concealed. Brandon stood, and despite his protesting muscles, began calisthenics to warm himself. What at first seemed impossible soon became pleasant as the exertion warmed and dried his body. After twenty minutes he sat again and relaxed himself, then used

Wovoka's concealment technique to reduce his biological emanations. His suppressed panic subsided and he began to feel at least temporarily safe once more.

Plans for the next stage of his trek began to form. He would chance taking the road to Tahoe so as to make better time. There he would try to look presentable and disappear into the crowds of tourists and hikers. He might find some food at picnic spots or near small fast food diners. With luck he might even find some clothing. What he had now was in shabby condition. Boots seemed an unlikely acquisition. His aching told him that boots would pose a long-term problem in this rugged terrain. When his shivering began again, Brandon repeated his calisthenics. This time he wore his long underwear in the hope that body heat and motion would dry the garment. It was hard to convince himself that there was improvement. He passed several hours alternating between calisthenics and planning his next steps. The combination helped him survive the cold in good mental and physical shape.

The rain ceased in mid-morning although the clouds still hung heavy and low in the sky. The air was chilly and fitful gusts of wind raised goose bumps on his arms. A careful search of his back trail revealed nothing moving. Whatever the outcome of the confrontation in the lean-to, the storm had effectively covered his tracks. His feet had a few stone bruises but no serious damage from last night's headlong flight. He examined the damp clothing and was surprised by its good condition. The socks were in shreds. He donned the pants and heavy shirt for their wind breaking potential and also to look presentable to people he might encounter. If the clothes dried out, that would be a welcome added benefit. He combed his hair back with his fingers, tucked his shirt into his pants, rolled up his sleeves to the elbows and started north.

Despite his concern about his feet, the walking quickly warmed them and their aches faded into the background. In half an hour he reached Route 89 to Tahoe. Traffic was light so he stayed on the edge of the road, stepping into the trees when he heard vehicles approaching. At the outskirts of the town of Meyers, he found a shuttered roadside stand named Herb's Garden Fresh Produce. It appeared deserted so he circled the little shack looking for anything edible. He found a treasure trove. Trash bins at the side were loaded with produce left over from the cold rainy days that had discouraged tourism. Brandon's empty stomach labeled it a feast. He ate voraciously of tomatoes, spinach, summer squash, oranges, apples and grapes. His pockets soon bulged with the firmer apples and oranges plus a handful of spinach. With a firmer stride, he started out again, leaving the highway to cut northwestward toward Fallen Leaf. He estimated it to be about four miles ahead at the southwestern end of Lake Tahoe.

There was a spring in his step as he strode past Fallen Leaf. The rain had held off, the clouds had parted several times to show the sun and his clothes were dry and warm again. An apple in each hand served to top off the lunch of vegetables he had munched while walking. Ahead of him the lodge pole pines stood tall and straight in orderly rows along the slopes. Their farther ranks disappeared into the mists of vagrant clouds from the far-reaching storm system. His eyes were drawn to the treetops and then to the broken clouds and patches of blue. The serenity of blue sky calmed his spirit. His attention drifted to the smaller fluffy cloud shapes that evoked gentle fancies of playful animals, fairy tale figures and dreams of happy times yet to be. The puffy clouds aggregated into larger masses evoking images of larger animals, forceful figures and massive looming structures. Soon the darkening clouds assumed more threatening configurations and alarmed him with visions of conflicting hosts moving in ominous formations across the sky. The uneasiness brought Brandon out of his reverie. He realized that these daydreams had relaxed his vigilance and dropped his Wovokian shield. Probing pings were eliciting responses from his mind. He looked fearfully behind him but could see no one. He knew, however, that his searchers were still on his trail. His own carelessness was making it easier for them to determine his direction. With two of them tracking him, they could even triangulate to get his position.

Brandon increased his pace. He withdrew his consciousness into himself insofar as he could while exerting himself strenuously. He wanted to make tracking difficult until he reached a shelter where he could relax completely and reduce his bioelectric emanations below the level of the natural background. Then he would be completely undetectable to his pursuers.

The vast expanse of Lake Tahoe was intermittently visible through the trees as the fugitive cut diagonally downhill toward the water. He hoped that he could conceal himself near a campground so that the biological emanations of other people would raise the background noise and so make the Wovokian technique more effective.

He became aware of a change in the probing pings of his pursuers. Two were still behind him, but a third signal was now coming from directly ahead. A car! Of course! The two trackers on foot had communicated with their driver and sent him to the point where his projected path would cross the road circling Tahoe. The boy's heart sank as his chance of escape dropped to near zero. He increased his speed as his whirling thoughts searched for a better plan.

The threatening clouds finally opened up in a torrential downpour. Rivulets ran down the slope. Gusts of wind turned a fire hose of rain upon him from varying directions. Visibility was severely limited. Thunder rolled and the crash of a nearby lightning strike could be heard above the storm. The probing pings on his mind were lost in the electrical static of the lightning. No one could sense him now. Brandon altered his course to evade pursuit and headed directly down slope. A fallen tree with upended roots lay across his path. He couldn't avoid it, so he slid under the trunk. The root mass formed a small cave into which he crawled, protected from the fury of the storm for the moment. The roar of rain and wind faded. The ground was dry. Immediately he sat in the lotus position and relaxed himself preparatory to diminishing all of his telltale bioelectric emanations. This must be his strongest effort yet or all was lost.

Faintly from outside he heard the shouting voice of the Sasquatch hunter. "I told you those bastards were after the kid. Following that truck has led us right to him. Keep your eyes open, Jack. He has to be hiding right near here."

Moments later Brandon heard the burping reports of fire from a semi-automatic weapon.

"There go the two who grabbed us!" yelled Jack. More shots followed. Indistinct shouts of pursuit faded away and all was quiet again in the boy's refuge.

Brandon felt a great relief and the tension washed from his being. He felt himself sinking into a deep well of velvet quiet. Even the erratic electrical waves of lightning discharges faded away. He knew he was going into the deepest level of Wovokian concealment. His last sensation was that of being lifted on a giant wave and being carried weightless into the ultimate darkness of inner space where no external stimuli penetrate.

The Hoag Ranch

Marly Hoag was awakened from a drugged sleep by a crash that rocked the van. The van continued to rock under the onslaught of what sounded like a gigantic fire hose. She donned a hooded jacket and struggled unsteadily to the front of the van but could see nothing in the pitch darkness. Turning on the headlights produced only a wan glow through the torrent streaming over her windshield and side windows. In a panic at being caught in a flood, she cranked the engine until it caught with uneven firing and then roared to life. She jammed the shift into reverse, gunned the engine and the vehicle jumped back twenty feet from the rock face which had become a waterfall in the torrential downpour. Her wiper and the pouring rain cleared away the mud from her windshield so that she could see the cascade in front of her. Twenty feet above she saw a tree trunk edging over the cliff under the insistent pressure of the water. She opened her window despite the rain so that she could see to back the van onto Route 89. She revved the engine and the van lurched in reverse out onto the road. A look back at the waterfall showed that a lake was forming in the turnoff and beginning to run across the road. It was time to get moving.

She looked back again and jerked the van around to head north on the highway. Marly rolled up her window, pushed her wet hair back from her face and turned to the front again. Two hands were sliding slowly down her windshield. She sat transfixed as vague recollections of horror movies brought unstructured thoughts of homicidal maniacs, vampires, werewolves and other monsters to her addled mind. The hands were followed by a head, shoulders, and then the entire body, which slid limply down the windshield to the ground. She backed away until her headlights illuminated the motionless crumpled body. Her panic subsided as she pulled her thoughts together and realized that this was the thump on her roof. A boy had been swept over the cliff by the torrent and flung onto her van.

A tremendous crash in the turnoff jerked her head about. She surmised that a rock or tree had gone over the edge. The stream across the road was now broad and deep enough to be moving the body across the road. Marly was galvanized to action by the danger. She opened the door and swung her hefty body down to the ground. In a moment she had grabbed the boy by the shoulders, pulled him back to the van, hoisted him in through the door and pushed in behind him to the wheel. Judging it too risky to stay where she was and useless to examine her rescued passenger, she put the van in gear and drove northward away from the immediate danger.

The winding road along the lakeshore was made treacherous by the darkness, rain, runoff flooding the road and occasional fallen rocks that had to be avoided. Driving required her complete attention. Her passenger moaned occasionally indicating that she had not wasted her rescue efforts. After a few miles she realized that she was shivering in her pajamas soaking wet from the thighs down. The boy must be wetter and colder than she. She turned on the heater to warm the van and looked for a safe place to pull over so that she could change their wet clothes. A flat turnoff on a small rise provided the opportunity. She undressed, toweled herself off and donned Levi's, a heavy Pendleton shirt and boots. The boy's ragged clothes she ripped off of him and threw on the floor. Despite some ugly bruises he appeared not to be an emergency case. Marly used one of her heavy shirts as a robe for the boy, wrapped him in a blanket and tucked him into the bunk. Rest and warmth seemed most appropriate now.

Back on the road again, she drove carefully while she pondered what to do with the boy. She didn't want to bring him to the police. They might poke around and find the drugs she was carrying up north. That would be a bad scene. Drug and van confiscation, jail time, withdrawal – all due to stupid sentimentality. She looked back to where the boy appeared to be sleeping naturally. No problem there. Well, he would still be back in the turnoff and probably dead by now if she had not been there by chance. Now her own safety was paramount. It was his turn to take the chances. He could ride with her for a while.

Her thoughts turned back to her own son. He was born in an RV camp near Cody, Wyoming, delivered by a nurse who was just an overnight camper. The nurse called him Cody when Marly couldn't think of a name. Cody Hoag. It had a virile outdoors ring to it. But Cody was a runt with delicate health. Some birth defect due to her doing drugs, maybe, she thought with a pang of regret. But he was the sunshine of her life, always sweet and laughing. He made the open road and camping out seem like an endless trip through paradise. Cody was quick and smart, sharper than any schooling would have made him. She didn't want to stay in one place and lose all his days to four walls and a stranger. He died at eight, curled in her arms and looking across the green clad and snow bedecked Grand Tetons in the spring. When his shallow breathing stopped with a final exhalation, she knew that his liberated soul had become part of the grandeur of that scene. He was now the laughter in the brook, the delicate sunshine that filtered through the pines to kiss her cheek, the breeze that gently wafted tendrils of her hair. She buried him there near that gurgling brook. Part of her soul lay there beside him.

Marly glanced back again to her sleeping companion. Tears flowed down her cheeks. Some of her void of loneliness had been filled.

The van crept north for hours through the night on Route 89. The wind-driven rain, crackling thunder and stroboscopic lightning flashes laid a heavy stress on Marly as she drove with her face near the windshield to discern the road ahead. Water on the road was like the surface of a storm-roiled lake whose depth she did not know. Wind bent trees seen in the intermittent lightning flashes stayed in her mind constantly during the darkness with their threat of collapse on her roof. Large rocks on the road were constant navigation hazards and threats to her tires and undercarriage. Sporadic mudslides threatened to engulf and imprison her or to sweep her over the edge of the road and down towards the lake. Her eyes were burning, her throat was dry and scratchy, and her hands were shaking on the wheel. She was strung out and terrified. She screamed aloud in her frustration and fright. Her eyes closed to deny the dangers outside. The van struck a rock and lurched to one side, its tail swung wide by the water flowing across the road.

She moaned, "Oh, God! Oh, God!" And slumped against the steering wheel.

A boy's voice cried, "Mama! Mama!"

Involuntarily, Marly responded, "Cody! Hold on! We're going over!"

Her eyes flashed open and focused on the road. Her grip on the wheel tightened and her shaking ceased as her maternal instinct to save her son galvanized her to action. She turned into the skid, gunned the engine and fishtailed crazily along the edge of the road sending a shower of spray before her. The strong hands on her shoulders steadied her own shaking body and calmed her spirit so that she could guide the van. The intensity of the storm gradually diminished. The road passed through more sheltered areas. Lights along the road indicated she was entering a populated section. The tension eased and the van picked up speed as the highway conditions improved. Several emergency utility vehicles passed her heading south. The worst of the storm was behind her. The roadway cleared even more, the rain was lighter, and the wind less blustery: driving became almost relaxing.

Marly took her right hand off the steering wheel and squeezed the boy's left hand. "Thanks, son." she said in a warm relaxed tone. "You saved us both tonight. I'm all right. You lie down now. You need to rest."

The boy went dutifully back to his bunk.

The bright lights of the Tahoe City intersection loomed up in another fifteen minutes, a welcome sight. Marly stopped at the gas pump of an all night station and ran in to pay the attendant, get coffee and use the restroom. He barely glanced up from his magazine as he took her money and rang it up. She filled the tank and climbed into the van again where she tucked the blanket around her sleeping companion before starting on the road again. The hot coffee, fading storm and clear road revived her spirits. By the time she reached Sierraville, the sky had lightened and the morning sun illuminated the beauty of the taller peaks. She thought of her own adventure. She thought of her son Cody's last months in the mountains he so loved and of which he was now a part. Her new Cody deserved that kind of youth. And after she delivered her vanload up north she could come back to her parents' ranch and show him all the beauty she had known in those near forgotten years.

Marly impulsively turned east on Route 49 and headed towards Chilcoot and Route 395. She would drop Cody at the ranch first and then come back to him. Delivery could wait a day. Route 49 stopped at the highway, but she found the familiar dirt road up Lawlor Canyon and crossed over into Nevada. Nine miles of rutted road brought her over a rise to a view once again of her childhood home. The ranch looked the same. Old weathered buildings sat in a grassy vale. A spring fed creek supplied water to the ranch. Paint peeling from the ranch house evidenced neglect. The house faced a dusty corral across the front yard. Two large sugar pines shaded the western side. A small vegetable garden was behind the house. When she drove up to the front porch, she could see that a few foundation geraniums still struggled to lend color to the drab surroundings. She lifted her eyes to the backdrop of mountains and blue sky. The beauty of God's creation compensated for the inadequacies of man.

A little woman wiping her hands on her blue-checkered apron walked out onto the porch shading her eyes to discern the identity of her visitor. When Marly dismounted from the van, the old woman seemed hesitant and uncertain with eyes squinted to sharpen her vision. A flash of recognition brightened her face but the smile remained uncertain.

"Marly!" she exclaimed, "Marly!" She descended the steps carefully, then spread her arms in welcome and walked quickly to meet her daughter. Marly stepped forward and hugged her mother tentatively at first, then returned her wholehearted embrace. Her mother held her at arm's length and looked her over carefully.

"You look tired, Marly. You've gained a lot of weight," was her matter of fact conclusion. Her voice was flat and monotonous, her facial expressions and hand motions emphatic in the manner of a deaf person unsure of her listener's comprehension. "Where's the boy?" she asked.

Marly's lips formed that resigned semi-smile reserved for parents who greet their children with critical candor. The daughter signed 'boy' and pointed to the van.

The boy was out of the van when they reached it. Marly's oversize shirt was draped about him. His hair was a wild shock. His hands barely reached the ends of his sleeves. His sturdy legs were exposed from the knees down. He stared at the two women with a puzzled look on his face.

The women stopped in front of him.

"He looks a lot sturdier than when he was two years old, last visit. Never thought he'd live long, traveling with you," said Marta Hoag, mingling her sound and sign languages. "Hug your grandma, Cody."

The boy watched her in fascinated non-comprehension. Marly pushed him forward and her mother hugged the non-responsive boy about the shoulders. She squeezed hard several times and then looked to Marly with an expression of approval. "Strong. You done something right."

She took the boy's hand and turned to the house. "Bring his clothes, Marly. I'll get lunch."

Marly touched her arm and signed awkwardly, "Boy. No clothes. Storm."

Marta took a good look at the dented muddy van, then nodded in comprehension and led the way into the kitchen. She poured coffee for both of them. The boy spotted the toilet through the bathroom door. He urinated in the commode without closing the door and turned to leave. Marta saw his actions and went in to flush the commode. She brought him to the door and said loudly, "Close door, Cody. Close door, Cody," swinging it open and shut several times. He watched impassively.

"He deaf?" the old lady asked her daughter. Marly shrugged non-committally, eyeing him thoughtfully.

"Give him coffee. I'll get your old clothes," said her mother.

A few minutes later she came in with several sets of overalls and shirts. Checking fit against his frame, she directed, "Try these on," and handed him the clothes. Brandon took them but made no move to don them.

"Retarded," she commented. Taking off his oversize shirt, Marta put the clothes on the unresisting boy. She then took out a comb to neaten his hair. She examined him critically, decided he was presentable and sat him at the table. She put the coffee cup to his lips and tilted it. He sipped but burned his lips and tongue. He turned his head away and would not try the brew again. His new grandmother then put a glass of cold water in his hands. This he drank thirstily.

"Needs teaching," decided Marta. "You staying long?" she queried Marly.

"Not now. Package to deliver. Can he stay?"

"How long?"

"Until I get back. Maybe longer. I want to get clean, get my act together."

"No drugs here!"

"I know, I know. I'll be clean." Marly got to her feet. "Where's Pop?"

"Reno. Back tonight."

"Sorry I missed him. I'll be back in a few days." She opened the front door.

"What about Cody?" her mother asked.

Marly looked at the boy who was sitting quietly, shuttling his gaze from one to the other as though making a futile attempt to understand their terse words, fleeting expressions and accompanying gestures.

"He's no trouble. Just a few days." Marly waved goodbye to the boy and then walked out on the porch, down the steps and climbed into the van. Her mother stood with one hand on the boy's shoulders and watched the van depart.

"Don't worry about your mama, Cody. She'll be back soon." The expression on her face belied her words and gestures.

The boy sat there without any show of emotion at Marly's departure. In his mind he tried the sound 'Cody' and the flashing hand sign. They seemed to be associated with him by 'grandma.' He experimented with several variations of it in trying to get it right but it did not seem familiar. A hand on his arm brought him out of his concentration. He realized that 'grandma' had been saying this name repeatedly. Raising his eyes, he saw that she was making the associated hand sign. He repeated this back to her and she responded with a pleased expression, nodding her head up and down. She repeated the sign and then pointed to him. He followed suit and pointed to her. Her head shook negatively. She signed 'Cody' again and pointed to him. As he had surmised, this was the name sign she attached to him. 'Cody' therefore repeated the sign and pointed to him.

'Grandma' beamed. She signed vaguely and muttered, "Deaf as a doorknob. Not stupid." Cody did not recognize these signs or the mumbled words.

She made a new sign and pointed to herself. He looked at her in a perplexed way. She repeated it several times while muttering, 'Marta.' At last Cody signed 'Marta' to her but followed it with the 'grandma' sign and a questioning look on his face.

Now she laughed delightedly. She signaled back the 'grandma' sign while muttering it verbally and then made a new sign with fingertips together before pointing to herself again. Now he understood. She had two names. He nodded in the affirmative and repeated both name signs separated by the touching fingertips and followed by pointing to her.

'Marta-grandma' laughed and cried, then hugged him tightly. He hugged her in return. They had made contact. He had an identity – Cody.

Grandma Marta toured the house with Cody to point out every item to the boy and give the associated sign for it. Unconsciously, she muttered the names along with the signs in the manner of one not deaf from birth. Cody realized the association of signs and vocalization that gave the names in two separate forms. He tried the names vocally and they seemed familiar but she did not respond at all to the sounds. Realizing that she could not hear any sounds, he repeated the names subvocally to himself but did not say them out loud for her benefit. He concentrated on her sign language and found it simple to grasp. Grandma hugged him and patted his head frequently to show how pleased she was with his quick progress. Cody found himself liking her very much and responded to her praise by trying to connect the names in ways that were meaningful or occasionally ways that were humorous.

"Poor little boy," she murmured without signing, "What might you have been today with proper training. Dad and I will fix that."

Cody gave no indication that he heard what she said for she did not realize that she had said it out loud and it did not seem to require a response.

When they reached the bathroom, again she made the sign for bathtub and then added several other signs including his name, Cody. The boy did not understand her message until she beckoned him toward the tub and indicated that he should get into it. After he did so, she turned the water on momentarily and demonstrated washing motions. When his expression indicated understanding and he signed, 'yes,' she had him get out again. She led the way across the kitchen and through the far door into a large pantry built at the back end of the side porch. She crossed the shed to a tank and lit a fire inside a little door under the tank. Grandma pointed to the tank and signed, 'water.' She then held his hand near the fire door and made a new sign while verbalizing, "Hot." Cody connected the signs 'hot' and 'water' and then touched the tank. He glanced around the shed and noticed bottles and jars on the shelves, several large white metal boxes with doors, and stairs leading both up and down to dark mysterious places. Grandma led the way back into the kitchen before he could ask what they all were.

The coffee cups were still on the kitchen table. She picked up his cup, held it to her lips and then gave it to him. She signed 'hot' with a negative sign and then 'Cody drink.' He obediently took a sip but made a displeased expression and put it down. She laughed and poured the coffee down the drain. She then mimicked his expression and made a new sign, which he interpreted to mean bad taste. They both laughed when he repeated the 'bad taste' sign several times, each time with more emphatic gestures than the last.

The tub was full of hot water at last and Cody undressed to step into it. Marta looked over his bruises carefully and decided that they would all disappear in a week or two at most. The boy gingerly tried the water before sinking into it gratefully to soak away the grime and soothe his aching body. Grandma carried his new clothes into the kitchen and began reshaping them to his contours. Cody soaped himself and then lay back to let his mind wander. He remembered a little of the van ride through the storm, the road up to the ranch and the events inside the house. Otherwise, his past was a blank. He was bruised and had therefore been in an accident. These people seemed to know him as their son and grandson. It was strange to think that he could not remember his past but it was comforting to be with people who knew him and loved him. He dozed off with a feeling of security knowing he was home with his family.

Heavy steps on the porch awakened him. The rumble of a deeper voice told him that a man had arrived, probably the 'Pop' that Marly had inquired about earlier. Cody got out of the tub, dried himself and walked out into the kitchen. A big older man was there conversing with Grandma in sign language. At the sight of the boy he signed 'Cody' and beckoned him closer. The old man's face broke into a delighted smile as he swept the boy up from the floor in a bear hug and swung him about. It felt wonderful to be so welcome and at home. Back on the floor, the boy watched the excited signing of the two but could catch only a few words such as 'big,' 'strong,' and 'beautiful' which he inferred were being applied to him. He smiled tentatively. When he smiled, the two older people stopped and beamed down at him.

Grandma Marta introduced the man to Cody by signs and muttered words as Grandpa Seth. She then indicated that the two of them were joined as Grandma-Grandpa-Hoag. To Cody's surprise and delight, she then joined together Marta-Seth-Cody and Hoag to include him in the family. They hugged each other in a tight circle with Cody sobbing happily. Now he was sure he was home at last.

Grandma Hoag broke free and walked over to the table, dabbing at her eyes with her apron as she went. She called the boy over and held out the reworked shirt and overalls to him. These he donned quickly and paraded around waving his arms and kicking his legs to show how well they fit. He went back to where she had sat and clambered in her lap. He awkwardly patted his chest and then hers, after which he kissed her on the lips and laid his head on her shoulder. Her tears fell on his cheek. Grandpa Seth patted him on the shoulder. Cody thought he could hear a sweet breeze soughing through the mountain pines, a perfumed breeze bearing a lost love home again. He knew that he was that lost love for them.

When they regained their composure, Grandma had Cody sign the names of all the objects in the house for Grandpa. Both were astonished that he knew them all without hesitation. Further, he was forming phrases and short sentences using the connections and space management that they used between themselves. Now they knew that they had a prodigy in their grandson, one who could add a whole new dimension to their lives. Convinced that he was a deprived deaf child, they made every communication a lesson in sign language. With the hints of their muttered vocalizations he was able to learn much faster than would otherwise have been possible.

A scratching at the screen door attracted Cody's attention, although it went unnoticed by his grandparents. Finally, the screen door was pulled open and allowed to slam with a force that vibrated the house. Both Seth and Marta responded to the vibrations. Seth opened the door and in walked a jet-black cat, a cat with a peculiar hopping gait. She walked confidently to each of the pair and rubbed her cheek against a foot. She eyed the boy speculatively for a moment, was apparently satisfied with what she saw, and walked over to rub her side against his leg. She then sat at his feet, waiting. Seth stepped to Cody's side and reached down to pet the cat. He signed for the boy to do the same. Cody did. The cat was satisfied with the mutual recognition. She walked over to lie beside her dish and turned an expectant face toward Marta.

Seth signed 'three-legged' and muttered 'tripod' after which he pointed to the cat. Cody recognized the sign as the cat's name, 'Tripod.' He was pleased when Grandma filled the cat's dish and allowed him to feed her. Tripod didn't seem to mind at all. She also accepted him as part of the family.

Candles lighted the table to make the evening meal a festive occasion. Every dish received an accolade from Seth. They sat quietly before eating with Seth signing some new phrases that Cody did not comprehend. The explanation seemed to involve something or someone expansive giving them food and other things. He remembered the signs for later explanation. His plate was large and food from each of the serving dishes was heaped on it. A tossed salad of leaf and romaine lettuce graced with red cabbage, scallions, tomatoes, mushrooms, green peppers and zucchini had a creamy ranch dressing. Hot vegetables included broccoli, Brussels sprouts and asparagus all covered with a cheese sauce. A baked potato dripped with butter. Hot fresh baked bread melted its buttery spread.

The odors made his mouth water. All, that is, but one. That was a large slab of a different texture and unpleasant odor. He pushed that to the side of his plate and ate hungrily of everything else. Grandma Marta noticed his neglect of that course and indicated that he should try it. He thought for a moment and then signed as he had for the coffee, 'bad taste.' She looked shocked for a second, then laughed and signed something new to Grandpa while muttering 'vegetarian.' She made no further effort to have him eat it. He was glad to be a vegetarian, whatever that might be.

That night he was tucked into a large soft bed and kissed goodnight. He couldn't sleep. He was too warm and the bed was too soft. At last he got off the bed, wrapped a blanket around himself and lay on the floor. With that he drifted off to sleep and dreamt strange dreams of storm and wind and rain that at last were warded off by Grandma and Grandpa Hoag. A deep and dreamless sleep took over. He was safe at home.

The days that followed were full of discovery, exploration and wonderment. Grandpa reshaped a pair of Marly's old boots to fit his wider and shorter feet. Grandma knitted socks for him and Grandpa gave him a broad brimmed hat. He strutted about in his new finery as proud as any peacock. He dressed like one of the family. He was even imitating Grandpa's walk with slightly bent knees and feet about eight inches apart. His grandparents laughed at that and signed the joined words 'cow-boy' for him but he did not grasp the meaning. They laughed at that, too.

The ranch house was simple in design. Grandpa Seth's father had built it in the 1880's. The house was 50 feet square with a porch across the front and halfway down both sides. The original house appeared to have been 50 feet wide by 25 feet deep. A back section of equal size had been added later. The front faced west towards the access road through the narrow lower canyon.

The front door opened into a wide area that included the kitchen and dining table on the left and the living room on the right. The back half of the house held two bedrooms and a bath in the middle. The bath was a modification of the early 1920's that brought the outhouse into the main house. The bath was 12 feet by 25 feet including closet space and the bedrooms were thus reduced to 19 by 25 feet each. There were no closets as such. Wardrobes and dressers provided much of the storage space. Each bedroom had a dressing table with mirror. There were windows in all the rooms to take advantage of the views of ranchland, creek and mountains. Cody was given the bedroom behind the kitchen. He spent a full ten minutes touching all the furniture in the room, testing the bed, and tracing the intricate patterns in the Navajo rug. He looked up the fireplace chimney and finally understood it was for smoke from a fire. He gazed long out the windows toward the far eastern end of the ranch where the creek emerged from a narrow gorge. An urge to explore grew within him. As he drank in the scenery he could feel himself striding across the pasture, wading through the cold refreshing waters of the creek, climbing the steep run of the gorge, and reaching an area perfumed by trees and flowers. The feeling of being home grew within him.

Grandpa Seth took him outside and around the house on the porch. The right side of the house, where the living room lay, overlooked the creek and the steeply sloping hills on the south side. As they walked back around the front of the house past the door, he could see on his left the entrance road coming in from the west and the hills defining the west wall of the canyon. Close in were corral and several buildings with large sliding doors. Straight ahead to the north the land sloped gently upward at first and then rose more quickly to foothills and eventually forested mountains in the distance. Turning the corner past the kitchen, he could see the large extent of the pastures back to where their little valley narrowed again at the gorge from which the creek flowed. Directly in front of them was the pantry, which terminated the north side of the porch. Cody tugged Grandpa's hand to go back to that intriguing place with all its stairways, food containers and appliances.

Seth obligingly opened the pantry door and entered with his inquisitive grandson. A flick of the light switch illuminated the 8x20 ft. room. First Seth led Cody up the flight of stairs in front of them. When Cody's head rose above the ceiling line, he saw a dim expanse with undefined boundaries. A strange fear of walls pressing in on him combined with a sense of floating in limitless space. He squeezed his grandfather's hand and began to back down the attic stairs. Seth found the light switch and flicked it on. Cody felt suddenly at home. The large attic was now a room containing chests and boxes and assorted strange things to be investigated. There was a rocking horse, a small chair with wheels, some tiny furniture, a little wagon, and a two-wheeled something and a clear covered box containing a big replica of a girl. The boy stopped at each item and looked without touching.

'Touch them. Lift them,' signed Seth, demonstrating the actions and muttering the words. 'Belong little Marly. Now big Marly. You take.' Cody gingerly sat on the rocking horse, sat on the little wagon, and stood next to the bicycle without comprehending how it could be used. He then turned to his grandfather and looked questioningly at the chests.

Seth threw open the lids on the first two chests. Inside were clothes for a little girl, all clean and neatly folded as if ready for use.

'No little mother now,' he signed. His eyes were moist as he remembered the happy years with Marly growing up on the ranch.

Cody felt a deep sorrow surrounding his newfound grandfather. He hugged him powerfully in return as if he could be squeezed into his lost daughter's mold. They stepped quietly downstairs, each lost in his own thoughts. Cody sensed that his mother had caused great sorrow to her parents by leaving them. It somehow struck a responsive chord in his own heart that gave rise to a sorrow he could not explain. With a heavy heart he feigned interest in Seth's explanations of refrigerator, freezer and washing machine. Only the taste of some home canned spiced apples brought him back from his gloom.

After dinner Seth built a fire in the living room fireplace to ward off the evening chill. He pulled three chairs before the fire, the middle one for Cody. They sat quietly for several minutes and let the radiant heat of the fire relax them to the bone. Cody's eyelids fluttered as the tension left his body and the bruises ceased their throbbing.

Seth had apparently been preparing to communicate with Cody. He waved to get the boy's attention and brought him back from his doze. The old man signed, 'You Cody. Me Grandpa for you.'

Cody nodded his comprehension and signed in response, 'Me Cody. You Grandpa me.'

Seth continued, 'House belong grandpa for me.' The boy nodded that he understood.

Seth signed further, 'House belong me now.' Again, Cody nodded.

This time Seth started with an unfamiliar sign. '_______ house belong Cody.'

Now the boy understood. 'No die!" he signed emphatically and began to cry. 'Cody take care Grandpa Seth.' With that he jumped onto the older man's lap and threw his arms about Grandpa's neck.

Seth held him tight and rocked him back and forth to soothe him. 'No die,' he signed. 'Grandpa and Grandma take care Cody!'

Grandma Marta came over and kissed his cheek, murmuring words that he could not quite get but which reassured and calmed him. Some communications require neither sounds nor signs but are purely heart to heart.

Life on the Ranch

The morning sunlight skipped across the mountainous desert of northern Nevada in uneven jumps. It illuminated the peaks, flowed backward down their slopes to the valleys below, and having gathered strength sprang forward again to the peaks of another range. It surmounted the Stillwater Range, ran fleetly across the Carson Sink, leapt over the Trinity Range, touched the Virginia Mountains, then gathered itself in the foothills and jumped over Pah Rah Mountain. Its first rays illuminated the Holy Place of the Water Children who brought life to Earth in the first days of Creation. They carried the message of the Creator to encourage all things to grow in grace and beauty and peace. The Water Children still bring the message of Manitou in the voices of rain, sea, spring and grotto. They carry messages of laughter, sorrow, wisdom and war to those who will listen.

The Paiute shaman 'Far Walker' was one who listened. He sat cross-legged by the spring of the Water Children patiently awaiting possible messages for him to bring to his people. Yesterday, in this small box canyon, he had fasted to purify his soul. Towards late afternoon he had bathed and donned his ceremonial garments. His raw cotton pants had a woven design of maize and bean plants. His cotton shirt was decorated with painted stylized representations of animal life of the desert and mountains. Over these he wore a knee length robe with intricate embroidery and beadwork that depicted the seven stages of creation of the world. On his head was a white headband in which were placed an eagle feather for bravery in searching for truth and an owl feather for wisdom to recognize the truth when it is found. At dusk he had smoked a pipeful of aromatic bark and let the smoke ascend to the skies as a prayer for revelation of truth and guidance in its use.

Through the night he sat there listening to the spring and brook babble in many voices and tongues, yet there were none that he could understand. Sometimes he thought that they were surging with excitement over a message whose time to tell had not yet arrived. In the morning when the first sun lit his face, he could hear the waters saying, "Come again next year. We will have much to tell you when the time is come."

Now birds were calling, two deer came to the brook to drink, and a light breeze was rustling the leaves. He was awake to the sounds of a new day and the whispers of night faded into the background. 'Far Walker' arose and carefully folded his ritual accouterments into his pack. He bid a respectful farewell to the Water Children and started eastward on the trail back to the Pyramid Lake reservation. Each year he made this pilgrimage. In his youth the voices of the Water Children told him about great events to come, events that could change his nation's destiny, and would be revealed to him in time. That time would come. Perhaps next year. Perhaps later. His faith supported his patience. That time would come.

The same morning rays that illuminated the spring traveled straight through the gorge, across the ranchland and into Cody's bedroom. For a few brief moments the beam entered his window, flashed upon his eyelids and then was gone again as the sun moved across the sky and off the straight path through the gorge. Cody's eyes opened, the afterimage of the flash still on his retina. He thought that he could hear joyous voices calling him to experience the wonders of a new day. The fading image in his eyes seemed to tell him where those wonders would eventually lead.

Outside all was dark on the ranch. To the east the sunlight illuminated the sky over the mountain peaks and rosy streaks were beginning to find their way through the passes. He sat on the edge of his bed and watched the ranch materialize out of the night. It was the dawning of a new life and he could hardly wait to rush out and embrace it. Somehow it had called to him. He wanted to shout back joyously, "Here I am!"

Another light entered his room streaming under the door. He recognized the light footsteps of grandma in the kitchen as she walked about and lightly clattered several pots and pans. He watched the growing dawn on the ranch and tried to pick out objects from memories of yesterday. Meanwhile he tried to picture what grandma was doing in the kitchen from the muffled sounds he heard. He was torn between the revelations of the morning sun and curiosity over her activities in the kitchen. Soon he could smell coffee, the hot liquid that had burned his mouth, and hear the pot's rhythmic percolation. There was also an odor like hot bread in the air. The emerging scenes of the farm faded from his sight as he tried to envision the kitchen.

He pulled on his full cowboy regalia and followed his nose to the kitchen. The table had been set and a basket of biscuits sat steaming in the center. All three sat and grandpa Seth asked 'God' to 'bless' the food and them and Marly. Grandma Marta then brought the food and named the items for him – 'oatmeal,' 'fried eggs,' 'grits,' 'gravy,' 'bacon,' 'coffee' and milk. Cody turned down the coffee and bacon. The gravy tasted a little odd but he took a little at grandpa's urging. They were amazed at how much he ate. So was he.

After breakfast grandpa had chores to do and took Cody along to see the ranch. They were met at the front door by Tripod who was sitting near her empty plate. She stretched, yawned and fell in beside them with her hippity-hop three-legged stride. The morning inspection was apparently perceived by her as one of her duties.

When they reached the corral, the two horses trotted over to greet them at the fence. The mare nuzzled Seth's shirt pocket insistently. He spoke to her verbally because he knew she could hear him. "That's my girl, Blue Bell. Want your morning sugar? Ask for it properly, now."

Blue Bell stepped back, tapped her right hoof twice, then returned to the fence and nuzzled the rancher's cheek. Seth grinned and said, "That's right. Good girl." He took a lump of sugar out of the pocket and let her take it from his palm. She punched his pocket again with her nose until he at last proffered another sugar lump. Taking that, she backed off and shook her head, satisfied. The filly stepped up to the fence cautiously, aware that her turn for the sweet had come but timorous about the human contact. Seth gave two lumps of sugar to Cody. He signed, 'You,' 'sugar' and pointed to the filly. The boy gladly took the sugar and thrust his hand out to the filly. She started and backed away, suspicious of the sudden movement. Grandpa placed his hand on the boy's shoulder and indicated to him that he should move slowly and gently so that the horses would not spook. Cody tried again and after gentle coaxing the filly approached, took the sugar lump and ran off to savor it. No amount of waving brought her back.

The rancher caught his grandson's attention and began signing to him. First he pointed to the mare and signed, 'name.' Next he looked about, found a blue clover and successively held it next to his denims and to his shirt. Since Cody had already heard the name 'Blue Bell' when his grandfather spoke to the mare, he gathered that the color blue was the common denominator among those objects. The repeated sign made by his grandfather was therefore the sign for 'blue.' The boy repeated the sign and touched each object in turn. He also added the signs for 'pants' and 'shirt.' Seth agreed with a flourished 'Yes!'

Seth now drew a strange looking object in the dirt and made a new sign for it. He began with the sign for 'blue', followed it with the new sign and pointed at the mare. Obviously the new sign was a bell. Cody repeated the signs and pointed to the mare, bringing approval in the form of a shoulder pat. The boy pointed to the filly and followed with name and question signs. His grandfather signed, 'name-none.' After a moment he added, 'Marly name Blue Bell.' A pause, and then he signed, 'Cody name' with a finger pointing to the filly.

The boy's face brightened with pleasure at the prospect of conferring a name on such a beautiful animal. He began thinking and thinking – and thinking. His brow furrowed. He frowned.

He did not know enough names to choose one that would be appropriate. Seth saw Cody's problem in choosing a name. His own taste in names was rather prosaic and tied to an animal's looks. Naming an animal 'Spot' or 'Tiger' or 'Tripod' like his three-legged cat was his style. The filly had a white star on her forehead and white stockings on all four feet. 'Star' or 'Silk Stockings' might be his choice for a name. Marly had named Blue Bell. He had bought the mare for Marly seven years ago to entice her to stay at the ranch with two-year-old Cody. She was thrilled at first and rode through the wildflowers every day, recapturing some of the light heartedness of her girlhood on the ranch. The name Blue Bell came from her love of flowers and the sight of the mare playing among them in the pasture. Marly's sparkle gradually dimmed, until one morning she packed her van, said a tearful goodbye to Blue Bell and took little Cody back to her hippie friends and drugs. He hoped that this time she and Cody were back for good. He watched the boy puzzling over a fitting name and recalled little Marly puzzling the same way over names for kittens, puppies, piglets and calves. He desperately wanted those days to come alive again through Marly's son.

Cody simulated reaching into his shirt pocket for sugar and then waved his hand to beckon the filly. She flipped her mane, swished her tail and cantered over to the fence. Changing her mind, she spun about, kicked up her heels, and ran back to her mother. Dancing from side to side and then back and forth to the fence, she kept tantalizing Cody with her approaches and retreats. The boy began mimicking her steps in a *pas de deux* that had Seth leaning weakly on the fence with laughter. Cody heard Grandma's mumbled voice behind him talking to her self as she signed to Seth, 'Are those two sillies dancing?' Cody spun about to see her closing signs, 'the Can-can?' The boy stopped short when he saw how heartily Grandpa was laughing at his wife's comments and the actions of the filly and him. He signed to Grandma, the question 'Can-can?' She, too, was laughing in good spirits. Marta grabbed Seth and spun a few steps in the dirt with her surprised husband. She signed to the boy 'dance.' Next she grabbed Cody and spun him about several times, signing again, 'dance.' The boy looked at her in puzzlement. Grandma Marta then picked up her apron demurely and began kicking up her legs rhythmically. She stopped and signed, 'dance' followed by 'name Can-can.' Grandma then pointed to Cody and the filly, waved her hand in a circular motion and signed 'Cody dance Can-can'. Cody laughed with them and kicked up his own heels, signing 'Can-can'. When he turned about he saw that the filly was repeating her own advance-retreat-heel kicking routine. He waved his arms high in a sign of solving his problem and shouted the words as he signed over and over, 'Can-can.' Turning towards his grandparents, he pointed at the filly and signed, 'Name Can-can.'

His grandparents stepped to either side of the boy, put their arms across his shoulders and danced together their own version of the Can-can. It was like having their little Marly home again. When they stopped dancing the filly was standing at the fence watching them curiously. Seth gave Cody another sugar lump that the boy held out to the animal. She took the sugar and stood there reaching out again to his hand. One more lump and she nuzzled his cheek. They were friends. Cody signed,

'Can-can,' and like Seth he vocalized the name to the filly. She stared at him for a moment, then threw back her head, neighed and trotted off. He thought that she liked her name.

Grandpa Seth walked around to the barn side of the corral with Cody close behind him. He lifted the lid on a wooden bin and removed two galvanized pails. Into these he measured some grain from a large covered barrel. He gave one to Cody and together they walked to the corral gate. The two horses recognized the pails and trotted over to the gate to meet them. The rancher emptied his pail into one of two troughs next to the fence. Blue Bell immediately put her head into the trough and commenced eating. Seth then indicated that his grandson should do the same in the other trough for the filly. Cody was learning that with ownership comes responsibility. Watching her enjoying the grain he saw it as a happy sharing and not an onerous task.

They walked into the nearby barn, which to Cody was a large and cavernous structure. There were eight stalls, four on either side. The stalls had chest high gates to allow the horses to look about while yet keeping them in. There were pegs for bits and bridles but all of the gear was kept in a tack room just inside and to the left of the door. Seth opened the tack room door and named the pieces of equipment for him, holding up a few of the items to indicate their functions. His grandson was most amused when Seth took the bit between his teeth to demonstrate its use. Slung over two wide half-round rails set waist high on either side of the tack room towards the rear were six saddles. Five were full size western saddles; one was a child's size for a small pony. Cody was intrigued by the dark leather made smooth and shiny by use and careful polishing and conditioning over the years. His grandfather gave him a leg up on to one of the saddles and adjusted the stirrups to fit him. 'Cody – saddle' made it clear that he was to ride a horse on this, his own saddle. He leaned over to embrace his grandfather but went a little too far. The saddle slipped around the rail, his grandfather caught his shoulders, and they wound up sitting together on the floor. When they got up again, Seth signed to him, 'Cody thrown by wooden horse.' The boy replaced the saddle and vaulted onto it again. He bounced up and down, signing to his grandfather, 'Cody ride again!'

They then headed back to the house as Grandma Marta came around the corner when they approached. Three medium sized long-haired dogs were with her. They were all similarly colored a mixture of brown, black and white. At the sight of Seth and Cody the three dogs excitedly headed their way. Not recognizing the boy, the dogs showed their differing temperaments. The oldest dog walked over to the older man, nuzzled his hand while keeping her eyes on the boy, and then turned to Cody to inspect him closely. She sniffed his feet, his clothing and then the hand he reached down to pet her head. The larger of the other two dogs had sat down about ten feet away and was giving Cody an intense visual examination. He moved to the boy's side as they approached, keeping his distance during the inspection. The other young dog was excitedly running a circle around them, barking occasionally, and pausing next to the sitting dog as if for advice. Seth stopped next to Marta and made the introductions. He took the boy's hand, had the older dog sniff it, and then had the boy rub the dog's head and neck. When the dog was sniffing, Seth said loudly, "Dark Eyes, this is Cody. This is Cody, my grandson." She accepted this with a calm stare, and then walked back to Marta. "Stalker!" called Seth to the sitting dog. That dog rose and walked over to the man's side. "Stalker, this is Cody. Cody, my grandson." Stalker at last approached the boy, raised his head for the mandatory caress, and retreated to a distance to sit watchfully again. The third canine, the smallest and lightest colored of the three, was now moving slowly and getting closer. Seth whistled and called, "Mischief! Come here and meet Cody. This is Cody." She had apparently been awaiting the invitation. Now she ran right up to the boy, jumped up on his chest and licked his hands as he tried to fend her off.

The judgment of the other two canines had reassured her that this was a new friend. Seth turned to his grandson and communicated the dog's names in signs and mimicking actions.

They had accepted him and sat quietly. He looked them over closely to note the differences in their markings. He also sniffed them as they had him and noticed their individual odors, particularly the strong male-female scent differences and the musk gland odors. He would know them now and where they had marked their territories. A hand on his shoulder pulled him up from his olfactory inspection of the dogs. Seth was wearing a strange look and signing negatively as he pointed alternately to his nose and to the dogs. Cody was puzzled but accepted the idea that people did not inspect dogs with their noses, although the dogs didn't seem to mind.

Sleep that night was full of dreams for Cody. Seth's full tour of the garden and farm had stimulated his imagination. He saw flowers, vegetables, grain and fruit trees delivering their bounty to his grandparents. It was so good to be here on the ranch with them. He wanted to be part of it all.

Growing Up on the Ranch

Cody awakened before daybreak each morning. He lay in bed and watched the stars follow their slow arc up from the far horizon. A brilliant flash of light that had awakened him on his first morning at the ranch did not reappear. The thought that it had been a signal calling him to the gorge faded to the back of his mind. Someday he would go there but it was not urgent.

Each day his tasks expanded a little as he gained insight into the purposes of ranch operations, familiarity with the chores and had his presence accepted by the animals. The horses now came to him for their sugar and grain treats, especially the filly 'Can-Can'. The cow rebelled at the touch of a new milker so that chore remained to Seth. The dogs responded to his commands although at first they looked questioningly at Seth for his approval. Very quickly the boy realized that the dogs gave their attention to the rancher when he called vocally but that much of the command information they garnered from his conscious and unconscious body language. Cody copied his grandfather's body language for commands and then expanded upon it so that the animals could better understand what he wanted. Seth soon noticed his grandson's way with animals but could not perceive nor copy the subtleties of the boy's communications. Cody accepted the rancher's visual perceptive limitations the same way he accepted his hearing deficiency. There must be 'deafness' of the eyes as well as the ears, the youth reasoned.

The animals had their own personalities and preferences that varied from species to species and animal to animal. The cats were self-contained and self-confident independent residents of the ranch. When called, they mulled it over before responding to show that it was their decision to come. Tripod was the dominant cat who commanded respect from all. She started her day with a meal from Marta and then followed the men to the barn for the early chores. There she accepted recognition from the other cats as she inspected the buildings and checked for rodents. The dogs ran over to her for cursory sniffs. The larger animals gave her only brief glances. After the morning rounds she stayed close to Marta and the house, presiding there over her principal domain. Part of the night she spent indoors near the banked fire. The younger felines had their headquarters at the barn but ranged out through the chicken yard, gardens and fields. The rodent population was low near the farm buildings. These cats had not forgotten that they were self-reliant hunters.

The three dogs associated more closely with the humans. They performed services upon command and basked in the recognition and affection they received. Routine chores – bringing in the animals, patrolling for predators, guarding the ranch buildings – they did on their own. Accompanying humans on their chores or sitting quietly near them on the porch was the dogs' pleasure. Cody felt that the dogs read more subtleties of body language and tone of voice than their humans suspected.

The horses loved to run and roam the pasture. They were not apt to brave the hills without a human for reassurance so being saddled for riding was the start of release and adventure for them. They usually resisted saddling to show independence and rebellion against domination but once mounted they were anxious to explore new frontiers with their riders. Cody felt this conflict of emotions in the horses when he first began to ride 'the paint.' The preliminary bucks after he mounted the gelding landed him on his hands and knees inspecting a recent cow flop. The paint seemed amused at the boy's inexperience at this game and did not run far so that Cody could quickly remount and get them moving. The wind in his face and the ground rushing past were thrill enough to compensate for a few hard contacts with the turf. The new equestrian soon found that he could anticipate the gelding's actions from the tensing of his muscles. Conversely, his mount could read the pull on the reins and the pressure of his rider's knees and thighs for guidance. They quickly became a unit when riding, enjoying the tactile communication, reveling in the ballet of guided and controlled exuberance as they flew over the ground. The surrounding mountains were less a daunting obstacle and more a challenge to adventure when the pair raced over the earth. Cody's horizons began to expand past the canyon walls. His grandfather rode along after them on Ironsides, content to watch the young centaur with pride. Seth's own exhilaration with riding in his youth returned to him and brought tears to his eyes – sadness for his lost youth, gladness for his rebirth in his grandson Cody. The bond with the boy strengthened with every shared learning experience, every skill transferred. Seth felt himself being reincarnated and immortalized in the memory of his grandson.

Gardening was Cody's favorite chore because it was a family affair. They would walk down three separate rows of vegetables pulling weeds and inspecting the plants for insects, disease and general good health. He was shown the harmful insect infestations and virus symptoms by his grandparents and then correlated them with the condition and color of the plants as Seth and Marta pointed them out. He quickly noted other symptoms which his grandparents could not observe and for which he had no symbols in their sign language. Some sick plants had altered auras and electrical fields about their affected growth. Dry plants emitted high frequency vibrations. Water lowered the pitch and stabilized the tone. Soon he could stand at the edge of the field and identify trouble spots from a distance. Cody could listen to the subtle murmuring of the plants to tell if they needed water and fertilizer. He could smell their chemical emanations that seemed to warn other plants of insects and plant disease so that they could generate defensive chemical mechanisms to protect themselves. This world of communications brought him to a kinship with the plants that went far deeper than Seth and Marta's generalized love for the land and plants based largely on visual externals. To Cody, the ranch was not a beautiful scene outside himself but a seething cauldron of life in which he was immersed. His grandparents were soon following his lead in gardening, confident that the drug induced failures in his body had been compensated by other gifts from God that brought him closer to animals and nature.

Cody often knelt beside a plant and appeared to listen to it. He might then give it an extra drink of lightly fertilized water, or spray its leaves with a soap solution, or carefully trim the infected foliage. His grandmother was touched by his caring for the plants and sometimes knelt next to him to watch his gentle ministrations. Occasionally she would look at him and murmur to herself in a rhythmical cadence a series of words that expressed some deep feeling that he did not comprehend. The words appeared to express a relationship with him, the garden and the whole ranch. Some of the phrases seemed to describe the bond he felt with the land when he sat quietly sensing the bountiful life about him, the individual growing things united in the fabric of life with their nurturing environment. Her phrases followed themselves through his mind, gliding to their own rhythms and tones, which refreshed his bond with Mother Earth.

"Alone in the garden at dawn,
The Father steals into my soul.
His voice is the sound of His lawn,
His message heals and makes me whole."

The garden produced much more than they could eat. One day

a week was devoted to canning some of the excess. This was another opportunity for the boy to pitch in on the chores, learning and doing with his devoted grandparents. They had to restrain him from his zeal in harvesting, lugging the baskets up to the house, cleaning and cutting the food, sterilizing the containers and sampling the results. It was new and exciting as he joined in the preparation, cooking, packing and storing in jars or freezer packages. The freezer, pantry and storage cellar were soon overflowing with canned and packed vegetables. Fortunately, they had the animals and convinced Cody to share the appropriate foods with them. Nature's bounty was for caring, preserving and sharing to him. Sometimes Seth took a load into town for sharing with people who had no farms. Cody did not go on these trips. The advent of cooler weather slowed down garden production and plots were therefore turned under to enrich the soil. Seth showed his grandson how to run the tractor and the tiller but the boy was not enthusiastic about the noise and gasoline fumes. He preferred working quietly by hand when he could. The grain fields were now ripe so they turned their attention to reaping. These crops of corn, oats, barley and rye were principally raised for animal fodder. Some sweet corn was for the house. Taking in the grain was a dusty and tedious job with the small tractor. Each phase of cutting, threshing, stacking the straw, shucking the corn, and sacking the grain was an extension of the teaching bond between the rancher and his grandson. He marveled at the boy's enthusiasm, strength and endurance but equated it with his own work when he was a boy on this ranch. The end of gardening gave them more time to relax.

One day at breakfast Cody asked in sign language for his grandparents to take him across the river to the orchard. After the morning chores, Seth and Cody returned to the ranch house. Marta served coffee and then pointed to her picnic basket on the counter. 'Picnic in orchard,' brought Cody to his feet applauding. A new area of the ranch was opening to him, the geometrically aligned trees that bore the fruit he loved. The boy's coffee with milk was downed in a moment and he jumped up to lug the picnic basket to the door, waiting there expectantly for his grandparents.

They laughed at his excitement and quickly finished their coffee. Seth retrieved two more baskets from the pantry and the three were on their way with Cody running ahead in his excitement and then back again to the older couple. The crossing was an irregular array of stepping-stones in the creek bed. The boy hopscotched across the steps in a moment. He turned toward his grandparents and saw that Seth was carefully selecting his footing and helping Marta to step across behind him. Cody set down his basket and went back to help his grandmother, playing the gallant gentleman to her delight. The steep far bank required teamwork from all three of them although Seth tried to make it seem a routine walk for him.

The orchard began not far from the top of the bank, orderly rows of several varieties of fruit trees. From his grandparents' signing and the unconsciously muttered names accompanying the signs, Cody was able to associate the pictures and descriptions in their gardening books with the trees in the orchard. Apple trees were first with fruit ripening on the upper branches but mostly picked from the lower branches. There were numerous dead branches on the trees and much of the fruit had dropped off to rot on the ground. Cody climbed several trees to the accompaniment of warning admonitions from below but concern was forgotten when he began dropping ripe apples to his waiting grandparents. In minutes a basket was full. They left the full basket and walked in the shade between the rows of trees, breathing the cool air spiced with the odor of apples. His grandfather showed him several other apples that he indicated were of different varieties. Cody insisted on getting several prime examples of each from the treetops. Seth and Marta were torn between proud admiration of the boy's agility and worry that a dead branch might break beneath his weight. They continued on through pear, cherry, plum, peach, crab apple and quince trees but found only scattered quince and crabapples still on the branches. The boy bit into those fruits but found them quite tart for his taste. Past the fruit trees there were walnut, pecan and oak trees.

By now they had traversed the hillside to a point opposite the house. Here on a rock promontory they spread their picnic and paused for lunch. From this point they had a clear view of the canyon. The ranch house was just across the creek and below them. On the left was the road coming into the canyon. The corral and barn were beyond the house. To the right of the house, eastward along the creek, were the garden and chicken coop. Further east was the grain field. The creek below them cut north across the canyon floor to form the east boundary of the grain field and then turned east again to disappear into the gorge. The creek separated the 30-acre high pasture from the 130-acre low pasture, which comprised the remainder of the canyon floor. Beyond the pasture to the north the land sloped gently up to the mountains. The lower slope was grassland sparsely studded with trees. These grew more thickly further up the slope until they gradually coalesced into a forest.

The trio sat meditatively as they ate, each absorbing the view in his own way. For Seth it was the family homestead where he had been born and lived for 60 years. The mountain and creek were God's eternal beauty; the ranch was his family's temporary mark, which expressed their reverence for nature, their aspirations, their commitment to the land and the continuity of their family. The three of them in this slowly deteriorating homestead signified an end to these aspirations and perhaps to the family line. Seth slowly bowed his head as he compared the lusty vitality of the ranch his parents ran with the evident state of decay now. Marta gazed out and saw the dreams of her youth when she was a young bride coming from a desert town to this magnificent canyon. She made the gardens bloom, ran a happy home with her mother-in-law and anticipated a happy future with a growing family. Her first child, Adam, lived but seven weeks and then died quietly in his sleep. It was nine years before Marly was born, a difficult birth. There were no more. The next 15 years were wonderful as they built the ranch and watched their baby grow into a wonderful and beautiful young lady. The family was small but their love and togetherness fit the beauty and grandeur of their mountains.

Then Marly became restless; she yearned for change and the excitement she did not find in this ranch country.

She left to live in Reno, and then moved to California. Her visits to the ranch became those of a stranger paying a duty visit and anxious to be on her way. Her letters became infrequent and said little. When she arrived with her two year old Cody it was a complete surprise. They tried to keep her but ranch life was no longer for her. She and her poor delicate baby went suddenly one morning. So did her mother's hopes. Now Marta looked at her grandson and smiled through her tears. Perhaps they were here to stay and her dreams of family could be reborn. She reached out to touch his hair to reassure herself that he really was present. Cody had no memories to color his perception. He saw only the beauty of the canyon and its surrounding mountains, felt the lure of the distant forests and peaks, was intrigued by the mystery of the gorge and wanted to belong to all this and to his grandparents beside him. Beneath his joy he could sense an undercurrent of sadness from his two grandparents. He resolved to share with them the joy he felt at being here and being loved and accepted so whole-heartedly. He put his arm about his grandmother's waist, leaned his head on her shoulder and signed, 'I love you, grandma,' with an all-encompassing flourish of his arms. Tears coursed down her cheeks as she hugged him back. After a moment Seth touched them for attention and signed, 'Time to go. Let's take fruit back. Marta make pie tonight.'

Cody noted that their path back into the orchard was wide and well worn. He pointed down and signed, 'Road?' His grandfather nodded affirmatively and pointed across the creek to a similar overgrown track near the house leading to the opposite bank of the creek. 'Was road, bridge. Water knocked down.'

Cody replied with expansive arm waves, 'I make bridge again for Grandma Marta. Walking on rocks too hard.'

His grandfather smiled fondly. 'You are sweet grandson. Big pie for you tonight.'

While they walked back the rancher pointed out to the boy the need for pruning, ditch and pipe repairs, and a retention pond repair up at the gorge. He indicated the hopelessness of reclaiming the orchard. 'Too much damage. Too much work. Trees dying. No need for bridge.' He sighed at the dejection in his thoughts. The boy did not reply. With the infinite self-confidence of youth, he knew that he could find a way to please his grandmother with the restoration of her orchard.

Marta sorted her apples for immediate cooking and had the others placed in the pantry. She set Cody and Seth to work coring, paring and slicing while she made pie dough and prepared four pans. Working next to her in an identical apron and following her every direction meticulously, Cody rolled dough, tamped a layer in each greased pan, aligned the apple slices in careful patterns, sprinkled sugar on top, covered the heaping apples, and left his fingerprints in the crimped edges. When the pies were placed in the oven he stood there pressing his cheeks with his flour-covered fists and wearing a broad smile of achievement. Happier than she had been in years, Marta wiped his face with her apron and kissed his cheeks.

Seth brought out a photo album to keep his grandson occupied. Almost immediately the boy had found pictures of the bridge to the orchard. It was a wooden bridge anchored to the outcroppings on the creek banks and supported by two large boulders in the creek bed. Beyond the bridge the orchard was green and healthy. Other photos showed Marly in her early teens on a ladder that her mother was bracing in front of a fruit laden tree. They were displaying prizes that they had just picked. The boy pointed to the bridge. 'Build again.' His grandfather was now less pessimistic about the enormity of the task. His spirits had been buoyed by the excitement of the day, the love in the house, and perhaps the heady odor of the baking pies. 'Maybe,' he started signing slowly, then with more animation, 'Maybe we can build again!' He arose and walked to the window with his grandson, looking from the photos to the bridge site and orchard. A frown of self-reproach crossed his face as he noted the deterioration. He glanced down at the eager boy and felt a resurgence of his own excitement when he had helped his father and grandfather repair the bridge and expand the orchard. Without a family to build for these past dozen years he had unconsciously let things decay around him. Seth gripped Cody's shoulder momentarily, then signed forcefully, 'Together, we will build again!'

The smell of the apple pie grew stronger. Marta was there next to them, looking out the window and perhaps seeing the bridge and orchard as Seth saw them. 'For my men!' she signed, but when they reached for the pie tin she drew back and added, 'Later.' Supper was a meal devoted to signing about the orchard, a conversation that taxed Cody's sign language capabilities. By the time the still hot apple pie was served the project had assumed the status of reality in their minds. It was unifying them and linking them with past generations and with the land. More than ever, Cody felt that he belonged. The next afternoon the rancher showed the boy plans for the irrigation system, the orchard and the bridge. They then walked to the ford, crossed over the creek and followed the irrigation ditch east towards the gorge. The ditch had been well made and was constructed of rocks lined with cement. Now it was overgrown, cracked and collapsed in several places, and almost indiscernible where gullies had carved the hillside. The ditch originated part way up the gorge where ancient rock falls had blocked the waterway into a small reservoir. A natural opening in the barrier spouted a steady stream that ran back down into the channel below the natural dam. Next to the opening a broken sluice gate hung uselessly, unable to divert water into the irrigation channel. A myriad of small tasks pyramided into a Herculean restoration effort. And this was just the irrigation system.

They walked back reviewing the reconstruction work necessary on the ditch and finally arrived at a small retention pond, now dry, at the upper corner of the orchard. Beyond the pond the irrigation ditch continued across the slope above the orchard and oak trees. It terminated at the top of a granite block on the bank of the creek where it could form a waterfall visible from the house. They backtracked to the place where the bridge had spanned the creek from near the rear of the ranch house. Holes were visible in the rock where the bridge had been anchored. The two large boulders in the stream showed little evidence of the role they had played as supports. Across the creek bed about 24 feet away and 8 feet below them could be seen low piles that had held the other ends of the bridge beams. The old road had apparently continued behind the house. Seth showed Cody the picture of the bridge again, which showed how the bridge access was ramped up on land to reduce the otherwise steep incline across the stream. Marta's apron-clad figure appeared on the porch waving to them to return. Back they went through the orchard to the ford and were soon walking around the house to the front door.

Marta stood at the front steps, obviously distraught. Her hands were clasped before her, the fingers nervously intertwining. She had been crying and her eyes held a deep resigned sadness. The tension in her cheeks and tight-lipped mouth seemed all that kept her face from dissolving in tears again. Cody started to run up the steps to her but she halted him with a firmly outthrust hand. She then beckoned Seth into the house out of Cody's view. The boy sat on the steps wondering why he was barred from the only family he knew. He caught occasional muttered words from inside. Marly, sheriff, Shasta, canyon. His grandmother's tone and demeanor indicated that a calamity had befallen her daughter.

After a few minutes Seth opened the door and invited his grandson inside. The sadness that the old man carried inside him was now on the surface. His eyes were wet, his face sagged and his lips were held pursed. The couple stood before the boy, regarding him with deep sympathy. Scth spokc with sadncss quavcring thc unconscious vocalizations that accompanied his hand signs. 'Marly van broken. Fell in canyon. Marly not found. Maybe dead. We are sorry. Cody mother gone.'

They put their arms about him and he could feel the emptiness in their hearts. Their little girl had been lost to them for years but now the faint hope for her return was gone. Cody embraced them in return and sobbed for their loss and their emptiness. They thought it was the cry of an orphan bewailing his mother. For Cody, he was sharing their sorrow. Marly he hardly knew.

Seth felt that his grandson needed both company and a physical outlet for his grief. It was still the dry season and water was very low in the creek so he started with the boy on rebuilding the bridge to the orchard. There was an abundance of lumber stored in the barn for he had intended to rebuild the bridge after the washout. With Marly's departure he had lost the desire to reconstruct. Now he took joy in showing his cagcr grandson how to anchor thc footings, attach thc posts and bolt on the crossbeams. With such an apt and agile pupil the work progressed rapidly. In four days the first beam was slid into position across the gully. Cody nonchalantly walked across the beam from the house bank to the orchard side while his grandparents suppressed their anxiety. With the first beam securely bolted in place, the second was guided across in minutes. Braces were quickly emplaced to stabilize the framework and the young bridge builder walked proudly back to help his grandfather with the decking. The loss of Marly faded from her parents' consciousness as they busied themselves working with him and reveling in his contagious joy of learning and accomplishment. As they tried to console him, he became their solace.

What had seemed such a monumental task was accomplished in two weeks. Seth drove the tractor across the bridge. Cody and his grandmother rode behind in the trailer, backseat driving as he negotiated the bridge and cheering when he reached the other side. A quick run through the orchard brought several bushels of apples, crabapples and quince into the trailer for the trip home.

That night dinner consisted of baked apples, applesauce, and a pie filled with apples, crabapples, quince and cinnamon. The house was steamy with all the apples cooking. The celebration of accomplishment muted the sorrow of their recent loss. After completion of the bridge they turned attention to the water supply. The natural dam and waterspout in the gorge had been modified with a frame and movable spout cover on the inside face of the dam. This was operated by a wheel and worm gear to control the water flow and stop it if necessary. This unit was operating. A diverter on the outside face could be moved by another worm gear and wheel to intersect the stream and cause part of it to flow into the irrigation channel and on to the orchard. This mechanism had rusted and broken. The labor here was heavy and awkward to remove the old mechanism, ream the holes, replace the anchors and mount new supports. Seth marveled at his grandson's endurance for he found that it surpassed his own. He was weary and relieved when the new diverter gate sent its first stream into the irrigation ditch. His own father would have been proud of their job. He watched the stream dwindle as Cody reversed the mechanism, laughing as he changed the size and direction of the stream.

When Cody stood, Seth put his hand on the boy's shoulder, squeezed it hard and gave a thumbs-up sign of approval to the boy. Suddenly his point of view changed. He was no longer looking down at his grandson but up at his own father who was beaming with approval and giving the thumbs up signal to him. His face contorted with emotion as his mouth returned the smile and his eyes fought to hold back the tears from an old memory. Cody felt the flicker of emotion and saw the fleeting change in the face above him. He knew that it was Seth's father and saw behind it other faces marching like images in a double mirror into a limitless distance. Their approval was an invitation to come into the line. Seth was surprised and embarrassed by this unexpected emotional contact with the memory of his father. He patted Cody's shoulder and turned away toward the ditch.

The rancher showed the boy how to clean the ditch, replace and realign the stones, and spread a new cement lining. After the initial instruction, Seth had to return to neglected ranch chores. Cody concentrated on the irrigation system. Seth let him drive the tractor now and the boy put it to good use hauling stones, cement, dirt and tools. When working alone, Cody found that he could lift heavier loads and expend greater effort for longer periods without getting tired. He thought that he must be getting toughened by the labor. Day by day he progressed along the ditch with his cleaning, repairing and sealing. Several washed out places required major effort; some long stretches were in nearly pristine condition. In three weeks he was near the dam site with only minor repairs ahead.

Cody was down in the ditch spreading cement when a shadow fell across him. He looked up, startled, to see Seth observing his work. The rancher had an incredulous look on his face as his arm gestured from end to end of the ditch and he then signed, 'How? Job too big for two men. I'm proud of you.' His expression mirrored that pride.

The boy beamed back at his grandfather. 'Tomorrow we bring water to Grandma.'

'Stop now. Come home. Rest. Finish later.'

Cody shook his head adamantly. 'Water tomorrow. Finish ditch now.' Shaking his head with wonderment at the boy's energy and determination, the rancher joined him to complete the task. That evening they were late for dinner and obviously excited about something. Despite Marta's wheedling questions they would only reply,

'Tomorrow.'

The next morning after chores they set a comfortable chair on the south porch, put a pot of tea on the table and had the curious Marta sit there to await her surprise. They drove off on the tractor towards the gorge in high spirits, bubbling over with the excitement of their surprise. There were no hitches. The diverter gate worked, water flowed through the ditch as fast as they could drive. They crossed the bridge to the house, ran up on the porch, and sat breathlessly next to Marta. After a few moments of expectant tension, she signed, 'Well? What is it?' Cody had been watching the other bank expectantly. He sprang to his feet and jabbed his finger repeatedly towards the outcropping where the old waterfall had cascaded. 'There! There! There!' Marta's eyes followed his pointing finger. Her eyes widened with amazement and pleasure as she caught sight of the water glinting and sparkling in the morning sun as it splashed down the rock face to the creek bed.

"My waterfall!" she whispered to herself, "My waterfall!" Her own tears of happiness cascaded down her cheeks to match its flow. "In all my life with Seth I wanted only my child and my waterfall. Now Cody has brought them both back to me." She reached out her arms to her grandson who felt himself swept up by her emotions. He fell into her arms and wept on her shoulder, unable to grasp the conflicting torrents of emotion that his surprise had caused to surge through them both.

Seth sat there with tears of sympathy in his eyes although he could not feel the depth of their emotions. He knew the joy she had expressed as a young bride when she first saw the waterfall. He knew that in times of trouble she would sit and listen to it, finding solace in its tinkling confidences. Why had he not repaired the waterfall years ago as a comfort for her rather than steeping himself in the same well of pity? Perhaps his tears were as much contrition for his own lack of understanding her needs over the years, as they were gladness for her joy at the sight of the waterfall. The boy had brought a perceptive element back into their marriage that had faded after courtship and wedding. His heart reached out to Marta from forty years of inattentiveness and suddenly he could see the sparkling rainbow of the waterfall through her eyes and hear its tinkling music in her heart. She looked at him and he could tell that she knew he finally shared her feeling for the waterfall. She smiled tenderly at him and a kaleidoscope of emotions and sensations coursed through him. There would be much to share in the coming years through this new window between their souls.

Cody left them for a while and returned with a fresh pot of tea. They were sitting together holding hands, the pressure of their fingertips more eloquent than gesturing hands. They drank their tea in the aura of their love and Cody felt twice blessed by the waters flowing from the rock.

The days marched by and the weather grew colder. The garden had nearly ceased its productivity except for the late pumpkins and tubers in the ground. The barns, cribs and silo were full. The chill mornings required heavy jackets. The horses were skittish and spirited when saddled for a run. The skies were often cloudy and spitting cold rain. Morning frosts were frequent. Seth and Cody trimmed the deadwood from the orchard. Thanksgiving brought a full day of cooking, basting and feasting along with solemn words of thanks to God who made this fertile Earth and blessed them with its bounty. When they relaxed by the fire, hints were dropped about the coming Christmas when a Child was born to save the world with His love; and, how presents were exchanged to remember the Magi who brought gifts from the East to the humble stable where the Child was born. Cody was overwhelmed with joy when his grandfather told him, 'You are our own blessed child who brought your love into this family and have saved our little world. We are doubly blessed this Christmas.'

Christmas Eve arrived at last. Cody helped his grandparents set up a small spruce tree in the living room and decorate it with shiny balls, tiny figurines, candy canes, garlands and tinsel. On the top was a large star reflecting the firelight. They read to the boy from the Bible about the birth of the Christ Child. Cody's fluency in their sign language, his ability to read and their unconscious subvocal mutterings enabled him to comprehend the story and relate it to his own situation. The world needed repairing but people in the world did not recognize the need for their spirits were low and they were used to the decay in the world. A Child was sent to help repair things. His parents traveled through cold and storm looking for shelter. His arrival was unnoticed and unwelcomed by all but his parents. Only because of a bright star in the sky at his birth were the mystical Magi able to find him and bring him presents and honor. Cody remembered his own flashing bright star in the sky on his dawn at the ranch. He wondered if his star would bring wonderful people into his life.

At the end of the reading he signed to Seth and Marta, 'If the Child had a grandma and a grandpa like mine He wouldn't have to be born in a stable. You'd take Him in the way you did Marly and me.'

They smiled at each other over his interpretation of the Christmas story. The boy went to bed feeling too excited ever to sleep. He anticipated the morning, seeing the tree in daylight, hearing the story of the first Christmas again, and exchanging the presents they had hinted about. When Marta looked in on him a few minutes later he was fast asleep. She could see a smile on his face in the pale moonlight. This must be his first real Christmas, she thought. Perhaps she could share her only grandson's first Christmas after all. She and Seth then retrieved the presents from the closet in their room and arranged their surprise for the morning.

Cody awakened before dawn and lay there watching for the first light. He wondered if the guide star for the Magi was still up there waiting to herald other sacred births. He wondered if the tree was still standing with all its beautiful ornaments in place. He wondered if he should take his flashlight and go out to inspect everything. He dozed off again in the midst of his wonderings. Dawn at last outlined the mountains against the eastern sky. The rooster crowed to let them know that there were chores to be done even on Christmas Day. Cody arose quietly, pulled on his woolen robe against the chill, and walked quietly to the door. He eased it open to suppress the hinges' squeaking. Peeking out, he could vaguely discern the outline of the tree. He pulled the door wide and was startled by the sudden shutting of another door. When nothing else occurred he ventured out into the still dark living room. He raised his flashlight towards the tree and pressed the switch.

The room came ablaze with color emanating from the tree. The star on top shone a brilliant white. On each branch there were lights of different colors, some steady, some twinkling. The colors reflected from the facets of hanging ornaments twisting gently on their hangers and from the myriad crinkles of tinsel. There was no time to fix the image in his mind for it was changing continually like sunlight seen through the blowing mist of a waterfall. Cody's mouth opened in wonder, his eyes widened with delight and he pressed his cheeks hard with his fists to contain himself.

"Merry Christmas, Cody! Merry Christmas!" his grandparents shouted and signed in unison from their bedroom doorway. Seth's camera flashed to catch the tree and Cody in his wonderment. Marta came over to hug him and he hugged her in return, although the boy's eyes never left the tree. Seth came over after a moment to join the family hug. He put his arms about the other two and swung them about just as the camera flashed again on its timer to record this moment on film as well as in their hearts.

Before any presents could be opened, Marta brought in spiced hot cider and cookies. They sat before the fire while Seth read the Christmas story from the Bible again. Cody signed along with his grandfather and murmured all the words in a soft voice with his lips barely parting just as his grandfather did. At the conclusion Marta went to the tree.

'Enough!' she signed to her husband. 'Cody must want to see his presents.' She picked up a gaily-wrapped box and handed it to her grandson. To his grandparents' amusement, the boy carefully opened the package so as not to damage the wrapping paper. 'Just like me when I was a little girl,' laughed Marta. 'Just like her now!' was her husbands amused comment. 'But not like Marly. She would tear it open and throw the wrapper in the air.' His gay remark stopped short and he frowned somberly as he recalled the happy holidays with his little girl.

Cody meticulously folded the paper before opening the box. His eyes lit up when he saw the boots inside. His own hand-tooled boots! Now he would look like grandpa when he rode Can-Can. Another box brought him a fringed leather jacket. Then came narrow-legged riding pants and a broad-brimmed low-crowned hat. He donned all his clothes and strutted in front of his admiring grandparents. He stopped suddenly as thoughts of them filtered through his excitement.

'Grandma! Grandpa! Presents for you?' They had forgotten their own presents while they shared Cody's thrills. Marta brought two more gifts from the tree, one for herself and one for her husband. She opened her wrappings and withdrew fold after fold of an iridescent knitted material. It was basically a deep purple in color with interwoven strands of red, green and gold. There was no repetitive pattern but the eye kept trying to discern mystical shapes that formed in the background weave and dissolved into other near-tangible forms with each ripple of the cloth. She drew it lovingly over her shoulders and let the ends hang by her sides. As she turned before them she became a mystical figure of the imagination and seemed to recapture for her husband both the mystery and allure of their courtship.

Seth stood with her, signed, 'May we dance?' and held out his arms to her. Marta smiled tremulously, stepped up to him, and they circled the floor gracefully as he hummed a waltz. Cody saw a new side of his grandparents' relationship, the love and understanding and empathy that had bound their lives together. He wondered if he would grow older and find such a partner. Seth received a red plaid Pendleton jacket and wool lined leather driving gloves. A bottle of White Shoulders perfume rekindled memories of youthful days in Marta. A sheath knife and two books were added to Cody's gifts. All the presents under the tree had been opened. Still arrayed in their treasures, the three gathered the papers and boxes into a pile so that Seth could take a final picture.

The rancher then went out to his morning chores. Marta busied herself making breakfast. Cody dressed quickly and disappeared outside. An hour later breakfast was on the table. The aroma of biscuits, sausage, omelet and steaming coffee was in the air. Seth had washed and was ready to eat. Marta was looking out the window for her grandson. She finally went out on the porch into the cold morning with her new shawl about her shoulders. Cody rounded the corner of the porch as she came out.

'Cody! Wash. Breakfast is ready. Grandpa's waiting. Hurry!' The boy looked mysteriously self-satisfied as he nodded his head in assent and ran inside. Breakfast was quiet. Cody ate quickly and looked expectantly at his grandparents' plates, obviously hoping to see them empty. He jumped to clear the table when the last bite disappeared.

'Coffee on porch,' he signed. 'Come. Warm in sun.' Suspecting that he had a surprise in mind, they feigned reluctance to go outside into the chilly air. Cody put all three cups on a tray and signed them again.

'Come. Porch nice. Sun is warm. Enjoy view.' He opened the door and ushered them out, then walked quickly ahead and around the corner with the tray. When Seth and Marta turned the corner they stopped short in amazement. The space between the house and the creek was transfigured. Cody had accumulated a pile of rocks next to the bridge ostensibly for his irrigation ditch repairs. Sorting these rocks and masking them with lumber and tarpaulins had concealed his real purpose. A small waterfall flowed from a stone well down its vertical stone face into a semicircular pool. A curved wooden bench graced the near side of the pool wall. A notch in the front of the pool wall allowed water to flow out into a stone-lined trough and then noisily down these miniature rapids into the drainage system of the yard. This drab ditch had been transformed into a burbling rivulet that carried the flow down to the riverbank and over the edge in a twenty-foot waterfall. A breeze in the creek channel wafted the small cascade into a drifting mist. Across the creek the orchard waterfall contributed its own spume to the drifting droplets. Sunlight shining through the mist produced a rainbow that crowned the beauty of the fountain and turned the garden into a fairyland.

Cody had placed the tray on the corner table and was watching their reactions, waiting expectantly for approval. He received more than he expected. His grandmother's face lit up in surprise and incredulity. Cody felt a wave of joy emanate from her and sweep through him so that he seemed to float above the decking and see a golden glow over the landscape. Marta rushed over to him, placed her hands on either side of his face, and looked at him with an expression of wonderment and love. She kissed him gently, leaving a lingering glow on the spot she kissed. Her surge of joy coursed through his nervous system and he felt it become a permanent part of his own being, a part of her that was now a part of him. She stepped back, keeping a hand on his shoulder as her gaze returned to her dazzling present.

'Oh, Cody!' she signed rapidly, 'you have given me my fondest dreams: first the waterfall, now a fountain, a meandering brook and a wondrous rainbow. It's my water wonderland. What can I give you in return?'

Her grandson allowed himself the vicarious pleasure of enjoying the fountain through her senses and perspective, feeling the rebirth of fairy tale daydreams of the young child, the new bride, and the young mother resurrected from sealed crypts of her memory. Although he had searched, he found no such vaults of remembrance in his own mind. He seemed to have been born of the storm that tumultuous night in Marly's van. For now he thrilled vicariously to Marta's realization of her girlhood dreams. Her tears of joy were reflected in his eyes. The blank pages of his memory were faintly traced from hers. He could see her childhood playhouse by a meandering stream; feel her gasp of wonder when Seth had first brought her into this canyon paradise; shared her playtime fantasies with Marly in the garden; and, felt the dreams fade into a dull grey despair when Marly drifted into her drug scene, the garden wilted, and the lilting voice of the creek turned into the keening of an anguished soul for its vanished dreams. Now a new memory was forming to take its place. It was a rebirth of dreams in rainbow colors, a new vision that returned meaning to a life that had degenerated into routine repetition of days that lead only to the oblivion of the grave. He was her spark of life today; their shared memories were her life hereafter. Though a part of her had died with Marly, yet she would live on through Cody. The boy felt the joy of giving life through love but he sensed also the long-term responsibility of keeping that love alive. He hugged her tightly as acceptance of that responsibility. Over her shoulder he saw Seth viewing the radiance of his wife's rebirth.

Seth felt an overwhelming happiness that the rainbow glow had returned to her life. Yet, lurking far in the background was a faint jealousy that the boy had instantaneously cured the atrophy of her dreams while he had buried acknowledgement of Marta's pain in the routine of chores on the ranch. He had failed to bring violets for her soul. The tears in Seth's eyes were not unalloyed joy but had traces of the acid bitterness that admitted his own blindness and futility while resenting the boy for bringing them so starkly to his attention.

New Year's Day started like all other ranch days with morning chores for the animals first on the list. Coffee time at ten o'clock was a pleasant surprise with a large wedge of strawberry pie covered with whipped cream. Marta announced that seconds were available and that work was over for the day. It was New Year's Day; a day to reflect on the events of the past year and to promise one's self to improve one's life in the coming year. The warm sun beckoned them out on the porch on the creek side where they were sheltered from the fitful breeze. They drank their coffee quietly and ate seconds of pie, which Cody happily fetched. Tripod lay in the sun licking whipped cream from her whiskers. The stream and waterfalls provided a random lilt that allowed the boy's thoughts to drift freely over his short span of memories. The waterfalls misted and sparkled in the vagrant breeze, creating a magic veil for memories he felt must be hidden there in recesses of his mind. Marta sat with hands in her aproned lap, a small woman who sat straight of back and held her chin high. Her lips were pursed, the skin held firm over her fine boned face despite the network of faint lines etched by weather and sorrow. Her eyes were seeing her thoughts in the flickering illumination of the reflections from fountain and waterfalls. Her ears were hearing their lilting melodies in memory. Cody's attention was caught by the faint whisper of her voice and flutter of her hands as she mused over her sorrows of the past and her hopes for the future.

"Marly's gone. Child of light, woman of despair. Broke our hearts, shadowed our lives. Her troubles ended. Her debt paid. Rest in peace, Marly. Rest in peace." She looked up and her eyes rested lovingly on her grandson.

'Marly atoned with a gift of love, her son. Sorrows fade, future bright. Cody is child of hope. We live again through him.' Seth was watching her, nodding in agreement with her musings.

He signed, 'Amen.'

Cody could remember only the chaos of the rainstorm at the lake and his acceptance into the loving family life here on the ranch. His resolve was simple. He wanted to love and be loved. He wanted to do things that would make them happy. He wanted to be here on the ranch and to be a part of it always.

A car made its dusty approach along their road and pulled to a stop at the steps. "Sheriff" was printed in large letters on the side. A bar of lights was fastened to the roof.

A tall man, thin and sinewy, alighted and called out, "Howdy, Seth."

The rancher called back, "Howdy, Arnie," and walked down the steps with hand outstretched, "Happy New Year!"

"Happy New Year, Seth!" the sheriff answered over-loudly and pumped Seth's hand. "Happy New Year, Marta!" he added, waving his free hand at her. His eyes took in the boy next to her. "Happy New Year, son!"

Marta returned his greeting with a wave. Cody tentatively emulated her brief hand motion. "Come in for coffee and pie, Arnie. Marta baked strawberry pie with lots of whipped cream, your favorite."

His curiosity about the boy as well as his appetite for strawberry pie brought the sheriff quickly up the porch steps with Seth. Sheriff Arnie Hopper took a chair next to Seth at the porch table while Cody remained in the corner staring at the big, loud visitor. The sheriff smiled encouragingly at the boy but directed his conversation to the rancher.

"Marly's boy?" he wrote on his pad. "Yep," boomed Seth, "name's Cody."

The pen scribbled on the pad, 'He okay?' while the sheriff stared speculatively at the transfixed youth. "Deaf and dumb," replied Seth.

"Any trouble?"

"None. Cody's healthy, strong as a horse, hell of a worker."

The sheriff noted in his book, 'handicapped,' after the name Cody Hoag

'Father?' was the next written query.

"Never mentioned one," came the reply.

'Plan to keep him?'

"He's all we've got left of Marly." After a brief pause, the rancher asked in a halting voice, "Marly. Did they ever find her?"

The sheriff answered, "No sign of her. Rugged country. No search team. I'll let you know." He put a hand on Seth's arm. "Meanwhile, she's missing. You take care of the boy until we hear." The sheriff closed his notebook and put it away. The rancher fell silent thinking of his daughter. Lost in spirit, now lost in body. An ill-fated end to life for such a beautiful child. He looked at Cody and wondered if those same ill-directed genes were harbored in her son.

Marta arrived with the strawberry pie. That put an end to the conversation. Arnie stood at last, rubbed his stomach to indicate satisfaction and with emphasized lip movement said, "Thanks, Marta. Great pie." Shaking hands all around, he went to his car and drove off. His farewell waves could be seen as the car rounded the bend in the road and disappeared from view.

Far Walker has a Vision

Far Walker strode uphill across the slope in a long easy gait reminiscent of the tireless lope of a wolf ranging his territory. He was tall, lean and supple, accommodating himself to the uneven upward climb so that he seemed to glide across the surface of the terrain. He followed no apparent trail. He left no new made trail behind him. His buckskin clothing blended with the dun colored hills. Braided hair descended to his shoulder blades. A decorated headband held his black hair from his face. His skin was dark and smooth, not revealing his years. A sense of mission and pleasure in his surroundings combined in his expression. The exertion of his uphill climb was not evident in his face or bearing. When he passed behind a tree the landscape was left undisturbed as if no one had been there. He might have been an apparition from days when Paiutes roamed these lands as their own tribal territory. He emerged from the small clump of trees, now with his path angling back across the slope. A sharp-eyed search of his back trail, which lay entirely across a grassy incline, revealed no one following. It was mere habit, instilled by his grandfather.

In earlier years there had been great interest in the location of the rumored holy place that had been sacred to the shamans of his tribe. Many of the curious from his tribe and others had tried to track them on their annual pilgrimage to seek counsel and guidance of the grandfathers through visions sometimes granted there. But interest had waned with the demoralization of the native peoples and discrediting of the old ways. Now he alone knew of the sacred place. He alone saw the visions, sometimes clear and sometimes unfathomable, that recalled the distant past of rich lands and a proud people; the recent past of a subjugated and disintegrating people; and, the near future with conflicting images of peril and opportunity that might mean disintegration of his people or a resurgence of ancient principles. He must know whether he was pursuing a lost dream by keeping the faith alive during this century of denigration of his people. He needed reassurance in the face of years of rebuff from the wasichu world and even from the younger members of his own tribe.

He continued up the slope through the trees, now and then glimpsing the twin peaks that were his guides. The mere act of being on the journey raised his spirits. He took three days to travel a deceiving and circuitous trail through the Virginia Mountains from his home near Sutcliffe on the Pyramid Lake to his sacred place of the morning sun. The lonely journey, wary searching of his back trail, the dogged pace through rough country that discouraged would-be trackers – all these factors brought him back to his youth and the excitement of a mystical journey to commune with his forebears of myth and legend. As he traveled he shook off the cynical weariness of reservation life and regained the youthful wonder he had felt with his grandfather. For him it was a journey into an exhilarating past of a wondrous people, powerful spirits and stirring visions. His pace quickened as he neared the end of his journey.

The unmarked trail led through a maze of diverging gorges. Tumbled rocks and sand swept clean by wind and rain left no signs of passage. He picked his way carefully but quickly, following without thinking the few landmarks engraved in his memory. He exited at last from the rough country and crossed a scree slope to an undistinguished cleft in a bluff face. The cleft seemed shallow but each time an apparent terminus was reached a sharp turn occurred and the path led deeper into the bluff and always upward. The trail gradually widened and then fanned out into a shallow bowl at the top of the bluff. The afternoon shadows were growing longer and the early fall air was chilling as he walked through the first sparse pine trees at this elevation. His careful steps left no discernible trail through the rocky meadowland. A depression in the meadow followed a short climb over a gentle rise. There before him was a vertical sided circular box canyon about one hundred feet in diameter and eighty feet deep. His narrow trail led downward approximately one quarter of the way around the wall. At the bottom the trail terminated on a flat rock twenty feet above the canyon floor. A small spring-fed pool of water fed a stream cascading around both sides of a rock spire at the far end of the pool and across the canyon floor to a narrow fissure in the far wall. This was the sacred place where his family had been accorded visions for many generations.

Far Walker put down his roll, sat cross-legged on the ground with both hands extended to his knees, and prayed silently for guidance. After several minutes he arose and went several feet back up the trail. Despite the deepening gloom he reached confidently to the wall above the trail and removed a stone from the mouth of a small opening, placing the stone on a ledge beside the opening. He returned to his seated position, wrapped his blanket around him and began to chant in a low voice, invoking the help of his ancestors and the spirits to grant him a vision that could help his people. He asked also for the wisdom to understand and communicate it. Intermittently through the night he chanted, prayed silently and quietly contemplated the unity and continuity of all Nature. Darkness descended, the world faded away, and Far Walker continued his vigil, purifying his spirit of worldly intrusions and seeking only his place in the Hoop of Life.

The shaman was no longer alone. He heard low snorting and snuffling sounds that he recognized as those of a bear. He knew that his best course was to remain still and not provoke the curiosity or hostility of the animal. A nose pressed into his shoulder tipped him on his side. A strong paw tentatively rolled him over while the nose snuffled around his body. He was rolled over again. Far Walker did nothing. He suppressed all reactions of fear, apprehension and incipient panic to lie quietly. He resigned himself to Nature's way. The bear backed off and sniffed the air. The shaman felt calm and peace suffuse his being. The bear padded away. A strong acrid odor overpowered that of the bear. It was not that of a lion, not of a grazing animal but a scent that touched a chord in his memory. He knew that it had been here, in the company of his grandfather that he had smelled this scent before. It was not fearsome. It was Sasquatch.

The shaman sat up again and remained quiet. Despite the stygian darkness he sensed that a large being had squatted before him and was silently regarding him. No words were spoken but a scene formed in the shaman's mind. It was this site. A vigorous middle-aged man and a young boy sat cross-legged side by side. He recognized his grandfather clad in the old shaman's regalia of woven grass and rabbit fur. The boy he recognized as himself. Tears started in his eyes as he remembered coming here with his grandfather for the first time. The Great War of the wasichus was engulfing the world and his father had gone overseas. The next morning they saw in a vision his father with the Grandfathers, the wounds of battle still fresh on his body but a supportive look on his face.

"Learn from your grandfather, my son. You must preserve our ways and our values. You will have a part to play in the emergence of our people from the shadows and the disappearance of the wasichus." The tears streamed down. Slowly the scene evolved. The boy grew into a man. His grandfather aged. And then Far Walker was alone, carrying on the tradition of his family. And all the while he was here now. A sense of approval from the being opposite enveloped him. They sat wrapped in their own thoughts, companionable but separate. Their longing for the old ways, sorrow for the current ways, and hope for future appreciation of the unity of Nature intermingled at times so that Far Walker felt himself striding with giant steps across limitless wilderness or gazing sorrowfully at naked mountainsides, clear-cut of trees.

And then he was alone. Or had he been alone all the time? Was his visitor merely a figment of his imagination, an ally he conjured up to renew his faith? Far Walker returned to his chants, prayer and meditation to prepare himself for the morning ritual of dance and invocation. It was the second of October, the fifth anniversary of Cody's arrival on the ranch. Six times now a bright light from the gorge had awakened him at dawn on this date. This time he wanted to be at the source when it happened. What was the significance of the light?

He dressed quickly and quietly left the house. The dogs watched passively as he strode to the barn. They had no duties at this hour. He did not call them. Can-Can came to the fence at his whistle, nuzzling him for sugar, dodging the saddle but once. She trotted across the pasture in the pale moonlight, carrying him swiftly to the mouth of the gorge. The sky was faintly gray when they arrived. Cody dropped Can-Can's reins and went into the gorge on foot. He trod carefully on the large rocks in the creek bed, hurrying to beat the dawn but watchful of the uncertain footing. He climbed over the small dam and hugged the wall of the gorge above the pond. The brightening sky illuminated his path so that he could move more quickly. He exited the top of the gorge onto a rock shelf at the base of the canyon wall, which gave him a complete view of the box canyon beyond. The canyon was small and circular with walls of vertical rock. The streambed crossed the center of the canyon to a spire of rock rising twenty feet from the canyon floor. Beyond the spire the rock was flat with a small spring-fed pool of water located at the near end. The water overflowed the pool and coursed down both sides of the spire into the streambed. Beyond the pool was a clear area in which sat a Native American in traditional clothing that included several necklaces of miscellaneous objects and feathers. The canyon was dark with the morning shadows except for the man himself. He sat in a small circle of light formed from multiple reflections of the morning sun – first from a spot high on the near wall of the canyon, secondarily from a spot about ten feet up the wall behind the man, and then apparently from some point on the other side of the rock spire. The man's hair was long and black, held in place by a decorated headband. He was chanting in a voice that rose and fell in volume and tone, chanting words that trembled in Cody's memory on the verge of recognition. The boy stood quietly attentive, letting the strange sounds flow through him in hopes that they would activate the chords of memory.

The man opened his eyes. When they focused on Cody the chanting ceased. The man called to Cody in that tantalizing tongue. The boy remained immobile, straining to catch the sense of the speech. The vocal query changed while Cody continued to concentrate on the sound bites. It took him a few minutes to reassemble the last syllables into the question in English. "Who are you, Grandfather?"

The shaman rose to his feet and began dancing to the rhythm of his own chanting. The words and movements spoke to Cody but again just beyond the pale of recognition. He was drawn to the platform and there joined the shaman in the ritual that his conscious mind had forgotten but his body now remembered. Through his inner vision coursed a tale of Creation, formation of the worlds, the advent of animals and man. Then the Paiutes came to a pristine world and joined in the natural order of things, respecting all Nature and being part of the Hoop of Life. This idyll ended with the coming of the wasichu, in whose greed laid the destruction of all tribes. A constricted world of darkness and despair became their lot. Their spirits were low. But ahead was a promise of rejuvenation. The wasichu world was beginning to accept the unity of Nature and to respect the traditions of the people. The young people were being reborn in their heritage.

The shaman sat cross-legged again and continued his chant of a hope that the people would regain their world. Understanding of the vision was coming to him. The wasichu would leave these lands as the Ghost Dancers had prophesied but not by force of arms or a mass exodus. Rather, their spirits would change. They would cease to despoil the lands and degrade the people. They would accept the native peoples' concept of the indivisibility of all life and its environment. The wasichu as such would disappear and be reborn in spirit to the ways of the people. The Hoop of Life would be restored and the Earth would return to fruitful. The chanting ceased and silence descended. Far Walker could hear himself breathing – alone. His eyes opened to the empty sunlit sacred place. His visitor was gone without a trace. There were no footprints on the rocks, no belongings left behind. No spoken message uttered.

Was there indeed a human visitor? Had the Grandfathers sent him a vision? If so, what did it mean? Was the message in the medium itself, the participation of a stranger in the rituals and memories of the native people? Were the people at last to be honored in their own land? Far Walker pondered these thoughts as he gathered his things. He replaced the cover stone over the crystal solar reflector mounted in the rock wall behind his prayer platform. The shaman climbed the path curving along the face of the canyon wall and walked slowly over the mountains deep in thought. A strange and wonderful thing had happened to him. The significance of this event might transcend his own powers of interpretation. He would bring this tale to the next Paiute powwow and consult with the other shamans. The sense of excitement and anticipation grew in him as he retraced his circuitous route to Pyramid Lake.

∞

After the third council meeting that he saw as a fruitless picking over long barren bones, Far Walker sat alone at a corner table in the coffee room, pondering the details of his preparation for revealing his vision to the tribe.

"You are very distracted, Far Walker. You have not made a single recommendation to the council. The spark and fire are missing – from you as well as from the council."

The familiar voice of Quiet Fox penetrated his abstraction. He raised his head and responded, "I cannot abide these petty problems while our world crumbles." She raised her eyebrows with an expression encouraging him to elaborate. "We are treating myriad symptoms instead of fundamental problems." He regarded her speculatively and then came to a decision. "I need your help, Quiet Fox. I was granted a vision in my sacred place last October. It has changed my outlook. I must bring this vision to the council, the tribe, the nation and the world. You must help me prepare for this revelation."

Quiet Fox felt the intensity of his conviction. Perhaps a vision of special interest had been granted to him. "I will help you," she replied, "But first you must reveal this vision to me privately. You know my niece's house near the junction of 445 and 446. Come for supper tonight. Arrah is going to the movies so we can talk privately there."

Far Walker nodded his assent. "I'll be there at six o'clock."

That evening at Arrah Bond's house, supper was unusually silent. Arrah Bond was used to lively arguments with Far Walker about his proposals on all the problems of school and social services that were her responsibility in the county office. This night he ignored her questions or brushed them off with a brusque, "Symptoms! Symptoms!"

Quiet Fox sat patiently waiting, studying the shaman and speculating about powerful visions in modern times. Was it a mid-life crisis of identity for the shaman? Were visions relevant to the modern world of the wasichu? Had the spirit world retreated to just vague memories of the elders? Her niece at last cleared the table, grateful that movie time had arrived. "See you later, folks. Show time."

Far Walker began without preamble, merely telling her that he had made his annual pilgrimage to his sacred place on October first. As he prayed and meditated that night a bear toyed with him. He stayed quiet and motionless hoping that the bear would leave after a casual inspection. Suddenly a feeling of peace came over him. The bear left. Although it was dark he knew that a huge strong-smelling creature squatted next to him. They shared dreams of previous times he had been there as a boy with his grandfather, even a vision of his father's death.

"It was Sasquatch, I know," declared the shaman. Quiet Fox nodded her acceptance of this view. He told her how the morning sunbeam from the crystals awakened him for the ritual. He opened his eyes to see a young man clad in fringed buckskin staring at him across the canyon. He could not sense a presence.

"Sometimes you are like that," he told her, "Seen but not felt." At this statement her attention focused. "Tell me about this young man. What did he look like? What did he say?"

Her interest sharpened his recall. "The boy was not tall, about five feet seven, and weighed about 160 pounds. Tanned skin. No beard, short nose." Staring at the image in his mind, he continued, "His eyes were wide apart and deep set. His hair was dark, home cut above the ears and square trimmed in back."

"What did he say?"

"Nothing. I spoke to him in our Shoshone, in English and in sign language. He never responded."

"What did he do?"

"He danced."

"Danced?"

"Yes. I thought he was a spirit vision so I continued with my ritual – chants and dances. He was suddenly there with me, following all the dance steps and joining the chants. We shared a vision that said the wasichus would vanish as Wovoka told us but they would not be driven out of the land. They would accept our vision of the Hoop of Life and unite with us in reverence for all Nature. That is the message I must bear to the world."

"Then suddenly he was gone, leaving no trace."

"He was not real, then?"

"I do not know. He sang and I heard him. His feet made noise. He breathed heavily from exertion. I smelled his sweat. He could be real."

The old woman became silent and reflective. At last she spoke. "This is a very important happening. It may be a true vision revealing your mission in life and explaining Wovoka's vision of the eventual disappearance of the Wasichu.

"Or," she continued, "You may have met a very Sacred Person whom I saw briefly five years ago. Others, very powerful people who can steal your inmost secrets, were tracking him. If he is the one you saw then your knowledge is dangerous to him. Until you can learn the Wovokian technique of absolute silence you cannot stay near him. You must go to visit our brothers the Oglala in South Dakota and stay hidden while you study."

There was protest in Far Walker's eyes and trembling on his lips. He preferred to bear the message himself.

"I cannot go!" he demurred. "I thought you would help me understand and present the vision. Instead you want to send me off until I lose the vision or die. I will not go."

"Turn around," she directed him sharply. "When you think that I have left the room raise your hand." Starting to refuse, he shrugged and complied. The set of his shoulders indicated that his refusal to leave still held.

Quiet Fox relaxed, quieted herself and withdrew to her inner self. In less than a minute Far Walker raised his hand and swiveled around. He was amazed to see her sitting in the same place.

"That's it!" he exclaimed. "I can sense if people are near. I didn't feel the boy. Now I don't feel you. How do you do it?"

"It is a technique taught to me by Wovoka to hide information from questioners. The boy I seek learned this method from me at Lake Sabrina to hide from his pursuers. He was not caught. He did not die. He just disappeared from in front of his pursuers. I do not know if your strange vision is this boy or not but we cannot risk his safety. If he was sufficiently desperate and used the Wovokian technique he may even be hiding from himself. You must go for now until we can be sure of his identity."

After her display of deep silence, Far Walker was ready to heed her counsel. "Perhaps my head is too high in the clouds for me to accept that I may not be the savior I hoped to be. But perhaps being a disciple is my fated role. First I will give you directions to my Sacred Place. Then I will go."

They went to the niece's study, which contained a detailed wall map of the area. Far Walker located the canyon on the map and gave her specific directions to reach it on foot from Pyramid Lake. He also told her about his ritual with the crystals, his prayers and chants, and his dance. Quiet Fox committed it all to memory. She questioned him about people living in that vicinity and was told about the Hoag ranch among others.

After Far Walker left she remained deep in thought laying out plans to visit the boy surreptitiously. She had saved him once when she had been probably the only person in the world who could have done so. Her intuition had been that their lives would be further intertwined. That intuition appeared about to be realized. She must prepare carefully so as not to endanger him. A key grated, the door opened, and her niece entered saying, "Hi, Auntie. Did you and Far Walker have a good talk?"

"Yes. Now you and I must talk."

"No way. I'm not getting involved in any of that shaman's schemes to resurrect the old ways in training our kids. Remember, I'm with the agency. We do things by proven methods to meet national scholastic standards. Going back to the blanket won't help anyone. It won't help my career, either."

The old woman tolerated her niece's flippant response and then commented drily, "Your 'proven methods' haven't done much for the country's public schools. But that is not my immediate concern. I need your help."

Arrah became serious. "Sorry, Auntie. I attend too many council meetings where they propose old remedies for new problems. I can't take those threadbare blankets to my boss. But anyway, how can I help you now?"

Her aunt's bright eyes caught hers and peered deep within them, searching for something she may have glimpsed there long ago.

"You can't help now."

"Then why are you staring through me with your shaman eyes?"

"I'm looking for a little girl, a little girl who used to play hide and seek with me. You can't help but she might."

"Hide and seek?" echoed her niece, looking backward through time to days when she lived with her aunt. They played many games. Quiet Fox could always find her in hide and seek no matter how well hidden she might be. One day, in response to her petulance at being found quickly, her aunt told her that to really hide she must be absolutely quiet – and then the old woman held her hand to guide her to the silence of Wovoka. A few days later Arrah hid in her most secret place under the barn and made herself very quiet. It worked – and kept on working. Her aunt could not find her. Neither could her parents when they arrived. The game became tiresome and she decided at last to come out. She couldn't. She had wedged herself among the rocks and timbers and couldn't move. She called out. No one heard. She screamed until she became hoarse to no avail. Darkness came. She fell silent, resigned. An idea came to her. If she could make herself quiet, maybe she could make herself loud. Expanding herself outwardly as she had previously withdrawn into her inner self, Arrah projected with all her strength. In a few moments she heard crashing noises above her and shortly light streamed down through a hole in the barn floor. She was gathered up and hugged and scolded and told never to hide like that again. She didn't. Returning from her flashback, Arrah said in a surprised tone, "You want me to be quiet again, don't you? Why?"

"I cannot tell you," her aunt replied gravely, "Until you have learned to be absolutely quiet."

"Not even a hint?"

Quiet Fox extended her hand to her niece. "Take my hand. We must overcome your fear of being helplessly lost before you can be truly silent within yourself."

Cody found himself without volition as he joined the shaman in his dance and shared his vision of the Hoop of Life and the changing fortunes of the native peoples. He felt the shaman's quest for guidance and the hope for rebirth of the peoples and disappearance of the despoiling wasichus. Cody knew he was not dreaming. It was the shaman's vision and ritual upon which he was intruding, drawn to it by many hints of near memory that eluded his attempts to recall. When the shaman finished the dance the spell was broken. Cody went back to his original vantage point, took a last look back at the seated shaman and left.

Can-Can was grazing. She raised her head and came when he emerged into the meadow. He walked her back home while he wondered about the meaning of the strange encounter. The flash of light that had first caught his attention three years before was reflected light from the dawning sun. The Native American's ritual made use of this reflected light on his prayer area by the spring. That it also awakened Cody appeared coincidental. He knew that he was not expected, that he was an intruder there. Why he joined the dance and even knew the dance steps was a mystery to him but it must be part of his forgotten past before he arrived at the ranch. The vision touched on some aspect of Native American myths and history that he had found in his grandfather's books. He must reread them. He was still puzzling over it when he reached the ranch house.

Grandma Marta, startled, paused in the act of pouring coffee at the table when Cody entered. 'You surprised me!' she signed with a laugh. 'I thought you asleep. Sit down and take your coffee.' Seth was already at the end of the table.

'Where have you been, son?'

Cody started to formulate a reply about his strange experience but found that he could not translate his thoughts into words or signs. The boy took a sip of his coffee to cover the pause and then said what he could. 'Woke early. Saw light flash from the gorge. Rode Can-Can to check it out.' Cody could not relate what he had seen, therefore he ended with a question, 'What's beyond the gorge?'

Marta interjected, 'Marly mentioned the light once when in her teens.'

'A flashing light? From gorge? I never saw it,' replied Seth to Cody. 'Other side of gorge is small box canyon. I never go there.'

'Why not?'

'Family tradition. My grandfather knew it was a sacred place to Paiute shaman. He agreed long ago to preserve it for them. I honor his word.'

'What do they do there, grandfather?'

'I don't know. Just small ceremonies. Saw a shaman once about this time of year. Never any trouble.' He went to the fireplace where he pointed to a decorated leather belt above the mantel to the right. 'This belt records the compact.' Cody nodded without comment. Perhaps his inability to relate his experience in the box canyon was due to the sacred nature of the site. He must learn more about it and how it related to him.

The heavy work of fall chores took up all their time during October and November as they stored hay and straw, canned and stored the rest of their produce from the garden and the orchard, and brought in necessary supplies from town. All the buildings were tightened and winter ized. Roof shingles were checked and repaired. Drains and ditches were cleared for runoff. Road markers were put along the road in the event that deep snowdrifts should form. Farm equipment was stored under the second barn that had been built against a hillside. The first snows came to soften the contours of the landscape, mute all sound, and ornament the trees with snow puffs and crystalline icicles. The snow brought all activities closer to the ranch house. Feeding the chickens was a remaining outdoors chore. Even the matriarchal Dark Eyes became more of a housedog and sought the fireside to doze. Tripod often sat inside on a window ledge to survey her domain, limiting her inspection trips of the barns to the warmest part of the day.

Without the rush of the fall chores there was now time to renew all the harness in the tack room, repair the building interiors, and get all the farm equipment in top shape for the spring. There was also time for Seth to reminisce about his forebears, the ranch, and the local tribes. Cody learned that the Paiute shamans who came to the Sacred Place above the gorge were from the Pyramid Lake reservation on the eastern side of the Virginia Mountains, about twenty-five straight-line miles away. They crossed the road-less mountains on foot to reach the box canyon. All this land had been their territory at one time but government troops and encroaching settlers constrained them to the reservation. Subjugation had left them in limbo with remnants of a culture no longer relevant to present conditions and with little acceptance by the dominant European culture. Seth doubted that the box canyon would continue as a sacred place beyond the current generation. Seth wondered if his ranch would continue beyond his own time.

Evenings at home were spent playing games, particularly cribbage, dominoes and checkers; reading; and, working at hobbies – Marta at decorative stitchery, Seth at woodcarving, and Cody at learning about the world from their small library of older classics. Neither Seth nor Marta cared about television and did not have one. Their current news came from the weekly paper. Cody's adolescence was much that of a rural past.

Winter loosened its grip, the snows melted away and filled the creek, and the wet grasslands quickly greened. The animals wandered further in the pasture now, sprinting about from the sheer exuberance of escaping winter's confinement near the barns. The softening breeze, the fresh odor of grasses and trees, the sights and sounds of animated small creatures similarly exuberant all contributed to the resurgence of vitality among the ranch residents. Tripod resumed her three-legged morning rounds of the barns; the three dogs joyfully rounded up the animals that playfully tried to elude them; the horses played hard to saddle and then raced towards the hills as soon as they were mounted. Adventure was in everyone's heart. Chores were soon forgotten.

Seth and Cody rode through the mountains together, often with Mischief and Stalker tagging along. The dogs darted about and scared up all sorts of small game and birds, which they chased enthusiastically all morning. By mid-day the small animals and birds received only mildly interested glances and several half-hearted bounds. In late afternoon the dogs had their heads down and tongues out as they wearily followed the horses home.

The rancher was not a hunter but he was a keen observer of animals, vegetation and the land itself. Cody learned much from him about the interdependence of all life on the ranch. With his grandfather, the boy felt the quality of the vegetation; checked the health of the pines and the abundance of cones; saw ground squirrels, mice and rabbits eating with wary attention around and above them; and, saw the predators gliding silently through the skies and trotting across the meadows. Now and then they saw elk grazing. A black bear with two cubs eyed them from a distance. Other evidence of wild life included footprints, droppings and claw marks on the trees. Through these signs they estimated the animal population. The old man was proud of Cody's progress. He was also amazed by the boy's ability to detect wildlife around them and his insight into the health of both plants and animals. Seth could not see the subtle variations in coloring, detect the slight temperature variations, or sense the electromagnetic auras and vibrations that indicated the status of each living thing. Cody could not explain to his grandfather what it was that he sensed. And so Seth learned from Cody without knowing about or being able to feel what the boy sensed.

Seth found that the boy had an uncanny sense of direction. No matter where they rode, through unfamiliar winding canyons and across heavily wooded slopes, Cody knew unhesitatingly the direction in which home lay and how far it was. When asked, Cody had no real explanation for this ability. He would indicate the sun or a specific peak or an unspecified 'feeling' that told him. He showed his grandfather that even blindfolded; when he turned himself about slowly he could 'feel' when he was facing homeward. The 'strength' of the feeling also told him how far away it was. Seth accepted it as a gift from the Lord to compensate for the boy's other handicaps. Eventually he came to rely on Cody's sense of direction if he himself was uncertain about a route.

They learned much about each other on these treks. Cody saw his grandfather as a person with a deep attachment to his land and a genuine concern for all the living things on it. He killed nothing wantonly. He did not intrude or disturb the natural order of things unnecessarily. He treated the ranch animals as friends and coworkers. The wild animals were co-inhabitants of this realm, not objects disposable to his whim. His stewardship was limited to acting as a buffer against human encroachment on their natural habitat and only rarely as an intervener to mitigate the effects of natural disasters on wildlife habitat. He was a man who took his stewardship of the Earth as an obligation rather than a license. Reverence, consideration and gentleness were dominant traits in his character.

On one occasion Cody saw the granite foundation beneath Seth's easygoing nature. They were riding through rough country northeast of the ranch house when shots rang out ahead of them.

'Stay here,' signaled Seth and rode towards the sounds. Cody, as with any teenager, stayed put a few minutes and then cautiously rode after his grandfather. The old man's loud voice led him to the scene of a confrontation. About fifty yards ahead of him, three men in their twenties were truculently facing his grandfather.

"I don't care what you thought, this is private land and I don't allow shooting at any time," his grandfather was saying.

The middle man stepped up to the rancher, pushed him vigorously in the chest, and shouted, "You're crazy, old man, if you think you're gonna tell us what we can or can't do. Get lost before we kick your draggy ass...."

The sentence remained incomplete as Seth stepped in and flattened the insolent speaker with a full-bodied overhand right. The man on his right lunged forward into a left hook to the body and another overhand right that dropped him beside his buddy. The third man, startled at this table-turning response, swung his rifle menacingly towards the rancher. Cody felt an unsettling discordant change in the rifleman's vibrations and reacted without thinking. He scooped up a baseball-sized rock and hurled it with all his strength at the man with the gun.

The gun flew into the air and the man fell to the ground holding his side. "Goddam son of a bitch!" he yelped, "Broke my ribs!"

Seth picked up the gun and waved it at the three men. "Back in your pickup and outa here!" he barked. He then walked to the truck and removed two more rifles and a shotgun from over the seat. "I'll leave these with Sheriff Hopping next week. This ranch is off limits to you!"

They straggled to the truck muttering threats and imprecations while sizing up their chances of jumping him.

"Scoot!" rasped Seth in his best John Wayne style, firing a round into the dirt near the rear tire of the pickup.

The three bravados scurried into the truck cab with startled expressions on their faces and a grudging respect in their eyes. The old ranchers hadn't all softened in the new West.

After they drove off, Cody remounted and rode over to his grandfather who sat with the guns tied behind his saddle. 'Thought I told you to wait,' he signed, then added, 'but I would have been in big trouble without you. Where'd you get that throwing arm? That pitch was a game-saver.' He put his arm across the boy's shoulders in an affectionate hug.

They watched the truck out of sight and then rode home feeling good about each other and their stewardship of their corner of the world. Before this Cody had felt a strong bond with the land that they worked in the valley around the ranch house because it was there that the fruits of their labor and dreams were evident. Now he felt Seth's broader sense of stewardship. They could not isolate their little valley from the mountains around them. It was only the health of this greater domain that made their little Eden possible. The boy could feel his soul expand to touch the far mountains as his sense of belonging and responsibility to this larger world grew.

Warm weather and the spring growing season brought a heavier workload and kept them close to the ranch house and fields. Cody enjoyed these days because he and his grandparents worked together in the fields, orchards and garden; sang their marching hymns with gusto on the way home; and, sat companionably on the side porch watching the waterfalls and the turbulent rapids of the creek. It was a time of beginnings, of plantings, of flower filled fields and burgeoning trees, of leaping spirits and bounding strides reflecting this internal exuberance.

When they sat quietly on the porch sipping their coffee, Cody's mind was active conceiving ways to make his grandmother's favorite haven into an even more attractive spot for her. Across the creek the flowering orchard on the hillside provided the backdrop for the waterfall with its wind-blown mist on the far bank. The small waterfall near the house sent its overflow to meander through the rock garden below them, the little stream sending out its joyful greetings in tinkling aural melody and twinkling glints of reflected light. Climbing roses at the ends of the porch, hanging baskets of pansies at the eaves, and fragrant roses below the railings framed this bower of sight, sound and scent. Grandma Marta's hand often lightly touched his shoulder in gratitude and affection for the realization of her girlhood dream of a retreat that satisfied all the senses and of a family with the sensitivity to share that dream.

On an afternoon in early June, the cool breeze flowing off the mountainside alleviated the heat of the day. The creek was flowing well and the waterfalls tumbled over the rocks with the first wind blown spume misting and cooling the air. Marta sat facing the smaller waterfall in the garden so that her view included the side garden, the bridge and the north end of the orchard. Her face was relaxed with a small introspective smile and dreamy eyes as she absorbed the beauties of her immediate surroundings. Seth sat in the corner facing south. His body was relaxed; his eyes were fixed on swaying trees and the distant hills that bounded his domain. His mind, too, appeared focused on distant time – perhaps his childhood on the large working ranch, perhaps the future when his stewardship must be passed to another. Indistinct emotions played across his visage to mirror the flow of memories in his mind.

Cody immersed himself in the scene, forgetting his ego and enjoying the interplay of sensations from the beauty he had helped create.

The contentment of his grandparents formed a pleasurable background for his own musings on ways to improve the gardens and waterways. Suddenly he felt rigidity in Seth's aura. A glance showed that his grandfather's eyes were now focused on something to the south where the road lay. A moment of concentration and the boy could hear a truck engine in the distance. He turned about to follow the rancher's gaze and saw a small utility type truck approaching the ranch house.

Seth walked around to the front of the house. Marta roused from her reverie, stood up and straightened her clothes, and then followed him to the steps. The boy walked to the corner of the porch so that he could see their visitor. The truck, which had a Nevada state emblem on its door, pulled up near the steps and the driver alighted on the far side. She was short, of medium build, with a broad face and high cheekbones. Her black hair was parted in the middle, drawn back, and hung in a single braid down her back. She was dressed in a cotton plaid blouse, a knee length brown skirt and short, tooled leather boots. She wore a friendly smile as she approached the steps to greet the descending rancher.

"Hi, Mr. Hoag. I'm Arrah Wilson from County Social Services." She extended her hand as they met. "I hear that you have a child here who is not attending school." Seth shook her hand briefly, then intoned in his flat voice, "Pleased to meet you. I'm deaf but I read lips some. Either speak slowly and clearly or write your message." He took a paper and pen from his shirt pocket and proffered them to her. Instead of taking the pen and paper, Arrah commenced to speak slowly and sign to him. 'Do you understand American Sign Language?'

"Some," replied the rancher, "we studied it a little but mostly sign to each other in our own dialect. Your lip expression is pretty good. I understand you."

"I am from County Social Services." She handed him a card, which he read. "Sheriff Hopping told me that you have a hearing impaired child here who needs special education."

"Our grandson Cody is with us. Deaf. Mother's drug problem, maybe. Hard worker. No schooling but we taught him reading and writing. He's smart and knows a lot."

"May I meet him?" she asked, looking towards Cody.

"Sure thing," replied Seth, turning about and beckoning the boy. Marta took his arm as he passed and walked down with him.

"Mrs. Hoag," Arrah greeted her with a warm smile.

"Marta," the old woman replied. "I'm pleased to meet you, Arrah." She indicated her grandson.

"Cody understands a lot. He's quite bright. Amnesia, though. Doesn't remember anything before he arrived here last time."

"Oh?" said Arrah, looking at the boy speculatively. "Does he understand American Sign Language?" His grandmother nodded affirmatively and prodded him to reply. Cody recognized that there were differences between his grandparents' signs and those of the visitor. He therefore limited himself to basic signs and elaborate gestures. 'I Cody. Know hand speak.' Arrah saw this as exhibiting only a rudimentary capability for communicating.

She replied in a similar stilted fashion. 'I Arrah. Teacher. You learn more.'

'I want learn more.'

'Good. You come school soon.'

She turned to Seth. "He is slow but probably teachable. Can he come to school at Sutcliffe in September? It could help him to lead a normal life outside."

The rancher looked at his wife. 'Think he'd be okay?'

'Of course,' she signed emphatically. 'What are the school hours?'

"Boarding school," interjected the social worker. "Five days. Four nights. Home weekends. Good to be with other children all week. Learn faster."

"We'll talk," replied Marta. "He hasn't been away before."

'I'll be back in two weeks," concluded Arrah, extending her hand. 'I hope you'll let him come.'

She shook Cody's hand. 'See you soon, Cody.'

The boy nodded absently. He was staring at the passenger in the vehicle. She was an older Native American, mahogany faced with braided hair. Her eyes were bright and piercing, fixed on him. Unlike the others, she had no aura and emitted no clues to her emotional state. He wondered if there were many people that quiet. The truck left. The family watched it disappear down the road. Each wondered how this visit might change their comfortable lives and introduce unpredictable outside elements. They went back to the porch but the coffee was cold and ill-defined clouds roiled at the borders of their idylls. They soon went inside for a quiet dinner, each concerned with his own projections of the future.

Arrah Wilson climbed back into the cab of her Blazer, waved again, and headed southeast towards Route 445. Not a word was spoken until they reached the paved road and turned north to Pyramid Lake.

"What makes the Hoag boy so special, Auntie?"

Quiet Fox turned a noncommittal look to her niece. "Who says he's special?"

"You do. That is, you didn't react at all. You blanked out. Your blank squaw stare is enough to shut out most people. Did you draw that Wovoka curtain for me? Or for that kid?"

"Your intuition is creating a dangerous problem, Arrah. Even now you suspect too much. I can tell you nothing until you regain your own Wovokian silence. We must do that tonight."

Quiet Fox's upraised hand ended the discussion.

Her niece's annoyance showed in compressed lips and a lead foot on the gas. Arrah's inner turmoil did not let her speak again until they were home.

She restarted their conversation abruptly. "I don't want to put my head in that black bag of Wovoka's. It almost got me killed as a kid. No way, old lady." Quiet Fox maintained her firm attitude. "You are in too deep already, little one. We must go back to your childhood, overcome your fears, and reawaken your ability for silence again. You, like me, are a descendant of Wovoka's line. You must assume your burden. Something important to our people is happening. I have been chosen to help by the Great Spirit. I think that you, also, have been prepared for a role. We must play our parts. It is in our blood. We are responsible for the fate of our people and ultimately of the world."

Her niece responded angrily. "I don't want any more mystic crap, old woman. You and the other shamans are living in a twilight zone. Our Gotterdammerung occurred with the Ghost Dancers and Wounded Knee – and our revered Wovoka, too," she added sarcastically.

Quiet Fox was unmoved by the tirade.

"Auntie!" the younger woman pleaded for understanding, "Our gods had their twilight and are now only fading memories among the elders. I am trying to save our people, our youth, in the only way that works. We will learn the white man's ways and laws and use them for ourselves to regain our lands and heritage." The old woman smiled thinly without amusement.

"So you would make yourself over in the white man's image, so thoroughly that you can beat him at his own game, and then return to your people and their ways? No, Arrah, you cannot go that far and still come home again. Only the faithful and the true faith can overcome. You cannot deceitfully embrace false ways and false gods to achieve good ends. If you want to reestablish the Hoop of Life in the world, you must first establish that vision firmly in your heart. Only then can you hope to establish it in the hearts of others. When all people believe in their intimate relationship with all other things, then it will be so."

Quiet Fox folded Arrah's hand in her own. "You have been denying your heritage for too long. How did you know that I made myself silent? Because you have inherited the same sensitivity from Wovoka's line that I have. Why do you feel that the boy is important? Because our grandfathers have told you so. Why did you enter into social work in education? Because the Great Spirit has prepared you to play a role in the next phase of our people's drama. Wovoka had the first vision of the departure of the wasichu but it was not to be in his time. I, Wovoka's kin, have been given a small part to play. You, also his kin, have a part in this. Have faith."

Arrah felt the oneness with her aunt that she had felt as a child. She could feel a limitless line of ancestors regarding her fondly and offering her their hands through those of Quiet Fox. She felt the terror of being trapped in the darkness under the barn evaporate as her father lifted her into the light and her mother enfolded her with love. Her ancestors ringed about in encouragement. She realized that they had been there with her in the darkness under the barn; that they had been with her through her years of denial in the spiritual darkness of the white man's schools; that they would be with her in the dark philosophical limbo ahead when she would be torn between the white man's egoistic world and the Hoop of Life. She knelt before her aunt with hands covering her face and placed her head on the old woman's knees. Her shoulders shook as her eyes emptied her soul of guilt for denying her own faith and embracing the white man's ways without faith; of guilt for urging her children to conform to the white man's image; and, of the pain of living her own life in a lie. She could see herself pushing her children out to aimless wandering in a spiritually barren land.

Arrah's sobbing ceased. She knew that it was time to listen to her heritage and make amends. She raised her tear drenched face to that of Quiet Fox, sat back on her heels, placed her hands on her knees, closed her eyes and quieted her whole being. She withdrew into herself, not alone now but in the company of her ancestors who enfolded her with love. The murmur of a faint rhythmic chant kept pace with the beat of her heart. She was not in a dark lonely prison but in a place of refuge and love separated from all sensations of the outer world.

Arrah opened her eyes to see her aunt smiling down at her, "Now I can tell you about this boy." The medicine woman began with the warning her tribe had received from their brothers in Tehachapi that a sacred person was fleeing northward through the Sierras. He would need their help to avoid pursuit and to continue north. Almost immediately strangers appeared at Walker reservation inquiring about a lost boy. They had a powerful presence and seemed to know answers to questions before you could say yes or no. Only the silence of Wovoka seemed to baffle them. While the others planned a rendezvous with the boy, she took a circuitous route to intercept and help the sacred person.

To her surprise it was a boy about nine years of age. Her only help was a warning and instruction in the Wovoka technique that he instantly grasped. He was in truth a sacred person who could touch your soul with love, understanding and a feeling of oneness with all Nature. He was a boy, yet like a grandfather.

"He left and his pursuers were close behind yet I never had a sense that he was caught. He disappeared from the senses of my soul. I did not feel the fading squelch of life. He was not dead. Where was he? Wrapped in the silence of Wovoka, I felt, and those hounds of hell could not track him there. Now and then I have sensed the hunters near so I knew they had not found him. It was not by chance that I was the one to meet him with a warning and with the silence, his only means of escape. No, I am a descendant of Wovoka and like him I was chosen and prepared for this role. I have been waiting nearly five years for him to come back for I feel that he is part of the vision of Wovoka and my role is not yet over."

"Today we saw this sacred person, now called Cody Hoag. He is not Cody Hoag, he is not their grandson. He is still wrapped in the silence of Wovoka, probably an unconscious protective measure. We must help him to learn and grow in safety. It is no accident that you are in a unique position to do this for him – a kinswoman of Wovoka and an official of the white man's schools. I cannot see the outcome but I tell you this, you have no guilt. You are an instrument of the Great Spirit. All of your trials have prepared you for this task. Only you can do it."

The younger woman resumed her chair. The tears had dried and her guilt had evaporated with them. A sense of calm and purpose had taken their place. "What must I do?" she asked.

"Carry out your normal work. Smooth his return to a normal life. He can hear, he can speak – if he will. He has other gifts according to the shaman Dreams With Manitou. He has a mother who was kidnapped. He has friends in Tehachapi who cannot yet be told of his whereabouts. These things I will tell you about later. Let his awakening happen as it will but do not let him become a public sensation in any way. For yourself, be wary of strangers with a strong presence. They must not find the boy until he is ready to find them."

Arrah nodded that she understood. "I will do as you say."

It wasn't an imposing edifice, just a small weather worn wooden building with a sign, 'Sutcliffe School,' hanging over the entrance. Seth entered the reception foyer with Cody to find a small administrative area set aside in a long hall with desk, file cabinet, bookcase, clock and a large monthly schedule hanging on the wall. They all had the appearance of battered retrievals from a government discard warehouse.

After a few moments of standing quietly, Seth called, "Is anybody here?"

The door on the right opened and Arrah came in carrying a cup of coffee. She smiled, set the cup on the desk, and greeted them in signs and spoken language.

"Happy to see you. Sign up now. Bring suitcase to house. School starts at 9:00."

Seth filled out the enrollment forms. The three then went outside and walked next door to Arrah's home. It was a modest single-story, two-bedroom, white clapboard with green trim. Visible behind it was an addition that appeared larger than the original house itself. They entered the front door into a hallway that extended the length of the house. On their right was a living room and on their left a bedroom. They proceeded down the hall past a bathroom on the left and then entered the next door into a bedroom. It was simply furnished with two single beds, a night table and lamp, a dresser, a two-shelf bookcase and a small student desk with its chair. Two reproductions of paintings of Native Americans from the 19th century were on the walls plus two old photographs identified as Standing Bear and Jack Wilson. A braided rug was on the floor between the beds. The beds were covered with handmade quilts bearing colorful geometric designs. The book titles appeared to be related principally to educational subjects. Through the windows could be seen a barren uncultivated yard.

"Your room now," Arrah signed and spoke to Cody. "Come see other rooms."

The door at the end of the hall opened into a large dining room with four tables having six chairs each. Other chairs were against the walls. The room was bright and airy with pale yellow walls adorned with colorful student drawings. Large windows at the left side and a glass paneled door at the east side let in the outdoor light. A pantry took up most of the right side. They walked directly across the room to glassed double doors through which an open area could be seen where several geraniums were surviving. On either side of the double doors a single door opened to a hallway running the length of two separate building additions that formed the sides of the open area. They entered the one on the right. Windows all along each hallway gave a view of the open area and lighted the hallways. The inner side of each hallway was lined with doors. The first door proved to be a large communal bathroom. Six small bedrooms followed and a large housekeeping and linens room was last. At the end of the hall a door opened into a utilities and heating area that connected the two wings and closed the end of the open space. The utilities area was divided in two by a wall that separated the facilities for each wing and prevented direct access between the wings. "Boys here," Arrah said. She pointed to the other wing and added, "Girls there. Seventeen students stay here. No empty rooms."

They exited the side door of the dining room and entered the school building by a side door directly opposite. This was a large high-ceilinged room that was mostly open space.

"Meetings, plays, dancing," their guide said.

A double door in the center of the inside wall led to a long hall. The foyer they had first entered was at its far end. Doors to four smaller classrooms opened off this hall.

"Should I stay awhile to see that he gets settled?" asked Seth.

"You may," she responded, "But be inconspicuous. Some students are afraid of strangers." The rancher and his grandson settled into chairs near the desk while the school supervisor readied herself for the influx of students. They arrived in small groups starting at fifteen minutes before nine o'clock. Most had been through registration before. Their parents signed the prepared forms, received the room assignments and went on to the dormitories with children and suitcases. Two women with young children went into the first classroom, scrunched into undersized desks and filled out the admission forms.

The number and variety of children fascinated Cody, more than he remembered seeing before. They ranged in age from less than one year up to the late teens. Two boys and a girl were older and taller than he. Only two of the younger children appeared to be Caucasian. The others were Native Americans. All were dressed in denims, flannel shirts, broad-brimmed hats and athletic shoes. Cody felt dressed in their style except for his riding boots. More than their appearance, Cody was fascinated by the variety of sensory impressions he received from the students. Some were bright, active and highly charged, almost bursting to communicate the thoughts that competed internally for expression. Several were quiet with gently pulsating auras that peaked only now and then when a significant idea clamored to be heard. One boy of five years or so emitted almost no bioelectric signals and exhibited body movements that seemed to be pushing away all external stimuli. Several children had erratically fluctuating fields about them and demonstrated a parallel hyper physical activity. The variety in his new classmates exceeded anything he had encountered on his infrequent visits to town with his grandparents.

His first class was a mild introduction to school. The teacher was a plain young woman. She was chunky of build, without makeup, dark hair drawn back and braided, wire rimmed glasses, and a loose fitting muddy colored cotton dress. How ever, she radiated warmth and her bright smile lighted not just her face but also the whole room about her. It was impossible not to feel at ease with Angela. The five younger children vied to sit next to her and basked in any special attention. The three older ones, perhaps eight years, were too polite to crowd the inner circle of infants but patrolled the perimeter of her attention to catch any stray glances. Cody at first stayed in the far reaches, content to observe the way in which she drew out the children to express their burbling inner thoughts with their halting media of limited hand signs, body movements and facial expressions. Only now and then did he catch the amused eye of his teacher upon him.

When the initial excitement of the students diminished, Cody found himself being drawn into the formalized training in communication. Each child had first to introduce himself or herself to the class. The three older children introduced themselves with carefully precise signs and letters. 'I am TONY.' 'I am SUNNY.' 'I am WANDA.' The younger children stumbled over their signs in their anxiety to perform but, with a little coaching from Angela, they each received the emphatic accolade sign for 'Good!'

Cody was not familiar with the variations in signs and stumbled badly in his spelling. However, with the teacher's instruction, he achieved near perfection in minutes. It was not a new language to him, merely a new dialect. He felt a flush of pride when rewarded with his, 'Good!' from the teacher. Pleasing her brought warmth that filled the room. It was a group game that made the day pass quickly as they reviewed the alphabet, simple spelling and signs for basic emotions, objects and actions.

When the children went to the playground after class, Angela asked Arrah into her classroom for a talk about her new student.

"Arrah," she said, "Cody is not a beginner in sign language. He makes many mistakes at first but quickly picks up corrections and remembers them. Perhaps he should be with more advanced students."

"I'm sorry, Angela, that I didn't have a chance to discuss him with you before class. He hasn't been tested. I don't know how much he has learned from his grandparents who are both deaf and use a mixture of Aslan and their own signs. I thought that he could learn the fundamentals with you and then we could test him on total comprehension when you feel that he is ready."

"Okay, but I have a feeling it won't be long. He catches on quickly and could become bored in no time."

The playground was full of the explosive release of energy from children concentrating too long in class. They played in groups of two and three, their excited gestures compensating for the minimal vocalizations. Shouts were usually the grunts of exertion and the yelps of surprise or pain. One boy sat alone making repetitive motions with his hands, oblivious to those about him. The biggest boy, not in Cody's class, made the rounds of each group, usurping their activity for a short while and then moving on. When he approached Cody, who was sitting on a board observing the activity, the boy signed, 'I'm Big Elk.' Cody stood and returned the introduction, 'I'm Cody.' 'You go. I sit,' signed the bigger boy and took Cody's place. Cody was nonplussed at the unaccustomed rudeness. He stepped to the other end of the bench. Big Elk slid down in front of him.

'I sit all over!' he signed forcefully. 'You go!'

Cody was perplexed and moved away to stand against the wall. He continued to observe Big Elk's behavior and recalled the way in which dominant animals demonstrated their dominance in similar fashion. It surprised him to see it in humans for he was accustomed to the politeness and courtesy of his grandparents. It was a trait to remember and avoid. However, Cody noticed that a surge of hostility arose in him whenever Big Elk asserted his dominance over the smaller children, a surge similar to that he had felt against the three men who had threatened his grandfather. Despite the resentment, Cody could not bring himself to stop Big Elk; he could not force himself to intervene. It was a strange conflict within himself that he had not thought about before. He wondered what it was that sometimes paralyzed his actions when others were around.

The children were assembled in the playground at lunchtime, sorted into groups of six and marched into the dining room in a loose route-march fashion. Two mothers took the hands of the youngest infants and a third led the strangely detached boy. Each preset table had a teacher and children of assorted ages. The children with their mothers were all at the two tables by the windows. A large amiable woman with a smile that included everyone headed to the other window table. On either side of her was an infant with its mother on the other side. Cody sat at the opposite end with a demure girl of about seven or eight years on either side stealing glances at him from the corners of their eyes and then looking at each other with suppressed smiles. A small thin man with steel rimmed glasses headed the other window table and black hair combed straight back. He appeared concerned and nervous about the restive teenagers at his table and especially Big Elk at the other end. Tables three and four were near the pantry and door to the schoolyard. A patient looking older woman who wore a pleasant smile over an underlay of sadness headed table three. His own teacher, Angela, headed Table four. The two older girls were at opposite ends of their respective tables, sitting nearest to the center of the room.

Arrah stood by the hall door and signaled for attention. The pushing, jostling, giggling and signing ceased and all turned towards her. She began to sign and many of the students joined with her. Cody recognized some of the signs from the grace before meals that his grandparents said.

'Thank you for the food we eat,
Thank you for the world so sweet,
Thank you for the birds on wing,
Thank you, God, for everything.'

He thought, however, that he remembered the third line was, '... birds that sing,' but he supposed that it had been modified for those who had never heard a song. A deep sadness stirred in his soul as he looked about at these children who would never know the beauty of a bird's trilling melody. Perhaps God would give them a better perception of the joyful song in motion that was a bird on wing.

Behind Arrah were two women wearing aprons. Their waves and smiles, which brought responses from two boys at Table three, indicated that they were mothers who had volunteered for kitchen work. The older children at the inner ends of the tables now stood and headed for the kitchen. Big Elk roughly pulled Cody to his feet and dragged him along. In the kitchen the cooks gave them serving platters for their tables. Cody immediately grasped his role and started back towards the dining room. He tripped as he passed Big Elk and only a miraculous recovery of balance avoided spilling everything onto the floor. A glance back showed the older boy grinning and drawing back his foot which had caused the stumble. Cody knew that this harassment would be an ongoing thing but he could not vent the annoyance that he felt. The inner turmoil spoiled his lunch for every time further table service was needed, the bully was there to jostle him. Cody could see that the teachers recognized the problem but their coping consisted of signs for Cody to be calm.

The meal was partly a training session for the younger children who learned the signs for the table settings, the food items, and requests to pass the food and condiments. Practice by the youngsters had those last items circling the table at a rapid pace. Occasionally a two-way conversation would get underway but it quickly degenerated into chaos as other children corrected the signs and interjected their own comments. For Cody it was a social event more than training in sign language.

When Cody finished his cleanup chores and put away the dishes and utensils he found himself the last student in the dining hall. The school bell and flashing light bulbs announced that class had begun so he hurried out the door to the yard. As he passed through the door he sensed the presence of Big Elk and the electric force of muscles tensed to spring. Cody sprang to one side as he exited. Big Elk jumped also but missed his target and instead rammed into the wall. Turning around, he glared at Cody for causing him to miss. The big boy rushed his target again, determined to bring him down. Cody felt his own resentment boil up and now there was no barrier to expressing it. He caught the charging Big Elk by shoulder and waist, easily lifted him and lofted him ten feet across the yard.

The bully gasped for air and rolled over on hands and knees, glancing back fearfully over his shoulder at his no longer docile target. Cody stepped forward to help him up. Fearing a further attack, Big Elk scuttled across to the school entrance and pulled himself erect. When Cody started to follow, the cowed bully slipped into the building and ran to the safety of his classroom. Cody followed slowly, wondering why he had finally struck back at his tormentor. Slipping quietly into his own classroom, he took the seat that Angela indicated.

Who Am I?

The barren surroundings of the dormitory and school depressed Cody. The porch vista at the ranch had spoiled him. Sitting there with his grandparents, he could feel the quiet aura of contentment and serenity that arose from the sound of waterfalls and creek; from the mixed odors of the garden; and from the sight of the burgeoning orchard above the mist of the tall waterfall on the far bank. The dark green of conifers formed a calming background rising to meet the spiritual blue of the sky. Here at school, barren dust cast its grayish brown pall over everything – buildings, sere trees, classrooms and on the children who trudged through it. He wondered if, inhaled, it deadened the heart and mind. It moved only in dust devils that attempted to stall the birds in flight and obscure the sun from view.

His second Monday, Cody arrived in the pickup with both his grandparents and a load of plants for the atrium between the dormitory wings. They pulled up at the office, dropped the tailgate and proudly presented the plants to Arrah as she came out from the office.

'You shouldn't!' she signed when she saw the greenery.

"Cody's idea," responded Seth.

"Enjoy the beauty," added Marta with a wide smile. Arrah's expression was more concerned. 'I love plants but we have no water for them. They will wither like hope on the reservation.'

Seth echoed, "No water?"

'None to spare for plants. Our funds are small.'

"Not even for these few?" asked Marta, crestfallen.

'Perhaps these few. No more. Green is a luxury here.'

They unloaded the pickup at the dorm with subdued spirits. The flats of greenery sank into the dust like ant-lions into the sand. Arrah fetched a bucket of water but the dust swallowed it without raising the local humidity. The truck departed and the plants wilted in the dry heat, longing for their home in Marta's garden.

Lunchtime surprised Cody. The children looked through the atrium doors and saw the vegetation sacrificing its fluids to the September sun. One at a time they tiptoed out to sacrifice their glasses of drinking water to the needs of the dehydrating plants. Each child wanted to adopt a plant and contribute his or her own glass of water to its welfare. It was apparent in a few days that the growing plants could not flourish in the children's drinking water, for the dusty soil and dry air competed voraciously with the plants' root systems for the little moisture available. Classroom discussions raised the question of where water would come from to nurture the garden. Gloom settled over the school as minds young and old sought a solution.

Cody walked with Aaron during recess to make sure that the autistic child did not wander off. This time Aaron had a purpose. He carried his glass of water to the atrium, straight to a wilting pansy in the farthest corner, and carefully poured every drop on the soil about it. As the water sank into the soil, Cody could feel the thirst of the boy as dryness in his own throat, a longing for the water he was sacrificing to another life. Cody touched Aaron sympathetically on the shoulder. An electric field seemed to engulf them both, a field that diminished slowly as the water was absorbed by the dust and evaporated into the air. The two arose and walked away hand in hand, startled into closeness by the strange phenomenon. As they walked past the kitchen the electric field grew to crushing potential and then diminished as they continued outside.

Cody's instinct was that the strange force was associated with the presence of water. He walked Aaron back towards the kitchen and then away, each time feeling the powerful electric field. Aaron was frightened at first but then found aspects of a game in generating this strange effect. Cody took Aaron outside and began to walk him about the school property. They detected a faint feeling of that same force fluctuating in intensity as they zigzagged back and forth across the grounds. A pattern took shape that made sense to Aaron. His course straightened to the southwest corner of the grounds. The now familiar force field increased with every step. Walking became difficult. Both of Aaron's hands were dragged down towards the ground before him. They slogged forward through this unseen viscosity. The younger boy's hands now hung vertically down and he ceased moving. Cody released his hand and the field diminished greatly but did not disappear. Aaron turned his eyes to his companion, more alert and aware than Cody had ever seen them.

Aaron pointed to the ground, then signed and spoke, "Water." This was the first direct communication that Cody had observed from the autistic child. They were late for class but no one thought it odd for Aaron. That weekend at the ranch Cody related to his grandparents about the flowers, the water shortage and the generosity of the children, and finally about Aaron's affinity for water. 'Dowser!' exclaimed Seth, slowly spelling the word for the boy. 'He feels water in ground. Maybe a well there.' 'Well!' responded his grandson. 'We dig?'

'No!' laughed Seth. 'We drill. Get machine from Reno.'

Next Thursday morning a truck with a drilling rig mounted on its flat bed drove up to the school. Seth sat next to the driver. They both waved to the gathered schoolchildren and then went into the office. Soon after, they went behind the school building with Aaron and Cody to identify the location for the well. Holding hands, the boys walked to the far corner where Aaron's arms pointed down to the spot. The dubious driller tried to raise Aaron's arm but found it to be pointing rigidly down. Shaking his head, Joe Bosworth muttered, "I've heard of dowsers and he might be one, but I've got to see water in this dust before I believe."

The children went back to class but attention that day was all on thc vibrations of the building as the drill bored deeper into the ground. At noon Joe and Seth ate with the children. Dusty clothing and tired faces showed their lack of success. At 2:45 p.m. the vibrations ceased. Five minutes later classes were dismissed. The children were brought out to the truck. Nothing was evident. Joe started a small engine next to the well pipe and the children moved forward to observe. Suddenly a fountain of water shot into the air and rain fell on the assemblage. The children gasped and screamed. A moment later they cheered and signed thumbs up. Discipline then broke down and they ran around crazily in the shower with mouths agape to catch the droplets. "Good fresh water!" shouted Joe toward Arrah, holding up a bottle he used for his preliminary testing. "You can use it for your garden now but wait for the lab tests before you drink it."

Joe turned off the water pump and the tumult decreased. The mud-spattered children dried themselves in the sun before being led into the dorms in groups of four to wash themselves. It was a welcome and joyful respite from class. Joe filled two barrels with the water to keep their garden growing until he could set up the piping system. Seth took out his wallet to pay for the job but Joe backed off with palms out in refusal. Through Arrah, Joe finally agreed that Seth could pay for the piping system, headworks and pumps. When the clean and dry children were assembled in the school hall, Joe formally thanked Aaron for finding the well. He then presented the boy with a company cap bearing their logo and name, "Water Boys." While the class waved their arms and shouted, Joe put the cap on the little dowser. For the first time

Aaron was attentive to the affair and appeared to respond emotionally. To Cody it felt as though the autistic boy's barrier against the world wavered at this moment.

Excitement ruled the ranch that weekend. Cody talked about adding plants from the ranch gardens to his small atrium garden at school. Seth brought out a plan and cost estimate for piping water directly to sprinklers in the atrium. Marta listened to their proposals without comment. When they were talked out she shook her head with a firm negative and walked away into her bedroom. Seth and Cody looked questioningly at each other, wondering why their little plans brought such a strong negative response.

Marta reentered the room in a moment carrying a large roll of cloth. Her face was now bright and shining, eyes alight, lips curved in a smile. She unrolled the cloth on the kitchen table to reveal a carefully sculptured garden plot sewn in multicolored threads.

'You men dream too small!' she signed in mock annoyance. Her surprised men flanked her at the table to study her colorful needlepoint. It was not Cody's meager splash of green in the dusty atrium. It was not Seth's spare lines of a pump, a pipe and a pot to bring underground water to a cistern for growing a crop of plants. Marta's artistry and needlework craftsmanship had been combined to express in infinite detail her girlhood dream of an Eden-like garden. Its colorful flowers and multi-hued greens wove impressionistic murals that lured the imagination into creating images to suit its needs. The garden displayed infinite and ever changing variation even as one delved into the artistry to discern his own dreams. Were those butterflies alighting on the stalks? Were those hummingbirds hovering over the flowers while drinking their nectar? Were those robins pecking insects from the ground? In truth, great art is more than what the artist puts into it. It is also what she entices us to put into it from our own dreams.

The prolonged stasis was more than Marta could abide. 'Do you like it?'

When there was no response or even notice of her question, she shook the two of them to gain attention and repeated her question in exasperation, 'Do you like it?' They didn't answer but simultaneously turned and hugged her tightly. Seth at length stepped apart and signed to her 'Marta, I fell in love with your beauty of face and figure when first we met but it was the beauty of soul I sensed within you that made me ask to marry you. All our married life I have sensed that inward beauty growing through the years. Now, for the first time, I see it with my eyes through this tapestry, a woven window into your soul. I cry for the years when I could have worshipped this beauty. Yet I know that if I had seen it when we were twenty-one, I never would have dared ask you to marry me.' The tears crept slowly from his eyes as they washed away the blindness of his inner sight. Marta cried also for now she knew that she no longer walked through her secret garden alone. Cody saw this interchange and felt the walls between their feelings go down and their spirits merge. He wondered if most people were like this, together physically but apart in all the deeper ways. If so, why could he feel these things that seemed only rare and transient revelations to others? School brought him more questions than answers.

Seth hugged Marta again and kissed her lips. He released her and signed, 'Your garden will grow at Sutcliffe.'

Saturday morning found the three of them at the school surveying the grounds. Seth measured off his irrigation system needs and decided to incorporate two water tanks with pumps. Marta sketched a garden plan to transfer her tapestry image to the school grounds. Cody estimated his needs in rock, concrete, shovels, picks, hoes and rakes to handle the project with the help of his schoolmates. He knew that they would enjoy it more if they built it themselves.

Arrah and her staff were dubious about the idea when Seth explained it from beside his loaded pickup on Monday morning. The tapestry, now framed, convinced them to give it a chance. The atrium came first. The students eagerly helped with the sprinkler system, not always with skill, but Seth and Cody checked every joint while praising the work. The younger students dug holes and planted flowers while older students used shovels to set the bushes. Big Elk used his strength to move rocks, carry large plants and dig the deepest holes. A fabric mesh between the dormitory wings shaded and cooled the atrium. At the end of the day Seth turned on the well pump and the children reveled in the garden shower. Formal schooling might be suffering but the children were being drawn out into sociability more through the shared experience than through all the abstractions of hand signs. The happy community feeling filled the air. Four weeks went by and the outside garden rapidly took shape. Young trees from Seth's orchard stood in groups near the far fence. Several had ventured out into the flowerbeds to cast their welcome shade in the heat of the day. The flowers created patterns from a capricious artist's brush. Here, they grouped together in formal array; there they intertwined their rows in swirling patterns that drew the eye in a dizzying whirl; and elsewhere their varying colors intermingled like those of children's balloons at a carnival.

The total effect was similar to that of Marta's tapestry but now the garden scene came alive through the eyes of children emerging from their shells. Her subtle weavings had erupted into a visual riot but still the soul of the artist shone through, shouting in color to be heard. On Saturdays Seth and Marta came down to bring supplies and to guide the overall configuration of the project. Several parents were brought in by their children to see the garden and then volunteered for heavy work with the Hoags. Under Marta's urging the water tanks were transformed by stone facings down which waterfalls tumbled into small pools below. Sod brought in from the ranch and some neighborhood fields transformed the dusty schoolyard into a green athletic field. Near the dormitory a formal garden of herbs was planted. A plaque in English and braille identified each.

The major work on the garden was completed by late September. Cool weather was slowing plant growth and most of the flowers had gone. At noontime one Saturday when all sat down for their picnic lunch, Arrah motioned for attention. Talking and signing, she expressed her gratitude and that of the whole school for the work initiated by the Hoags and completed with the help of many volunteers. In recognition of the part played by Mrs. Hoag's vision for this beautiful garden, several of the men had made a gate for the main path. At these words two of the fathers carried forward a gate framed by posts and a small trellised arch. This they placed in prepared postholes and stepped back. A carved sign over the gate read, 'Marta's Vineyard.' Everyone applauded. Two climbing wisteria were then planted at the base of the trellis.

Seth and Marta came forward and thanked Arrah for her laudatory words. The rancher brought Aaron to the front with his parents. Speaking and signing, he told them, "You all know the real hero of this project. Aaron found the water. Without that we would not be here today. Let's applaud our talented boy, Aaron, who brought us water from this barren soil." Aaron's eyes sparkled, his face was animated, and his hands appeared to be drawing in the adulation rather than pushing back the crowd. His mother and father, tears coursing down their cheeks, stood tall and proud behind their son.

In October, Cody rode toward the gorge under the slowly lightening sky. The sunrise beacon was calling him again to the Sacred Place. He must ask the shaman who he was, why he was calling Cody, what was the meaning of the dance and the vision. He clambered through the rocky gorge and emerged onto the perch from which he could view the ceremonial platform. The shaman sat there quietly with head bowed. The dawn terminator moved down the wall behind Cody. When it reached the embedded reflecting crystal a beam of light sped forth to illuminate the Sacred Place. The shaman began to chant in an almost inaudible voice. The boy dropped lightly down to the canyon floor, crossed to the spire at the foot of the platform and climbed in two jumps to the level of the shaman. The questions rising to his lips were stilled when the chanting ceased and the shaman's face lifted toward him. It was not the man who had been there last year, the man with whom he had danced and shared a vision. This was a woman, an old woman. Her face he had seen before in the cab of the county truck when Arrah had first come to meet him at the ranch. He wondered then about the strange quiet surrounding her. He wondered then and he wondered anew about her interest in him. She smiled at him. "Welcome, Cody. I am pleased that you have come again." With a gesture she indicated that he should sit facing her.

"Who are you?" he asked, "Where is the shaman? Why are you here?"

"Far Walker has traveled to the Dakotas. I am here in his stead to greet the sun and to seek a vision for our people. My name is Quiet Fox of the Paiute tribe at Walker Reservation."

"Why should I join you? I saw strange things last year. I do not know what they meant. Do you know?"

"My people believe that our ancestors sometimes speak to us through visions. These visions can sometimes be invoked with proper preparation, spiritual cleansing and rituals. Performing these rituals in a sacred place can help. This has been the Sacred Place of Far Walker and his fathers for many generations."

"But why me? What do I know of your ancestors or your visions?"

"Only you can answer these questions. You are here, called by the Dawn Light. You have danced and sung, unbidden. You shared a vision with Far Walker. Join me and perhaps we shall both know why we are here."

Cody stood, his mien intense and wary. "No. I am afraid. You are bringing a dark cloud into my mind. I'm leaving." She halted him with an upraised palm, a look of concern on her face. A wave of sympathy emanated from her to envelop and calm him.

"Wait, Cody. You have asked questions. I have a story to tell of my people. Perhaps it will have meaning for you." Reluctantly, he sat again.

Quiet Fox began to chant softly in that strange language of the Shaman, Far Walker. Cody understood it although he did not know where he had learned it. The chant told a story in a repetitious manner that allowed images of the tale to form in his mind. He began to chant the repetitious phrases with her for it seemed to clarify the images that formed. She rose to dance and beckoned him to join her. The dance also helped connect the images into a story.

The tale was about a sacred person of her tribe who had lived near here long ago. At that time the foreign invaders, called wasichu by the native peoples, were subjugating the tribes, taking away their lands and confining them to reservations. There they were reduced to beggars living on the handouts of their conquerors. Their spirit was beaten down. Their culture was taken away. Their children were 'Americanized,' even though they were the real first Americans. Hopelessness engulfed them.

And then Wovoka, called Jack Wilson by the wasichu, had an important vision. The grandfathers told him that all was not lost. They taught him a dance that would cause the wasichu to disappear and the beautiful hunting grounds to flourish again. The dance was one of peace, brotherhood and unity in the Hoop of Life. Other tribes sent emissaries to learn of this vision and the wondrous dance it taught. Angry Dakotas, Lakotas, Sioux and Oglala who were still smoldering from brutal wasichu military campaigns and repression learned the Ghost Dance. They changed its message to one of conflict and revolt. The wasichu forbade the Ghost Dance, repressed the people more, and even Sitting Bull was killed. The tribes appeared broken. The Ghost Dance is remembered but its message is lost. Her dancing ceased and her chant ended on this despairing note.

Quiet Fox turned to Cody and said wearily, "Let us sit."

She took his hand. At that moment the lost chords of memory

from Wovoka reverberated again in her mind. They danced again, but now the message of the Ghost Dance became clear. The tribes were not to fight the wasichu; the Dance was not a ritual battle to extinction. Instead, the Ghost Dance was a dance together in which the wasichu would learn from the native people about brotherhood and unity in the Hoop of Life and reverence for the ancestors. The invaders would disappear as ravaging wasichu and become as the native people in their respect for all things in Nature, animate and inanimate. Then the whole Earth would be lush again and repopulated with a natural diversity of life. They sat. The face of Quiet Fox was now serene. Her eyes were still on the vision of a reborn people and the lands Eden-like again. Her aura pulsated gently as she sat rapt in her renewal of Wovoka's vision.

Cody broke the silence. "I have seen your vision and a promise for your people. But I am not of your people. Now tell me, who am I?"

The old woman returned from her spiritual journey and considered her answer carefully.

"I think you are a sacred person who has been sent to help us find the meaning of our message. You must discover for yourself who you are and what your own mission in life is. I think that the thread of your mission is interwoven with mine. I will protect you until, in time, you will find yourself."

The boy was thoughtful all day wondering about this unknown mission that Quiet Fox mentioned. There was also the problem of his memory. He knew that the unlocked memories were those of the old woman and possibly one of her ancestors, this Wovoka. He had helped her to unlock her memories. Why could he not find his own memories of the time before he was riding through a storm with his mother? Why could he not find a single ancestor in his memory, not even his own mother?

He was preoccupied that evening at dinner, not his usual communicative self.

Marta at last asked him, 'What's troubling you, Cody?' The boy hesitated a moment, then signed almost unintelligibly, 'Who am I?'

His grandparents were taken aback. 'You're Cody, our grandson. Marly's little boy,' Seth responded.

'But why can't I remember back before I came here?'

'You were hurt in an accident, Cody, in a storm. You were all bruised when you arrived here.'

'But why can't I remember?'

'Sometimes when you are hurt the mind doesn't want to remember the pain and just blanks out everything. It's called AMNESIA,' said the rancher.

'Do you remember me before that?' probed his grandson.

'Of course we do,' his grandmother reassured him. 'Marly traveled a lot. You were born in WYOMING. Near the city named Cody. Marly brought you here when you were two years old. A skinny little boy, very shy, with big eyes and a serious face. How we loved you and wanted you to stay. But Marly was restless and left with you. We didn't see you again until you came to stay after the accident.'

Who was my father?'

'We don't know. Marly never said.'

'Will I ever know who I am?'

'Come to me, Cody,' invited Marta.

When he came near, she enclosed him in her arms and kissed his cheek. 'You are our grandson, Cody. This is your home. We love you and nothing can change that. Whatever else you remember, always remember that we love you. You are Cody Hoag, the best grandson in the world.'

Cody kissed her and Seth, comforted by their response. He conversed about school, his classmates and the garden, laughing with them over all the humorous events he could recall. That night he lay awake searching the corridors of his mind for unopened doors. He found none. Quiet Fox's rituals, chants, visions and talk of a sacred mission receded to the level of an old woman's chatter. He was just Cody Hoag, an ordinary boy with wonderful grandparents. The blank in his memory was just a blank to be filled with his grandparents' memories and items from Marly's rare letters home. He could have any memories he wanted. Better than having bad memories.

The excitement over the school garden gradually subsided as early frosts ended the growing season. Only the atrium garden, sheltered by the walls of the house, continued to bloom. The small herb garden of rosemary, sage, oregano, coriander, thyme, dill weed and chives spread its enticing scents to every corner of the atrium and into the dining hall and dormitories. When Cody worked in the garden various younger children would wander in to help, to visit and to enjoy the variety of sights and odors. The two blind infants were frequent visitors. They felt all the plants and delighted in the odors. The herbs were their favorites.

Cody spent time with the children, sorrowed by the sensory losses that deprived them of much of the beauty of the garden. He sat with them and had them trace the braille patterns while smelling the leaves and flowers. He began a game with them by tapping the braille symbols for the plant names on their wrists while the children read the plaques with their fingertips. They caught on quickly and soon were tapping the symbols back to Cody's wrist and to each other. Cody tried to fool them by switching plaques but after the initial confusion they quickly corrected him. In no time they could identify all the plants in the garden by smell. Then, given a plant name, they could unerringly go to it. This skin telegraphy soon developed its own shorthand and expanded vocabulary so that they communicated more than Cody had dreamed possible when they started their little game.

The game took another quantum leap when the children began to respond to his questions before he tapped out his message. He observed them more closely now with all his inner senses. They communicated now without touching. The tensing of muscles prior to a motion generated a bioelectric signal that the children could sense. Their concentration and selectivity were so great that this initial signal sufficed to carry the message like a radio wave. He realized that they could read his emissions as well. There was no further need for tactile communication. Now they began to read the hand signals of Ameslan and joined the class in their sign language drills to the amazement of teachers and classmates.

Cody thought that there might be a further use for this talent. He stood the two children between himself and a wall, and then tensed his body to the utmost to project a strong signal. They located him instantly as the source but then turned part way to the wall as though sensing a signal from that direction. Cody could also feel the signal reflected from the wall. After a few tests the children realized the import and began using their own bioelectric signals as radar to locate the wall and then other objects in the room. A new confidence developed in their ability to cope with their world.

These discoveries forged a strong bond between Cody and the two infants, Little Dove and Silent Owl. They often roamed the school grounds together, permitting them to form a mental map of the area. At times they would sit together while Cody signed to them a description of all that he saw – trees, far hills, clouds in the sky and birds winging past. A hawk swooped down near them one day, snatched its prey from the ground and rose swiftly aloft again. In his excitement, Cody grasped the wrists of his two friends to describe the encounter. The children sat completely still, intent expressions on their faces.

Cody tapped out the question, 'What's the matter?'

In unison they signaled back, 'I saw! I saw the bird!' Their finger-tapped vocabularies were inadequate to describe the picture in their minds but Cody was convinced that somehow they had 'seen' the bird. He was thrilled at the miracles evolving from his grandmother's challenging dream of a garden for the children at the school. He smiled down at the two blossoming children in Marta's Vineyard and knew that the gift of her dream would brighten lives for years to come.

It was the fifteenth of December and school was closing for the winter recess. The children's bags were packed and all were waiting now for their parents to come after them. To pass the time a holiday program was underway in the school assembly room. There were games, skits, story telling, poetry recital, soda and cookies. Everything served to heighten the expectancies of the holiday.

As the festivities drew to a close, Arrah seated the children around her and rose to tell them the story of a Native American hero, Chief Sitting Bull.

'Today is a special day of remembrance for our people. It was on this day in 1890 that this great man died in a tragic incident at the close of the period of military subjugation of our people. We do not mourn him on this day. We remember him with pride because he stood firm against overwhelming odds in his struggle to defend our land and preserve our culture.' In signs and pantomime she recounted how Sitting Bull had rallied the tribes about him to protest broken treaties and encroachment on tribal lands. 'When negotiations failed, he, in concert with other chiefs and braves from many plains tribes, led a military campaign that frequently defeated the forces of the United States in battle. The destruction of Colonel Custer's 7th Cavalry Regiment at Little Big Horn is the most famous of the victories of the Native Americans. These victories were not enough. The unlimited weapons, resources and manpower of the United States government and their destruction of the food supplies on the plains wore down the Native American fighters and their families. One by one the tribes succumbed to the pressures of starvation and surrendered to be confined on reservations such as our Pyramid Lake. Sitting Bull was the last to become a prisoner of war in July 1881.'

'Ten years later a Sacred Man of our tribe, Wovoka, had a vision from the grandfathers. This vision showed the despoilers, called wasichu in our language, disappearing from the lands on condition that our people would perform a ritual dance taught to Wovoka by the grandfathers. Some leaders from the Dakotas took this to be a war dance and began fomenting rebellion. The United States Army suppressed the rebellious groups by force. Sitting Bull was killed when he resisted arrest at that time. We remember Sitting Bull because he upheld our honor against impossible odds. He did not waver in his defense of our land and our way of life. He could not be bought by the United States. He knew who he was as a Native American. He knew what he must do to preserve our customs, our beliefs, and our way of life. He knew why he must do this. He had to keep faith with the grandfathers and the Great Spirit to maintain the Hoop of Life so that all creatures might live in harmony with Nature. We, also, must keep the faith and one day despoilers of the Earth will disappear.'

'Join hands now and heed this prayer in memory of our Chief Sitting Bull.'

'Great Spirit who created all the Earth and all living things;

Gods of the four winds who refresh the land with the rains and the seasons;

Our Grandfathers have taught us to live in harmony with Nature;

And with our brothers the wild animals of the mountains and the plains.'

Cody looked about him and saw that the audience were sitting tall, eyes on Arrah and listening with rapt attention. In his own head he could sense the presence of Sitting Bull; hear the chief's sonorous voice in a strange tongue that he could yet understand; and, see behind Arrah the great man's face with its stern lines, determined mouth and high forehead. He knew that all the others heard and saw this, too.

Arrah continued,

'Help us to stay firm in our faith, our customs and way of life;

Help us to maintain the harmony and balance among all living things;

Help us to bring the wasichus into the Hoop of Life;

And restore our heritage lands to their beauty and abundance,

As a fit abode for the Spirits, the Grandfathers and all your grandchildren.'

Behind Arrah and the face of the chief, the apparition gained greater depth and became crowded with figures of tribal elders in traditional ceremonial dress. They were dancing now to the rhythm set by Arrah's rendition of the prayer. In deference to the presence of the grandfathers the children rose and swayed to the rhythm of the dance, stepping softly in time with the ghostly dancers. The circle of dancers expanded to include the children and then grew more and more tenuous as it enlarged to embrace the school grounds, the far mountains and then the world. The dance finished, the dancers disappeared and the children stood reverently motionless.

At the conclusion, Chief Sitting Bull's face relaxed into a smile that lit up the whole room and the soul of each person in it. Cody felt the sense of brotherhood, family bonds, and ancestral pride that traveled the ages in both directions. All were changed, each questioning his or her contribution to this vision. The parents wondered about the subdued offspring they brought home from school that holiday.

Late spring found the Sutcliffe School a verdant island in the dry county acreage. Nearby Pyramid Lake was low because of the extended dry spell. Farm allotments had been cut so that some brown fields interspersed the irrigated working acreage. Rivers were barely flowing; creeks were dry. Despite the drought, the well on the school property continued to supply ample water for the luxuriant gardens. This was a blessing for the children, each of whom seemed to have adopted his own plot for special care in addition to contributing to overall care of the grounds. A small riding mower, donated by the local farm supply company, was the special pride of Big Elk. He kept the grounds meticulously manicured, had learned every detail of maintenance for the machine, and carefully supervised training of those over twelve years of age in its operation.

Cody was garden supervisor and instructor for the younger children. He had found that his powers of observation, the wavelength range of his vision, the ability to sense the vibrations of the plants and to interpret their needs, and the ability to differentiate among the odors were far beyond the abilities of his classmates and teachers. Yet each of the children could sense these things when holding his hand and each child had some capability with a specific sensory talent. He thought of Aaron who dowsed water; the blind tots who had great olfactory discrimination and bioelectric sensitivity; the two girls who read body language so well; and, Big Elk who could sense the slightest erratic vibration in his mower. Often it seemed that those who were most deprived were best able to discover and utilize compensatory senses. He wondered if these little used special senses were inherent in all people but were dormant because they were not needed in everyday life. Why then, he wondered, did they show up in him, but only when others could not observe them? Perhaps these were the answers that Quiet Fox intimated he would discover when he found out who he was and what mission in life had been assigned to him by the Great Spirit and the grandfathers. But, did these grandfathers exist or were they merely hallucinations brought on by the rituals and some form of hypnosis? Would he ever know?

Arrah found Cody leaning on his rake, staring west across the Virginia Mountains into infinity. She moved into his range of vision and signed, 'Cody, I have two people whom I want you to meet. Please come to my house.' He came back to the present, nodded his assent, and followed her into her home. A man and a woman in the living room rose to greet them.

Speaking now without signing, Arrah introduced them. "Cody, I would like you to meet my friends from Reno, Maria and Pasco Tallman. They teach at the community college there." They shook hands with Cody in turn, smiling and murmuring their greetings. Both were closely observing the boy and listening to his speech.

"Sit down, please," requested Arrah. They sat facing each other, the couple on the sofa while Arrah and her pupil took the two chairs.

"You have learned all that we have to offer here, Cody," Arrah stated. "You are accustomed to school, now. You are older than most of our students. It's time for you to move on to a broader education and a wider world. Maria and Pasco have agreed to give you the opportunity to attend their school."

"Thank you," said Cody agreeably.

"This is not yet an offer of admission,' cautioned Maria. "We travel to rural schools looking for special candidate students who are not qualified by normal certificates of high school graduation. We are authorized to give promising candidates the exam for the High School Graduate Equivalent Diploma or GED. If you would like to take the test we would be glad to give it to you. We know Arrah well and trust her judgment." Cody looked questioningly to Arrah.

"Take the test, Cody. You will pass and your life will be changed and expanded to a broader world. You may find answers to your many questions." That decided the boy. He took the proffered examination sheets and sat down at the table.

To Reno and College

Cody slid his bag behind the seat back and clambered into the cab beside his grandmother. He could see the flats of plants covering the truck bed and there were several small trees secured in the corners. The Tallman's old Victorian house in Reno had a large lot but the two teachers had only a few foundation plants on either side of the front steps. What spare time they had from their school duties had all been devoted to restoring the house, first outside and now inside. The Hoags agreed with their grandson that in return for the Tallman's hospitality Cody should contribute to the property renovation. His hosts had approved the idea without any concept of his ambitious plans abetted by his grandparents.

They drove out the dirt road to pick up Route 395 South near Constantia. Each was occupied with his own thoughts as they bumped and swerved along the access road. When they turned onto the highway Seth spoke.

"We're going to miss you a lot, son. When you came to the ranch eight years ago you were a lost, withdrawn boy with big eyes and a trusting heart. We were two old fogies who had forgotten why we were together and why we were here. You rejuvenated us and gave us back our dreams. You surprised us continually with your gardening, your construction and your way with animals. Then last winter we found that you can hear and talk. You're a wonder and we'll miss seeing you grow day by day."

"Most of all, Cody," added Marta, "you brought back the love that we thought we had lost when Marly left. Sitting on the garden porch with you in the evening, just feeling close, is the greatest gift God could have given us. Seeing the kind of young man you have become, I guess that sending you out into the world is our repayment to Him. We know that you'll have to stay in town a lot to keep up with schoolwork and outside assignments but come home whenever you can. You can rest at home and I'll pamper you no end."

Cody signed back, 'I love you, grandma and grandpa. You know that I'll be home often. I'll miss you, the garden, the ranch, and Can-Can and Tripod. How could I ever leave you all?" He squeezed her shoulders with his arm and they rode along silently sitting close together, their emotions intertwined. They drove south on Route 395 to Reno and took the business branch past the University campus. Several blocks past Route 80 they reached East 4th Street and North Center Street. This was about a one-mile walk to the campus. It was also near the gambling casino where Pasco enjoyed low stakes gambling while he tried to develop mathematical approaches to beating the games. Since he was trying to refurbish an old Victorian house in his spare time while the casinos were erecting monumental additions to their facilities, it was obvious that he had not yet found the right technique.

The Tallman's house was one of two old Victorians on a street struggling back from long years of creeping dilapidation. The varying architectural styles and stages of neglect showed that attempts to rebuild were intermittent and short-lived. The house sat on a one-third acre lot commensurate with its large size. A wrought iron fence in good shape bordered the lot. Two large oaks were spaced on either side of the front gate. A gated driveway on the far right side led to a weathered barn that had once sheltered horses and carriages. Wide curving steps led up to the front double door. Four chimneys rose above the roofline showing that fireplaces had once provided the heat. Despite the obvious need for repairs and a partially completed exterior repainting job, it had been a grand house in its day. It seemed an overwhelming task for two people to undertake.

They found the front door open when they climbed the steps. The smell of paint permeated the neighborhood. A call of "Come in!" sounded from some nether region in response to their pounding on the door. When they entered, the paint-splattered couple was descending the stairs. Hugging and handshaking were avoided as greetings. They laughed at their condition but shrugged it off as a way of life when living in a massive fixer-upper.

"Hi, everybody. Come into the family room and have a soda. We need a break anyway."

Cody and the Hoags followed them down the wide hall, passing a parlor on the left and library on the right. Stairs occupied the right side of the hall. Further along were a dining room and kitchen on the left and a large family room on the right just past the stairs. At the end of the hall a door led to the back porch. Cody was awed by the size of the house, the 12 foot high ceilings, the large rooms, the number of fireplaces and the stairs leading up to even more floors of rooms.

"It's a little larger than we needed," laughed Pasco, enunciating deliberately for lip reading or translation by Cody. "The card table and folding chairs we brought with us. The upholstery department of the campus theater refurbished the chairs as a house gift when we moved in. The pool table was too big and ugly to move or sell, so it came with the house. Same with the dining room table, the two master bedroom sets and the library table."

Maria brought a tray with the coffee pot and five mugs to set on the table.

"Why did you buy it?" wondered Marta. "You two will rattle around in here."

Pasco smiled at that question. "No, no. We'd never buy this barn. It was donated to the school by the estate, probably for the tax deduction. The school couldn't sell it so they decided to make it serve multiple functions economically. Maria and I are the house managers, watchmen, painters and refurbishing coordinators. For this we get free rent, the master bedroom, run of the house, and all the paint we can spread. The college departments will use this as a lab and demonstration project for construction technology, electrical engineering, furniture design, decorating classes, handicrafts and gardening. It could be used for informal off-campus faculty meetings. The rooms upstairs could house new faculty and students temporarily. As you can see, it's a bare canvas and we can use our imaginations freely."

"What about me?" asked Cody.

Maria replied, "We saw what you and Mr. and Mrs. Hoag accomplished at Arrah's school. It was marvelous!" She pointed out the window at the unkempt yard and added, "You can see the challenge here. We told Arrah that you could stay in the house so that we can help you with schoolwork as necessary. Meanwhile, if you wanted to plant a few petunias it would brighten all our lives." The challenge of the project and the promise of help with schoolwork were enough to convince them that Cody should stay with the Tallmans.

"Things are in a real mess upstairs," Pasco told him as they entered the house. "The smell of paint is enough to asphyxiate you. Maria and I are sleeping in the parlor. We thought that we could put up a cot for you in the library this week. By next week the master bedrooms on the second floor should be ready. Later on you may have to move into a front bedroom because the master will be needed for couples." Entering the library, Pasco showed Cody the cot and bed linens. "Not fancy, Cody, but it will do for a week."

The boy agreed and put his bag down by the door. They moved the large table from the middle of the room closer to the inside book shelves.

Cody then proceeded to set up the cot in front of the bay windows looking out on the porch. "You can clean up in the bath for the left-hand master bed room," Maria told him. "We'll have dinner about six o'clock. Chinese takeout from over on Virginia Street. You like Chinese?"

"I don't know. I guess so. I never had Chinese food," he replied.

"Never had Chinese? Your life will be enriched. Clean up and come to the family room. I'll call in the order – Moo Goo Gai Pan, Cashew Chicken, Szechuan Egg Plant and Shrimp Egg Rolls. Anything else, Pasco?"

"Sounds great," her husband called down the stairs. "I'll take a quick shower and be down to get the order."

"You take your shower, Cody. I'll follow Pasco and be down by the time the order arrives."

It was a strange dinner for the boy. There was no warm kitchen with familiar strong odors, no solemn grace before eating, and no grandma to serve plates heaped high with food. It was unlike Arrah's school with its strict order, four large tables of students signing their Aslan, and waiters scurrying to keep up with the appetites. Here they relaxed before the fire and filled plastic plates from myriad cartons on the card table. Pasco and Maria sat in the armchairs, resting their weariness after the day's painting. Cody was in a folding chair next to the table. He sniffed carefully before trying out the strange dishes. The spices and vegetables were unfamiliar to him so tasting was his only recourse. He quickly decided that he liked this adventuresome cuisine.

He lay on his cot that night thinking about the new vistas opening to him. He was sleeping in a room filled with more old books than he had ever seen. Outside there was the constant noise of traffic from the nearby highway. Through the side windows to the south he could see the dawn-like glow of the lights in the casino area, the streets that never slept, that tried to overcome the diurnal rhythm in Nature. A mile to the north laid the college campus where he would be introduced to the larger sphere of learning so that he could work in the 'outside' world.

What was wrong, he wondered, with staying on the ranch where life was so simple and enjoyable? Why was he being urged towards a more complex and unsettling environment?

Cody rose at dawn. He had coffee, two oranges and oatmeal in the kitchen. There was no sound from the Tallmans' room so he went outside. Everything was quiet and motionless except for an occasional vehicle on the highway several blocks distant. Unaccustomed to being without chores, he went to the barn for a shovel and set about spading one of the garden plots.

"Cody!" came a shout from the back porch. Tousle-haired and clad in a plaid bathrobe, Pasco stood there holding aloft a coffee mug. "Thanks for the coffee. Come on in for breakfast in a few minutes. Maria is fixing an omelets, potatoes, biscuits and preserves."

He looked at the yard and whistled. "Man! I'll tell her to make you a double helping."

Everything smelled good inside, a lot like coffee time at the ranch after the early chores. He thanked Maria for his heaping plate and joined Pasco at the serving table near the hall door. "You must have hired a backhoe, kid. The yard is dug up from end to end," joked Pasco.

"I rise early," answered the boy with a self-deprecating smile.

"Yes. The ranch chores. Well, on this ranch we keep a different schedule. Classes don't start until nine a.m. at the earliest. Sometimes we study late, sometimes friends drop by and shoot the breeze until the early hours of the morning. You can get up with the chickens if you want to but you'll be out of synch with the academic world. Except for the athletes. They've probably done their ten mile workout and are chowing down at the training table."

"I like the early mornings, Pasco. Everything is fresh. Everyone is eager to get going."

Maria patted him on the shoulder and sat down at the table with her plate. "My dear husband sees only two worlds. If you aren't large enough for football, tall enough for basketball, or lean and fast enough for track, then you're one of us – condemned to be a bookworm. Pasco thought that he wanted to play in the NBA but only his brain was star quality." She ruffled Pasco's hair and gazed fondly at him. "Well, maybe not only his brain." Her mouth curled up in a little grin as her mate caught the last remark.

Cody felt the warm undercurrent between them and wondered whether he would find a similar relationship some day. The Tallmans rode bicycles to school and let their guest choose one from several extras in the barn. The school usually had several older bikes left behind in the dorms at the end of each school year and gave them to the younger faculty members. These at the Freeman House were intended for guests who would be quartered temporarily at the estate. Cody selected a single speed balloon tired bike because it was similar to Marly's bike that he used to ride around the ranch yard.

Traffic was fairly heavy on the roads so the trio kept close to the curb and maneuvered warily across traffic. Pasco's casual remark that one small accident per year was standard for riding to school kept all of Cody's senses alert. His biggest problem was the crick in his neck from constantly looking over his shoulder. Pasco told him laughingly that he was beginning to look like Igor the lab assistant in an old horror movie. He felt relieved when they turned in at the campus gate only to find that pedestrians became the major hazards. Students were running, walking, standing and even reading while crossing the street, never watching for traffic. Bikes had no rights on streets or on sidewalks. Occasional ten-speeds threaded their purposeful paths through the Brownian motion of the student mass. The first day of class was mainly a confused search for forms, offices, buildings and classes.

Maria had already put her ward's registration forms through the administrative process and now they were merely directing him to his classes. They had agreed that three courses would be enough of a load while he was being introduced to formal schooling. Landscape Architecture 100 seemed a natural based on the work they had seen at Arrah's school – and they had a large lot at the house to do homework for this course. Humans and the Environment 100 dovetailed with that same sensitivity for his surroundings. Cody selected the third course, Introduction to Anthropology 101 when he saw the brochure featuring Native Americans in ceremonial dress. Maria agreed that she and Pasco could help him with homework for that course. If all went well Pasco felt that they should consider introductory science courses for the near future. Depending on Cody's aptitude, tutoring at home might give him the prerequisite math and computer skills to qualify for those courses as early as the Spring semester. Pasco saw it as a personal challenge because he taught introductory courses covering all the sciences for non-majors. The breadth of the new subject matter in this complex scholastic world overwhelmed Cody; but he was encouraged by his sponsor's enthusiasm.

Cody had memorized the campus map and so had no trouble finding the Anthropology lecture room. A student monitor took his class registration card without a word and waved vaguely towards the ramped rows of student desks in response to his seating question. Unaccustomed to so large a crowd, the new student climbed to the upper row and sat down. Below him the other students were milling about greeting each other and seeking seats near friends.

Cody noted the differences in appearance and mannerisms that set him apart. His Levi's, flannel shirt, boots and short, neatly combed hair was apparently modeled on his grandparents' past. From his vantage point he saw shaven heads, flat tops, windblown locks, spires rising six inches, and hair trimmed into initials; tank top shirts and tee shirts bearing personalized messages predominated; loose shorts, Levi's cutoffs and leotards abounded; logoed athletic shoes and sandals were the accepted footwear. His own wardrobe included none of these. His instinct was to blend in with the others but the styles did not appeal to him. He would have to discuss this with the Tallmans and his grandparents.

The class buzzer sounded and all settled into their seats at the behest of the young registration card collector. He announced that Professor Anza would not be there and he, Duncan, would project the film, "Orientation in Anthropology" for them. A screen came down, blinds were closed and with a thunderous musical fanfare the world was created from chaos. Lightning flashed in the primordial soup of carbon compounds, organic type molecules formed and rearranged themselves, one-celled animals appeared and suddenly dinosaurs marched across the screen. Meteors impacted the Earth, species and phyla disappeared, and soon mammals dominated the scene. Only in geologically recent times did primates begin their evolutionary journey towards modern "man." *Homo habilis, H. robustus, H. neandertalensis* and other branches blossomed along the way but disappeared in the competition for adaptation and survival. Within the past 60,000 years modern man (*Homo sapiens sapiens*) appeared without specifically traceable ancestry, quickly replacing Neanderthal Man and then becoming the dominant creature on Earth.

Duncan told them, "This Introduction to Anthropology is concerned with the cultures that modern humans have developed in the past 20,000 years. The older cultures that have been well documented historically can be traced back about 6,000 years. The first American peoples have records going back about 2,000 years. We will look at worldwide cultures for the general view of dominant trends. Because we are in the heartland of the disappearing culture of the Native Americans, we will study their beliefs and ways of life to understand why their culture seems relegated to oblivion.

Even this view of anthropology shook many young students' conceptual foundations. The Earth was nearly a million times older than the Bible's creation about 6,000 years ago. Humans were not created as full-blown masters of the world but was only the most recent to bear that distinction. There were many concepts of culture that related humans to their environment. The concepts changed with time, changed with environmental conditions and with the accumulation of knowledge. *H. sapiens* is probably not the end point of primate evolution. Modern culture will probably not be the culture of 100 years hence, let alone a thousand or a million years. How can modern Europeans and North Americans claim to be the ultimate species with a culture applying to the entire world for all time? Conflicting in Cody's mind were the literal Bible centered and land-oriented lives of his grandparents; the longings of the Native Americans for their traditional ways of living in harmony with a bountiful nature; the self-indulgent childish rebellious fantasies of his college classmates; and, the kaleidoscope of evolutionary concepts in the film. How did they all fit together? What did his visions mean? What was his own role, if any?

The classroom had emptied before he rose to leave. The quadrangle between classes was too much for one accustomed to ranch life, solitude and the gentle murmur of animate life in the background. Here, a cacophony of rock music dominated the aural range, pouring from the public address system and from portable stereo units carried by a large fraction of the students. Students were everywhere – lying and sitting on the grass, greeting friends from last semester, intently rushing between classes, strolling and reading, tossing frisbees. Disjointed superficial phrases, overlapping auras and bioelectric emissions, odors of perfumes and sweat, people passing him, bumping him – all these sensations overloaded his senses so that he couldn't focus on any single signal or thought. He had an unaccustomed feeling of panic rising in him, so he turned sharply to his right to head for the garden walk behind the east buildings. He stepped into a bicycle and tipped it against a girl walking it. Quick reflexes saved him, the bike and the girl from tumbling in a heap.

Embarrassed, he flushed and mumbled, "Sorry! Hope you're okay." Her arm was smooth and firm in his grasp; the faint odor of perfumed soap was pleasant with its musky undertone of perspiration from her ride to class. Her startled look softened to one of concern for him and then humor at the incident. She looked down at his hand on her arm. "Strong grip you have there, cowboy. I think I can stand alone now." He quickly released her and, confused, started walking away towards the garden again.

The girl fell in beside him. "I'm Kim. I saw you in the bleachers at Anthro 101."

He sensed her casual friendliness and looked her way. She was as tall as he with an athletic physique. Her long dark hair was braided down her back. Her face was without makeup and deeply tanned. So were her bare arms and her legs below the spandex bicycle shorts. Her sleeveless oversize athletic shirt bearing the university logo hung down loosely below her hips. All in all, an attractive person.

"I'm Cody. Sorry about the collision. I was a little confused by the crowd and decided to walk out here where it's quieter. I'm going to Environmental Sciences." Kim was watching his hands with interest as he talked. "Are you deaf or something? You're using sign language when you talk. My girlfriend Kathy is deaf so I learned some from her." He self-consciously clasped them behind his back. "No. I was raised by deaf grandparents so I learned to speak with them." She laboriously signed, 'Hello. I am Kim,' to him. "See? Not fluent, but workable."

"Where are you from, Cody?"

"We live on a ranch about 50 miles northwest of Reno. It's nice mountain country."

"I'm from the mountains, too. Near Incline Village. Ever been up to Tahoe?"

"Not that I know. We stay pretty close to the ranch."

"Here's Environmental Sciences. What course are you taking?"

"Humans and the Environment 100. I'm just starting here."

"We must have the same counselor, Cody. That's my class, too. We mountaineers have to stick together down here in Flatland."

He felt much more at ease with a friend at school. The ride to the Victorian was less harrowing now that Cody knew what to expect. He still breathed a sigh of relief when he turned off the main road and cycled the side streets to the house. He wondered why homes were not kept in repair, why the gardens were neglected, why letters and symbols were painted on walls and fences. The people must not have dreams like Grandma's.

Wednesday's Landscaping class with Mac Windish was disappointingly basic to Cody. The information about soil types, drainage, plants and watering was at the most fundamental level. The lecture's end was a welcome relief.

"This class has lab work in the garden," announced Mac.

"Let's stretch our legs and get some dirt under our fingernails."

They trooped out behind the instructor with shoving and horseplay to expend their repressed energy. The entrance to the garden site had a large glass-covered bulletin board with an artist's multicolored rendition of the planned garden. Beyond the board was a sere wasteland packed hard by many feet trudging between parking lots and classrooms. A few hardy plants braced emaciated stalks against the onslaught of the sun. Heat-toughened rose bushes protected their meager turf with a long-thorned barricade. They wasted no strength on blossoms. The planned paths were bricks neatly stacked on pallets. Within the pile of rocks at the northern end there was surely a waterfall whose tinkle was waiting to be heard.

"This is our sandbox, students. It can become whatever we have the imagination and perseverance to make of it. When and if you go into landscaping, you'll find out that this is as good as development land gets." The class groaned at that.

"Lab is a minimum of two hours per week at whatever times you arrange with the groundskeepers. You will rotate jobs – digging, shoveling, raking, paving, installing an irrigation system, making streambeds, and, finally, planting. After you do the dog work, you'll appreciate design work more." Another groan rose from the class.

Mac led them around the plot, describing at every step the beauties soon to appear. Dust caked on their sweaty faces and bodies. They at last returned to class via a water fountain and rest room detour. "Sign up for your lab work! Remember, when you leave on vacation the school will have more to remember you by than a littered campus and bubble-gummed desks." Cody started the movement and the others struggled up to make their job and time slot selections. The big debate was over the choice of the least onerous tasks. There was little discussion of the garden they intended to construct. Cody started his own sign-up with the waterfall and watercourse, then paving paths, and then the irrigation system. He wanted to lay the outline and backbone of the garden before getting into planting. Two large and muscular athletes signed on behind him. "We're in this for the exercise, kid," the redheaded Alan told him. "Hope you can keep up."

"Hey, man, ignore him," laughed the dark and barrel chested Randy. "Al can lift beer better than he can rocks. Those aren't muscles on his arms, just silicone implants." They both laughed loudly. Cody joined in with a tentative smile. He couldn't separate the friendliness from the competitive challenge.

Life at the Victorian was a whirlwind of change. A parade of helpers from campus applied plaster, paint and wallpaper. Light fixtures were changed. Wiring was updated. The house was reroofed. Caulking plugged all the leaks. Furniture arrived from many sources – alumni donations, estates, transferred students, stage props and upholstery shop homework. The upstairs rooms were decorated and furnished. The Tallmans moved to the north Master Bedroom at the rear of the house on the second floor. Cody was assigned the south bedroom on the street side. Volunteers brought their own work clothes, tools, beer, wine and soda. After work there was usually a barbeque or a takeout dinner, some joking and laughing, then a music party. Cody was slowly drawn into the party activities because, although reticent, he was one of the regulars and often cooked for the crowd. He usually just listened to the conversations. After being coaxed into dancing, he found that he loved it, quickly became adept and was a sought-after partner. He often invited Kim and they soon became the prime dance couple at the house. He found that when he danced his shyness left him. Dancing was self-expression and communication with his entire body. Kim had the same approach and was a joy to watch.

The Victorian garden was a favorite relaxation area until the weather became too cool. Flowers in various patterns delighted the eye. Scents of flowers and herbs delighted the nose. The splashing waterfall and warbling brook delighted the ear. Winding paths invited a stroll. Benches and swings said to stay a while. Neighbors dropped by to chat, to compliment, to sit and visit. Soon other gardens bloomed, graffiti disappeared, and the whole neighborhood became more friendly and relaxed. It became a community brought together by beauty – beauty that soothes antisocial impulses.

Trips back to the ranch became like visits to another land and time – a place of solitude, natural beauty, a slower pace and talk of problems connected with ranch operations and animals they knew individually. Masses of people, global scope, geological time spans and anthropological evolution were beyond the scope of their concern. Cody talked less and less of the informational panorama that was opening to him at school. His life became two separate parts and he reverted to the teen-age grandson when at the ranch. His grandparents had replaced their lost teenage Marly with him. He didn't have the heart to take that away again.

Thoughts of Extinction and A New Family Life

Protect the environment? That's a laugh! Mother Nature herself causes the most pollution and damage. Volcanoes, earthquakes, epidemics, meteorite and comet collisions, fires initiated by lightning, ice ages, competition among species – these natural phenomena have made more species extinct than man has. A meteorite extinguished the dinosaurs; ice ages have regularly wiped out vegetation over large areas; melting glaciers have flooded land and seacoast, exterminating more species. Even the liberation of oxygen on Earth by stromatolites 2.5 billion years ago is thought to have obliterated most of the anaerobic life forms then populating the planet. Ninety-nine percent of the species that ever existed are already extinct. Can man do more?"

Dr. Hagen sat back in a challenging pose, lips curled to sneer at any rebuttal from the environmental "bleeding hearts."

Professor Hammond took a sip of his Perrier and twist of lemon. He leaned forward with elbows on knees and hands clasped before him. Chin forward, lips pursed and eyes narrowed in concentration; he gazed into the embers in the fireplace as though reading portents of the future. His ruminative tone did not directly confront his aggressive opponent.

"Nature's catastrophes are random events of a mechanistic kind that cannot be countered by a plan or act of humans. Disasters on the simpler biological level, such as the prolific stromatolites poisoning the atmosphere for other species with their oxygen waste product, are not part of a rationally conceived plan to modify the environment for good or ill. Humans, the current dominant species, are a rational creature who can reason from cause to effect. We can identify changes in the environment and evaluate whether they are favorable or unfavorable in promoting our own existence and that of other creatures with whom we share this planet. Humans can cause great changes in the environment because our species is so numerous and we employ a great deal of fossil and mineral fuels in our activities. We produce waste products that pollute the environment for all living things. And we eat most other creatures, or consider them pests and exterminate them, or ignore them as "useless" and take away their habitats for our own purposes. Worst of all, most of this damage is done for short-term monetary gain spent on transient diversions. Only a species bent on suicide would behave this way intentionally."

Ugo Hagen pushed himself forward to rebut these arguments. "Come on, Trent! You drive a car. You eat dwindling species such as salmon. Radioisotopes were used on your sister's cancer. Your parents had eight children. You spray insecticide on your roses. All these things harm the natural environment. You even teach nuclear physics. How can you preach this crap and live as you do?"

The physicist unclasped his hands and raised them to support his chin as though the weight of these contradictions was bowing his head. "You're right, Ugo. I'm living a lie. Short-term money and luxuries subvert my rationality for greed instead of good. I've decided to quit teaching physics at the end of this year and work with an environmental group called Life Cycles. They believe that all life is connected. They want respect for all life to become an eleventh Commandment."

"You're serious about this?" asked Pasco. "You're going to give up a good career and go off into the ozone with the weirdos? What difference can one man make against all the economic interests exploiting Nature? Forget it! We'll build a good department and send our graduates off into the fray. It's a waste of your talent, Trent. Stay here and have a life."

Ugo, an instructor in the Business School, supported Pasco. "He's right. I've been researching the interconnections of the multinational companies. They have assets greater than any single country. Exploitation is their modus operandi – exploitation of people, animals, minerals, land and sea. Your environmentalists may be tolerated as gnats if they are ineffectual, but if they tread on the toes of the multinationals they'll be squashed. And you'll be the squashee."

Trent stared into the fire, perhaps seeing his own turbulent future. "Yes, it's daunting. But I can't live a lie."

"What do you think, Cody," Pasco asked his ward. "Is environmental activism worthwhile?"

"I don't know about populations, exploitation and depletion. I do believe that all things are connected in what the Native Americans call the 'Hoop of Life.' All things communicate if you listen closely. Many sad things exist in the city. If Professor Hammond can make one living thing happy, his new work will be worthwhile. He will feel worthwhile. And the world will be a better place."

"Thank you," smiled Hammond. "Your plants must be happy here."

"They are," replied the young gardener in a matter-of-fact tone. "They make the whole neighborhood happy."

"Happy and poor," retorted Hagen. "A shoe factory on this plot would feed everyone in the area and make them comfortable as well as charmed. They could hire gardeners if they wanted a garden."

"You must express your love directly to every living thing in order to benefit each thing as well as yourself. Hiring a gardener may make the plant happy and the gardener happy, but it will not make you happy."

"You're getting too metaphysical for me, young man. Money is the highest good. Everything else can be bought," stated Ugo.

"Not Professor Hammond," observed Cody.

The discussion ended. They all mentally reviewed their positions as they sipped their drinks and watched the fire die.

"Are you going home this weekend?" Kim inquired.

"No. The winter season is slow at the ranch. I decided to hit the books and get ready for finals."

"Finals? They're two weeks off. You're way ahead. Take a break. Come up to Incline this Friday."

"I don't know, Kim. I don't visit much except home."

"You need more socializing. And not with the faculty. There's snow, skiing and partying. You'll love it, Cody."

"But I don't know that partying crowd and...."

"No buts," she said emphatically. "I'd like you to meet my family, see Incline, do some skiing and partying. I'd like to show off dancing with you, too. You're my favorite partner."

"Okay, Kim. If I can dance with you, it's a weekend well spent."

The drive from the Victorian to Incline took forty minutes in Kim's Bronco. When they turned off the highway on the road to her home, she shifted into four-wheel drive and took to the snow without hesitation. The road wound through icicle-laden pines and bare-branched aspens for over a mile. She turned into a driveway between close pressing trees and, after a hundred yards, stopped before a large rustic house in a clearing. With a follow-me wave, she grabbed her bag and ran up the steps to the porch and opened the door. Cody barely caught the door to follow her inside. A trim woman in her forties caught Kim in her arms, with the squeals of "Mom!" and "Kim!" Happy, inquiring eyes over the girl's shoulder surveyed her companion. Kim stepped back, turned to pull him forward, and introduced them.

"Mom, this is Cody I've been raving about. Cody, this is my mother."

Cody dropped his bag and tentatively offered his hand. Mrs. Westing just laughed and pulled him in for a quick hug. "No formalities, Cody. Call me Connie. If you're here, you're family. Care for some coffee? It's fresh made."

Connie crossed the high-ceilinged sitting room and ran up five steps to the kitchen which was enclosed by a railing and entirely open to the sitting room. A door on the left opened to a large family room with a fireplace visible on the front wall. A similar fireplace was on the front wall of the sitting room. Kim went up the stairs and Cody followed her to a dining area on the right end of the kitchen. The glass walls looked out across a broad canyon to pine covered mountains. The waters of Lake Tahoe shimmered blue one and one-half miles away, stretching 20 miles to the south. Evergreens rose out of the snow covered slopes. White peaks were all about. The scenic beauty transfixed him until Connie set the coffee cups on the table before them.

She regarded him with friendly interest and began drawing him out about his background.

"You seem quite taken with our view. You haven't been to the mountains before?"

"This is the most beautiful sight I've ever seen. No, I haven't visited these mountains before. I live on a ranch with my grandparents 50 miles northwest of Reno. The ranch is in a canyon with mountains all around."

"That's dry country, isn't it?"

"Pretty much. But we have a permanent spring on the ranch and irrigate several hundred acres of pasture, garden and orchard."

"Kim tells me you're a great gardener. Right, Kim?"

"Fabulous, Mom. You should see the Victorian garden he made, it's a showplace! And the school landscape garden – his work is best of all."

"Who taught you to garden, Cody?"

"My grandmother, Marta, mostly. She envisions beautiful gardens and I help to build them. We made one at home, one at the Sutcliffe School, the one at the Victorian in Reno, and I'm working on another in Architectural Landscaping at the University."

"Was your mother a gardener, too?"

"I don't think so. She was lost in an auto accident in California."

Connie's expression became solicitous. "I'm sorry."

"It was long ago," he replied evenly. "I don't remember much about her."

"Your father?"

"I never knew him. Nor did my grandparents."

"Oh! Then you were raised entirely by your grandparents. They have certainly done a fine job." She smiled approvingly.

"They're good people. We love each other and work together."

"Was your school near there?"

"No. They taught me at home. They're good to me."

"They are good teachers. You are very well spoken."

He took her comment literally and responded, "They're deaf and use mostly sign language. But they speak sometimes and sing."

Kim fidgeted at the long interrogation. She broke in at last. "Enough questions, Mom. His folks are wonderful. They're deaf, but they talk and read lips pretty well. Cody knows sign language. Better than I do. Sometimes I think he reads my mind, he does it so well."

Her mother flushed self-consciously. "I hope I didn't embarrass you with all my questions, Cody. I do like to know Kim's friends. And you're the friend I've been hearing most about lately."

He looked to Kim for a cue. She steered the conversation away from his background. "Cody has never been skiing, Mom, so I wanted to bring him here to see the best. When will Dad be home?"

"Pretty soon. He went to pick up your brothers at the slopes." Connie seemed relieved for the change herself. For Cody there had been no strain. He was merely responding straightforwardly to her questions. Kim began to point out some of the landmarks visible through the window wall and the conversation stayed away from personal items. By the time the coffee was finished another four-wheel drive vehicle pulled up near the steps. Kim's two brothers, Jeff and Terry, tumbled through the door in a struggle to be first. They yelled their greetings to mother and sister, then said, "Hi" to Cody and took a close look at him.

"Track," said Jeff, the younger. "Too small for football or basketball. Too puny for wrestling and gymnastics." "Brain, maybe," opined Terry. "Finals are coming up and Kim needs help."

"Gardener," stated Cody, smiling.

"You ski?" asked Jeff.

"Never tried it."

"Great! At last she brings someone who won't blow us off the slopes. What size ski boot? A pair of our old ones should fit." Kim stepped up for a belated introduction. "This is my friend Cody from school," she told them. To Cody she added, "This is Jeff and that is Terry. Little brothers," she intoned with emphasis. Her father came in just then and chimed in, "I'm Howard, father and peace keeper. Glad to meet you, Cody." He extended his hand.

"Let's eat," said Terry, his interest in the visitor waning when he smelled dinner.

"About thirty minutes to dinner," stated Connie. "No snacks. Take the bags upstairs and wash up while dinner cooks." The boys bolted for the stairs up from the kitchen at the middle of the house.

Kim took Cody's hand. "With luck there'll be some hot water left for us when we reach our rooms. My brothers like that Niagara feeling." At the top of the short flight was a broad landing. The boys' rooms were in front and, from the splashing sounds, each had its own bath. Another short flight brought them to the master suite located over the kitchen area. A partly open door on the right revealed a large sitting room with fireplace. The next landing had a layout similar to the boys' level with two bedrooms over theirs. On either side was a bath with door opening on to the landing.

Kim pointed up the next short flight. "Two spare bedrooms on the lake side and a storage area on the uphill side. Mom and Dad like company."

"You get the left room and bath. Hillside view and glimpse of lake to the south. Remember, thirty minutes to dinner. Casual clothes. Just come as you are."

Cody nodded, still taking in the size and layout of the house. Each floor was as large as the ranch house. The view from his south window was magnificent with evergreen and snow covered mountains all around plus the lake stretching for miles. After dinner they all repaired to the game room at the other end of the ground floor from the kitchen, under the boys' rooms. Howard kindled a fire. They sat around the hearth drinking coffee while Connie played the baby grand at the left of the fireplace. After finishing his coffee, Jeff took her place and played sing-a-long tunes. They were surprised that Cody knew none of them until Connie mentioned that his deaf grandparents had raised him on an isolated ranch. She coaxed him into joining on a few simple songs and soon he was singing lustily if not well.

The warmth of the family reminded him of his work-with-song days with the Hoags at harvest time. He had often wished that he could be part of a family like this with other young siblings. Most often he felt like a stranger watching through a plate of glass, unable to touch or be touched. He even imagined that he was seeing cardboard cutouts with no depth, so that when he tried to get inside to their feelings he found himself out on the other side. Cody put these thoughts aside and gave himself enthusiastically to the songfest.

Sung out and laughed out, they sipped the last of their coffee and turned to other interests. Terry stood and suggested, "Let's get Cody outfitted for skiing. Then we can start early tomorrow on his lessons."

They trooped downstairs to the ski room and rummaged through their stock for suitable gear. There were racks of skis, poles, boots, socks, jackets, pants, thermal underwear, goggles and facemasks. A workbench at the rear of the room had extra bindings and tools.

"Sit down and we'll get you outfitted," said Terry, waving a shoe sizer toward a chair.

Cody was astounded at the gear. "This looks like a store."

"Right. Dad owns a ski shop in the village and a rental shop on the slope. Some of this is surplus stock; some is damaged gear that we've repaired. It comes in handy for our friends who drop by without gear. You fit into our beginner category, recruited by our sister who picks up strays."

Howard stepped forward and shook Jeff in mild reprove. "Don't let them bother you, Cody. We have lots of equipment. If you want to ski we can outfit you and have you on the beginner's slope first thing in the morning. Kim is a great instructor and the boys will be too busy to bother you. We'll need Kim in the shop in the middle of the day. We could even use you if you need a break from skiing."

Cody gave a shy smile. "I've watched skiing on television. It looks exciting. I just hope I can stand up, let alone jump off a cliff and somersault."

Howard laughed. "Jump? Beginners don't go off cliffs. We'll start on gentle slopes and see how far you want to go." Cody's medium size made him easy to fit. In no time they had set aside a complete outfit and set bindings on his skis. He was ready for morning.

Before daybreak they downed a breakfast of fruit, cereal, eggs and pancakes to carry them through the cold day. Hot coffee took away the morning chill. As they finished, the sky brightened and sunlight hit the mountaintops across the lake. As the sunlight moved down from the peaks and reflected from the snow, it seemed that cool white lava was flowing down the slopes. At last it reached the tree line where the dark evergreens came brilliantly alive with sunlight refracted by the ice crystals into myriad rainbow glints. The ice palace called the child within to come out and play.

Jeff jumped to his feet and slapped Cody on the shoulder. "Let's get going. We'll put your things into Kim's Bronco and head for the slope shop. Dad, Mom and Kim will open the village shop. Terry and I will get you started before the crowd arrives. When the morning rush drops off, Kim will come up to take over your education."

"Or kiss your boo-boos!" interjected Terry. "No fear, Cody. You're in good hands. When the morning crowd arrives you'll be on your own for a while to practice."

"Ignore them, Cody," called Connie. "Howard and I kissed all their boo-boos better when they were learning. You'll be fine."

"He'll be great," opined Kim. "With his balance and dancing ability he'll out-ski those two clods by mid-afternoon." With that they all picked up their gear in the basement and loaded the vehicles.

The drive to the slope took twenty minutes. By then the morning sun had illuminated everything into brilliant white. They left the Bronco in a parking spot near the ski shop. After stretching, they put on their skis and made their way over the comparatively level ground to the beginners slope. Standing proved easy. Gliding over the snow was not. Just when Cody got the hang of the step-step-push-glide cross-country locomotion, the upgrade steepened and he slid backwards into a cross-legged heap. That led to a quick introduction to the herringbone and side-step uphill techniques. Again, just as he had that under control, the slope turned down and he nosed into the snow in a spraddle-legged heap. A little untangling by Jeff and Terry, then a push on the right side with both poles and he levered upright… only to fall on his left side.

His companions stifled their laughter and soberly went through the exercises with him half a dozen times to be sure he understood the mechanics. Cody doggedly followed their directions, keeping his inner vision of a swooping glide kicking up a plume of snow across a virgin slope. Anything that beautiful would be worth the effort to learn.

The first cars entered the parking lot below. Cody was left on the slope to practice his fundamentals. He gradually achieved more glide across level ground. He herringboned his way up the slope each time, sidestepping up the steepest climbs. His snowplowing-braked descent transformed more closely to a parallel technique and picked up speed. A liberal coating of snow all over confirmed that he was constantly testing the limits of his capability.

Confident now, he felt the wind of the descent in his face as he ran straight down the gentle slope.

"Atta boy, Cody! You're a real schussboomer." Cody turned his head toward Kim's cheering voice, followed it with his shoulder, and presented himself in a ball at her feet. "Oh! I'm sorry, Cody. Are you all right?" He unrolled and gave her a woeful look. "I wanted to surprise you with my progress. Have I?"

She waved towards the bodies strewn about the slope. "Par for the course. Actually, you were doing fine until I called. Why don't we get some coffee and take a rest. Then we'll do a little more before I have to help in the shop. After that you can keep practicing or give us a hand with the crowd. Okay?"

Once Cody picked up the rhythm of Kim's graceful movements, skiing beside her became akin to a dance for him. He could sense the changing tensions in her muscles, the flex of her knees, the lean of her body. He modified his own movements to be an image of hers. More than that, he could feel the wind in her face, snow particles contributing a stinging excitement as they impacted her skin, the bumpy rise and fall of the track massaging her feet and leg muscles. He could sense her emotions of anticipation, apprehension and satisfaction as she went through a maneuver. The enveloping joy in being, feeling, daring and almost flying brightened it all. With Kim beside him, skiing became an unsurpassed joy. Later, in practice, he had only to envision Kim beside him to regain that ultimate joy and grace of movement.

The afternoon shadows lengthened and shop activity diminished. Terry came out to help with the instruction but after briefly watching Cody and Kim he waved goodbye and drove off to the village shop. An hour later, Jeff closed shop and drove home with his sister and the ecstatic new skier.

That evening at dinner, the youths regaled their parents with anecdotes of Cody's initial tumbles and then his extraordinary competence by the end of the day. They insisted that their visitor must demonstrate his ability then and there outside the house. He tried to downplay his accomplishment but finally acquiesced and took a run down the road. It impressed Howard. "It's not just how much you have progressed in one day, Cody. It's your instinctive grace, rhythm and strong movement. You could be an excellent skier. It's in your soul. You must come again during the week so that we can teach you what we know. What you do with it is up to you."

That night they went to a Rathskeller where they drank a little beer and danced a lot. To Kim and Cody it was like floating in a dream. Several of Kim's friends danced with her early in the evening but they were overawed by the way the couple danced together, lost in each other's complementary movements. Cody, for his part, enjoyed the variety of dances. He reveled in the driving beat and sheer energy in the modern popular dance styles; but he was swept away by couples dancing. He lost himself in the shared grace of movement in the older classical styles, whether waltz, tango, or foxtrot.

Connie danced once with Cody. Later she observed them thoughtfully, appreciating their dancing but worried by a formless concern hovering at the border of sensibility. Later, at home in her bedroom, she tried to unveil the feeling in a talk with her daughter.

"You and Cody are a perfect dance team, Kim. You seem to know each other's every move, every rhythm, every feeling, every intention."

"He's wonderful, Mom. But you danced with him. What did you think then?"

"Oh, Kim! He must be the best partner in the world. Not only did he foresee my every move, but also I thought that I knew his. Not even your father, good though he is, can do that. It's eerie!"

"Not eerie, Mom. Sensational! I'm lost in a dream when dancing with him."

"Are you in love with him?"

"Love? I don't know. I'm infatuated with him. I'm tremendously in like with him. Sometimes I'm in awe of him. But we've never even kissed."

"What? Never kissed him? You've kissed all the boys in Tahoe and probably at the university. What's wrong with him?"

"There's nothing wrong with him, mother. We're just friends, just very special friends. We do lots together. We talk a lot. I feel closer to him than anyone outside of the family. But we're just friends, that's all."

Her protestations raised questions in her own mind that she had repressed to maintain the tenor of their relationship. She rose to leave. Connie put restraining hands on her daughter's shoulders and stared intently into her eyes. "You're so much 'in like' and you're so warm hearted. Tell me honestly, haven't you considered for even one moment how it would be to kiss him – to feel the stir of romance – and more?"

Kim searched her memories for incipient sparks with Cody. There were none. "Honestly, Mom, he is just the most wonderful friend. He makes me feel good about myself. Sometimes my spirits soar and I feel as though we're flying when we dance. I can sit with him for hours just watching frogs and butterflies and birds. We can even listen to the plants grow and be fascinated. He makes me feel like a part of everything about me. But Mom, it's not directed at him. It's more like he gives wings to a spiritual essence within me."

"Is he homosexual? He's sensitive to so many things, he makes your spirit soar and yet there's no sexual attraction between you."

"No way. He never mingled with that crowd at school and they're indifferent to him."

"What then? Is he asexual?"

Kim laughed aloud. "And you danced with him?"

Her mother looked sheepish. "You're right. Just testing. He's strong and confident and masculine. He's like a lion. You look and admire his strength and maleness, but you don't feel attracted. Maybe he's just not for us Westing women."

"Don't sweat it, Mom. I enjoy what I have with Cody. I don't need a boy friend like Kenny Merer again to turn my brains to mush. Remember the crush I had on him at fifteen?" She giggled, and then gagged at the memory. Connie laughed along with her. The worry, contention and embarrassment had faded over the years. They hugged and parted for bed.

Cody and Kim

Kim slipped out of bed in the pre-dawn quiet, washed up for morning, then tapped on Cody's door and entered. He was sitting in bed without pajama top, reading a National Geographic. She stood in the doorway in her flannel nightgown and regarded him bemusedly. His eyes questioned this early visit. She surveyed his conventional good looks – nothing remarkable. Wide spaced and deep set eyes; a nose that was short and a trifle broad; full lips; a short chin; flat cheeks; and, broad, strong teeth. Sturdy neck, shoulders of medium width, and an absence of bulky muscles on arms or chest. Detail by detail, just middling in appearance. Yet, somehow, there was a composite impression of solidity, strength and self-confidence.

"Good morning, Cody. This is a big day on the slopes. We start early and work late. All the weekend warriors are out today." Cody threw back the covers to rise. Kim sat on the bed beside him. She bent to kiss him, and then lay beside him propped on her left elbow. She put her right hand on his chest and looked down at him, a question in her eyes.

"We've known each other four months now." She paused. He nodded encouragingly, wondering where she was headed. "I like you more than anyone I know. I enjoy your company doing almost anything. I'm amazed at your insight and understanding of people, animals, our environment, and particularly me. I really look forward to seeing you. And yet there's no spark of romance between us. It puzzles me." He tried to formulate a reply but she silenced him with a gesture.

"I'm not hurt, Cody, just puzzled. I've necked with boys who didn't attract me at all – and sometimes they got me pretty hot. Dancing with you, I've felt as though we're one person soaring to some kind of high. Then we finish with a platonic kiss on the cheek—and," she smiled, "maybe a pat on the other cheeks. With all that we've got, all the shared affection and excitement, shouldn't there be just a little romance?" Cody searched for a reply.

Kim swung her feet onto the bed and turned over to lie partially on him. She placed his hand firmly on her breast and pulled his body against hers.

"Kiss me," she commanded gently, and placed her lips on his. He hesitated an instant, then pulled her closer with his other arm and pressed his lips firmly to hers. She felt a common surge of tenderness and affection that circulated through them both. Her hand grasped his buttocks to draw him closer. She could feel his firm body against the whole length of hers. Warmth and security and love flowed between them.

But not passion.

The power of their embrace lessened. Their lips disengaged and they laid their cheeks together. His hand slid around to her back; her hand moved up to his back. They lay there embracing for several short moments while sorting through their emotions. Her futile attempt to generate passion and his minimal attempt to respond faded away. An underlying warmth remained that she at last defined. It was mother's love that had enveloped her as a child and even now served as a refuge from her troubles. Kim raised her head and recognized a similar comprehension in Cody's eyes, plus apprehension about its meaning for their relationship. She kissed him gently on the lips and then raised herself on her elbow.

"I love you, Cody, and I always will, but I'm afraid that we're not destined to be lovers. Be my best friend." The crisis in their relationship passed, a crisis that had troubled him in prospect.

He kissed her lightly in return. "You are my best friend, Kim, and I'll always be yours." A shadow of concern lay in his eyes. When the warm glow for their mothers had supplanted the abortive attempt at passion, he had not envisioned Marly as his refuge. Indistinctly, he had seen a shorter, darker woman with sad eyes gazing down at him. Who was she?

The three boys opened the ski shop and prepared for the morning rush. After the set-up Cody was free to ski while Terry and Jeff outfitted their customers. Cross-country instructions were being given to a group of novices by Johnny Linfeld, a pro who worked out of the Westing's shop. He beckoned the newcomer to join his group.

"Fall in, Cody! Enjoy some real scenery, peace and quiet. See this wonderland at a slow pace, as it should be seen, not at breakneck speed while schussing down a manicured slope." In response to the invitation, Cody joined them in limbering up exercises and then in the rhythmic cross-country routine of slide, slide, push with the poles and glide. The array of novices pushed off with the precision of a Laurel and Hardy comic routine. Tangled skis and poles plus inadvertent turns produced a traffic jam on the flat practice field. Johnny's patient determination restored order. In fifteen minutes the platoon coordinated their moves like seasoned veterans. Johnny signaled for attention. "Great form, team! Now peel off from the right in single file behind me. Aare Kinisalo will bring up the rear. Let's go!"

He led the way at an easy pace along the base of the slope and then in among the trees. His students followed, straining to match his leisurely pace. Cody joined the end of the line and Aare fell in behind him.

Cody's awkward motion quickly gained in gracefulness as he picked up the rhythm. Aare corrected his form and soon he was gliding along the trail with minimal effort. The glide became as natural as walking so that he could drink in the scenery without worrying about the placement of his feet. Deep snow blanketed the ground. Lodgepole pines covered the slope and limited the view until a clearing was reached. Then the grandeur of the mountains provided the perfect backdrop for soaring dreams of unbounded freedom, limitless fields of virgin snow, and fresh air tanged by the scent of pine. Much too soon they exited the pines back at the foot of the beginners' slope. The lesson had ended but the exultant expressions on the faces of the class said that the cross-country experience had just begun. Johnny and Aare shook hands with each pupil and told them that group trips were posted in the ski shop for most weekends. For the more dedicated and experienced, extended camping trips were organized monthly. Part of the group went back to the ski shop; some took the rope tow up the beginners' slope and the rest headed for the lodge and hot drinks.

Cody practiced his technique on the level field. On the road he observed several boys racing easily along with ice-skating strides. He pushed out onto the road, mimicked their actions, and promptly sat down hard on the heels of his skis. The boys passed him going in the opposite direction.

"Fill in your sitzmark!" yelled one boy, pointing to the indentation his backside had left in the snow. Observing them closely, he realized that they were leaning forward to shift their weight centers ahead of their feet. Rising again, he scraped snow into the sitzmark and then skated ahead with altered technique. He glided forward as easily as they. Stopping short obviously required using the ski edges. He lifted the heels of his skis, made a quarter turn jump and dug in the edges. He stopped short as he had intended, but lying on his side rather than standing. Another technique modification was needed, he realized.

The blast of a car horn swiveled his head to glance behind him.

"Better hop in, Cody. The condors might mistake you for a road kill," teased Kim.

The road kill sat up, loosed his bindings, and sheepishly loaded himself and his skis into the vehicle. "You caught me at an inglorious moment, Kim. You should have come when I was skimming over the snow like an arctic owl."

"Sorry I caught the inglorious landing. It's noon. I've brought lunch for you guys. After that, I'm free to join you on the slope."

The boys were too busy to eat. Kim and Cody helped them until the crowd dwindled. They ate quickly and headed out the door.

"We'll be back at four to catch the afternoon rush," she called to her brothers.

Cody led the way to the trail. "Cross-country," he informed her. "Johnny and Aare took me with their class today. I loved it."

"Lead on," she responded. Cody headed into the trees with a smooth rhythmic pace. He lost himself in the cadence and pushed along effortlessly on the now familiar trail. The cold air on his face, the patches of sunshine and shade, the scent of pine, and the faint soughing of the wind through the tree tops all served to unite him with this environment. He entered the first view clearing and was halted by the grandeur of the mountain view. Kim pulled up beside him moments later. "I never tire of these mountain vistas. I know that I could never live anywhere else, not for long."

After several minutes, Cody pulled his gaze from the distant peaks. He turned his skis up-trail. "Ready?"

She poled past him. "Let's go at my speed. Either those two are the greatest teachers or you're a fast learner. You had me sweating to keep pace."

They continued at a more leisurely pace that allowed for greater appreciation of the woods they traversed, with snow crystal and icicle decorations on every branch. Sun glints and rainbow colors of prismatic refraction scintillated across the stark black and white background of the tree trunks and snow. Cody lost himself in the magic of the surreal landscape. The trees flashed by, but now they were dripping rain. The snow turned to mud. He was running. Someone was gaining on him. He must hide… hide completely.

"Cody! Cody!" He flattened himself in his shelter and remained quiet.

"Cody! Are you all right?" A hand shook him by the shoulder. He could hide no longer. He opened his eyes to see a strange girl staring anxiously.

"Are you all right? What happened?" She rubbed snow on his face. Snow! What happened to the rain and mud? He sat up and looked around, felt the snow, and stared hard at the strange girl.

"It's me! Kim. Are you all right, Cody? Say something."

Recognition returned to his eyes. Skiing… cross-country… incline… Kim. No one was chasing him. He struggled out from under the fallen tree and shook off the snow. He was twenty feet off the ski trail. Everything worked. Nothing hurt.

"I'm okay, Kim." He headed back to the trail.

"What happened? You sped up, left the trail, and skied right under that tree. Then you didn't recognize me. What happened?"

He faced her. "I must have been daydreaming. Everything was different. Warmer weather, pouring rain, deep mud. Someone was chasing me. I hid under the tree to escape. Then you called. You weren't part of my dream so I didn't recognize you. Now I'm awake. And confused."

"Has this happened before?"

"No. Not exactly. But you know how sometimes, if we listen closely, we think that we can see and hear and feel what birds and animals sense? This had that feeling of virtual reality."

"What does it mean, Cody?" she asked with concern.

"I don't know. Maybe it happened to someone else here and I'm sensing his or her vibrations. Maybe it happened to me. Most likely it's only a dream."

She put her arms around him. "I'm always here for you. Never forget it."

He felt her warmth and caring enfold him as it had this morning, just like a mother's love. A nagging thought from his dream struck him. His pursuers stole his mother's love – but the hazy mother figure was not Marly.

They arrived at the ski shop in time to check in the rented skis and boots, and to make last minute sales to the snow bunnies. Confusion ruled as the party mood took over before the weekenders headed home to the flatlands. Terry distributed discount tickets for food, drink and future ski trips. The jovial crowd vied for tickets and dispersed to their *après* ski partying.

Kim's arrival brought cheers from school acquaintances who hugged, kissed and invited her to join them that night. She begged off because of a family get together but promised to drop by all the popular watering holes during the evening. Cody kept busy in the back to avoid the mob scene at the counter. After the torchlight parade, business dropped off to a few stragglers. Kim and Cody drove home to clean up, leaving her brothers to close the shop.

"Hi, kids," Howard greeted them at the door. "How was the skiing?"

"Super, Dad!" bubbled his daughter. "You should have seen Cody. One lesson from Johnny and he goes cross-country like a Finn ski trooper. I'm proud of him."

Howard looked to Cody who commented, "She called my technique 'early road kill' at one point." Her father roared while Kim told him about finding their guest flat on the road when she first arrived.

"I'm going back to the town store," Howard told them as he donned his jacket. "Your mother will come home to clean up and change, then we'll all go to the chalet for dinner. Okay with you?"

"Perfect. We can dance there for a while, then Cody and I will barhop to see everybody."

"Good. Connie and I can get to bed early."

"We'll be home before midnight, Dad."

"Have a good time." He kissed her cheek.

Kim led the way upstairs. "*Après* ski wear tonight, Cody. Casual. And shoes you can dance in." She finished her shower and went down to the kitchen to make coffee. Her mother came in as she started back upstairs. Connie eyed her daughter. "Where's Cody?"

"In his shower." Her mother's eyebrows arched. "And you're running around in bikini and bra? It seems you two are always in pajamas and undies. Are you sure there's nothing going on?" A smile softened the interrogation.

"Oh, mother! Cody is someone so special." Her tone softened. "I can't describe how special he is, how sweet, how understanding. I love him. Really. But he isn't my lover, just the friend you find once in your lifetime."

Wistfully, she added, "I wish I could say that we were in love, but we aren't. Can you tell me how to make us fall in love?" Her mother hugged her close.

"I found my one love and my lover in Howard. You have to follow your heart."

Kim looked up moist-eyed. "When he holds me, it's like you holding me, all warm and supportive. When he introduces me to nature, it's like Dad teaching me to ski – he knows and feels things more than I ever could. Sometimes, when I was a little girl, I wished I could grow up and marry Dad. And keep you, too. But I knew I never could. Cody is like that in my heart. I want to keep him forever but I know that it's just as my friend. My dearest friend."

Connie followed her up the stairs. Slim and trim, firm body, wide shoulders and a sleek feminine muscularity, Kim's figure caught male eyes in any setting. She moved with a natural grace enhanced by the discipline of skiing and dancing. Attractive features, flashing smile and an intelligent outgoing personality wrapped up a package that had boys flocking around. So far it had all been youthful camaraderie with several flings at puppy love.

Cody emerged from the shower in his briefs. His tanned body had the sleek suppleness of a seal. No bulging muscles, no knotted veins. A smooth continuity translated from one muscle group to the next, his shoulders sloped gently to his neck. He didn't project raw power, but suggested latent strength flexed beneath a velvety exterior. Connie realized that she viewed them as a matched pair with their sleek bodies and nonassertive muscularity.

Kim glanced down to see her mother watching, then mischievously patted Cody's butt and teased in a stage whisper, "Nice buns!" She darted into her room.

The slap, the comment and the astonished look on her mother's face threw him into embarrassed confusion. Before he could react, the two women vanished into their rooms, leaving him standing in the hall in his underwear. An impression remained that the playful swat expressed Kim's bafflement at the lack of sexual overtones to their relationship. It also carried a daughter-to-mother message that defined the intimacy of that relationship. From Connie he received mixed sensations of mild shock, amusement and then compassion. The episode played out the complexities in a dialogue that made him the medium of their communication.

He went into his room and mulled over this encounter while he dressed. He sought a way to simplify their friendship but none came. He made a statement about their relationship whether he expressed affection or studiously avoided it. Kim and her family and friends interpreted that statement in the light of their own personal and social expectations. He had to resolve this problem.

Connie leaned against her bedroom door, eyes glistening with sympathy for the confusion in her daughter's heart. For the first time affection had gone beyond the superficialities of instant physical attraction and exploratory caresses. Now Kim had the complexities of another personality entwined with her own concepts of romantic love and sexuality. The absence of sexual attraction in this relationship with Cody brought a novelty that may have overemphasized other facets of their attraction. She realized that she had to learn more about Cody. He filled Kim's social life and perhaps blocked her from meeting a man like Howard who could satisfy all her dreams.

A young beer-drinking crowd jammed the chalet, singing and dancing in a festive mood. The "oompah" band in lederhosen and Tyrolean hats kept the room bouncing with German songs. Steaming German dishes filled the tables. While waiting for their table the Westings greeted friends, joined in the choruses and circled the floor with fancy polka footwork.

"C'mon, Cody. Dance time," invited Kim.

"I don't know the polka."

Pulling him onto the dance floor, she directed, "Waltz a little faster," and spun him out into the throng. In a few moments he caught the rhythm, and by the end of the set he whirled her with enthusiasm. "Great!" panted Kim. "Next time, circle to the left to unwind me."

The music commenced. He dutifully circled to the left. One of her friends cut in so she gave Cody parting instructions. "Watch the dancers and pick up more steps. It's a fun dance."

Cody joined the Westings at their table. He caught only brief glimpses of Kim with a different partner every time. A pang of jealousy burned in his chest. He was used to her undivided attention. He knew she was popular but they were nebulous strangers mentioned casually in conversation. Here they were real, handsome, socially adept and monopolizing her. He felt himself to be a minor interest in her full social life. This resonated with a distressed chord repressed in his memory. The Westings, parents and sons, conversed excitedly about acquaintances they had seen during the day, events at the shop and accidents on the slope. Except for a brief recount of his cross-country lesson,

Cody participated little. He caught glimpses of Kim dancing, talking and laughing with friends, the vivacious center of attention.

Cody's thoughts turned darkly to how he would ignore her when she came to the table; never dance with her again; and, shove off early with Jeff to pack for the return to school. In his mind's eye he pictured her sitting disconsolately with her parents in the late evening. Clumsy partners had trampled her toes. She was miserable but ashamed to go home to the friend she had ignored. And he, sleeping contentedly, had already forgotten her. He smiled at the prospect.

"Cody! Why didn't you rescue me? Even with only one step you're better than anyone I've danced with tonight." Kim's voice punctured his reverie. "Why did you abandon me?" Her hand on his shoulder conveyed the sincerity underlying her jesting tone. His daydream dissolved into a petty puddle of baseless jealousy. He knew in transparent shamefulness that she could sense the jumble of discordant emotions sloshing through his psyche. Her teasing tone softened. A warm glow enveloped him as the tender side of her nature came to the fore. She leaned down to speak softly in his ear.

"I'm sorry you feel rejected. I have to be me. I have to fly free. But you're never forgotten, never alone. Not when you're here in my heart."

Two lips touched his cheek and the room pulsed with life again. The odors of the family style serving dishes whetted his appetite. He smiled foolishly at everyone. He knew that this day would never end. It would live in his memory as one that had excited strange emotions and stretched them to their limits. The remainder of the evening blurred past. Savory dishes thrilled his palate. Kim's hip against his at the crowded table reminded him that their fancied emotional rift had vanished. His heart kept time to the oompah beat. When they danced his feet wove new choreography that Kim partnered perfectly. When she danced with others, he saw the beauty of her free movements as he would the graceful flight of a hawk. Only once that evening at another bar did he have to rescue her from a large leaden-footed inebriate who rejected all attempts to cut in. The girl's major annoyance and mild alarm brought Cody angrily to her rescue. His tap on the shoulder buckled the big student's knees. His hand on the elbow propelled the drunk back to his rowdy but concerned friends. They caught the flying body and guided it into a chair with a resounding thud. Several restrained him as he struggled to rise. Two half-rose to break back in on the dancing couple. A table of Kim's local friends swiveled to stare at the rowdy table. The waiters converged on them. The band played louder; the waiters circled the table and sang, "*Ach, du lieber, Augustine*!" The crowd joined in and the dancers stomped heavily to the beat. The tense moment passed in a rousing songfest. Youthful exuberance prevailed.

Driving home, Kim harked back to the incident. "Not too many people toss Karl around the way you did, Cody. He's a super heavyweight on the wrestling team. Pretty good, too. You handled him like a ninety-seven pound weakling. You don't even lift me that easily when we're dancing. How come?"

"I didn't do anything special. He must have been turning and lunging when I pulled his arm. He just sailed off like a Frisbee. It surprised me, too."

"He'll be after you at school. He doesn't take a putdown lightly."

"Thanks for the warning. I'll avoid him."

"You amaze me. With all your unexpected talents, you are the most unassuming person I know. You seem to be deliberately avoiding attention."

The remark bothered him. "You know me better than anyone else. I'm just a country kid from an isolated ranch. I know a lot about nature and the outdoors. I've had little formal schooling. I'm just trying to fit into a new world, Kim. What you see is me. There's nothing else."

She laughed to break the tension. "I know you're not a phony. It's just your unexpected facets." Becoming serious, she added, "Maybe it's frustration with our relationship, too. I like you. I love you. I enjoy being with you. You open up new worlds to me. Yet there's a barrier we can't cross. There's no sexual attraction. Not even in my dreams. Not even when I try to imagine us together." Facing this frustration made her eyes tear.

"I'm sorry, Kim. I've tried to find the passion. It just isn't there. In every other way, you're the most wonderful person I know."

"You're not gay?"

"No. I've never felt romantic towards another man – or woman. Maybe there's no romantic desire in me."

"None at all? Not even a twinge?"

"I do have erotic dreams. About girls. But I can't see them clearly and don't know who they are. And they talk to me without vocalizing, all in a body language that seems familiar to me."

"Like mime?"

"Yes, but much more detailed, full of subtleties and nuances."

"Do you remember any?" she asked with excitement.

"Yes," he hesitated, "but it's like a word on the tip of my tongue that escapes me. I know it but I can't say it. Or do it."

He looked away from her and asked in turn, "Do you dream about men?"

"Oh, yes!" she chuckled. "All the time. Recently you've been getting into my dreams."

"And?"

"Nothing romantic with you, I'm afraid. But when I do get romantic with some hunk, you appear, look disapprovingly and, poof, he's gone." Cody smiled at his role of chaperone.

She continued in a humorous tone. "It's not enough that you chase my boyfriends away in real life. Like tonight. Now you're turning them off in my dreams. You must want me to stay a virgin."

Howard and the boys cooked Monday's breakfast at a leisurely pace. Business at the shops would start late and remain slow. Connie would open the town shop. Kim would go to the slope shop at 9 am. Jeff would go to classes. Howard and Terry promised Cody a sightseeing cross-country tour on the local mountainside after breakfast chores were done. They hurried the others off to work and school, packed the dishes in the dishwasher and in fifteen minutes they were in the basement donning their ski equipment.

Terry broke trail. Cody followed and concentrated on his technique. Howard brought up the rear with encouraging comments on the beginner's progress. After less than a mile, Howard took the lead.

"You're looking great, Cody. Follow me closely, and if you see me do anything that you like, try it. But don't try to copy me exactly. Do it the way that suits you. I think you have the ability to develop your own style. Let's go!"

They glided ahead enjoying the rhythmic motion, the cold clean air in their lungs, the pine odor, and the challenge of the slope. Minor mishaps were frequent, although Cody felt that some were staged by his companions to help him feel better about his own capability. They stopped for tea from their thermos bottles, and then headed downhill for a spectacular view. They were paralleling a precipice when Howard disappeared. A split second later Cody felt himself free falling in a white cloud. When the flight ceased he was entombed in a mass of powdery snow. There was no pain. He could breathe through his scarf. He waited a few moments to orient himself, then moved his arms to clear a hole to daylight. At full length his arms broke through the snow. He worked his feet free of his ski bindings and in a moment was on the surface. Looking back, he could see Terry standing far above him near the edge. Cody waved his arm.

"Where's Dad?" Terry called.

Cody looked about. There was no sign of the father. Relaxing himself, he searched for sign. There was none. The jumbled snow and ice of the collapsed arch gave no clue as to his whereabouts. Scanning with all his senses, he was drawn to a spot fifty feet away near the edge of the fallen snow mass. Digging down, Cody encountered Howard just a foot beneath the surface. He was lying atop a rounded boulder. He had not fallen as gently as Cody. He was unconscious.

Waving his arms excitedly, Cody called, "Here he is! Here he is!" Working carefully, Cody cleared the snow from Howard and then examined him. No broken bones. Numerous bruises. Blood seeping from scrapes. Shallow breathing. Shock, perhaps.

"How's Dad?"

"Unconscious. Nothing broken. Maybe in shock." responded Cody in a calming tone.

"Listen!" shouted Terry. "I'm going for the ski patrol. We need help to get him up the cliff. You keep Dad warm. I'll be back within an hour."

With that he turned and started up the back trail. Cody listened to Howard's breathing. It rattled in his chest. He felt the pulse and found it erratic. He sensed a slow decrease in body temperature. An hour's delay could be serious. He dug into his own exit hole and retrieved his skis. They were serviceable. Looking up at the rocky cliff, he saw that climbing was possible. Alone, he could easily ascend. With Howard along it would be difficult. Cody listened to Howard's breathing becoming more ragged. He touched the man's chest inside his parka and felt the erratic rise and fall. Cody's concern heightened. Panic rose in the back of his mind. He forcibly pushed it back. What should he do? He envisioned himself carrying the man up the cliff face. He selected a chimney that ran the height of the cliff and followed it in detail to the top. It was impossible. Howard was bigger and heavier than he. Howard's breathing rattled. Cody arose and tentatively hefted the unconscious man. He didn't seem heavy. With a quick lift, he hoisted Howard to his shoulders and walked to the foot of the chimney. Putting the man down, he retrieved their gear. At the cliff face, he took two lengths of rope from Howard's pack. He tied one length of rope to a pack, stepped on the end of the rope, and tossed the pack to the top of the cliff. He then secured their skis to the rope. He tossed the second pack to the top. Lifting Howard to his back, he secured him with the second rope. He then started his forty-foot climb. He was amazed at the ease of the ascent despite the burden of his friend. He clambered over the edge and retrieved the packs and skis. Moving to a clear space, he tramped out a message in the snow for Terry, 'A-O-K GONE HOME'

Cody again lashed Howard securely to his back, stepped into his skis and headed for home, hefting the burden. He traveled rapidly but carefully and arrived with no mishaps. He carried Howard to the basement sauna, turned it on, and undressed Howard to give him the full benefit of the heat. That done, he undressed and sat there enjoying the steam, feeling the pain of his own bruises and exertions fade away.

Howard moaned. "Where – where are we? Oh, the sauna." He pulled himself straighter and looked around. "How did we get here? What happened?"

"We fell over a cliff. We climbed out and made it home. Are you okay?" Cody moved over next to Howard and looked him over. "Yes. Yes, I guess so." He moved his limbs, his neck, and twisted his back with just a few grimaces. "Everything seems to work. Everything seems to hurt, too." He glanced at Cody. How about you?"

"Lucky. I fell on a soft spot. You hit on a boulder and were unconscious when I found you. You look groggy still."

"I am, I am. I don't really remember coming home."

"It was a drag. We followed our back trail straight to the ski room and sauna. This heat feels so good."

Howard stretched gingerly. "Where's Terry?"

"He went for the ski patrol. I left a message for him to meet us here." The older man nodded, then leaned back to doze again. Cody did the same. Tiredness was overtaking him. Terry's anxious voice roused them. "Dad! Cody! Where are you?"

The sauna had shut off automatically. It was cool now. Howard went to the door and called back, "We're in the sauna, Terry."

His son burst into the ski room, saw them in the sauna door, and rushed over to embrace his father. "You had me worried, Dad. You were out, Cody's a tenderfoot and help was an hour away. How did you get back?"

"It was a struggle, but we slogged home. It's all hazy until the sauna brought me around. Plenty of aches and bruises but nothing broken."

Two ski patrol medics entered. "Hello, Howard. Terry told us you went over the edge. How are you?"

"I feel okay, Eero. A headache. Sore legs and back. Nothing serious."

"Mind if we look you over?"

"Glad you're here to do it. Ready when you are." After a good visual examination, flexing of the joints, and delicate probing of sore spots, they pronounced him fit.

"Nothing urgent. See your doctor in the morning to be sure." Eero turned to Cody.

"How about you, young man?"

"No problems. I landed on soft snow." A quick once over by the medic confirmed his own evaluation.

"You're lucky guys. How did you get up the cliff and back home?"

Howard hesitated. Cody spoke up. "We found an easy chimney climb, used our ropes to retrieve the equipment and then just backtracked on our trail. The sauna seemed like the best medicine we could have." They accepted the sketchy outline and left. Terry made coffee in the kitchen while they dressed.

The incident diminished to a minor mishap by the time the women arrived for lunch. Short explanations sufficed during the rush when Kim and Cody packed the Bronco and headed back to Reno. They rode in silence for a while, and then Kim stated in a matter-of-fact tone, "You're a space alien. I know that cliff you went over. I learned to climb there. It's a tough climb in good weather. Dad never could do it all banged up. You saved him."

She caught his eye briefly. "I'll never tell. I'll never ask again. But at least I know why we can't be in love." A tear gathered at the corner of her eye and coursed down her cheek. "I really wished we could be in love – sexy love. But I'm glad we have the love we do."

She dropped him off at the Victorian. Her kiss tasted of farewell to a half-visualized idyll. Her embrace betokened a desperate determination to keep tight the bond that did exist.

Howard creaked and groaned as he pulled his pajamas over his patchwork of scrapes and bruises. Connie applied salves and liniment copiously to these souvenirs of the accident, marveling that he had such extensive bruising without serious injury. "You must have tremendous reserves of endurance to recover from that fall, scale the cliff and ski home. It's unbelievable."

Her husband lay there luxuriating in the rubdown and her soothing ministrations. He stared without focusing, trying without success to recall the incident. "It's unbelievable to me, too. I have zero recollection after going over the cliff until I awoke in the sauna. It's not a fuzzy memory as I said downstairs. It's blank."

He turned his head to look at her, grimaced, and turned it back to the pillow. "You know how hard that climb is in good weather when I'm in top shape." He extended his hand. " Hold my hand." He exerted a tremendous effort to squeeze her hand but she barely felt the pressure. "See how weak my grip is in this hand. There's no way I could have climbed that icy rock, even forgetting the rucksack and skis. And I didn't ski home. The left ski binding is broken. Connie was incredulous. "Then how did you get home?"

"I don't know. Cody did it somehow. And he doesn't seem anxious to take the credit."

"Well, he should! If he saved your life everyone should know that he's a hero."

"That's just it, dear. He saved my life. Can I do less than respect his desire for anonymity?"

She mulled this over, "Well we should at least thank him."

"Perhaps we can, by being quiet. He apparently doesn't even want us to know what happened. "We can thank him best by leaving it his secret."

Lost Spirit

Cody felt alienated from everyone in the ensuing weeks. Through his mind kept running questions of identity: who he was, what he was, how he differed from those about him. He felt invisible, detached, standing aside and watching the world parade past. Other couples held hands, walked arm in arm, kissed and merged their emotions. Couples talked seriously and became involved in each other's dreams. Groups formed, shared their feelings and became a social entity for a time before re-forming elsewhere in different combinations to become different entities. He walked alone. He shared with no one. He felt that others were two-dimensional shadows projected on a wall. They looked real from a distance but lost substance as he approached. Even the bull sessions at the Victorian became empty rhetoric, canned opinions voiced by puppets that had never experienced the real world.

When Kim came to the Victorian for theater sessions, she also took on this shadowy insubstantiality. Even when dancing with Kim, he felt as though he was in a dual-faceted costume of man and woman, dancing with himself in a dolorous masquerade. The world was slipping away and he was powerless to embrace it. He worked harder, studied harder, and gardened longer hours. Nothing filled the void or brought the world closer.

The Tallmans and the other residents went to a campus lecture.

Cody mechanically hoed weeds in a *papier-mâché* garden. Nothing stirred, perfumed the air, or vibrated with life. A shadow fell in beside him and silently joined in the gardening. Weeding, clipping and mulching they worked their way to the end of the flowerbed. Cody carried his tools to the shed. His companion followed. They went up the back stairs and entered the kitchen.

"I miss you, Cody."

Kim appeared small and distant as though seen through the wrong end of a telescope. Her voice had the muted tone of distance. Her eyes were hazy and clouded. Woodenly, he responded, "The world seems far away and without value. I don't know if I miss you or not." She turned toward the stairs.

"I'm going to use the guest room tub."

She ran the tub while he took a shower in the hall bath. In a few minutes he wrapped himself in a towel and carried his clothes back to his room.

"Cody! Cody!" called Kim. "Bring me a towel, please." He retrieved a towel from the linen closet and brought it to the bathroom door. He knocked.

"Bring it in, Cody. I'm decent."

He entered to find her immersed in suds, her hair braided high on her head. She extended a hand for the towel. He handed it to her. She took the towel, dropped it with a mischievous smile, and snatched his towel, tossing it across the room. She clasped his hand and pulled him to the tub.

"Come on in. I think we have to reach an understanding."

He stood there, reluctant, but she coaxed again. "This is just between friends. Step in." He stepped in and sank into the suds. Kim turned her back, handed him a scrubbing loofa, and directed, "Now do me. All over."

He tentatively rubbed her back and shoulders, becoming more

enthusiastic as she hummed with pleasure. At last she turned about and held one leg above the suds. "Start with the toes. I'll tell you when to stop."

He smiled for the first time. "This little piggy..." he began, and they burst out laughing. They became hilarious when the fifth little piggy went, "Whee, whee, whee! all the way home."

Her legs and thighs received a good scrubbing. Her arms, shoulders, and stomach followed. "Gently," she cautioned when he reached her breasts. She took the loofa and had him do that soaping by hand. Kim turned around again.

"Nice buns!" joked Cody, reminding her of the Sunday night teasing for her mother's benefit. She dissolved in laughter at that memory. "Oh, Cody! Can you ever forgive me?"

"I'll get even!" he threatened, slapping her buttocks with the loofa. "Don't try to sit down tonight." He finished the rubdown. She slid down into the suds. He rose.

"Please, Cody. Stay."

He hesitated, and then sat down facing her, a look both questioning and apprehensive on his face.

She laughed at his expression. "Cody, you're not the least bit sexually aroused. Neither am I. But we both had a lot of fun and I think we broke through that growing icy wall. I don't know what there is between us. I just know that I can't bear to lose it."

"Kiss me, Cody."

He leaned forward to peck at her lips. She slid forward to press her body against his and kissed him hard and long. She released him and stepped out of the tub. When he followed she stepped up to him, put her hands on his buttocks and pulled him close. Reflexively, he did the same.

Kim looked deeply into his eyes and moved her body forcefully against his. "I want you to remember the touch of my body on yours and the emotions you feel right now." She put her head on his shoulder and held him tight. "When you hold another woman, remember this moment. If this is all you feel, dump her. This you have from me. I want you to find a woman who makes your soul melt and your passion flame." She searched her memory. "The way I felt when I had my first crush on a boy at fourteen – only a thousand times stronger and more mature."

She felt his erection beginning and stepped back hastily. "Don't get hot on my second-hand romance," she chided. "Go build your own memories with that lucky girl." Cody blushed at her insight into his pseudo passion. Momentarily, he had adopted her emotional memory as his own feeling. He toweled her back.

"Thanks for the memory, Kim. Now I know what I'm seeking. I wish it could be you." They dressed and had tea downstairs. Kim then insisted on a dreamy dance in the family room, just to be sure the barriers were down. They lost themselves in the music and the movement as they had done before. A burst of staccato applause and shouts of approval brought them out of their reverie. The lecture crowd stood watching them.

"Beautiful dancing, beautiful!"

"Like Fred and Ginger! Made for each other." Kim and Cody exchanged intimate glances. Not made for each other, perhaps, but they had the next best thing, friendship with thorough understanding.

Schoolwork kept Cody busy as the spring semester advanced. Some landscaping students lost enthusiasm for the university gardens. The remainder shouldered the burden to achieve a beautiful area for informal graduation affairs in June – and a display for their visiting parents.

Anthropology traced the physical and cultural lineage of humans and their relationship with animal and plant life. It demonstrated that knowledge of our cultural past shows rather different life styles among our closest relatives while our genetic lineage includes close relationship with the Neanderthals through cross-breeding, with many people of European ancestry carrying a small percentage of Neanderthal genes. Anatomical and genetic similarities showed a proximate relationship with chimpanzees, but a lineage that was long separate. Fragmentary skeletal evidence indicated a possible hominid evolutionary path covering several million years during which numerous other primate species evolved and vanished into dead ends. Biology and Horticulture demonstrated the potential for breeding dissimilar varieties of the same species but did not clarify how species differentiation occurred. Conversely, it also showed that selective breeding could produce similar appearing varieties of different species. He learned a lot but found that new questions always outnumbered the few new answers in his educational progress. 'Who am I?' remained forefront in his mind. He recognized his inability to cope with abstract mathematical concepts that were second nature to others. He saw, heard, smelled and otherwise sensed biological phenomena that did not exist to his classmates and teachers.

Worse, he could not exhibit or describe these capabilities to others, not even to Kim. Some subconscious block prevented the words from coming, the knowledge from being expressed. Even his physical strength, which could be extraordinary when he was alone, was ordinary when with others. Was he really different or was he a schizophrenic who had developed an overpowering dream existence to compensate for his inadequacies in the real world? Was he hiding something that didn't exist?

Despite these inner conflicts, he did extraordinarily well in chemistry, and developed an interest in how fragrances are sensed and created. He wanted to create and study perfumes. His counselors made him aware of the demand for specialists in perfumery where talent created its own well-compensated niche. His ability to identify scents and recognize the subtle interactions of perfumes with individual body chemistry gradually brought him a small clientele of coeds who sought his advice on the best commercial scents for each of them. At first he made some major blunders when he found that scents that delighted his olfactory senses did not necessarily please other people. His experiments with skunk musk made people turn away. It didn't take long to learn that his preferences for powerful musk were not the norm. He adjusted his recommendations to account for others' odor preferences and soon was modifying commercial brands to suit individual women. To him it was an intriguing game. To the women he was becoming a guru of allure.

Cody's reputation for perfumery extended beyond the campus when one of the women brought samples of several of his modified commercial brands to Langlois' Perfumeries in Reno. The owner asked to meet Cody. The young man's ability to recognize scents and, more importantly, to tailor them for conformity with individual body chemistries led to the offer of a part time summer position at the salon. Cody accepted. He needed to meet more people, especially women. There must be someone out there for him.

Cody heard voices in the Victorian rec room so he picked up a soda in the kitchen and went in to find out the subject of the evening's discussion.

"What did you think of Larribee's paper today? He says that the common ancestor of the primates is not as far back as we thought. DNA analyses show that chimpanzees and orangutans are our close cousins."

"For you, Toby, I'd suggest the gorilla as a closer relative," joked the slender Tomcek.

"*Touché*," grinned Toby, pantomiming a stab wound to the heart, "however, he did mention that chimps can have vocabularies of tens and possibly hundreds of words. Even the ability to construct sentences. All sign language, of course. That seems to put them on a par with some humans."

"Quite subpar," chimed in Huber. "Perhaps a three- or four-year age level."

"You forgot their sense of humor and ability to use simple tools. And the ability to pass on knowledge to their offspring," added Tomcek. "Perhaps better than a three-year-old level."

"Let me ask," Toby proposed, "Would you surgically implant electrodes into the brain of a three-year old cousin of yours and then shock him electrically to see which areas of his brain react?"

"Of course not!" retorted Huber, "But these are animals, not humans."

"They're cousins, Franz. I think it's just the degree of consanguinity that's in question."

"They're animals! They don't reason the way we do. There's no moral basis for not using them in any way to benefit man. Food, clothing, medical experiments. Even sport. Any beneficial way. In a humane fashion, of course."

"Electric shock treatment?"

"Oh, come on, Toby. We don't torture them for no good reason. They are not rational beings."

"Then you must be in favor of abortion?"

"Of course," replied Haber with annoyance. "Up to the age of one or two years, I suppose?" concluded Toby.

"What?"

"And euthanasia for everyone with an I.Q. lower than your magnificent 173?"

"Toby! You're just stretching the limits of our discussion to rile Franz," Tomcek intervened. "What point are you trying to make?"

Toby leaned back and clasped his hands across his stomach. "You're right. The seminar brought together several ideas that bother me. One is the word primate. We are self-designated as 'prime' – number one – so that we are above all other species. Then we call ourselves '*Homo sapiens*'- the thinking hominid. Again we put ourselves above all other species, even other primates. We say that there is no law to protect other species against exploitation. By whose legal system? Ours!"

"That's the way it is," stated Haber smugly. "We're Number One."

"That's fine," agreed Toby. "We're Number One. Perhaps we exterminated the mammoths, the moas, the lemurs, the passenger pigeons, and the Neanderthals. Maybe we'll soon eliminate the elephants, tigers, pandas and other species on our endangered list."

"Maybe so. Man, *Homo sapiens*, and his needs come first, Toby."

Toby pursued his line of speculation. "Aren't there any laws but our game laws to protect other species? If they can reason and communicate, couldn't they pass their own laws to forbid hunting, pollution and even human overpopulation?" Dina Tomcek smiled. Haber guffawed.

"Numero Uno makes the laws. No one else matters. Children don't make laws. Animals, even animals with an IQ of 30, don't make the law. Only '*Homo sapiens*' law for '*Homo sapiens*' benefit counts." Haber poked his index finger into his own chest. "I am the law." Pointing to his temple, he amended, "Or rather, my mind is the law. That's how it has to be. It's Darwin's immutable law of Nature. Survival of the fittest."

Toby relaxed, leaned back, and clamped his hands behind his head. "With those convictions, Franz, I gather that you would gracefully step aside if an indigenous or extraterrestrial species with a superior intellect appeared. Say, an IQ of 1000 or 10,000."

"That's preposterous! We don't even have a test to score at that level!"

"And if their laws allowed them to use *Homo sapiens* for hunting, eating, conducting medical experiments and mounting your head on a wall, you would consider it a natural right of the superior intellect."

Irritably, Haber replied, "You carry everything to extremes. There are no such super-beings. If there will be in the future, they will evolve gradually from us. We'll never notice the change over the next ten thousand or hundred thousand years."

Toby pressed on. "But is gradual evolution of species the rule? Modern Man, *Homo sapiens*, appeared on the scene about 100,000 years ago. Today's seminar interpreted recent findings in the Middle East to say that Neanderthal and modern man cohabited the Middle East for as long as 40,000 years. What happened to the Neanderthals? Some speculate that we killed them off because they were different. Some suspect they were driven off the habitable areas and suffered gradual malnutrition to extinction, since our ancestors did this to each other as well. On the other hand, the latest DNA evidence indicates that there was some crossbreeding between Neanderthals and us, so there are some of their genes in our own population. Maybe there are even purer descendants of Neanderthals among us today? How would we know? A few people believe that the fabled Yeti and Sasquatch, now roaming the Himalayas and the American Northwest, are survivors of Neanderthals or earlier *Homo robustus*. Do you think that *Homo sapiens* could be reduced to a nearly extinct remnant species in several tens of thousands of years?"

Patiently now, Haber expressed himself. "Pre-*Homo sapiens* primates are not humans. Our laws classify them as animals. They have no place in our society. If, and I emphasize that this is a speculative hypothesis, if any such semi-intelligent Neanderthal primates exist, then they might be put on the endangered species list or captured and raised in captivity for biological and psychological studies. That's all."

"And the high IQ species – chimpanzee, porpoise, Neanderthals, super beings? Is that how we treat them, as specimens for study?"

"The animals would again be lab curiosities, as long as they did not threaten us. Any high I.Q. superman would naturally be a part of our society, subject to our laws, so long as he did not threaten us. To some extent, he would also be a lab subject." A pause ensued while Haber smiled self-contentedly over his own arguments. Toby tried to assimilate Haber's ideas into a coherent philosophy. Tomcek waited expectantly for the final clash of ideas. Pasco Tallman had just entered with a coffee and wondered what had led to the last several comments.

Cody, who had been quietly following these concepts new to him, spoke up. "Professor Haber. What gives *Homo sapiens* the right to treat all other creatures as objects to be used without consideration for their feelings and ways of life?"

Reverting to the pedantic, the professor explained, "Intellect, young man, intellect. The ability of *Homo sapiens* to reason in the abstract, to grasp the larger context, to organize and to plan ahead is unique with us. We have the brain, the will and the organized power to control the Earth – and we do, for the benefit of our own species. This is what Nature intended."

"Isn't it strange that Nature has created such a diversity of life forms when the goal was only one dominant form?" mused Cody.

"Not at all. There are multitudinous minor tasks to be performed to maintain the ecology for man," responded Haber.

"Animals plan ahead. Bees build hives and maintain them; beavers build dams to create ponds; whales, birds, eels and even butterflies migrate thousands of miles to have their young in favorable surroundings. Is that not planning?" asked Cody.

"Instinct," responded Haber condescendingly. "They are preprogrammed to follow seasonal cycles. They cannot alter their programs. Man envisions the larger context and acts creatively within that context to attain his long range goals."

Toby chipped in, "What about the use of tools and training the young by chimpanzees?"

"Yes, yes," agreed Haber. "But all this is at the three-year age level. And it does not show appreciation for the broader context and longer range goals." He looked at his watch and rose. "I must prepare my outline for tomorrow's lecture. Thank you for showing me the misconceptions I must overcome in my students." He walked down the porch steps to his car.

After a brief silence, Toby commented, "There goes a reason that I think *Homo sapiens* may become another dead branch on the evolutionary tree."

"He represents main stream thinking," said Tomcek. "I must say that I agree with most of what he says. We cannot sacrifice the welfare of our species for any other species – whether they are below or even above us on some human standard or species-specific IQ scale. We must pursue our own destiny."

Cody spoke up softly. "I think that I prefer the Native American concept of the Hoop of Life. We are all interconnected across species, across space and through time. We must respect one another. Every kind – animal and plant – has its own feelings, emotions and destiny. All together, we are Nature. No one species should have stewardship of all others, or sacrifice the others to its own concept of creation. That would lead only to a sterile world and the end of all life – including *Homo sapiens*. The Ring would be broken."

Pasco stood and nodded in agreement. "The old reverence for all life is gone. The sense of kinship with other species is gone. *Homo sapiens* has conquered all other species and eradicated many. Now *Homo sapiens* is preying on itself with guns, drugs, antibiotic-resistant bacteria, and pollution. It may be a close finish between species suicide and pulling down the pillars of Nature's temple to destroy all life along with itself. Who was it who said, 'I have cried for my people for years. Now I cry for all life.' Are we on our way to oblivion and powerless to stop it?" He went out on the back porch and looked up at the empty sky from the deserted yard. Tomcek joined him. Cody followed and took the railing space between them. The emptiness of the night absorbed the lonely cries of their souls. Cody placed his hands on top of theirs and listened for the night sounds. A frog croaked. A nighthawk twittered. A bat squeaked above the human sound range, but they heard it. A moth's wings flapped. An earthworm crawled through the garden loam. The petals of a flower closed. They joined the rhythms of the night. The Hoop of Life was not yet broken. Perhaps it need not be.

Search for Identity

Seth picked Cody up at the Victorian on Thursday for his monthly long weekend at the ranch. The road north carried him back in time. They detoured from the highway to visit Arrah's school, talk to the teachers and children, and inspect the latest improvements to the garden. Driving the access road to the ranch brought back the enfolding warmth of five generations of family history. Best of all, Marta welcomed him on the porch with hugs and kisses.

The steamy warmth of the kitchen was fragrant with favorite dishes for dinner. She placed cookies and hot tea on the table so they could hear of his latest adventures in college while enjoying the congeniality of a family snack. It brought back memories of breaks from chores when they came in from the cold to rest and chat. "How's school?" she signed and spoke. "How is Kim? When are you going to bring her for a visit? Are you comfortable at the Victorian? Do you get enough good food? How are Pasco and Maria? Are you making friends? Is your garden finished? How's your perfume job?"

Cody smiled at the barrage of questions. He put down his tea and combined vocalization for lip reading with signing to give her all the details.

"Kim is a very good friend. She can't come until after Spring Break when skiing falls off at Incline. You'll love her. And her family."

Tripod rubbed against his leg to register her notice of his arrival and to condescend to be stroked. He leaned down to pick her up but she rolled away from his grasp and presented her head again for stroking. Half a dozen strokes sufficed. She sprang onto a chair and then to the counter to her window position from which she could survey the yard. One cocked ear indicated that she deigned to listen to the familiar tones of his voice.

"The Victorian is great. We share cooking and chores. Our guests are sometimes good cooks and bring new recipes to our menu. To Maria and Pasco we're all family. I have more friends there than I do at school. And I learn more from the discussions at night in the family room than I do in most classes. Both gardens – school and the Victorian – are looking good, even for winter. When they're in full bloom in spring you'll have to come see them."

He paused to get his breath. "Langlois is great. He knows a lot about scents and compatible blends. He thinks some of my ideas are far out, but he listens. He knows what his clients will buy. But my nose is better than his. I can name minor traces of essences in a blend that he can't even detect. He says he will teach me to handle clients when I can work full time in the summer."

"Full time?" his grandmother echoed with dismay. "We thought you would work at the ranch. There's a lot to do."

"I suppose you do have to start thinking about a career," his grandfather temporized, "but we could use your help."

"It's not really full time," responded Cody, trying to allay their fears that he would be deserting them the way Marly had. "He wants me just Wednesday through Friday plus 10 am until 2 pm on Saturday. I'll be home from Saturday afternoon until Wednesday morning, if you can drive me to work by 10 am, Grandpa. I'll be home more than half the time."

Marta's fear of losing him was not allayed. Cody sensed that she was looking for more personal reassurance of their family ties. "It's all adventurous, but it's not home. It's not you and grandpa; it's not the ranch, the fields, the orchard, the garden and waterfalls. It's not our quiet mountains. It's not our animal friends, Tripod...." He was interrupted by an uncharacteristic gravelly meow that came from the matriarch, who had turned her gold-flecked eyes upon him. Marta put her hand over his. "We all miss you, Cody. Every day comes alive when the rays of the morning sun gently awaken each plant and animal in turn, giving them their moments of meaning and glory. You are our morning sun. You make us aware of our own individuality and hint that something special will happen this day."

Cody took his grandfather's hand also and gently squeezed. "And you are my family. No others make me feel like this."

Loud neighing and barking from the barn area caught their attention. "The rest of the family is calling for attention, too," observed Seth. "We'd better go out with a few treats in our pockets."

Greeting the animals was a ritual. Old Dark Eyes was on the porch ready to sniff Cody, have her head caressed and then lead them to the barns. At the foot of the steps Stalker and Mischief respectfully but all atremble waited for permission from Dark Eyes to approach for their caresses – and a bone apiece. As the coterie approached the barn, the cats came forward to rub briefly against the men's legs, accept their treats, and then strut ahead of them with tails held high. At the field gate the horses stood with heads over the rail, whinnying and snorting with excitement. Cody felt the sensation of galloping across the fields with the wind of passage riffling his hair when he stroked Can Can's muzzle. Sugar cubes and handfuls of oats disappeared quickly. A cow mooed in the field and her calf scampered around her.

The men assimilated the sights and sounds of their home and the subtle vibrations of its harmony. "This will always be home to me, Grandpa. It's so peaceful, far from the noises and smells and chaos of the city. Here I can listen to individual sounds. The clean air lets me identify and savor each scent. The absence of crowds and humming machines lets me feel the fundamental vibrating chords of the Earth and the gentle harmonies of each living thing, the harmonies that play together to compose the symphony of life. In the city I can be lonely in a crowd because individuals are drowned in the din. Here, I can focus on one at a time and feel companionship in what city dwellers might see as an empty land."

"Then why do you go to the city? You have a home and your life's occupation here on the ranch. As the only heir it will be yours when we die. You'd be the fifth generation Hoag on this land. You love it and care for it. Would you want it to go to an uncaring stranger?"

"I don't know what I want, Grandpa. My mind is filled with questions – about the world, about people, and especially about me. Who am I and how do I fit in? Only by meeting other people, talking to them and living among them can I find answers."

Seth looked away toward the distant peaks. He spoke slowly and softly, his hands providing an unconscious emotional background for the soft tones. "Everyone harbors questions about the meaning of life and death. Answers may be hard to find among crowds of people bursting with questions. Many wise men have gone to the solitude of the mountains and desert to seek wisdom. Most have returned more humble. A few have returned wiser."

"How can they find wisdom where there are no people?"

"Within themselves. Every creature has its own wisdom given at conception by Mother Nature. We used to call it instinct but nowadays they call it genetics. Each of us is given a store of unconscious knowledge about how to grow and assemble the body from cells, how to make cells function together as a unit, how to assume a specific role in Nature and perform predestined tasks. Beyond that our heritage must include knowledge of how to think and spiritual knowledge of what is morally right to harmonize with Nature. You may find external knowledge by watching others. I think that true wisdom of mind and spirit can only be found within yourself."

His grandfather's depth of perception surprised Cody. For the past eight years he had seen Seth laboring in the fields and barns with uncomplaining fortitude. Now he perceived the underlying philosophy that put him in tune with his environment. He played a supportive role on the ranch that enhanced the environment and from this enhancement respectfully drew a portion for himself. In many ways his concepts followed the precepts of the Native Americans.

"How can I discover the wisdom and morality that you say I have stored within me, Grandpa? What did you do?

"I think that you must seek answers in contradictions, Cody. You must seek the infinite in the microcosm of your cells. You must seek companionship in loneliness. You must seek complicated solutions in simple truths. You must learn about yourself from others – and about others from within yourself. You must learn about the breadth of this moment from the depth of yesteryears. You must learn about God from man and about man from God. You must see your questions as answers and your answers as new questions."

"But Grandpa, what you have said is self-contradictory. We have a word for that in college. An oxymoron."

Seth smiled. "That's a good word for Life. How can life be constructed of non-living elements? How can we isolate ourselves from other entities when we exchange the air we breathe, the germs and viruses, the food and excrement, every moment of our lives? We are individual but we are one. You have inherited more of me than I could ever tell you. Go to the mountain. You are the product of all your ancestors. You store all their wisdom and more. Each year you add to it. When you pass it on to your children be sure that it is a fruitful inheritance. It will last until the end of humankind."

"That's a heavy burden, Grandpa. Not only will my children copy my looks but they will carry my knowledge, my morals and my relationship with the world."

"Yes, Cody, it's a great responsibility to think about on the Mountain. You carry the burden of my years and those of our forebears. What you create in your children may be our Heaven or our Hell. You are your own immortality. And ours.

Dinner talk was limited that night. The burden of his ancestors and the responsibility for his descendants occupied Cody's thoughts.

After dinner, he told his grandparents, "I'm going for a long ride tomorrow. I have to shake off the city and school life, and get my thoughts straight." Marta looked a question to Seth, who signed, 'Finding himself.'

They said grace, did the dishes and went to the living room. Seth read briefly from the Bible. For what doth it profit a man if he gains the whole world and suffers the loss of his own soul?" Cody interpreted that as encouragement for him to seek wisdom within himself rather than in urban sophistication. And in what corridors of his mind were these memories buried? How could he gain access to them? Could he discriminate true ancestral memories from borrowed memories such as Kim's erotic remembrances?

He slept fitfully that night. The early spring morning was cool and dewy. Can-Can was frisky as they angled across the northern slope of the valley towards the higher peaks. At the edge of the trees he sent Stalker and Mischief home. He needed to be alone with his memories. Cooler air above the tree line led him to dismount and free his horse to select her own path. The walking rhythm and concentration on the terrain allowed his deeper thoughts to wander freely. He hoped that travel through unfrequented byways of his mind would uncover memories of his early life that had so far eluded him. Perhaps these memories would help him understand the differences between himself and other people. The acuity of his senses; his physical strength and agility that functioned only when he was unobserved; his rapport with nature; the missing sexual attraction in his life; and, his inability to discuss these things with anyone else.

Was he an *idiot savant*, a schizophrenic or a freak of nature? Should he ask doctors and scientists to examine him? Should he isolate himself on the ranch and live a lonely life away from the world peopled with cardboard cutouts?

An aluminum beer can under his foot interrupted his thoughts. It was shiny and new. The ground was pockmarked around it. A quick glance picked out several shell casings. Cody searched the vicinity and found deeply ridged tire tracks past a small rise. An off-road vehicle had been here. The direction of the tracks showed they had come in on the fire road from the east. Remembering the three truculent vagrants he and Seth had run off several years ago, he wondered if they were trespassing again. Closer examination indicated that the tracks were a week old. He crushed the can and put it in his saddlebag. Though he put aside thoughts of the intrusion, he no longer felt the same sense of tramping alone in empty mountains to find himself. The snow line was not far above when he turned into a small canyon to savor the luxury of being alone. He had been here before; it was a special place. The entrance was a narrow vertical fault in a red rock wall. This slit zigzagged through the rock in short runs before finally opening into a grassy bowl dotted with boulders fallen from its walls. Water trickled from the far wall into a stream that ran into a pond at the center of the bowl. The runoff went underground and exited by the slit he had entered. It surfaced again on the lower slope.

He removed Can-Can's saddle and bridle to let her drink and graze. The overwhelming sensation that he experienced in Reno of noise on every sensory path always diminished when he returned to the ranch. That impinging cacophony diminished several orders of magnitude further when he entered this canyon. The red walls and restricted view blocked the emissions of the exterior world and magnified the bio-vibrations of nature in this chamber. He sat facing north and gazed at the few snow-covered peaks visible above the canyon walls. Stately in their broad-shouldered stolidity and dignified in their white capes, these were the slowly changing memories of Mother Earth. They recorded on their flanks the transient impacts of recent seasons, storms and drought, and the short-term restless movements of the planet's surface. Deeper rock strata and faults recalled ever more ancient orogenic processes that laid down the strata over the eons and jumbled them in short cataclysmic upheavals. Throughout the strata could be found fossil records of the ephemeral biological species living in each era.

"Where to look?" he wondered. He leaned back against a rock and relaxed his body element by element. He ignored external stimuli. He directed his attention inward to hear the breath in his lungs, the beat of his heart and the surge of blood through his vessels. He diminished this physical awareness and focused on an imagined core of his being. A hall led off to the compartments of his mind. A corridor branched to his library of memories. Moving into alcoves, he could recapture recent memories in detail. These memories were nearly transparent so that older memories could be discerned in the background, waiting to be recalled and reinforced. He moved slowly, enjoying the detailed cameos of Kim, the Victorian, the University, Arrah's school, ranch life, the Hoags, Marly, and a terrifying drive in her van through a raging storm.

There were no further transparencies in the background. The corridor of memory ended. He searched frantically for another path, rounded a corner, and was back in the core of his being. He strove to move back to his memories to no avail. His calm was destroyed. His pumping heart became a thumping drum. Stiff muscles begged to be unlimbered. A vagrant breeze played in his hair. Can-Can nickered. The cool of evening descended. He awoke perplexed.

Why did his chain of memories begin with a rainstorm? What had happened then? What was his previous life? He ate a cold supper and slipped into his sleeping bag. The constellations spun around the pole but he found no answer written in the stars.

Nor in his dreams.

Instead, he found more questions that night and the following morning as he became better acquainted with his own recent life. His differences from other people became more noticeable as he pulled these memories from his files and assembled them. In fact, was he even "human"?

Physically, he appeared to be a middling specimen of the human race in size, countenance, build and musculature. When among others his strength and agility were average. When alone or in an emergency situation where his actions would go unnoticed, his strength and endurance greatly surpassed that of any men he had seen. He thought at times that it was wishful thinking that he had carried Howard up the cliff and skied home with him on his back. He had effortlessly thrown a big wrestler across the dance floor. He had emplaced boulders in the ranch water system that Seth could not budge. Yes, evidence existed of extraordinary strength and agility but this power was subconsciously repressed when he was among others. Another area of difference lay in his sensory capabilities. His sense of smell was sharper and more discriminating than that of anyone he knew. He could immediately recognize anyone he had ever met by body odor alone. He could also detect fear, anxiety, emotional distress and some illnesses. No one else he knew could do that.

In parallel, his palate was also more discriminating than that of his friends. His vision was not sharper than the best of his acquaintances but he knew that he could see much better in low light levels. Warm bodies stood out clearly in darkness, indicating that his eyes were sensitive to infrared radiation. His hearing was also acute and extraordinarily selective. He could remember bird and animal sounds and correlate them with individuals. In most cases he could mimic these sounds exactly. Human voices were very informative. Better than most people he recognized voices and accents immediately. Beyond that, he could read the emotional state of a speaker from stressed overtones. These were all examples of capabilities much better than those exhibited by above average humans. Still, individuals could be very strong, have keen eyesight, acute hearing, and be very discriminating in taste and smell.

His ability to detect and categorize electric fields from animals, inanimate objects and electrical systems seemed quite rare in humans. Numerous fish and some birds sensed electric and magnetic fields. Come to think of it, water dowsers probably sensed electromagnetic field variations when detecting water. Body language contributed much to communication by supplying emphasis and the nuances of attitude to the vocalizations. Animals made extensive use of it. Humans largely ignored it whether they were talking or listening. He often found human body language confusing because it did not corroborate spoken words. Humans had hidden motives that they sought to conceal from others in this confused babble of communications. The popularity of games such as poker probably stemmed from the need to practice this technique of concealment and misdirection. He had tried poker at Reno's casinos but quickly dropped it. Reading the body language of other players made winning akin to stealing. The cacophony of sound, light, odor and electrical pulsations made playing a torture.

Entering rapport with other people and animals was not usual among humans. Through rapport he could share sensory impressions, emotions and memories. This had been especially strong with Kim and Quiet Fox. When alone he often entered rapport with animals. Rapport experiences enhanced his belief in the unity of all Nature that the Native Americans called the Hoop of Life. Cody finished this enumeration of what he considered positive differences. Significant negatives also existed. He found that his senses were often overwhelmed and jammed in crowded environments. Lights were too bright, noises too loud. Manufactured chemical pollutants paralyzed his olfactory sense. Interfering electric fields disoriented him. Strong spices and sauces masked the subtle tastes of most foods. Chemical insecticides and additives upset his digestive system and caused allergic reactions. Even tap water could be sickening. Devotion to organic food and ranch fresh spring water had become his rule. Reading body language took on the aura of invasion of privacy because humans wanted to hide so much of their lives, emotions and motives. Rapport was limited because people were afraid to see into themselves and experienced the guilt of voyeurs when peering into the souls of others. Being sighted in the realm of the blind carried a burden of shame rather than joy for a gift. Mental differences connoted defects. He retrieved physical sensations, correlations and concepts as experiences and images. Abstract reasoning, particularly in mathematics, had no niche in his storage system. Did these mental differences make him an *idiot savant* wired in a new way? Had some abstract processor been omitted from his brain or atrophied due to his mother's drug habit?

Emotions puzzled him. He loved the Hoags and shared their feelings about many things. Pleasing them was his pleasure. His mother Marly left a blank in his emotional memories. Thinking of her brought not the least tinge of affection or dislike. Kim he loved. Maria and Pasco he loved. He had respect and admiration and an undefined affection for Quiet Fox. He could love other people.

Kim attracted him most of all his female contemporaries. She was physically ideal, outgoing and affectionate, and danced beautifully. She was straightforward and honest in word and body language. She entered rapport without fear of revealing her inner self. She returned his love. She wanted them to be sexually attracted to each other. They weren't. Love and sexual attraction were separate. Only vicariously, through

Kim's memory of her first infatuation, had he experienced sexual attraction. Was there somewhere a woman for him or was he also missing the genes for sexual attraction?

The sun warmed the canyon wall. Cody arose and washed. He resumed his seat by the rock and made his breakfast on bread, water and an apple. He reviewed last night's memory search. If the answers to his questions lay within his memories, they were not now accessible. The key to his self-knowledge must lie elsewhere. Marly might have told him of his birth and early life, but she was gone. Quiet Fox presented an enigma. She hinted that she might know something about his life prior to the Hoag's ranch. He decided to ask Arrah to arrange a meeting with her. In his earliest memory, he rode with Marly through a cloudburst. Pines lined the roadside. Lightning flashes occasionally illuminated a large lake lying to the right of the road. They drove through scattered settlements and small towns. They reached the Hoag ranch in less than half a day. Marly dropped him off and continued her journey north. They might well have been driving up the west shore of Lake Tahoe! Cody examined closely his eidetic memory of that ride. He was naked and wrapped in a blanket. His soaking wet clothing lay underfoot. Marly leaned over the steering wheel and peered intently down the constricted tunnel cut through the deluge by the headlights. She feared the dark, the winding route and the runoff streams slewing the truck across the road. His hand on her shoulder communicated to her feelings of calm and confidence. Delving deeper into that memory, he realized that Marly was a stranger. Filial attachment was absent. He pitied her for the pressure she was under. She needed his calming hand to fit her for driving. His hand! It touched dry hair! Marly had not been out in the storm as he apparently had. When they unloaded at the ranch, she had a load of her clothes to wash. His only clothes lay sodden in rags on the floor.

It all fit together. Marly was not his mother! She had picked him up on the road. He was a lost child, possibly an orphan whose parents had been washed away. Somewhere there must be relatives and friends who had known them. He must find them.

He rode back to the ranch faster than he had ridden up the mountain. He had a mission now. He would find out who he was, what he was and perhaps why he was. First he must ask Arrah to contact Quiet Fox. Next he would seek his earliest memory at Lake Tahoe. Perhaps from there he could take the next step into his past.

Backtracking

This is Tahoe City," announced Kim. "If your mother – Marly Hoag – was headed for the ranch from the west side of the lake, she would have stayed on Route 89 at least to Interstate 80. That means she would have left the lakeshore here. She must have picked you up between here and Camp Richardson where Route 89 leaves the lake at the south end. That's a 25-mile stretch to survey. She flashed an exasperated glance to Cody. "Don't you have any landmarks to delimit our search?"

"I've told you all I can remember. It was a terrible storm. Rain, wind, washouts. We passed through a couple of small towns before Tahoe City."

"Homewood and Meeks Bay. That cuts our search in half."

"It seemed a long way to the first town. We traveled slowly. Marly was terrified. Being washed into the lake was a real possibility."

"Okay. Let's go to Camp Richardson and backtrack. Call up your memories again and search for clues." Cody relaxed in his seat, cleared his mind, and relived the events of that chaotic night. He was in the van, standing at Marly's shoulder. Reverting further, he awakened beneath a scratchy blanket on a bunk that tossed and swayed. Where was he? He remembered being washed from beneath a fallen tree by a mighty gush of water that lifted him through the air to fall jarringly on a flexible metal surface. That thought disappeared. He re-ran it over and over looking for clues. The tree was on a hillside. He was hiding. The downpour was like a waterfall. Thunder rolled incessantly. Lightning tore through the night. Gunshots roared nearby. Gunshots? Then a great wave lifted the tree and spurted him from beneath it. He arced through the air. A lightning flash showed a small parking area with a lone van. He crashed again on the resilient metal. The memory blanked. He felt the rough blanket, the tossing bunk, and wondered, "Where am I?"

A hand shook his shoulder. "Wake up. We're at Camp Richardson, turning around. Keep your eyes open." He opened his eyes and looked confidently into Kim's. "We can find the place, now. I remembered more." Her eyes widened in surprise and elation. "Oh, Cody! I'm so happy for you. I feared this would be a wild goose chase. What have you remembered?"

"The place she found me is a small turnout on the left side of the road heading north. It's cut into the hillside so that the back is a vertical drop of fifteen feet or so. How many turnouts are there?"

She spun the wheel and crossed the road into a turnout. "Quite a few, I'm afraid," she sighed. "The whole lake area fills with tourists and campers in the summer." They proceeded north with frequent disappointing pauses. After a brief glance, Cody shook his head at each. Their elation diminished. Another turnout and another. Kim wheeled in and out continuously. Another turnout. Cody halted his reflexive headshake and signed for a stop. He stepped out and gazed up at a massive tree root jutting out over the parking lot from the hillside above. He grinned with satisfaction. "This is it, Kim! This is where I dropped in on Marly!"

With a scream of delight, Kim jumped from the Blazer, grabbed him in a bear hug and swung him off his feet. She let go and ruffled his hair, laughing and whooping all the while. She took his face in her hands and planted a congratulatory kiss on his lips.

"We did it, Cody! We did it!" She dropped him onto a roughly hewn tree trunk and sat beside him. "Tell me all. I'm dying to know who you are. Missing prince? Kidnaped billionaire? Lost camper from a foreign family? Woodland spirit who took on human form? Tell me, tell me!"

He smiled ruefully. "I'm afraid it's only a small step into my past. See that tree above us?" She glanced up and nodded. "I was hiding under that tree. People searched for me. The rain came down in a deluge. Thunder rolled. Lightning flashed. Several shots rang out. Then a flash flood lifted the tree and spouted me out like Jonah from the whale. I flew through the air and landed on the roof of Marly's van. That's all I know until I awakened in her van as she drove north on Route 89. I'm not her son. She rescued me and dropped me off at her parents' ranch to avoid contact with the police. She was transporting dope. By accident and coincidence, I became the Hoag's grandson."

"But who are you really?"

"I know who I'm not. This is just the first step on the back trail to my identity."

"What about the Hoags? How will you tell them?" He considered this carefully. "I don't think that I will tell them yet. They're the only grandparents, parents really, that I know. Marly's child must have died because he wasn't with her. Therefore, I'm their only grandchild. I can't take that away from Seth and Marta. They love me. I love them deeply. No, I won't tell them until I have to, unless I have to."

"They're bound to find out if you become a news sensation. 'Lost Child Found After Dozen Years!'"

"I don't think that will happen. Nothing so dramatic. I may never get beyond this step. My trail of memories stops under that tree."

She jumped to her feet. "Well, let's go up and see. Maybe the trail starts again on the other side."

It didn't. A washout had occurred. The fallen tree had slid down the hillside and slewed to lodge among other trees. Dirt and rocks had filled in any remaining crevice beneath the root mass. There were no bullet holes, no bodies. No sign of a relentless pursuit and dramatic escape remained. The trail was cold. It did, however, point south.

They searched the map that night at the Westings' house but found no clue. He might have come from anywhere. Two months passed before a message from Arrah reached him at the Victorian. Quiet Fox would talk with him. She would be at Far Walker's Sacred Place at dawn on the Saturday after next.

Cody clambered over the rocky path through the gorge and into the box canyon of the Sacred Place. Quiet Fox sat on the flat ceremonial area facing the gorge. The old woman gave no sign that she saw him. The young man quietly seated himself cross-legged facing her. He relaxed in the stillness of this spiritual refuge. Peace and serenity filled his being. External sensations faded. Psychological stresses and mundane worries evaporated. He reached out spiritually to the shaman. Her aura was trembling from inner conflict. It flared with the expectation of major achievement. It constricted to a dark sheath of dread at the prospect of turmoil and danger. He withdrew into himself and let her spirit calm itself.

She looked up. "You have matured. You seek your identity. The Great Spirit has prepared you to assume your mission."

"My what?!"

She ignored the exclamation. "You are not the son of Marly Hoag."

"I know. I recalled the night that she rescued me near Camp Richard on Lake Tahoe."

"You know?"

"Just that night. I was afraid and hiding under a fallen tree. A storm raged – rain, thunder, lightning. Men shouted. Several shots were fired. A flash flood washed me over a cliff and onto Marly's van. She rescued me and dropped me at her parent's ranch without saying who I was. They accepted me as her son, Cody."

"And before the storm?"

"Nothing. My life began under that tree."

"Then I can help you another step into your past. A call came to our tribal council at Yerington from the shaman 'Dreams With Manitou' of the Kitanemuk tribe near Tehachapi. A sacred person, not a Native American but a blood brother of the tribe, was fleeing north along the Pacific Crest Trail. Powerful people pursued him, people who could see into minds so that no secret was safe from them. The fugitive was a boy of nine years who would need help. We must help him but avoid his pursuers."

"What happened?"

"A park ranger, Spotted Owl, alerted us to his route and schedule. Our council decided to meet this person with supplies. Then the strangers came with their prying minds. I knew that they would find the rendezvous and capture the boy. I went alone to Lake Sabrina and intercepted the fugitive. It was you. I warned you of the pursuers. Then the providence of the Great Spirit became evident. Only I possessed the secret of complete quieting given to me by the Paiute Holy Man, Wovoka. When I became quiet the strangers could learn nothing from me. This secret I gave to you, the one called 'Soars With Eagles' by the Kitanemuk shaman.

"Then who am I? What is my name?"

"You are 'Soars With Eagles.' That is your name. You are Cody Hoag. That is your name. If you have other names I do not know them."

"Where can I find 'Dreams With Manitou'?"

"He is with the Great Spirit. He is dead."

Cody's chin fell to his chest. "Then you have helped me very little."

Quiet Fox looked at him compassionately. "More than a little, I think. 'Dreams With Manitou' commanded high esteem in his later years. He, too, learned the quieting technique. He trained several novices. You will find them."

"How will that help?"

"You must have lived there for a while. You had a home. You had friends. They can tell you more."

He stood. "Thank you. I must go to Tehachapi. I must know who I am."

She motioned him to be seated. "You cannot leave yet. There are other things you must know about your pursuers and about us before you go. Otherwise you may put yourself and your mission in jeopardy."

"But I want to find my parents now."

"First you must find yourself," she told him in a stern voice. "You cannot remember back beyond the tree refuge because it was there that you invoked the Wovokian silence. What you do not have is the key to unlock your silence. My niece Arrah nearly died because she became locked into the silence. I cannot give you your key. I can demonstrate my key for you. Under standing the basis, you must then search for your own particular key. Now, hold my hand and enter rapport."

Cody took her proffered hands and attuned himself to her. He felt her breathing and pulse. He saw through her eyes and heard through her ears. They were one. They moved along her neural networks, pulling shutters down against all incoming sensations. They imploded to the core of her being and paused, listening. No signals penetrated. They expanded again, blocking all bioelectric neurotransmitter paths behind them. They reached the outer world. Their hands parted.

He stared at the shaman. There was an illusion of semi-transparency to her image like that of a store window. If he focused on her surface he could see her plainly. If he searched for depth he saw only the background behind her. He concentrated his senses at all levels to no avail. Except for a slight surface reflection, she was not there to his probing. There was nothing he could detect of her. She took his hands again. "That is the silence that Wovoka taught me. Now follow me as we use my key to unlock my shuttered pathways."

He reentered rapport with her. An all-encompassing cloud confined his perception to the immediate vicinity. There were no forms, no direction. His attention was drawn to a slowly increasing brightness in one sector. Her spirit soared as at the dawn of a new day. The haze lightened until a narrow beam broke through. Quiet Fox took control of the beam and swung it in a widening arc. The haze evaporated before this onslaught. The corridor to her inner self reappeared. The beam shortened in length. Barrier after barrier was touched and evaporated with the haze. They continued unhesitatingly through her core and back again. Their hands unclasped. Cody could sense the full depth and richness of her being.

"You have experienced my key, Soars With Eagles. It is an allegory of the rebirth of my soul. To use Wovoka's silence at will you need both lock and key. When first we met I had time to give you only the lock. In your desperate escape you set the locks but you do not have the key. Like my little Arrah, you have lost part of yourself in the silence."

He implored her, "You must help me find my key. I must know my parents. I must live my life as the true me." Sympathetically, she responded, "I cannot retrieve your lost years for you. I can teach you to use the silence now to protect yourself against your pursuers. When you are thus armed, go to Tehachapi. More of your life may be waiting there. Perhaps that knowledge will enable you to bridge the barrier to your past. Now, let me teach you to use the silence properly." They joined hands and became one.

Kim's Bronco pulled up by the steps of the Hoag ranch house. She alighted and immediately became the cynosure of attention. Tripod hopped down the stairs and sniffed the new arrival. Satisfied, the feline rubbed against her leg, accepted the head scratch, and strode back to the shaded porch. Green Eyes, the granddaughter of Dark Eyes, trotted in from the barn with head and tail high to make her inspection. Old Stalker and Mischief followed more sedately. After approving sniffs by the dogs, Mischief showed vestiges of her youthful frivolity by circling Kim several times and then squeezing between her legs for stroking. Stalker squatted and viewed them impassively. Horses neighed at the fence, the cow mooed, and several barn cats sat at a distance and watched the excitement. Marta, followed by Dark Eyes, came from the house wiping her hands on her apron. Around the corner of the house raced Cody, shouting, "Kim! Kim! Welcome to the ranch." He ran up to her, gave her a hug and kiss, then swung her in the air. Marta smiled and waved her welcome. Seth came striding around the corner of the house, a broad smile on his face. They were happy to have a visitor, especially this girl of whom their grandson was so obviously fond. They had met her at the Victorian and were duly impressed by her.

Kim ran over to hug Seth and then up the steps to hug and kiss Marta. "What a beautiful valley, Marta." She combined vocalization with the sign language she'd been practicing with Cody. "I wish that I could have visited sooner but we're just overloaded at Incline during the ski season."

Marta led the way to the sitting area on the east side of the porch. "No apologies necessary. Any time that you can come is a pleasure for us. Sit here and I'll bring coffee and cakes. No, no. You sit and relax."

Kim turned to the railing and gasped at the view. The garden was in bloom with a dazzling display of color. The waterfall tinkled. The stream burbled over its rocky bed. Across the creek a fitful breeze blew aloft intermittent curtains of spume. The irrigation ditch on the hillside formed a semiprecious necklace of shining wet stones, sun glistened watercourse, and chain of small retaining pools.

"Oh, Cody! Did you do this? It's so beautiful!" He deprecated his part in it. Seth and Marta observed him from their chairs.

"This is the product of five generations of Hoags, a family affair. Great Granddad built the reservoir in the gorge. Seth and his father constructed the irrigation system, the bridge and the orchard. Marta and

Seth expanded the orchard and started the garden. Marta had the vision for the garden as it is now. Seth and I supplied the labor."

Marta laughed her rebuttal of this version. "Don't listen to him, Kim. The garden and orchard were a shambles when Cody got us started again. He repaired the sluice gate on the dam, rebuilt the irrigation ditch, rebuilt the bridge, put in both waterfalls, and did loads of work of the orchard and flower garden. She turned adoring eyes on her grandson. "It may be my dream come true, but Cody brought it to life." Her flowing hand signs caressed him through the air.

"Don't worry, Marta. I know him. He's always trying to evade credit and make the rest of us feel that we really deserve it. I can see it all here – the family heritage, your dreams and the efforts of Seth and Cody. It's overwhelming." Marta tried to phrase a fitting agreement. "He's a wonderful young man." Her hands were more eloquent than her voice. Kim smiled at the sales implication. Marta saw her as an acceptable candidate for Cody's future.

He stared into the distance, ignoring the embarrassing adulation.

Kim put her hand over his. She put her feelings into emphatic gestures for his grandmother's sake. "He's all I would ever want in a man."

Cody, startled, blushed under her wry adoring gaze. Another reference to the platonic stasis of their relationship. She jumped to her feet. "The coffee and cake perked me up, Marta. Thank you." Turning to Cody, she said, "Now that I'm revived, how about showing me the orchard and waterworks?" He rose and reached for the tray.

"Don't bother," said Marta. "Seth and I will clean up. You take your young lady sightseeing."

They strolled through the garden, making small talk about the flowers, stream and waterfall. Kim took his arm and walked with him sharing the sights, fragrances and gurgling water. She played at romance as they walked, partly to tease her companion and partly to gratify his grandmother who obviously saw her as a potential mate for him. After some initial discomfiture, Cody realized her game and played along. To the observer they were ideal young lovers.

In the shade of the orchard they were out of view of the house. Kim released his arm and walked beside him. She asked the question that had motivated this visit. "What did you learn from Quiet Fox?"

"A little more but not enough. She first met me on the Pacific Crest Trail at Lake Sabrina. She confirmed that I'm not Marly's son. It was just a chance rescue." He hesitated, wondering how much more to divulge.

"And? I have to know. We're too close for me to be excluded from your mysterious early life."

He nodded in assent. "You've a right to know. Strange people who could almost read minds pursued me. Apparently, at nine years of age, I walked the Pacific Crest Trail from near Tehachapi to Tahoe. I was helped by Native Americans who considered me to be a – a special person. I would probably have been caught were it not for Quiet Fox. She taught me to be absolutely quiet in a special way she had learned from the Paiute holy man Wovoka. Unfortunately, she didn't have time to teach me how to come back completely from that silent state. When I was about to be caught, I must have used that technique to conceal my hiding place under the tree. I escaped but now my old memories are locked away and I have no key."

Kim had been listening attentively. She had picked up his brief hesitation. "No hold backs, Cody. What kind of a 'special person' did she call you?"

Uncertain of his response, his eyes pleaded with her not to pursue this question too deeply. She ignored the plea. "How special, Cody? Tell me." She would not back off.

"A 'sacred person' were her words." He looked down as though to deter further questions.

"How sacred?" she pressed.

"Quiet Fox does not know."

"Who does?"

"Her contact was a Yakut shaman named Dreams With Manitou. He's dead. Perhaps his successor would know."

She brightened at that. "Well, let's go to Tehachapi. The answers must be there." He didn't respond. They walked in silence to stand at the creek bank overlooking the waterfall made by the irrigation stream. Shc brokc thc silence. "Well? When do we go to Tehachapi?" He responded negatively. "I go alone, Kim. I don't want you to be involved in this. I don't want to see you anymore."

"Whoa! Back up! What else did that old witch tell you?" The concern in her voice mirrored her expression. "What are you involved in?"

His voice was strained as he sought words to explain himself and to justify an abrupt break in their friendship. "She told me that these people are still hunting me. They know I'm alive. They expect me to show up between Tahoe and Tehachapi. Since they can almost read minds, only the silence of Wovoka can prevent detection. She instructed me further in its proper use. Only people with this knowledge can block them out. You would be in danger."

She glared with anger. "You can't keep me out, Cody. I love you. You are closer to me than anyone else in the world. We've shared our innermost feelings that no else can reach. Not even my mother. And I know you saved my father's life. I won't let you push me aside. Not again."

He accepted the tirade with a hurt look in his eyes. "I'm not rejecting you, Kim. I'm protecting you."

"Forget it! I'm in this all the way."

"Another thing. I'm different. I don't know if it's this sacred person thing or if all my genes are mixed up. I thought about it on the mountain two weeks ago. I'm just different."

She laughed out loud to relieve the tension. "Of course you're different. If you weren't I'd be all over you under the trees right now." He smiled at that.

"Now, come over in the shade and sit opposite me," Kim directed.

She reached out for his hands. "Teach me to be silent. I want never to reveal anything that might harm you."

Their drive south initially traversed the magnificent national parks on the east side of the Sierra Nevada range. They found that Spotted Owl had retired from the park service. Their route dropped down to the full afternoon heat of the Mojave Desert. Tehachapi, at 4000 feet altitude, gave welcome surcease from the desert heat. Just off the highway they found an excellent Japanese restaurant close to a motel. They ate and decided to stay the night and search for the Yakut shaman in the morning.

At the motel, Kim showered and slipped into her bed while he rinsed off. Cody came out drying his dark hair with a towel. Kim lay under the sheet, her hazel eyes following him fondly.

"You're fun to be with, Cody. You throw yourself into things and get the most possible enjoyment. You're interested in everything. You bring new talents to view in whatever we do. I really like you. More than anyone I've ever known. Maybe more than anyone I'll ever know."

He stopped toweling and smiled down at her, "You captivated me that first day in the quadrangle at school when our bikes entangled. Our hearts and our lives entangled, too. Forever."

She threw back the sheet. "Cuddle me, Cody. I need to feel your arms about me, your body next to mine. I'm so lost with loving you but you're always beyond the reach of my heart." He hesitated, and then slipped in beside her with a look of fond acquiescence that both thrilled and infuriated her. She turned her back.

"Just hold me, Cody, nothing more. I want to go to sleep like this, secure in your arms. Now, kiss me goodnight." He gently kissed her cheek. His arms enfolded her with the strong gentleness of a deeply caring friend, not the passionate embrace of a lover. She took what she had, relaxed in his arms, and was soon fast asleep.

Cody took her hand and led her through the dappled shade of the trees. Blossoms of pink and white relieved the green shades of the foliage. Birds sang, squirrels chattered and half-seen lithe shapes darted through the grass and light underbrush. Occasionally she spied another couple arm in arm, walking, engrossed in each other. They reached a clearing containing a small spring fed pond. She darted ahead and knelt on a rock to look down into the clear water. Small fish swam lazily. A heron walked towards her, eyes searching the bottom. A pair of ducks with their brood drifted past. All was quiet. She could hear the faint gurgle of the spring and the splash of the heron's steps. Underneath, she could sense the throb of life in all these creatures. This was an Eden for lovers. Kim turned to have Cody kneel by her, to join her in sensing the pulsing life in everything around them. This was the essence of being. Not to be alive in isolation but to exist in conjunction and harmony with all about you. Especially to be united with the one you love.

He wasn't there. She stood in alarm and searched the forest. There! He was dashing through the woods, pausing at every startled couple to peer at the girl, then running off again. Kim knew that he was seeking that special girl who would be his love. She rose and ran toward him, shouting inside herself, "Cody! I can be your love. I can!" No matter how fast she ran she could not get closer to him. At last she fell to the ground and cried great heaving sobs. Strong arms lifted her, enfolded her, and held her against a familiar chest. A soothing voice called her name. "Kim. Kim. Wake up. Wake up. What's the matter, dear? You're safe with me."

The forest glade disappeared. She was sitting in bed, sobbing against Cody's chest.

"What's the matter, Kim?" he repeated softly. She raised her tear-dimmed eyes. "I can't help it, Cody. Even in dreams I can't stay close to you. Sometimes I wish I didn't love you so."

He was silent, regarding her with sorrow and regret. "But not when I'm awake," she added. Smiling through her tears, she told him, "Now get back to your own bed. We have a big day coming tomorrow."

Claymore was their fifth stop, another undistinguished town off Route 58 west of Tehachapi. They gratefully left the searing midday heat for the cool interior of the small diner. The counterman and owner welcomed them.

"Hi, folks. How about ice water for a start?"

They downed it without speaking. "Not many tourists this time of year. You lost?"

"No, not lost," responded Kim with her engaging smile. "We work in Las Vegas and spend our spare time looking for unique Indian jewelry and handicraft."

"Are you big time gamblers?" he asked with a grin on his gaunt leathery face.

"No. Just landscape gardeners."

"Go on! You don't look weather-beaten enough to be desert gardeners. You're too pretty to be out in that sun, anyway."

"You're right on that," she laughed. "I spend most of my time indoors doing design. He shovels the dirt." Cody joined in the laughter.

"What kind of salad do you have?"

"Fresh fruit and yogurt or cottage cheese. It all comes in from the valley and the coast. I pick it up in Tehachapi three times a week. Can I fix you one?"

"Sounds good."

"How about you, Miss?"

"Make it two. Anything cool sounds good." When they returned from the washrooms their salads were on the counter.

"You spoke about Indian things. We have a little shop just down the street. Nothing fancy. It's off the beaten track and may have something different." Their gazes followed his pointing finger to a single story wooden building just beyond the hardware store. Its sign proclaimed 'Indian Village.'

Settling up, they walked to the weathered building. The inside was warm. A noisy swamp cooler fought an uneven battle against the desert sun. No clerk appeared. They browsed among the usual souvenirs and then examined some locally made jewelry. "Can I help you?" A deep melodious voice surprised them from an alcove. They faced him.

"I hope so," replied Cody. "We're hoping to find a Yakut shaman who knew Dreams With Manitou." A young Native American dressed in Levi's and decorated vest stepped forward. His penetrating eyes studied them while his face remained impassive. He spoke in deep rolling tones. "Who sent you?"

"Quiet Fox of the Walker Lake Paiutes."

Their questioner showed no recognition of the name. Cody could read no reaction in his body language or aura. This man was employing the silence. He turned to a cabinet, unlocked a case, and brought them two rings.

"Go home, Soars With Eagles. Wait there."

He turned, stepped through a doorway and was gone. They went to the front of the store. A girl in her mid-teens sat at the cash drawer. Her eyes opened wide when she saw the rings. Her aura expanded with excitement. A brief pulse of energy touched Cody. Then her silence descended. "Ten dollars," she told them and put the rings in an envelope "Who is he?" blurted Cody. Unreadable eyes regarded him from her impassive face.

"Goodbye."

They went out to the empty street, climbed into the Bronco, and irresolutely backed into the street headed further up country. The cashier at the window shook her head negatively and pointed back towards Tehachapi. Kim made a U-turn and headed home.

Encounter with the Agency

"Going out again, Cody? Where to tonight?"

"Harrah's, Maria."

She smiled broadly. "It must be Wednesday. Big Band Night."

"You know my routine better that I do."

"You're in a rut, Cody. Work all day. Dancing at night. Alternate weekends at Tahoe and the ranch. You're as predictable as a pendulum."

"It suits me. I'm not anxious for a change until I find a good reason to change."

"What are you looking for?"

"Girls! Girls! What else do men look for at dances?" interjected Pasco from the doorway.

Maria clamped her lips together and gave her husband a pitying look. "Girls! With a girl like Kim in love with him, why would he have to scout the dance halls?" She turned back to Cody. "Marry that girl. You'll never find a better one. And she dances, too."

He grimaced ruefully. "It isn't that easy, Maria. It just isn't that easy."

He headed for the door to end the conversation. "I'll see you later."

Maria shook her head in annoyance. "I don't know what's wrong with those two. Kim adores him. They're a beautiful couple. They dance together like a dream. And I'm sure he loves her. Men! What is he seeking?"

Pasco smiled at her frustration with Cody. "Adventure. Intrigue. Strange passion. Maybe her love is too tame for him."

"Men!"

"Come here, tigress!" She gave him her most mysterious, intriguing and alluring smile, walked into his embrace and then led him upstairs.

Cody went to Harrah's lounge where a seven-piece band valiantly emulated the big band sound. The audience ranged from white haired retirees who had lived through the heyday of the big bands, to baby boomers who had watched their parents dance. The silver smoothies glided across the floor. The boomers adapted the basic steps of the 1940s to their own frenetic style. Cody sat at his usual table near the wall opposite the bar, two steps from the dance floor. From there he could survey the lounge and get a good view of the dancers.

"Cocktail, Cody?"

"The usual, Tina. Club with a twist." He rarely drank. A glass that looked like a mixed drink gave the image of a *bon vivant*.

He returned to his observation of the lounge. Nothing interesting. Several capable dancers, one couple his own age. The girl was good but not in Kim's class. They all fell short of Kim.

"Your drink, Cody." The young waitress smiled down at him. Nice face and figure but nowhere near Kim. "Find yourself a partner yet?"

"Not yet. You see any prospects?"

"No. Mostly seniors. But I get off at eleven." He paid and tipped generously, smiling noncommittally at her come on.

She walked off gracefully, perhaps swinging her hips a little more than usual. Enough to snare surreptitious glances from the silvered heads.

He resumed his inspection of the crowd. He often sat like this, enjoying the music, the dancing and the murmur of voices. Sometimes he would lose focus and the people became cardboard cutouts; faces pale and vacuous, movements stiff and jerky; body language garbled; voices flat and toneless. It happened now. He scanned the cardboard crowd. Surprised, his scanning ceased. Next to the dance floor were three young women. One face, one figure stood out. A dark haired, dark eyed girl spoke animatedly. Every expression, every movement of her body communicated intelligibly. He was frozen, fascinated. Their eyes met. She had idly glanced his way. Startled, her gaze fixed on him.

He was drawn to her. He heard himself ask, "Dance?" She stood, almost fearful, and let herself be guided to the floor. Cody moved and she followed without effort. He had no sense of leading her. They were one. This sensation of free floating movement intensified to a rhapsody of motion. An erotic undertone grew to overshadow the pure joy of the dance. Her eyes became frightened. He felt a combination of reciprocated desire and the panic of flight. The music stopped.

Pandemonium broke out. Two men rushed out onto the dance floor, pushed him aside and ran towards the exit with the girl. Whistles blew. Men ran into the lounge and towards the dance floor. Cody ran to the exit, not wanting to lose sight of the girl. He paused, looked about, and saw them disappearing around the corner. He was enveloped in a bear hug. Several bodies bore him to the ground. Moments later a car pulled up, he was bundled into the rear seat and they sped off.

"Who are you?" The question came out of the darkness for the hundredth time.

"I've told you. I'm Cody Hoag. I live in the old Victorian on Fourth Street. It belongs to the University. I just completed my studies. I work at the Perfumeries. Call the school. Call Pasco and Maria Tallman at the Victorian. Call my grandfather, Seth Hoag. Call Ferdi Langlois who owns the Perfumeries. I'm just Cody Hoag."

He could sense that his questioners had already checked him out and knew who he was. They continued the pressure hoping that something new would escape him.

"Who was the girl you were dancing with?"

"I don't know. I never saw her before."

"Then why did you dance with her?"

"I ask lots of girls to dance. Ask the bartender. Ask the band. Ask Tina, the waitress. I go to Harrah's often." A door opened and one of his questioners left. Cody could hear the low voiced message.

"They got clean away. The young guy's story checks out. He's just a limp wrist from the perfume place."

The door reopened, room lights went on and the glaring interrogation lamp went out. Three tired men in business suits stood looking at him. Cody was relaxed and appeared fresh despite the all night barrage of questions. "Your story checks out, kid," said the slender intense leader. "We've been tracking some elusive terrorists. We think that your dance partner is one of them."

"She didn't seem like a terrorist to me."

"Maybe she is, maybe she isn't. Can you describe her to our artist?" The man's demeanor told Cody a different story. The girl was his quarry but he did not fear her. She was no dangerous terrorist. Cody could not classify her. Their brief encounter had brought a kaleidoscope of emotions and events. She was the first woman to arouse him sexually. He knew that she was also aroused. And she feared it. She feared him. He had to find out why. Perhaps he could use this agency to help him find her.

"Well? Can you describe her to our artist?"

"I'm recalling her face. It was all such a hassle." Her face was engraved in his memory.

"Sure, sure. Do your best. We need your help to suppress terrorism." He extended his hand. "By the way, I'm Les Harlan." A cold hard hand imprisoned Cody's. A pseudo smile matched its warmth. Cody sensed the permafrost in Harlan's core. He was a stranger to frail emotion.

A session with the artist produced a sketch of Miss Middle America. He accepted a lift to the Victorian. Dawn brightened the sky when he let himself into the kitchen. A pot of coffee steamed its welcome. Pasco and Maria sat talking at the table. They fell silent, then jumped to their feet and rushed to greet him, both talking at once.

"Cody! What happened? Some police detectives grilled us about you. They said you were involved with a terrorist group and had been arrested at a secret meeting. 'Impossible!' we told them. It took hours to convince them. How are you?" They paused to examine him.

"No sweat," he replied, calm and amused. "First, I met the girl of my dreams in Harrah's lounge. We danced on air like the earliest autumn leaves spinning off a tree. The place was raided. She escaped. I was caught."

Pasco was incredulous. "You were arrested for dancing? At Harrah's? Come on!"

Maria saw it more personally. "What about Kim? Is she forgotten so easily?"

"This is different. Kim and I are friends. I love her deeply but only as a dear friend. This – this is sexual attraction. I never felt like this before. I only read about it or talked about it or sensed it in others."

Maria was matter of fact. "Infatuation. It won't last. Not like Kim's love. Besides, this girl is apparently a fugitive and you have no idea how to find her."

He defended himself. "Those agents aren't police. She's not a terrorist. I don't know why they want her. But I'm going to find out. They want me to help them find her. I agreed, but only because I want to use them to find her for me."

"Don't get involved with spies," warned Maria. Pasco regarded him with admiration.

"Using the agency that wants to use you! You're not the naive boy who arrived here a year ago. You're out of your cocoon and ready to fly." Cody was caught between the dour warning and the open admiration.

"I'll be careful. Emotionally and conspiratorially. Things are moving fast now." He went to the door. "I'm going to bed. It's been a long night. Thanks for waiting up."

"Good night, Cody."

"A few hours in the sack would do us good, honey. I have to prepare an agenda later for the tribal education council at Arrah's school on next Saturday."

Maria nodded. "Yes. I've volunteered for refreshments and entertainment. Cody will want to pitch in."

Enter Elaine

The blinking light in the laboratory signaled that a customer had entered the store. Cody looked through the one-way glass to see the embodiment of haute couture stride toward the outer desk. She was taller than he and slender with silken musculature. Her composed face had striking highlights at eyes, lips and cheekbones. She wore a knitted beret at a jaunty angle. A gray silk sheath clung to her body, sliding provocatively over her understated curves. He could almost see the inaudible whispering sound it must be making. Each foot was placed exactly in front of the other, toes pointed and turned slightly to the outside, as a dancer would step. Her arms swung freely but close to her body, matching the precision of her stride.

He stepped into the store. "Good afternoon, Mademoiselle. I am Cody Hoag. May I help you?"

She gave him a devastating smile that may have been too large for her doll-like face but which could carry across a room – or a stage.

"I was hoping to find you here, Cody. I am Elaine Pendragon. She extended her hand to him, palm down. He bowed, raised her hand to his lips and murmured, "*Enchanté.*" He joined her play of manners. It intrigued and amused him. This agency watchdog might be fun.

"My friends tell me that you are uncanny in your selection of perfumes to complement the natural attractions of your clients. I have yet to find a scent that I really like. Can you help me?" He walked around her, repressing his mirth while trying to look soberly professional. Appreciating her figure was a bonus for his walk. Without uttering a word, he walked to the consultation room and motioned her to enter. Observing her walk was another bonus. He held her chair and sat facing her. "Relax, Ms. Pendragon. Breathe easily. Think serene thoughts."

He was quiet while waiting for her to relax. As he expected, her controlled tension came from a lifelong training in the dance. Total relaxation provided her bridge to rest. Cody rose and circled her again. He sniffed audibly for effect while deciding how to approach her. The theater must have accustomed her to blunt appraisals from directors and critics. Her eyes followed him, a glint of amusement only half suppressed. He played it straight and sober. His voice dropped an octave. "May I speak frankly, Ms. Pendragon?" She was ready to laugh at this poseur. "Of course, Mr. Hoag. Cody. And do call me Elaine. Tell me the awful truth."

Her expression was one of gentle encouragement to a novice. He cleared his throat, simulating embarrassment. "I'm afraid that I can't help you."

She waited for more. This response did not fit in with her directions to get close to him. She held her smile and added a *moue*. "Am I such a lost cause that the renowned Langlois cannot offer hope? What am I to do?" Appearing flustered, he sought to explain his flat statement.

"No! No! Not a lost cause. It's just that you are already doing everything right."

"I'm flattered. But isn't there some small improvement that the fabulous Langlois Perfumeries can make?" She leaned forward and radiated a plea for help. The young perfumer plunged into his analysis with growing confidence.

"You are a trained dancer, Elaine, and you practice very hard. Your diet is largely vegetarian with herbs and garlic. You do eat some fish and chicken. Balsamic vinegar and olive oil are on your salads. You are muscular with little body fat. Your sexual attractive scents are suppressed. You compensate for this in your perfume with a musk base and the heavier floral scents."

He paused, wondering how far to go. He wanted to gain her confidence without revealing himself entirely. "Go on. What else does your nose detect?"

"Please walk for me," he requested.

She was surprised but rose and walked across the room and back. Cody sensed her movements and muscle discharges at all levels. He concentrated on sorting them into a description of the factors that had left their imprint on her physical dynamism. He surprised himself with his growing insight and the sympathy it engendered for her. She was not his enemy but her own. Her teasing voice ended his concentration. "Are you awake, Cody? Men don't usually fall asleep when I walk by. Tell me all."

He decided on a *tour de force* for her sake as well as his own. She resumed her chair. Cody relaxed now that he had made his decision. "Not asleep. Entranced. You are the most graceful woman I have ever seen... however--"

"I knew it! First the candy, then the medicine. What's my problem?"

"Talent, discipline and perfectionism. You've worked all your life to perfect your dancing skills to someone else's standard. You've done that. You're perfect. But in doing it you've repressed your individuality. You don't express your self in your dancing anymore. You're an automaton. You're a valued member of the *corps de ballet* but never a soloist. Less talented dancers take the starring roles. You're frustrated. Now you've become self-destructive. Hired escort. Spy. You're dying inside like a tree with ring rot. These twisted emotions suppress the production of attractive scents. You are your own problem, Elaine."

"Shut up!" she shouted, resentful and angry. "What do you know about my career? What do you know about anything?" She waved her arm in a sweeping gesture to include the entire store. "You're just a naive kid with a wet nose sniffing underarms and underwear. You're a dog at a fireplug. Who are you to tell me about dancing, my life?" Her face had lost its haughty composure. Her eyes ceased their angry flashing, as she looked inward to her own soul. Her shoulders slumped. She put her face in her hands. "Who are you?"

Cody echoed her words. "Who are you?" He reached out to put his fingertips on her arm. "Who are you, Elaine?" Her faded memories of childhood dreams and aspirations focused into clear images. A wide-eyed child of four years watched fascinated as white-clad women glided across the stage in unison with dainty steps on pointed toes. A soloist leaped and turned; conveyed her emotions through every graceful posture, gesture and movement; and, finished to a thunderous standing ovation. From that moment, Elaine knew that she would be a ballerina. She danced everywhere she went, expressing herself in motion until motion and emotion were one. Ballet school was inevitable. It was the glorious focus of her life. The theater performance was her reward. She tried so hard to please her teachers and choreographers that she suppressed her own interpretations of movement and expression. She knew that eventually as a soloist she could be herself. She suppressed so well that she hid the spark that had supported her through the years of arduous training. She had become a pretty piece of background. Dancing had become a frustrating chore in a gray world devoid of emotion. She was dying from the inside.

Cody took both her elbows and lifted her to her feet. He began walking slowly and rhythmically with her. He concentrated his feelings on the sheer joy of graceful movement and communicated that joy to her. Elaine's spirits lifted. The images and emotions of her teenage years in ballet school returned. When Cody felt the dulling cloud of repression forming again, he concentrated on the sense of freedom and self-expression that Kim always projected in her dancing.

Elaine felt this freedom growing in her. It brought forth the same freedom and creativity that she had suppressed for so long. She escaped Cody's touch and executed a series of leaps and turns in the small consultation room. A smile of exultation was on her face. She was alive again!

At the completion of the circle she leaped into Cody's waiting arms, flung her left hand into the air and threw back her head. They were immobile for several moments listening to the applause of her imaginary audience. Cody set her on her feet. Elaine put her hands on his shoulders.

"Who are you, Cody? Who are you?"

"Your friend, Elaine. The naive wimpy perfumer with a wet nose." She blushed, and then kissed his nose.

"You know that I've been hired to spy on you. Why would Les Harlan want to know your every move?"

"His agency is hunting for some ecology activists whom he sees as terrorists. By accident, I danced with one of his suspects at Harrah's. He feels that I may provide a lead to them. Actually, I know nothing but I would be interested in dancing with that girl again. She was great."

"I'll bet you are, too. Why don't we go dancing and look for them? Harlan will pay, we'll see all the clubs and satisfy both Harlan and you with the search. It could be fun." The thought appealed to him.

"When do we start?"

"Tonight. Harrah's lobby at eight for dinner, then out on the town. Okay?"

He nodded assent. Through the one-way glass they saw Langlois approaching the front door.

"Here comes the boss. Our time is up."

"Wrap up a bundle of expensive goodies for me. Harlan will pay. Langlois will be happy. We can even showcase his perfumes when we go out. Everybody wins." She went through the consultation room door, smiling back at him as she left. "Send everything to the desk at Harrah's," she said for Langlois' benefit. "I want to wear your perfume tonight."

Cody hurried after her, introducing her quickly to Langlois who was holding the door for her exit. Cody explained to his employer that, after a consultation, she had decided on a complete set of one of their more expensive lines of custom toiletries. He added that she wanted him to go out with her that evening when she would wear the perfume. Langlois became thoughtful.

"I've seen that woman dance. She's no star. She has no money unless she found a sponsor at the stage door. Something's afoot that I don't understand. Maybe they're after the store. Be careful, Cody. And let me know if any hint is dropped."

"Yes sir!" snapped Cody. I'd better hurry with her order if she's to get it this afternoon."

"Put it together," directed Langlois. "I'll call for a messenger and then give you a hand."

The Corvette convertible drew all the valets when it pulled up to the hotel. Traffic stopped when Elaine alighted and walked to the door, leaving a smile and a greeting by name to each attendant. Conversation and movement ceased in the lobby as she crossed to the restaurant where Cody waited. Her pale green sheath with emerald accessories set off her reddish gold hair. Her gliding walk, slim symmetrical legs rising high to her short skirt, erect posture and proud set of her head would have made her regally forbidding were it not for the warm smile and friendly eyes. She was royalty with a plebeian heart.

The waiting list for tables on which Cody had registered became immaterial. Philippe came out and kissed her hand. Not a frown of annoyance showed on the faces of those waiting for tables. "Cody!" she greeted her date with a kiss on his cheek. "How kind of you to meet me. Philippe has the most wonderful restaurant in Reno – and possibly the world."

She turned to the *maître d'hôtel*. "Philippe, I would like you to meet my very special friend, Cody Hoag." Philippe bowed slightly in acknowledgement.

"Welcome, Mr. Hoag." Cody repressed the impulse to extend his hand and merely repeated the name, "Philippe." The maître d' led them to a conspicuous table set apart from the others.

Two waiters stood by their chairs. When they were seated the sommelier popped a bottle of champagne, poured a courtesy dram for Cody's approval, and then filled their glasses. Elaine's smile and nod of acceptance satisfied the sommelier. Elaine was a trophy companion.

A selection of appetizers appeared. No menu was proffered. Philippe approached the table and spoke to both of them although his eyes were on Elaine. She glowed – in her element as the focus of attention, and pleased with her escort, the restaurant and the special attention by the staff.

Philippe's demeanor had relaxed and he could not help but reflect her smile and sociability. "Armand tells me that your entree will be served in thirty five minutes, if that pleases you."

"Oh, Philippe! Armand would be devastated if it was not eaten at the moment of perfection." She covered Cody's hand with hers and gave him a warm glance. "We'll be quite happy together until then."

"Thank you, Ms. Pendragon." His smile became avuncular as he observed the clasped hands. "Is there anything else I can do for you?"

"Will the orchestra be playing soon? I'd love to dance."

"They will be playing in a few minutes." With a brief bow he took his leave and strode to the stage door.

"They really don't start until eight thirty but Philippe is sweet about having them start early if I ask." Cody shared her elation through the touch of her hand. Every one in the room could read it in her face.

What they couldn't see was her sense of rebirth and freedom plus her gratitude to him for this new start with her first love, dancing.

The orchestra began the Waltz of the Flowers. After an expectant moment, she inquired, "You are going to ask me to dance, aren't you?"

"Is dancing expected at dinner time?" he responded awkwardly. "There's no one on the floor."

"I asked for the music, didn't I? I feel so happy that I have to express myself in motion." She took his hand. "Come on, Cody. I'm asking you."

All eyes followed them. To him it seemed like a stage entrance rather than a social dance. They began with basic steps as she accustomed herself to his lead and he evaluated her responses. She had no confusion about his strong lead. Her reactions were so definite and precise that reading her bioelectric impulses gave him clear indication of her impending moves. Elaine became more inventive and expressive in her movements. Unhesitatingly, Cody complemented her every step. Soon it became a game as well as a dance. There was an impish look in her eyes on several occasions when she improvised and syncopated steps. He smiled back and lifted her high off the floor when they closed and spun.

The music ended during a lifting twirl. Cody slowed, set her gently on her feet and swung her to arm's length. She gave an elated laugh, then released his hand and curtsied to him.

Applause resounded from the diners with cries of "More! More!" Recalled to the present from the rapture of the dance, Elaine curtsied to each section of the room. She then indicated Cody and directed him in a low tone, "Bow. You're on stage." Embarrassed, he bent slightly and shook his head deprecatingly. Taking her hand, he held it while she curtsied and he bowed again. Her compliments to the orchestra brought another round of applause.

They started off the floor but the orchestra began the 'Tango de La Rosa.' A ringsider offered Elaine a rose from a vase on his table. She put it between her teeth and slinked back to her partner in tantalizing fashion. He had no recourse. They tangoed to the delight of the crowd as well as their own enjoyment. Elaine's reborn sense of freedom of expression made it a terpsichorean adventure for both of them.

They returned to their table. Chef Armand, who was tall, spare and mustachioed, stood next to the waiter preparing to serve their *vichyssoise*. Tears glistened in his eyes. He kissed her hand. "*Magnifique! Mlle* Elaine and *Monsieur*. I hope only that my dinner will please you as much as your dancing pleased me."

It did. Armand came to observe their reaction to his own braised duck Balanchine and *mousse cygnets blanc et noir*. Other diners had risen to dance, displaying more than usual elegance, creativity and élan. Elaine was their inspiration, Cody noted. Several of the couples stopped by their table to express their admiration. Even the hotel manager expressed his appreciation. Cody found himself enjoying the celebrity status.

Cody at last asked the waiter for the check so that they could begin their search through other clubs.

"It has been settled, Monsieur."

"No, Robert, the bill has not come."

Robert looked to Elaine for help.

"There is no bill, Cody. The hotel has picked it up." He looked uncertain, and then proffered a twenty-dollar bill to the waiter.

"No thank you, Monsieur Hoag. I have been taken care of."

"This is extra. For you, Robert. Take it." Again Robert looked to Elaine. "Thank you, but I cannot." She touched Cody's arm. "It's a house rule, Cody. I assure you that everything has been settled. With a generous gratuity. Shall we go?"

Robert, relieved, held her chair. They walked the edge of the dance floor towards the exit. The dancers noticed them and began applauding. The band changed tempo to an upbeat fox trot. Philippe approached apologetically. "So many of our guests have expressed their hopes that you would dance again that I am emboldened to ask for this favor. Would you please dance for us?"

Elaine bestowed her devastating smile and handed him her purse. "Philippe! Could I refuse you anything?" She turned her eyes to Cody. "Would you mind, darling?" They stepped onto the floor. The other dancers melted away and tendered their preliminary applause. They were not disappointed. Elaine and Cody, sure of each other now, improvised a fast paced dance that drew a standing ovation when they left the floor. The orchestra played their own tribute, "Goodnight Elaine," Philippe kissed her hand and shook Cody's. "You've made this a special experience for our diners and our staff. I am indebted to you.

Their car was waiting at the door. Again, a tip was refused. For Elaine, everything was complimentary. They toured the clubs. Cody was enveloped in Elaine's elation. The dancing, the applause, the celebrity treatment – these were her life. She had much to give to the world. Her spirit expanded when the world returned its love. How could he not add his?

Elaine Meets Kim

Kim stalked into the Victorian lot to find Cody cultivating the garden, the garden built with many hours of shared labor. The late afternoon sun threw drooping shadows across the listless plants. The leaves were silent in the breathless gloom. The flowers exuded no perfume. Her voice was bright and brittle.

"I see you made the entertainment pages dancing with Miss Tutu. Only your back, of course, and her legs up to the armpit. All that nightlife made you too busy to call."

His warm smile and welcoming, "Kim!" was too much.

"Damn it, Cody! If you've found your dream girl, at least have the guts to tell me. Don't let me discover it in a throwaway gossip rag. I deserve better."

Her eyes sparked, her lips stretched tight, her voice raised an octave. Hands on hips, head high, she confronted him with his perfidy. His smile changed to concern. He sought explanatory words for his escapade. "It isn't what you think. She's just a friend. She's helping me."

"Helping? The tabloids now, TV next? Does she consider the danger? Do you? Does she know anything about the searching we've done? Can she keep a secret? You make me sick! Your damn hormones go to sleep around me but they run away with your brains with every other girl you meet. I'm through helping you look for your mama. I'm through with you!"

She strode off. Cody matched her pace. "Kim. Kim. It's not like that at all." She accelerated.

"I didn't pick up Elaine. Harlan hired her for the agency, to spy on me. If I contact those people Harlan wants, she's supposed to call the agency immediately."

"That's a stupid story. Why would they hire a second rate charm girl to tail you?" The ice had melted. He had her attention.

"Please, Kim. Sit here. I'll tell you everything." He extended his hand. She took it and sat next to him. Her features softened. Hope replaced antagonism.

He began with Elaine Pendragon's appearance as an ostensible customer and his consultation with her. Langlois feared a plot to take over his business. Cody knew that Les Harlan had instigated the visit. The agent wanted the strange girl he had met at the disco. So did he. It seemed natural to play along with the agency to help his own search.

"And after you find her?"

"I don't know. I know several players but I don't know the game or which side I'm on. I do feel it involves my search for identity. I have to keep going."

"And what about your ballerina? How do you feel about her, really?" She wanted an answer to sustain her own hope.

"We're friends now, Kim."

"Really."

He essayed a smile. "Not like you and me, Kim. Just friends. Dancing is her only love. Now that she has recovered her freedom of expression, I think she can revitalize her career."

"Is she a better dancer than I am?"

"It's her life, Kim. She's a better dancer for ballet than you." She probed for a more satisfactory answer.

"But do you like dancing with her more than with me?"

"Never. With her I'm just a supporting partner. With you it's a communion of souls."

She sighed and relaxed her head on his shoulder. "Hold me, Cody. I so want you to find yourself but I'm afraid it will mean losing you, at least the part of you that I have." He put his arms around her and held her close. "I do love you, Kim. No one can take that away. I don't know why I'm not sexually attracted to you. How often I wish that I were. Perhaps when we find out who I am we'll solve that problem also."

"Let's go to the ranch. Arrah invited me to an open house at her school. I think she has word from Tehachapi. I want you there. We could plan to stay at the ranch for the weekend."

"Oh, Cody! Another clue. I wouldn't miss it!"

Their arrival at the ranch elicited a homecoming response. Marta and Seth came to the pickup for hugs and kisses. Tripod, the matriarchal cat, descended the steps with her hopping gait to rub against their legs. Only after her return to the porch did the dogs come sniffing and licking hands. The horses whinnied from the pasture knowing that there would soon be treats and a ride across the field.

Small talk over coffee preceded a change of clothes before they went out to ride Blue Bell and Dancer. The sense of freedom and the wind in their hair blew away the constraints of city and school life, the uncertainties of their relationship and the convolutions of the search for his identity. They were companionable blithe spirits riding the wind.

The after dinner conversation brought a somber note initiated by Seth. "We've had a lot of visitors lately. Some seemed official. Everyone was interested in you."

"In me? Who were they, grandpa?"

"Two smooth fellows in a big car. They showed I.D. saying they were with the Inter-Agency Investigation Bureau. Asked about your birth, your mother, how long you've lived here, your schooling and such. We told them. Didn't see any harm in telling the truth. They knew all about Marly's disappearance. More than we did, I think."

"What did they look like?"

"Like government men, I suppose. Mid-height, trim, well-spoken, sorta formal suits and ties. Smooth hair, one blond and one brown, but no real distinguishing features. I couldn't pick them out of a crowd now. Gavc thc namcs Mr. Brown and Mr. White. Appropriate."

"Who were the other visitors?"

"A woman and a man who said they were from the State Business License Board. They asked a lot about your schooling and the perfume job. The woman admired the gardens and waterfalls, too. Nice girl. Pleasant."

"Hmph! Nice and pleasant," interjected his wife. "She was medium height, black hair, very attractive. Absolutely charming. Your grandfather followed her around like a puppy dog. Her name is Rava, his is Brock. He was quiet and observed everything. Looked like the girl."

"Let me tell it, Marta. This girl Rava knew some sign language and was very expressive when she talked. She didn't have to write anything down for us."

Cody leaned forward with heightened interest. "Was she solidly built and strong looking in a feminine way? Brown deep-set eyes, a short broad upturned nose, and a very wide smile? Was she graceful and agile? Did she talk with her whole body the way I do?"

Seth searched his memory. "She was shorter and more compact than Kim. Big smile. Brown eyes, Marta?"

"Yes, brown eyes."

"She skipped up and down the stairs and over the garden rocks like a mountain goat. Strong hand grip." He looked again to his wife.

"Deep set eyes and short nose. Yes. And her gestures were like yours, Cody. Very expressive."

Kim's interest had a forlorn edge. "Your night club girl."

In his excitement, he missed the undertone. "She may be." He addressed Seth. "Did she leave a card or an address? How can I find her?" The strong response surprised his grandparents. "She didn't leave a thing. Just her agency name. Must be in Reno or Carson City. You could phone her."

Cody's excitement diminished. "Probably a false lead. But at least they're in the neighborhood. Elaine and I may find them yet."

"Who?" asked Marta in surprise.

"I'll tell you later, grandma. What about the other visitors, grandpa?"

"The sheriff stopped by. He said that neighbors reported those three rambunctious cowboys on the back road several times. I'll have to check on any mischief they might be doing."

"Careful, grandpa. They might be real trouble if you go alone. Anyone else?"

"An old friend, Far Walker. He came in the back way and met me near the gorge. Asked if he could bring in some tribesmen to the box canyon in October. I said yes. It's their holy place. We're just caretakers. That's the whole crowd, Cody. Strange that they should all come so close together. What do you make of it?"

"I don't know yet. Your description of Rava seems like the girl I met in the nightclub when those agency people raided the place and picked me up. They claimed some terrorist links against her. Now that same agency has enlisted me to help find her. I seem to have danced into a quagmire. The three cowboys may be just drifting vandals. We can find and evict them. Far Walker I've met before. He came to his sacred place last October, so this visit is probably coincidental." Cody spoke casually to allay any fears. "I think that the agency knows all it needs to know and has me under surveillance as a precaution. They shouldn't be back. The same for Rava. Sunday we'll look for those troublemakers."

He brightened at another thought. "Arrah's open house at school is tomorrow. I'll ask her about Far Walker's conclave. That should wrap everything up this weekend."

Seth concurred reluctantly. "Too much coincidence. I don't like the sound of international terrorism. Stay away from Rava. She was too charming for any government investigator." Kim smiled a wan agreement. Now Cody noticed the sadness in her eyes and realized that Rava was the cause. He was torn between his regard for her as his best friend and helper, and his compulsive desire to see Rava. Did they have to be exclusive? His smile faded and his eyes dropped to the table. They finished their coffee in silence.

All four arrived at school in Seth's king cab pickup. Kim sat close to Cody in the rear seat, enjoying the proximity that was threatened by Rava's appearance. The school had the air of a picnic ground. Flags, banners and balloons draped the walls to welcome parents, students and visitors. Vehicles overflowed the parking lot onto neighboring roads. Brightly dressed children dragged parents toward the garden and waved excitedly to classmates. Children proudly exhibited their personal plants to any one who came near.

The approach of the Hoags elicited hugs, kisses and a flurry of sign language bragging about the state of their individual projects. The garden was a community project and a source of pride for both individual and group achievement. The Hoags were soon split apart and drawn to different parts of the garden. Seth went to the waterworks. Marta went to the flowerbeds around the waterfall. Cody and Kim went to the herb garden for the blind. They covered Cody's eyes and brought him plant after plant for identification. He was infallible until they reached the far corner. The boy holding Kim's hand squeezed it hard. Cody sniffed. He sniffed again. He stood puzzled. The children laughed. One signed a name that Kim could not read. Another trial. Stumped again. Another name Kim couldn't catch. Cody straightened and removed his blindfold. He signed and spoke. "Where did you get these herbs? They're all new to me." The children giggled.

"Tell me. I'll never guess." At last one relented. "Grandma Marta sent away for them. She played a joke on you." They laughed and resumed their progress around the garden. At eleven, the forum opened for parents, teachers and administrators to discuss the school's program and progress. It served mainly as a vehicle for praise of the work, the development of the children and the cooperation of the parents. Arrah especially praised Marta and Seth Hoag for their contributions in finding water, building the waterworks and planning the garden. Cody was not mentioned. Kim interrogated him with a questioning glance about this. He shrugged.

The forum concluded and the dining room opened for lunch. Arrah paused briefly at Cody's side. "Come to my living room. There is a meeting you must attend." She passed on without waiting for a reply. He found Kim in the garden, separated her from the children and scooted them to the dining room. "Arrah wants me at a meeting. I think it must be word from Tehachapi. I want you there. It's your search, too."

The group in the living room surprised them. The storekeeper from the shop near Tehachapi sat facing the door. Far Walker and Quiet Fox sat with an older Native American to their right, flanked by two young Native Americans Cody had not seen before. On their left were two dark-haired Caucasians, a girl about sixteen and a man about Cody's age. They were all casually dressed befitting the open house. All eyes were on the arriving couple. "We expected you to be alone," spoke the storekeeper.

Cody understood their concern. "Kim is my closest friend. She can be quiet." Arrah put two chairs for them facing the others. The storekeeper spoke first. "We are all your friends. We have come together to help you discover who you are."

"How can you help me? Who are you? What do you know about me?" Fear of a blind alley restrained his mounting excitement.

"Let me introduce your friends from Tehachapi. I am called 'Dust Devil,' shaman of the Kitanemuk tribe in the Tehachapi area. On my right is my clan brother 'Walks in Spirit Lands.' On his right is 'Thundercloud.' Beyond them are two of our neighbors, Dan and Emily Costain." Each acknowledged the introduction.

Arrah pointed to the older man on the far right. "This is Spotted Owl, a ranger in the Sequoia Forest. He is from the Yakuts." Arrah added for Kim's benefit, "This is Far Walker from Pyramid Lake."

The shaman continued, "You are awakening to your own identity. We believe that this is a sign from the Great Spirit for us to reveal what we know. Whatever role the Great Spirit has given you to play, we know that it is bound to the fate of our people. We were fated to protect you as a child in your time of concealment and escape. We are now here to help you return to your own identity and mission."

Cody, angry, jumped to his feet and spoke vehemently to Quiet Fox. "You knew this all along and kept silent? How could you? How could you keep me from my family?" His hot glance swept around the room. "All of you! You decided what was best for me! You made me an orphan. You hid me from my parents. Now your Great Spirit wants you to exhume me from my crypt of ignorance. What kind of fanatics are you? How loving is your god to do this to me?" He challenged them. "Well? Tell me who I am. But I myself will decide what role I shall take in your cosmic drama. If any."

Cody felt an overwhelming upwelling of sorrow and sympathy within his being. He saw tears streaming down Emily's cheeks as she watched him with deeply understanding eyes. The room faded and he felt himself being drawn into a turgid kinship that frightened him. He drew back physically and psychologically. With an effort, he turned to Dust Devil.

"Who am I?" he spoke forcefully but with a pleading note.

The shaman responded thoughtfully. "We do not know exactly who you are, although we have known you from the time you came to Tehachapi at age six with your mother. You fled into the mountains three years later when your mother was taken away by her pursuers."

Cody shouted, "My mother! Tell me!"

"Your mother came hiking across the desert with you. She was an interesting woman, not ordinary. Physically she was about five feet three inches, dark hair, tanned, brown eyes, and not wasichu, yet not of the tribal peoples. She was strong-willed and strong in body: very sturdy and self-confident. She bought several acres of land and made the two of you a home. She found water and dug a cave for a home and a flower nursery. Her name is Brisa. She helped our village find a permanent water supply. And you were a very special boy: you befriended our sorry old shaman, Dreams With Manitou. You reawakened his tattered dreams into a hopeful tapestry for our future when the wasichu, the despoilers, shall vanish.

"You played with us as a child, you renewed our kinship with our brothers, the animals and birds. You helped us to hear the voices of the trees and flowers and Mother Earth herself. You put us in touch with the visions of our grandfathers.

"The Costain family, mother and father plus Dan and Emily, squatted on government land. We all played together. One day we gathered peyote and shared it in our own make believe ceremony. It was a disaster. And it was a miracle that changed our lives. We became sick. A vision was revealed to us. It showed us world evolution to its present condition, a vision of hope for the future with reestablishment of the Hoop of Life. But Emily became lost in the vision. You brought her back. We all hold some of that vision, Emily most of all."

Cody glanced at Emily. Her eyes were still upon him. The whirlpool exerted its pull again.

"We regarded you as a special person, a sacred person. You improved our lives. You brought us closer to our Mother Earth. You renewed our bonds with our ancestors and our culture. You gave us hope for the future.

"We knew your mother concealed herself from powerful people. She had us teach you an escape route to the north, to Mt. Shasta. After three years, the pursuers came. They took your mother. You fled. Our brothers helped you to the Pacific Crest Trail. You would have been caught at Lake Sabrina but for the intervention of the Great Spirit through Quiet Fox. She was the only person in the world who could have saved you from these mind readers. She taught you to quiet yourself. You escaped but lost yourself in the Silence. Quiet Fox had faith that you lived and searched for you. You know the rest."

Cody's breathing labored with strong emotion. "But where is my mother? Is she alive? Who took her? Where are they?"

Emily spoke. "Brisa gave my family your home. She said that her own people might find her and take her north. We mourned her leaving as well as yours."

"You knew my mother? You live in her home? What was she like?"

Emily opened a folder and removed a detailed sketch of a dark haired woman and a boy standing in a garden. A trickle of water came from the wall behind it.

"That's you, Cody!" exclaimed Kim. "And you resemble your mother. She's beautiful."

He absorbed every detail. "My mother. She is beautiful."

He looked to Emily. "Where is she now? What happened to her?"

"Three men and a woman arrived unexpectedly. Your mother knew them. My mother and I were there. They ignored us. They spoke little. I heard them say, "Your boy?" Your mother did not answer. The woman and man went outside. The woman returned wearing a triumphant look. We thought you had been caught. Brisa left with them. We never saw or heard from her again."

Dust Devil picked up the tale. "We in the tribe helped you escape.

You are blood brother to the three of us. You are a sacred person. When you ran up the escape canyon we confused the trail. We overran your footsteps. We dragged some of your old clothing up blind trails. We lit creosote smudges. We turned on our radio transmitter. The strangers gave up the search when a thunderstorm rolled in over the mountains. We contacted friends by telephone to assist you on your journey."

The story passed to Spotted Owl. "We knew your route. Four of us met you on the old migration trail and drove you to the Pacific Crest Trail near the Little Kern River. We gave you directions, supplies and quick instructions in our survival lore. We had misgivings when you strode out of sight. Your strength and self confidence gave us hope you would safely reach your next contact."

Cody was still looking at the picture and only half listening to the escape highlights.

Quiet Fox spoke next. "You know, I think, that I met you at Lake Sabrina and gave you the quieting technique that led to your escape and also to your amnesia. You remember Marly Hoag rescuing you and bringing you to the ranch."

"There is a little more to the story," added Spotted Owl. "A couple of rangers picked up the three hunters at the south end of Lake Tahoe. They were waterlogged and suffering from exposure. Claimed they had encountered two Sasquatch and barely escaped with their lives. No one believed them. Boomer Bomano is a Big Foot cultist who hates the Sasquatch. He's always claiming close encounters. Says he senses their vibrations. You were there. Did you see any Sasquatch?" Cody shook his head in the negative.

Far Walker clasped the hands of those on either side. "You have helped us to remember by touching us. Take our hands. Perhaps we can help you to complete the circuit of your memories."

They formed the circle and sat silently. Quiet Fox murmured, "I remember a young boy at Lake Sabrina. He learned Wovoka's Silence from me and then ran off with his pursuers close behind."

Each recalled past times with Cody. The murmuring voices merged into a powerful tide that swept him back through the corridors of his memory. He made unexpected turns. Blocked paths opened. Hidden files appeared. Each link to his past formed an element of his mnemonic key. Once more he trekked the sand in his mother's footsteps, searching for a new home. The faces in this room became familiar.... They were friends... and he was Brandon, son of Brisa. Her last shrill warning to flee echoed through these newly opened corridors. The trail to Shasta became clear. Brisa waited there, he knew. She would give him his identity. Hands unclasped. Too many memories and emotions poured into the circle. They did not want to intrude on each other's private thoughts. Quiet Fox broke the silence.

"There is more involved in this than finding your mother and recovering your memory. Some mysterious and resourceful people, whom your mother knows, have been seeking you for more than a dozen years."

"They have been seen near our cave intermittently, and in Claymore," interjected Dan.

"The Silence may have been your only protection against them," continued the old woman. "You are also involved with our legends and our culture. Many of our young people have forgotten the old ways and now espouse the ways of the wasichu. They sell tribal lands, open gambling casinos and forget our bond with the land, the trees, the animals and each other. You may be able to restore validity to the old ways. Wovoka's vision of the disappearance of the wasichu and return of fertility to the land may be true. It simply was not for his time. The Ghost Dance was misinterpreted as a weapon. Rather it is an enlightenment and metamorphosis for all people. The Hoop of Life can yet be restored. You may be part of this restoration, a Sacred Person sent by the Great Spirit to guide us."

Cody listened intently, and with growing fear. His own view of his life took on a broader, but unwelcome perspective, laid out as yet another journey accompanied by many hazards.

Quiet Fox leaned forward and emphasized the importance of her words. "A new element has been introduced. You met a girl at a nightclub to whom you were instantly attracted. I think she is like your mother, a member of her tribe or people."

Cody nodded in agreement, staring at the picture of Brisa. "Yes. Not only in looks but also in her expressive use of body language. I'd never seen anyone like her – not until I remembered my mother just now."

"Your unexpected appearance startled her. She may have realized you were Brisa's son. She showed up at the ranch because she now connects you with Harlan."

"What about him and his government agency? What do they want with Cody and Rava?" asked Kim.

"We know him and his thugs," responded Thundercloud, his tone indicating low regard.

"Yes, we know him," added Emily emphatically. "They show up at all our ecology meetings. They cloak pollution and resource exploitation in the guise of jobs, housing and business development. They also sneak around taking pictures of environmentalist opponents. Thundercloud and I are prominent in their rogues' gallery."

"Why are they after Rava?" wondered Cody.

"I've seen her at environmental meetings with the activists. I guess they want her picture for their gallery and a better line on what her role is. Some aggressive activists stay underground so they can surprise Harlan and his people." Cody's brow furrowed as he puzzled over the linkages.

"You tell me that the Great Spirit has sent me to defeat the wasichu, who are the polluters and despoilers. You then tell me that the people pursuing me are the environmentalists and they kidnaped my mother.

So I'm now working with the polluters. I'm confused. Whose side am I on? What is my role?"

Quiet Fox rose. "Each partial answer brings more questions. You can only follow the trail laid out for you and in due course the pattern will emerge. You can see in this room that you have already influenced many people. Who knows how far the ripples may spread?"

The Native Americans filed past, each shaking his hand and Kim's as they exited. Dan approached with Emily and briefly touched hands. The diminutive girl put her arms around his waist, dark head on his chest, and hugged him tightly. She looked up with tear stained face and quavered, "I've been desolate without you, Brandon – Cody. You twined your soul with mine when you saved me from my dark vision. I'm only half alive without you. Come back to the cave soon."

He held her shoulders and patted her back. "Now I remember, Emily. That was a special time. I'll come back."

Dan regarded them with a dark enigmatic look. Emily released herself, gave Kim a tremulous smile, and left. Cody's eyes followed her, mirroring fond memories of their youth. Kim stood with arms folded and shook her head ruefully, with a small crooked smile.

"What chance do I have, Cody? You're soulmate to every girl you meet. And they're all so darned beautiful." He didn't respond to her levity.

"Let's get the folks and head back to the ranch. We've a lot to discuss. With each other and with Seth and Marta."

Back at the ranch, their eyes were on the beauty of the garden and waterfalls; their thoughts were on what to tell Seth and Marta about the revelations at Arrah's school. When his grandparents came out to the porch with the evening coffee and a plate of oatmeal cookies, Cody opened the subject.

"We had a surprise meeting with Arrah's environmentalist friends at school today. They threw some light on the recent inquiries about me."

"Oh?"

"The Native Americans are concerned because they are attuned to nature. They've suffered many ecological problems involving incursions for mining, logging, hunting and fishing into Indian lands and nearby government-controlled lands. They're fighting back. They told me that Les Harlan is an agent for the despoilers and polluters; that he carries out a government policy that gives financial advantage to those who would take from the poor, from the people's heritage, and grow richer. He tracks the environmentalists to frustrate and discredit them. Because I danced with Rava, they see me as a possible lead to her group. However, I'm an unknown quantity. No one is sure of me. Everybody's checking me out."

Marta chuckled softly. "Well, I could have told that girl you're on her side. Just looking at the ranch would prove it." Cody remained serious. "I don't want to involve you and grandpa in this. There might be fanatics on either side who would commit violence out of frustration."

"I've read the newspapers," agreed Seth, "but I think I can handle anything that happens on my ranch."

"Who would have thought that perfume would get you involved in a big ecology war?" mused Marta.

Cody gave Kim a glance combining frustration and amusement. He could not bring himself to tell them he was not their grandson and that forces from his real mother's past were threatening him. Seth clung to his self-reliance, ready and willing to defend his property.

"When we go riding tomorrow we'll have to look for tracks of those three troublemakers." Seth had dismissed the environmental factions as a negligible threat.

Early morning brought a surprise. Elaine's red Corvette rolled up to the steps. She leapt out garbed in cowgirl regalia from Stetson down to riding boots. She skipped up the steps and greeted Cody with a hug and kiss as he came through the door. "Cody, darling! I hope your invitation to visit any time is still valid. I awakened early and decided that fresh mountain air – and you- are just what I need."

Seth and Marta came out, gaping at this magazine picture of what a ranch girl should be. Tall, lithe and fresh faced, her clothes tailored to perfection on a figure trained for display. She surprised Seth with the strength of her grip as Cody introduced her. "This is Elaine Pendragon, a client from Langlois."

He responded warmly to her as all men did. He patted her hand, returned the smile and glanced teasingly at Cody. "We've heard much about you, but Cody's a master at understatement. Welcome to our home, Elaine."

She turned to Marta, bypassed the tentatively outstretched hand and greeted her with a hug and kiss. Still holding Marta's shoulders, she looked to the waterfall and said, "Mrs. Hoag, you must show me your garden. I see now where Cody gets his love of beautiful surroundings."

"Please call me Marta, or even grandma," the older woman replied. "And my husband is Seth. But not grandpa to beautiful young ladies," she added with a twinkle in her eyes. "You're welcome to explore and enjoy anything on the ranch – especially the garden. It's mostly Cody's work, you know."

Kim had been standing several steps to the side, coolly observing the newcomer captivating everyone. Her own self-confidence dwindled before this paragon of beauty, grace and charm. She felt awkward and hated Elaine for putting on this theatrical act for these nice but gullible people.

Elaine turned to her. Kim stood frozen. She despised herself for not smiling or extending her hand. All she wanted to do was turn and run. Elaine's smile softened and the radiance of her face took on a warm glow. Her eyes expressed – admiration! Her voice became velvety with intimacy. They might have been alone.

"I've wanted to meet you, Kim, since the first time that Cody spoke of you. He danced with me and said that I was well trained BUT – I could never be a star until I learned to put self-expression into my dancing the way that his friend Kim did. I could have kicked his shins! I could have stomped on his feet! Who was he to tell me, a ballerina, about dancing? When he finally made me understand, made me feel dancing the way you do, I experienced dancing again the way I did as a child. Do you mind if I say how grateful I am that you have become part of my dancing, part of my life?"

Elaine stepped forward, took Kim's face in her hands and kissed her on the lips. She then enfolded the girl in her arms. Kim's arms went around Elaine. How could she have been so cruel and hateful and jealous without knowing this woman? She knew that it was fear of losing Cody that caused it. She now realized that Cody saw qualities in her that she did not see herself. There was hope for her love. The two women walked arm in arm to the side porch above the garden. The others discreetly went inside to complete breakfast preparations.

Intruders

Marta set out a family style breakfast of hot biscuits, fried eggs, bacon and refried cabbage and potatoes. Coffee, milk, butter and preserves completed the spread. The women vied to do the serving. After Seth said grace, they dug into the food with mountain air appetites.

"I'm riding over to the back road this morning," stated Seth. "I'll be back for lunch."

Cody recalled that the three truculent vagrants had been seen there. In a casual tone he asked, "Do you mind if I tag along, grandpa?"

"No need, Cody. You ride around the pasture with the ladies. Take them out to the dam. Show them the orchard. That's an easier ride."

"Ignore this dude ranch outfit," laughed Elaine. "I can ride. My Lochinvar is a quarter horse. We still enter an occasional cutting competition. Win some, too. And I'd like to see more of your ranch."

Once on horseback, Seth led them toward the hills at a steady pace. The younger horses playfully startled at nothing and ran off their excess energy until the slope steepened. They then fell in behind the experienced Patchwork and followed the trail he pioneered.

Scattered rocks and dry vegetation offered little inducement for the horses to dally on the lower slope. The uphill ride in the climbing sun soon had them sweaty and dust covered. The scattered trees closed ranks about them providing welcome shade, cooler air, the resinous aroma of pine and its soft carpet of needles. The gold, red and brown of deciduous trees streaked the evergreen cloak on the mountainside. Occasional ground squirrels, rabbits and a marmot paused in their dining to watch curiously as the party passed. A startled deer bounded off through the trees. Their horses' hooves clopped softly in the wooded silence.

They cleared the ridge and heard the soughing of wind through the pines. The cool breeze and easy downslope were a relief from the dusty climb. Seth angled left across the slope. Uphill, the rise became near vertical. He paused at an outcropping and signaled a halt.

"What is it, grandpa?" called Cody as he pulled up behind the girls.

The horses moved restlessly. Seth raised his hand for silence. Talking ceased. They quieted their mounts. Faintly they heard the tinkling notes of water splashing. Seth proceeded around the outcropping. The other horses followed eagerly. A narrow waterfall fell through a cleft in the rock into a small pool. The overflow went into a rocky basin and disappeared from view. They dismounted to let the horses drink. The rancher walked past the spring and up the hillside twenty feet to a lookout point. He gazed down the canyon. "Cody. Step up here."

When his grandson stood beside him, Seth pointed below. "What do you make of that dust cloud on the road?"

Cody squinted. "Looks like a pickup headed out."

"That's what I thought. I wonder if that's our trespassers? Where were they? What were they doing?"

"Shall we backtrack on them?"

"What about Kim and Elaine?" worried Seth.

"They can follow at a safe distance. I'll see if these guys left anyone or anything behind."

Seth studied the mountainside and selected their route. "This trail forks two hundred yards down. The right branch meets the road about a half mile below the canyon." They rejoined the women and warned them about the possible danger ahead. They agreed to wait on the trail just before the intersection with the road. The carefree attitude vanished and they remained quiet on the descent. Seth took his rifle from the scabbard when they reached the road. He offered it to Cody.

"No thanks, Seth. I'm just out to reconnoiter not to get into trouble." He slipped from his saddle and grounded the reins. "It's less than ten minutes up the road to the canyon. Keep lookout here for the truck."

He walked quickly up the road. Out of sight, he paused and listened with all his senses. Nothing. He moved ahead, pausing at intervals to listen. Fresh tire tracks led into the canyon. He entered warily, keeping to one side and listening intently. Still nothing. The tracks ended. There, neatly arrayed, were at least 200 small plants in containers. He recognized them: marijuana. A small, cultivated plot lay beyond them. The intruders were about to set out the plants. This had to be stopped. He went back to the road, erasing his tracks with a sheaf of brush. The rocky side of the road held few footprints so he made good time. He signaled Seth for silence.

"No one there. Just a campsite and preparations for a marijuana crop. Let's bring the women back home and come back to clear it out."

When they reached Kim and Elaine, Seth told them, "No one there. They may have gone for a ride and turned back at the top of the road. I'll check it again next week."

"I'm glad," said Elaine. "I was afraid there'd be trouble." Cody sensed her genuine concern and more, a hint of hidden knowledge driving that concern. Kim watched them, an unspoken question in her eyes. Seth looked at his pocket watch.

"We should be heading home. Marta will have lunch ready. I know you have to head back to town." Kim kept her silence. Seth led them home at a good pace, bringing them in at eleven o'clock. He went straight to the house while the young people unsaddled and carried the gear to the tack room. Marta shooed the women out for a shower and change of clothes while she finished luncheon preparations. They emerged to find a quick meal of sandwiches, pie and coffee on the table.

Elaine and Kim carried the table talk. They described the scenery, the animals, the waterfall and the truck sighting. The men were quiet, eating and half listening. Seth broke in at a lull in the conversation. "I need some help from Cody on the irrigation system. I wonder, Elaine, if you would mind bringing Kim home?"

She gave him a radiant smile, "I'd be happy to do it." She squeezed Kim's arm. "We have a lot to talk about." Kim looked to Cody and accepted the invitation.

"You're a godsend, Elaine. I do have to get back."

Right after lunch they packed, gave effusive thanks for the weekend, and roared off in the Corvette.

"All right, Cody, what did you see?" demanded Seth when they reentered the house.

"There's a marijuana field ready to plant in the canyon, grandpa. I'm worried. It's too late in the year for planting. I think we have to go back now and get rid of it."

"Why bother? Nothing can come of it. Only idiots would plant now."

Marta watched both, reading signs and lips.

"Right, but I think there's more to it. Elaine knows something about it. There's a federal law: your land can be confiscated if you grow drugs on it," Cody explained.

"That's impossible! No jury would believe that Marta and I would grow drugs. Sheriff Hopping wouldn't believe it."

Cody became impatient. "No one has to believe it. An informer's accusation is enough. A quick raid, a few plants, and the ranch is theirs. You'd have to fight the federal government to get it back. Even if you won, the legal fees would bankrupt you."

Seth stubbornly looked for a way out through innocence, then angrily conceded.

"All right. All right. Let's get it done." They saddled Toulouse and Strutter, and pushed them hard on the return trip. Dust from the trespasser's truck hung in the still air when they cautiously approached the canyon entrance. The three men were assembling the plastic pipe to carry water from the spring to the cultivated field. Young plants in the pots had been set in neat rows waiting to be planted. Using the truck as cover, the two ranchers moved close to the field. They noted the full gun rack in the truck's king cab. Cody rounded the truck and approached the men.

"Excuse me, fellows, but you're cultivating the wrong ground." Anger made his voice hard.

"What the hell?" exclaimed one man. He spotted Cody, then looked beyond and saw no one else.

"Grab him, Harry!" The nearest man crouched with arms wide and rushed at Cody. His anger at what the three men were doing to his grandfather overcame Cody's ingrained suppression of his physical abilities. He sprang into the charging bigger man with his shoulder, stopping him dead in his tracks and straightening him up with the impact. He grabbed the shaken man by neck and crotch, raised him high and smashed him back to the ground. The leader couldn't comprehend the sheer strength of that quick move. He pulled his hunting knife.

"All right karate kid. Try your stunts on Sam Bowie."

Unhesitatingly, Cody stepped in and enveloped the man's hand with his own on the hilt of the knife, holding hand and arm immobile. The leader put his other hand over Cody's to no avail. The knifepoint turned and moved toward the man's eyes. He watched the inexorable approach with growing fear, and then turned his head to his remaining companion.

"For God's sake, Tommy, jump the bastard! He's going to blind me." A blazing look from Cody and Tommy backed off with hands raised to his shoulders in submission. He wanted no part of this action. The leader fell to his knees and turned his head away from the knife. A bullet kicked up dust near the group. The shot echoed in the small canyon.

Seth's crisp tones cut through the sudden silence. "Don't move, fat boy!" he ordered the one Cody had thrown, who was now on hands and knees.

"You with the knife. Drop it!"

Cody, whose ire had simmered down, slowly unclasped his hand. The knife dropped from his assailant's numbed fingers. Cody kicked the knife to one side and stepped over to recover it. The rancher gestured with the rifle. "You two. Sit next to Harry." They complied in sullen subjugation.

He smiled down at them in a fatherly manner. "I want to thank you boys for all the trouble you went to digging up this plot and piping the spring water. It was right neighborly of you. But I'm afraid we're going to refuse delivery. You'll have to load them up again." They were relieved at his mild tone.

"Harry. Stand behind the others, facing me." His voice took on an edge. "Now! Hands on top of your head!"

"Cody. Take his weapons. Search him head to toe." His grandson recovered a short sheath knife and a pocketknife.

"Sit, Harry. Tommy. You're next." Another sheath knife from his belt. "Down, boy."

"You. Knife fighter. On your feet." The man rose slowly. "What's your name?"

"None of your god-damned bus..." A shot smoked past him. His face whitened.

"Buck! It's Buck." Cody frisked him, took his keys and sat him down. "Now, boys, I want you to load that truck of yours. Fast but neat. Up!"

They scrambled up, wary of the soft-spoken old rancher with his hair trigger temper. They loaded the plants and then gathered the plastic irrigation pipe, and lashed it to the roof rack and tailgate. Cody used a sheaf of brush to cover traces of the work and many footprints.

"Can we go now, old man?" asked Buck impatiently.

"Turn around!" barked the rancher. They did. "Hands behind your backs." He handed the rifle to Cody. He took the lashing rope from the truck and cut three short lengths. "Grab your wrists, Buck." He made several turns of the rope around the wrists, a quick turn between them, pulled it tight and knotted it. He tied the others similarly.

"Sit."

Buck protested, "Hey, old man."

The rope whipped around his ankles and yanked him to the ground. Seth knelt on his legs and hog-tied him in seconds. The other two submitted without protest.

"Stow them in the back, Cody." He stacked them in the rear seat like cordwood. Seth took his grandson out of earshot. "You know where this back road intersects the highway just across the California border. Take the horses to the ranch. Meet me at the highway as soon as you can."

Cody assented. "Okay."

Seth climbed into the cab and headed down the road at a leisurely pace. Cody mounted Strutter and led Toulouse at a quick canter back to the ranch. Telling Marta that Seth was all right and they would explain later, he sped to the rendezvous. Seth waited off the road one hundred yards from the overpass. His grandson pulled up beside him in the fading light. "Everything okay, Seth?"

"Sure thing. Climb in and we'll rack up the truck." Muffled shouts from the rear were ignored. Seth wheeled the truck up onto the highway, gunned the engine and like a seasoned stunt man ran the right wheels up on the railing. He shifted into park, turned on the emergency flashers, and removed the key from the ignition.

Back at the ranch, Seth put his hand on his grandson's shoulder. "You've been quiet a long time. What's bothering you?"

"It's the timing, grandpa. If there is a drug raid planned, it's going to come soon. It could be violent like the ones we read about. I'm worried about staying in the house. You and grandma could get hurt."

The rancher pointed to his gun cabinet. "No one comes in here unless I invite him. And what I can't hit, Marta can. We can take care of ourselves." Cody shook his head.

"You don't understand. A SWAT team comes in today with automatic weapons, tear gas, battering rams and air support. It's a mini-war."

"That can't happen here! Not to law abiding citizens. That's just in drug dealing neighborhoods."

"You read the papers. I'm worried."

Marta agreed with her grandson. "I've read those articles, Seth. Drug enforcement is getting as violent as the drug deal. Seth picked up the telephone and dialed, then handed it to Cody. "Tell Sheriff Hopping what you think. He'll tell you, it can't happen here unless he knows about it. And then it won't happen."

Cody listened and returned the receiver. "There's no dial tone."

"Now I'm really worried, Seth. Maybe we should do as Cody says and leave." Her husband slammed his fist into his palm. "I'm darned if I'll let some haywire posse run me off my property. I'm not going."

Cody spoke calmly. "We don't have to leave the ranch, grandpa. We could cross the bridge to the orchard and camp out for the night. The fruit's ripe, the weather's mild. We could watch the stars." He smiled in fond reminiscence. You could take me camping the way you used to do."

Marta rose. "I'll put the rest of the coffee in a thermos. Get our pack, Seth."

He retrieved their light camping packs from the closet. Cody brought out his sleeping bag. They donned jackets and boots, Seth took his rifle and they hurried off to the orchard. They camped under the trees next to the irrigation stream that fed the waterfall on the creek. The site commanded a clear view of ranch house and access road. They reminisced about rebuilding the orchard, the irrigation ditch and the waterfall. They traced the constellations in the sky. The coffee gone, they rolled into sleeping bags and settled down for the night.

The constellations wheeled across the sky and the faintest hint of dawn showed over the mountains to the east. Cody awakened to sense the proximity of a group of people. No noise or lights accompanied them. He strained his eyes down the access road. The faint infrared halo of a warm engine moved towards the ranch. Then another. He awakened his grandparents, pressed their lips for silence, and pointed down the road. They saw nothing but nodded understanding.

Five vehicles in all came into view. They stopped out of sight of the house. He noted faint human figures approaching the yard. At last the dogs barked and came running toward the intruders. Two of the trailing attackers stopped and sprayed the dogs that yelped and ran back behind the house. The rest of the raiding party ran up the steps, broke the windows and threw something inside. A battering ram smashed the door. The first one into the house ran out a moment later wearing a black fur headpiece. He screamed, tore it off and threw it on the porch. A staccato burst of shots from a machine pistol followed. Immediately, other guns fired until a small war erupted. A bullhorn amplified commands to the force. A helicopter swooped down and illuminated the area. Shots from the barn stampeded the horses. The rooster crowed and hens squawked. Pandemonium reigned. The shooting ceased. Men ran out of the house front and back. They regrouped under instructions from the bullhorn voice. Their vehicles pulled into the yard with headlights on the house, adding to the illumination of the rising sun. "Come out with your hands on your heads!" roared the amplified voice.

Nothing moved. "It's your last chance! Come out or we commence firing." No response. Several flat reports. White smoke billowed from the windows. No one came out. The SWAT team, gas masks on and weapons ready, moved forward. A cloud of dust swirled on the road. Flashing lights and a wailing siren identified the patrol car. It pulled to a sliding halt in the middle of the yard. Sheriff Hopping stepped out. "Who's in charge here?" he bellowed. A SWAT team member confronted him.

"You're in the middle of a drug bust, trooper. Get lost!"

"Drug bust? Who the hell are you?"

Cody strained eyes and ears to follow the conversation, relaying it to his grandparents.

"I'm Inspector Carver, federal drug agency. We have a warrant to enter these premises."

"Well, I'm Sheriff Hopping. No one busts anybody in county territory without checking with me. Show me that warrant." A paper was handed over.

"Justice of the Peace Lem Loblaw! He can't even perform weddings in my jurisdiction. Call off your dogs."

"Sheriff, you don't know..."

The sheriff put his face down to the inspector's level. "Call off your dogs!" he bellowed. The agent waved his troops back. Sheriff Hopping ascended to the porch. "You in there, Cody?" When no one answered the sheriff entered. A minute later he came back to the porch. Hands to his mouth, he shouted, "Cody! Cody Hoag! This is Sheriff Hopping. Can you hear me?"

Seth's voice came back. "He heard you. Is it safe to come down now?" A relieved tone in his voice, the sheriff inquired, "You all right?"

"Just fine!" came the answer.

"Then come on down. I'm in charge now." The three came marching across the bridge, wary eyes on the heavily armed SWAT team.

The sheriff came to meet them. He put his hands on Marta's shoulders and looked in her eyes. "You all right, Mrs. Hoag?"

"Yes," she replied in a chipper voice. "I'm real glad to see you here."

He shook hands with the rancher. "Sorry I was too late to stop this, Seth. I just got word something was going on about a half hour ago."

"What's going on, Arnie?"

"Some half baked drug bust, Seth. They got a warrant from Lem Loblaw to break down your door."

"Lem Loblaw? He's not a real judge!" exclaimed Seth.

"These fellows don't know any better. Let's see what they want."

Hopping turned to the impatient inspector. "What is it you want in this house, inspector?"

"We have a warrant to search for drugs."

The sheriff turned to the rancher. "Would you agree to a search, Seth?"

"I guess so, if it gets them out of here."

Inspector Carver raised his arm to signal his men into the house. The arrival of two more patrol cars carrying five troopers interrupted his command. The troopers walked over to the sheriff, eyes on the heavily armed SWAT team in gas masks. "Any trouble, sheriff?"

"No. Just some misdirected drug bust authorized by Lem Loblaw." The troopers all smiled broadly.

"Shall we show these boys the way out?"

"Not yet, Sergeant Hancher. Seth agreed to a search."

Inspector Carver made a thin smile and raised his arm again.

"Just a moment, Inspector. Only two of us will search the house, accompanied by Mr. Hoag." Chagrin clouded Carver's face. "Now, sir, remove your jacket and empty all your pockets on it." Carver didn't move.

"Do it! Now!" He reluctantly complied with the sheriff's order. Looking beyond him, Hopping commanded the SWAT team, "The war is over. Stack your arms next to my car. Then form a column of twos and stand at ease." The men looked about uncertainly and then complied. Hopping had taken charge. The inspection lasted only a few minutes.

"Nothing here," Carver told his troops, "but now we'll have to check out the aerial photography."

Hopping regarded him quizzically. "Check out what?"

"Aerial photography." He pulled out a large photo from a carrying tube and presented it. "See this corner blowup? Those are marijuana plants in a field on this ranch. These people are major growers."

Hopping turned to Seth. "Will you allow these men to trespass?" Seth felt in a stronger position with the SWAT team disarmed.

"No," he responded and gestured to the house. "They trample everything like a herd of buffaloes. I will allow the inspector alone to take a look if we can catch those spooked horses."

"No need for horses," said the agent, "we'll take the helicopter." The three men entered the idling aircraft and shortly disappeared over the hill. They returned in half an hour. Carver wore a black look. The sheriff was grim and annoyed. Seth smiled. The deputies had gradually drifted between the ranks of the SWAT team and their stacked weapons.

When they returned to the yard, the sheriff said in an amiable voice, "Well, Carver, we've searched everywhere on the ranch for drugs. Since you're technically an intruder, why don't we inspect your vehicles?"

"No. We're satisfied. We're leaving."

"Inspector Carver. I order you to open your vehicles."

"I won't allow it." He ordered his team, "Load up!"

The sheriff roared, "Ten Shun!"

The SWAT team stood rigidly at attention.

"Sergeant Hancher. Deputy Gomez. Search those vehicles."

They returned in a few moments, each with a plastic sack. "Looks and smells like marijuana, Sheriff," said Hancher. The sheriff gave Carver a frigid look.

"Would you mind coming to headquarters and explaining this operation to me?" The inspector looked worried. "You have no authority to do this. I'll have your badge. You're interfering with a federal drug interdiction operation."

The sheriff's face hardened. "Would you like handcuffs and a gag?"

Carver shut his mouth. Malevolence twisted his features. Hopping turned to the SWAT team.

"You men. Turn in your ID to Sergeant Hancher. Take off your ski masks and battle gear. Get back in your vehicles and follow him to headquarters. You'll be questioned and released on your own recognizance." One of the unmasked squad was bleeding from long slashes in his face. "What in the hell happened to you?" exclaimed Hancher.

"Their damn cat attacked me. I hope I killed it." As if in response, Tripod came onto the porch with her three legged hop and skip. The troopers laughed out loud.

"This SWAT team had better stick to mosquitoes," Gomez jibed. Tripod showed her teeth in a cat grin, possibly taunting the despondent team.

"Inspector Carver. You come with me," ordered Sheriff Hopping. He turned to the rancher, "Seth, this is the darndest thing I've ever seen. I apologize to you and Marta. Whatever damage there is, I'll get that agency to pay for it. They can't get away with this high-handed activity in my county." The caravan exited the yard. The Hoags and Cody went into the house to survey the damage and see about breakfast. Except for numerous bullet holes and a carpet of splinters, there was surprisingly little damage. The machine pistols had been used as spray guns rather than point target weapons. Luckily, random events are more often misses than hits. Only Tripod, now the center of adulation, had drawn blood. She seemed surprised at all the doting attention she received just for expressing her feline territoriality. Nobody entered her domain without permission.

A quick survey of the kitchen and pantry revealed one dented pan, a leaking bag of beans, and three shattered jars of preserves. Marta at last shooed the men out. "Enough cleaning! Go see to the animals while I make breakfast."

Seth and Cody went out the front door. There at the foot of the steps were the dogs, nervous and apologetic because they had not driven off the intruders. Like shamed puppies, they wriggled closer to beg forgiveness. Seth's rough head rubs and rump slaps showed acceptance. They ran circles around the two men and then led the way to the barn. "Dark Eyes is limping, grandpa."

"I noticed. We'll take a look at her."

They caught up with the dogs at the gate. Seth called Dark Eyes and held her, then sent the other dogs after the horses at the far end of the pasture. A sensitive lump on her thigh appeared to be a bruise.

"Seems like one of those bullets kicked up a stone, Cody. She should work it off in a day or two." The horses arrived in a skittish mood, too nervous to come close for their treats. Ironsides hung far back despite the dogs barking at his heels. There were no wounds visible on the horses until they finally got close to the old horse. The hair on his left flank was matted with blood and covered with flies.

"Get a rope, Cody. We have to take a look at Ironsides." Cody ran for a rope and gave it to Seth. A quick flip of his wrist and the reluctant old horse was brought in. Cody held his head and murmured in a soothing fashion while Seth examined the wound.

"Just a long shallow crease. Ironsides is a fit name. Walk him up to the tack room. I'll clean the furrow and rub on some antiseptic grease. If I'd seen this earlier I would have kicked Carver's butt all the way to the gate. Those SWAT fellows shouldn't be allowed to play with guns. They're more of a menace when they're helping than those drug growers are when they're threatening. God save us from the government."

Ironsides stood patiently for the medical attention. He walked calmly back to the pasture when it was completed. The other horses took their cue from him and turned to quiet grazing. The cows had trailed in behind the horses, lowing irritably. Milking time was long past. The ranchers brought them into the barn and milked them quickly, speaking in soothing tones. Once milked, they resumed grazing in the meadow. Chores finished, the men went back to the ranch house. Marta saw them coming and had breakfast on the table. Grace was said with deep emotion. They had survived. Over dinner they laughed at the ineptitude of the raid, its failure to implicate them with drugs, the probable plight of the vagrants with their cargo of marijuana in California, and Tripod's heroics in defending the house.

After dinner brought more serious talk. "What's going on, Cody? Why is this happening? What are you tangled in?" asked Seth.

Cody shook his head ruefully. "I don't know, grandpa. Really. Some powerful groups are fighting over ecology, trying to take control of resources so a few wealthy people can get wealthier. Because I asked a girl to dance just before a police raid at the disco, I'm a suspect for both sides. They're confused. I'm confused. I think this drug raid was instigated by the big business group and their political ties, maybe as a warning, maybe to isolate me. I'm sorry it involves you. I thought I could use the agency to help me recover my past. Now I'm in over my head and involving everyone I know."

"And what is your past, Cody?" asked Marta gently. "Wouldn't it just be memories of traveling with Marly?" Cody realized that he had said too much. He could not tell them a direct lie. He did not want to break a presumed direct tie to their daughter. He sat in silent consternation, not knowing what to say that would preserve their relationship.

Marta asked again in gentle persuasion, "What do you know of your past, Cody?"

He looked down, shoulders slumped, and sighed. Squaring his shoulders, he looked up at the two of them, and speaking and signing, blurted, "I'm not Marly's child." More gently, he added, "I'm not your grandson."

They showed no shock. They regarded him sympathetically.

"What do you know, son?" asked Seth softly.

"Marly found me in Tahoe during a big storm. I was swept over a small cliff onto the roof of her van by a flash flood. I had little recollection of what happened to me before that, but now I know. She rescued me and brought me here. She let you assume I was her son."

"And?"

The boy rose. "I have some pictures to show you." He brought Emily's photos to them. "I was just given these by people who knew me at Tehachapi as a child. This is my mother, Brisa. We lived in a cave that was, and still is, a plant nursery. We were in hiding from Rava's people. They found us. My mother told me to flee on foot to Mt. Shasta. Native Americans helped me. At Lake Tahoe I would have been caught but for the storm. But for Marly and you I wouldn't have survived." The Hoags examined the photos closely.

"You favor your mother, Cody. She's beautiful and looks very self-reliant. You're like that, handsome and independent. No wonder she trusted you to travel alone all that way."

Cody regarded them with astonishment. This calm acceptance was not what he had expected.

"Grandma, you knew! You know I'm not Marly's child. Did she tell you?"

Marta shook her head slowly. "No. She said nothing. I suspected right from the start but wouldn't accept it. When you arrived that day you were naked. Only the dirty shredded clothing on the van floor was yours. There wasn't a toothbrush or a toy for you. Nothing. Marly never showed you any affection, never hugged or kissed you, not even when she left. The one time she brought her little Cody here she doted on him, showered him with kisses and kept him in loving view. He was her life. She could not have changed that, yet she ignored you. It bothered me then but I suppressed it thinking I could ask her when she returned."

"Four years passed before I accepted her loss and opened the boxes she had left. One was Cody's. There were clean little clothes, some brand new, that never could have fitted you. There were several pictures of a frail child who looked about six or seven years old – and it wasn't you. A tear spattered poem said goodbye to a delicate flower that God had sent briefly to brighten her world. I knew then that Cody had died. I felt that you were sent by God as the new flower rising from the seed of love planted in Marly's heart. By then you had blossomed in the new spring of our lives. You are the grandchild God has returned to us."

"Seth?" Cody questioned the rancher.

Marta put her hand over her husband's and answered, "I told him when you went to Tehachapi with Kim. I sensed that something was troubling you and felt that you must be recovering your memory." She sighed, "I've been anticipating, and dreading and hoping for this moment. I want you to know who you are."

"Why didn't you tell me?"

"So many reasons, Cody," she replied, sadness and guilt moistening her eyes. "I wanted to protect you. You were, I thought, deaf and unable to talk properly. You had trauma and memory loss. You were probably an abandoned child from Marly's hippie crowd. I didn't want to send you back to that drifting, drug filled life. Or, if not that, I didn't want you in an uncaring state hospital or a succession of foster homes. The ranch life was better, much better than that. And I didn't want to lose you. You'll never know the happiness you regenerated in our lives. We pray every day to thank God for bringing you to us, the replacement for Marly and her poor little Cody. Of course, there was your state of mind. You remembered nothing before us. Could we burden you with a mysterious past to which we had no clues? We felt that only the return of your memories should reopen that part of your life.

"But grandma, what about my mother? What about her loss?"

"I reasoned that she must be dead not to have looked for you. Perhaps she is, Cody."

"Brandon: she named me Brandon." Marta stiffened. He immediately regretted the retort. "She isn't dead, grandma – Marta." Pain showed in her eyes. "She isn't dead. Somehow I know that. She knows that I'm alive, too. If I were to die, she'd feel it in her heart. She just doesn't know where I am because I've been unconsciously hiding myself from her people – from my people." His grandparents reacted with surprise to this statement. "When I was fleeing through the mountains, I was being trailed by my mother's people. They could sense my presence, my location, in some way. The same as she could. The same as I can. Quiet Fox met me at Lake Sabrina and taught me to be absolutely silent so that no one could sense my presence. When I was trapped under a tree above Lake Tahoe, in desperation I quieted myself. Unfortunately, Quiet Fox did not have time to teach me to recover myself. My memories were blocked. Then the flash flood spurted me onto Marly's van. And here I am."

"Who are your people, Cody? … Brandon?"

"I don't know. The girl I met at the nightclub, Rava, and her friend – they seem different from other people, like my mother. Maybe I'm different, also, Marta."

"Mrs. Hoag." Cody-Brandon, was taken aback. "Mrs. Hoag?"

"You're getting formal with us."

"But I'm not your grandson. I'm a stranger."

"Are you, Brandon?" she asked. "Are your new found memories of your first nine years to be your only reality? Are the eighteen years with us an illusion? Or are we also now an indelible imprint in your memory, a physical part of you?"

Brandon sat silently and looked back through his years. Those at the cave, those at the ranch, those at the school, and even several ancient inherited memories he did not understand. There was no difference. They were all physical as well as conceptual parts of his self. He looked up repentantly.

"You're right, grandma. I'm sorry. Whatever else I may be, I am your grandson." He knelt and embraced them.

Elaine and Kim

The red Corvette angled into the space next to Kim's Bronco. Kim vaulted out over the door. "Riding with you is a white knuckler, Elaine. I can see why you chose Strutter to ride. You're kindred high steppers." Elaine rewarded her with that brilliant smile. "I take that as a compliment. I'm glad I met you, Kim. It has been a wonderful day."

"Thanks for the lift, Elaine. 'Bye."

"I'm still thirsty from that ride. Would you have any ice water in your fridge?"

"Of course. Come on up. There might even be frozen yogurt."

Elaine stepped out of the car to follow her. "Better lock your car, Elaine. It won't last long unlocked in this neighborhood."

The ballerina laughed. "Steal it? Steal 'LEGS'? Where would they take it, China? They wouldn't get out of Reno." In Kim's apartment, they sat and talked about the day's ride, the waterfall, and the beauties of the ranch. Also about their sudden departure.

"Cody's nice," commented Elaine, "and I enjoy searching the clubs with him, but he's naive. He doesn't know the power of the people involved in this, whatever it is. They have unlimited money, connections and a global network. I'm just small potatoes. They can make or break my career in a second." She looked squarely at Kim, "Cody found something on that back road that worried him."

Kim's interest was aroused. "What do you know, Elaine? What do you think he found?"

Elaine played down her own role. "I don't know anything. I heard the Hoag ranch mentioned. They said they wanted Cody isolated to control him."

"Who said?"

"People with Harlan. People in tailored business suits. I thought Harlan was big but he's just an enforcer. Other people pull his strings. People with big projects and big money. If Cody doesn't deliver what they want, they drop him or squash him. I'm supposed to watch him but I want to keep him out of trouble. I like him."

"So do I," said Kim.

"Like him?" Elaine gave her a knowing look. "I think that love would say it better."

"Yes. Love. That's it."

"How does he feel, Kim? I've never gotten a rise out of him. And I've tried. It's a challenge to me."

"He likes me a lot, Elaine. We're close. I know he loves me. But he isn't sexually attracted to me." She chuckled. "And I've tried."

"I owe him," stated the ballerina. "And a lot of what I owe him comes from you. He told me I had to dance with your freedom of expression and somehow he made me feel what you feel. I'm moving up to featured roles already. More than that, I know that I'm communicating with the audience. My dance, my career, my life is reborn because of Cody – and you." She stood and began dancing slowly and expressively. "Put on some music, Kim. Anything danceable." Kim selected a real oldie: 'I Get A Kick Out Of You.'

"Dance with me, Kim." Kim looked surprised. "I need a partner," pleaded Elaine, "And I do want to experience dancing with you because Cody made me feel it only vicariously. Come on, dance with me," she coaxed. Elaine led her into a fox trot that started simply and grew in complexity. Kim was surprised by the ballerina's strength and the sureness of her lead. It reminded her of Cody. She thought of him as they whirled and was sorry when the final dip ended it. Elaine applauded them.

"Brava! Brava! More! More!" she encouraged. Kim put on some old favorites. "You remind me of Cody. You're the first girl I've enjoyed as a partner." At last Kim called it quits.

"Elaine, I'm beat. I have to take a bath and rest. You can use the shower if you like." Kim filled the tub and luxuriated in the hot water and bath oils. Elaine took a long shower, letting the needle spray relax her tension.

Kim soaped lazily and swabbed the loofa at her back in desultory fashion.

"Allow me," said Elaine, kneeling at the side of the tub.

"You'll never come clean that way." She scrubbed Kim industriously from neck to waist until her friend's skin tingled.

"Enough! Enough. You're down two layers already."

"Now your arms," ordered the scrubber, and worked fingers to shoulders on the nearer arm with the loofa. That done, she reached across the tub for the right arm. "Scooch forward," she directed, and seated herself behind Kim. The right arm received the same meticulous attention. "You have beautiful skin. It's like velvet."

"Why thank you, ma'am." She rubbed Elaine's legs. "You're pretty smooth yourself."

"Ever share a tub before?"

"Not with a girl."

"What!"

"Only with Cody," Kim giggled. "I told you we were close friends. There's just no sex involved."

"Oh. Well, just think of me as Cody and relax." Kim closed her eyes and thought of Cody, the man she loved and wanted to desire her.

Elaine discarded the loofa and washed her tenderly. Stomach, breasts and thighs. She kissed Kim on the neck and told her what a beautiful body she had. Kim stirred from her fantasy of Cody.

"All right, Elaine. Let's dry ourselves." They stood facing each other while toweling. Kim's eyes were wide and thoughtful. "I've never met a woman like you before."

Elaine's arms enfolded her. She kissed her on the lips, seeking an answer to the unspoken question of love. Kim returned the kisses warmly but with a limiting reluctance. "I love you, Kim. I've always wondered why I never loved before, none of all the men I've known. And now I know. My soul has been awaiting you."

Kim held her close. "Oh, Elaine. I'm so confused. Your kisses tingle like champagne. Your body feels like part of me. We dance with the same expressiveness. I want to be close to you. And yet, I love Cody. What's wrong with me? I don't know what to think." Elaine twirled her out in a slow dancing step.

"I've never loved a woman before. I don't know what to do. Lie down with me. Please." They lay down side by side. Elaine turned to Kim and kissed her. Kim drew her head back, searched the ballerina's face, and saw only love. She buried her face on Elaine's shoulder. "Hold me, darling. Just hold me."

They stayed locked in each other's arms until Kim went to sleep. Elaine slipped out of her embrace and looked tearfully down at her newfound love. How could she be so vulnerable? And to a mere child who loved an unresponsive man? She left angry. Angry with herself for feeling love that she did not want. Angry with Kim for loving another. Angry with Cody for not returning Kim's love. Elaine left in turmoil.

Threat to the Ranch

A knock brought Cody to the living room door. He sensed one person outside. "Who's there?"

"Far Walker." Cody opened the door and signed to Marta and Seth. The Paiute shaman shut the door behind him.

"Good evening, Mrs. Hoag. Mr. Hoag." He shook Cody's hand.

"Soars With Eagles, we have been worried about your safety. We have been hearing disquieting rumors about your ranch. Rumors that it was wanted for mining, for a waste dump, even for a nuclear dump. We have been near the Sacred Place, waiting and watching since Wednesday. Yesterday two of my brothers followed you to the box canyon. They were prepared to help, but you did not need it." He smiled at the thought. "It was a well executed engagement. We guessed that you dumped them somewhere on foot when Soars With Eagles rode back to the ranch and then went to pick you up."

"Better than that!" laughed the rancher. "We delivered those guys and their marijuana plants to the California Highway Patrol. They'll be a while getting back."

Far Walker nodded approval. "But we did not expect the immediate drug agency raid. How did you escape?"

"That was all due to Cody's uneasiness and a dead telephone. I would have stayed to try and defend. Probably been shot, too. These two dragged me off to the orchard." He glanced fondly at his family.

"You were fortunate, my friend. My tribe became familiar with dawn raids on our families when others in power wanted our lands. There were always excuses for murder."

"Well, we did have prime seats for a SWAT action. Lots of shouting and shooting but not much damage. Don't know what they would have done if we'd been there. Only casualty was an agent clawed by old Tripod. Sheriff Hopping came and settled things down before they blew up the house. He's reading the law to them now. They won't be back."

The shaman disagreed on this point. "The same agents may not return, Mr. Hoag, but the ones behind them will keep after your land in different ways."

The prospect of unrelenting pressure perturbed Seth. It meant a need for unceasing vigilance. "Let them try. They'll find out they ran into a buzz saw," he muttered with forced bravado. His wife and grandson followed the conversation with concern.

"A buzz saw might be seen as a direct challenge by those who rely on brute force. I would like to propose an alternative – a swamp," suggested the shaman.

"A swamp? You want me to flood the ranch?" Seth was incredulous.

Far Walker smiled broadly. "The white man's swamp. The law and politics. Your family has befriended mine for many years. You have protected our sacred place and permitted us to hunt and to gather berries and pine nuts on your ranch. This has maintained our links with our customs and our ancestors. Because of our friendship and to preserve our heritage, I want to propose a way to help you. Our young people are beginning to look back on our heritage with pride. The ranch was once a small part of our lands. The sacred place, the springs, the pine trees, the game and the mountains are remembered in our religious and cultural background. We would like to use your ranch in traditional ways to reawaken this heritage among our young people. In return, we will help protect your ranch against intrusion. Patrols will watch your boundaries and roads. Our lawyers will fight in court any attempts to usurp your lands. We will claim protection for our sacred places, our ancestral burial grounds, and for continuation of our traditions. We will ally ourselves with environmental groups. We will protest against possible pollution of aquifers and Pyramid Lake. We will build a paper swamp to daunt any industrial or political invader."

Seth turned a perplexed countenance to his grandson. "Does any of this make sense to you, Cody?"

"Grandpa, it's perfect. We can't outgun or outman them, but we can bog them down in stinking legal mire up to their company logos. Let's do it!"

Seth stood, as did the other men. He extended his hand to Far Walker. "It's agreed. We work together." The shaman took his hand.

"Agreed. I have to return to our camp. We will work out details at Pyramid Lake during the week. We'll return for your approval next Friday." They talked about the ranch and the possibilities for cooperation. The shaman recounted details of the ranch and its history that amazed Seth. More details lived in memory than had been committed to books.

Kim's Bronco pulled into the driveway of the Victorian. Cody double-timed down the steps and over to the vehicle. To his surprise, Elaine was at the wheel.

"Hop in, Cody. Kim and I thought we'd both take you clubbing tonight." Kim, wearing a mischievous smile, occupied the passenger seat. Cody did as he was told.

"I never expected a double date." He noted Kim's more sophisticated hairdo, makeup and dinner dress. Elaine's influence. "And with the two most beautiful women in Reno."

"Elaine thought that another pair of eyes would help our search," offered Kim in explanation. "Hope you don't mind my tagging along."

"Great idea. I love it," although wondering how to handle the two at once.

The valets at Harrah's didn't recognize the vehicle but they certainly knew the driver. When she pulled up to the entrance there were valets available to help both ladies descend before Cody could unsnap his seat belt. He saw the inevitable head turning by bystanders, male and female, as he walked with one on either arm to the casino restaurant.

Kim basked in the VIP reception, the procession to their prominent table, and the instant service of wine and appetizers by the attendant waiters. Her glow of excitement and sparkling eyes heightened her allure. Cody felt the warm friendship of their table expanding to fill the room.

The orchestra appeared and began the Merry Widow waltz. Elaine turned to Kim. "Would you mind if I dance first with Cody. It's a way I can repay them for their hospitality."

"Of course not. Anyway, I've never seen you two dance." Cody found Elaine more challenging and mischievous in her dancing than ever before. The varying tempo of the waltz taxed their inventiveness but her dedicated training and his sensitivity to her improvisations made it a tour de force. The dinner crowd watched the dance and applauded enthusiastically. The orchestra entered into a fox trot for an encore but Elaine surprised them. She ran to the table and brought Kim out to partner Cody. The new duet was different but equally appealing. Kim's movements lacked the precision of Elaine's, her posture was less schooled, and her timing less accurate. Yet she danced with a sense of joy, expressiveness and abandon that overcame any deficiency in schooling. She was the audience idealized in their own minds. Again the diners applauded the twirling finale.

"Encore! Encore!" filled the air.

The orchestra struck up the Tango de La Rosa. Again Elaine surprised them. She walked out to the couple, took Kim's hand and sent Cody back to the table. She danced with Kim herself.

The audience became quiet as the women danced the erotic steps of the tango. Passion, fire, desire and restraint were displayed in slashing movements, expressive pauses, and sensuous dips. The audience sensed desire, uncertainty, mixed emotions, burning passion and controlled fire. When they were drawn together at the closing beats, the audience was silent, caught up in their own tangled emotions of love, hate, jealousy, desire and self-sacrifice. A tale of love had been pantomimed. The lights dimmed to a spot on the dancers. Pandemonium broke out in applause and cheers. They had communicated with the audience – and with each other.

The girls curtsied to the room, embraced and returned to the table. The performance fascinated Cody. What tied these women together?

Elaine said to Cody through her smile, "You bastard. What have you done to me? You've made Kim a part of me. I can't give her back." He looked at the radiant Kim, enjoying her VIP night and the two people she loved. What had he done, he wondered? And how did he feel about this emotional conflict? Their night of clubbing, dancing and searching for Rava generated unexpected crosscurrents. Cody tried to fathom the emotions of his companions as well as his own involvement with them. How were their hearts intertwined? He watched them laughing together as they walked arm in arm to the powder room.

Who are you, Cody? The words reverberated in his head. The little he had learned about his early years had only complicated his quest. *Who are you, Cody?*

He realized that the echo was outside his head. He turned to find

Rava seated beside him. Her face expressed her puzzlement over how to categorize him.

"Rava!" A rush of emotions suffused his being. He leaned toward her. She pulled back, alarm lurking behind her questioning gaze. Cody separated out the elements of his startled reaction. Love for his mother, brought to the fore by a woman who resembled her and communicated with full body language in the same way. He longed to be with others who shared his communications, his sensory abilities, his capability for rapport, and his store of memories. He hoped for a woman with whom he could share his every thought and emotion.

She spoke, combining a few words with her totally expressive body language that contained subtleties he could not grasp. "Who and what are you? You are like us in your use of language although sometimes you express yourself like a child. You look like us. You smell like us. I think that you sense bioelectric emissions although I cannot sense yours. And you're sexually aggressive towards me but not towards your beautiful escorts. Who are you?"

He searched for a response but could not answer immediately. Too many other lives were involved. Rava stood. "Let's dance." He followed her to the floor. They merged in a smooth flowing fox trot. He could feel her every intended motion. He removed his barrier of silence and let his biorhythms merge with hers. His mind was lulled by the music and the motion. His thoughts drifted through his recent past – the perfumery, Incline Village, the Hoag ranch, the stormy ride with Marly, and – and then he realized that his thoughts were being guided back. Rava was in rapport and reviewing his memories. He raised his barriers, swung his partner out and eyed her accusingly. She shrugged.

"I must know who you are. You can be a threat to us. We'll meet again."

He held her hand. "Where are you going?"

"Your friend Elaine is on the telephone, probably to Les Harlan.

Give them my regrets, but I must go." She withdrew her hand and walked quickly to the exit.

Cody returned to the table. Kim and Elaine joined him.

"Who was your partner, Cody?" asked Elaine. "You should have had her join us. You dance beautifully together."

"She's your mysterious nightclub lady, I bet," commented Kim. "How did you find her?"

"She found me. She just came to the table and asked me to dance. She is a good dancer. Not like you two, but good."

"Where did she go?"

"I don't know, Elaine. She said she had to leave and went."

"No late date?" teased Kim.

Cody felt a surge of tension in Elaine. Her gaze was fixed on the main entrance. He glanced behind her to the mirrored wall and saw the reflection of two conservatively dressed men at the door. Harlan's agents, no doubt. Her eyes flicked towards the exit Rava had taken. A nod of understanding and they strode through that portal. He steered the conversation from Rava. The ballerina's loyalty appeared battered by the conflicts among ballet career, financial sponsorship, gratitude to him, love for Kim, and jealousy. An unstable ally at best. Worse still, how would Kim's loyalty be affected?

Les Harlan was seated at the desk in his suite when Cody entered. His thin smile belied the forced heartiness in his voice. "Well, we got close to that mysterious girl again but she eluded us once more. You should have detained her for a few more minutes," he chided Cody.

"I thought we would dance a while longer, Les, but she was alarmed. She saw Elaine on the phone and surmised that your men would come quickly. She broke off the dance and left."

"Who is she, Cody"

"Her name is Rava."

"Rava who?"

"She didn't say."

"Where is she from?"

"I don't know."

"What organization is she with?"

"I don't know."

"Well, what the hell did you talk about?"

"We danced. Very little talk. She asked me to dance and we did. That's all."

Harlan's look softened. "That's enough for young people, I suppose. Did you agree to meet her again?"

"Not exactly. When she left, she said we'd meet again."

"No matter. We'll find her eventually." He became more affable. "In fact, that's what I wanted to talk to you about. There's going to be a meeting of a core group of environmental activists at Mt. Shasta in two weeks. I'd like you to come along and look for this Rava and her friends. If she contacts you, let us know right away. We want to talk with her and with her friends, find out what they really want, and come to a mutual understanding."

Mt. Shasta! The destination his mother had given him. Cody moderated his enthusiasm as he agreed to go. "Of course I'll go. I'm grateful for all you've done. I'm also against terrorism. I want to help."

"Fine, fine. We'll make the arrangements.... Oh, another thing. I heard about the raid on your grandparents' ranch. No serious damage I hope."

"No, not really. Just several bullet holes in the house."

"Good. That would never have happened if I'd heard of it beforehand. We could have vouched for you as one of our associates and squelched the raid. Remember that if your grandparents are troubled again, I can be a good friend."

"I'll keep it in mind." And also the converse, he thought.

"I spoke to Carver, the SWAT team leader. He told me that three suspicious people they had tracked to the back road on the ranch had disappeared. Any idea what might have happened to them?"

Cody saw no harm in revealing an outline of that episode. Elaine must have relayed her suspicions. "My grandfather saw that trespassers were using our back road. We surprised them planting a small marijuana patch. Seth escorted them to the highway and told them to take off."

"In California? Maybe that explains why they haven't been seen. I'll tell Carver."

Harlan rose and escorted Cody to the door. "A very resourceful man, your grandfather. I admire his kind. Remember, I can help him. And you can help us." Again Cody sensed the veiled threat. The ranch incident might be the beginning of the pressure, not the end.

Tripod was on the porch to greet him when he arrived at the ranch Friday evening. Careful repair concealed all evidence of the attack. His grandparents were in the kitchen in the midst of preparations for a larger than usual meal. He jested, "I know I eat a lot but this is too much. I'll be wearing two sizes larger after dinner.

"You're welcome to fill your plate, son, but we're having guests for dinner. Several of Far Walker's friends have been setting up a security system for the ranch. They said they'd be in about dusk."

"Security? What are they doing?"

"They'll explain when they come in. Meanwhile, I'd appreciate a hand at the barn." Two unfamiliar pickups stood near the barn. Out in the field a dozen extra horses grazed.

"Far Walker's horses?"

"Yes. They're for patrol. And for the young people to use to experience their cultural background."

They reached the trucks. "They brought ten saddles. I put up two more racks in the tack room. We'll store them there." They carried two apiece to the tack room and swung them up to higher saddle racks. Bridles were hung over the horns. "How long will this security go on, Seth?"

"Indefinitely. It's a mutual thing. Protecting the ranch protects their sacred place and allows them a private domain to train their youth in traditional ways. I have a feeling that they are also concerned about you, Cody."

Four horses trotted across the field, two with riders and two pack animals. Seth waved them to the tack room door where they quietly unsaddled and stored their gear. "This is my grandson, Cody. And these are Far Walker's kinsmen, Craig Reynolds and Ron Brasher." They shook hands and gave their tribal names, Far Talker and Tumbleweed.

"I was an electronics technician in the service," Craig explained. "Far Talker was a takeoff on my uncle's name. It stuck."

"I was always roaming, even as a little boy," said Ron. "I'd rather be in the desert or the mountains than in the city."

After dinner they sat in the living room and discussed the security installation. Craig described their work.

"The ranch is too large to patrol all the time. Remote sensors and radio relay give the best solution. We've put sensors on the back road, the fire roads and three canyons to the north. Two radio relays connect the network. Here by the ranch we've placed sensors on the road, the gate and the fire road on the ridge across the creek. To the east we have sensors on the trail to the Sacred Place. Two receivers, one here and one at our camp just beyond the Sacred Place will monitor the signals."

"How will your patrol keep in touch?" asked Cody.

"Smoke signals," replied Ron with a straight face. "We have brushwood stacked on the hilltops with blankets and water. All laughed.

"We're using portable phones for the patrols, all tied to the net. It's like a cellular phone system," explained Craig.

"Isn't this an expensive setup?" wondered Cody.

"It would be if we bought it retail. Luckily, it's all government surplus. We can buy from military warehouses for reservation purposes such as education. This is for cultural education on the ranch. Some of our brothers in the Quartermaster Corps did a search for what we needed. This old and obsolete equipment cost us $25 in fees."

"What about the ranch house and outbuildings?"

"All included. If anything moves in the secure zones – the house, the barns, and the bridge – we'll know and be in contact. Another surprise raid is unlikely."

Cody changed the focus of the discussion. "I spoke to Les Harlan several days ago. He told me that the raid was a mistake and he could have stopped it if he'd known beforehand. I told him about the three men with the marijuana plants that we escorted over to California. Les said he would tell Carver where they had gone."

Seth slapped his knee. "Damn! That explains it. Sheriff Hopping stopped by this morning. He told me that a friend of his in the California Highway Patrol called. A federal lawyer brought an order to release those men, claiming they were transporting the marijuana for a sting operation. Looks like we got stung by the government."

"I think I had better pull out of this affair, grandpa. It's getting too dangerous. Harlan has powerful connections."

"Far Walker and Quiet Fox believe that you have powerful connections, Soars With Eagles. Connections with the Spirit World and with the sleeping giant, the Native Americans. A lot is at stake for our people – our culture, our identity, the Earth we revere and try to protect. You are helping to bring us in touch with the ways of our ancestors, with the spirits who guide and protect us. You are helping to reintegrate us with all of Creation in the Hoop of Life. After more than a hundred years of broken promises and despair, we are fighting for this opportunity to live again as the People."

"Craig is right," agreed Seth. "You brought Marta and me out of our despair. You made our land and us bloom again. I'd rather burn the ranch to the last blade of grass than abandon it to people who would desecrate it."

A New Vision

Cody and Kim clambered through the rocky gorge to the Sacred Place in the pre-dawn light of early October. A silent group sat cross-legged on the ceremonial platform. Cody recognized Far Walker as well as Quiet Fox, Arrah, Craig, and Ron. There were three Native Americans in buckskins whom he had not seen before. Opposite them sat Yakuts from Tehachapi: Dust Devil, Manuel and Gabriel. Far Walker rose and climbed several steps cut into the rocky wall behind him and uncovered a reflective surface inside a small depression. He returned to his seat and began a soft chant that was joined by the other Paiutes, the welcome to the rising sun and thanks to the Great Spirit for the commencement of another daily cycle.

The sunlit line crept down the far wall of the canyon. A dazzling circle of light illuminated Far Walker. It was a beam reflected from the far wall to the overhead depression, and to the spire of rock at the end of the platform and then onto the shaman. Cody knew from experience that a shaft of that ray passed through the small hole in the spire and fell on his bed at the ranch house. It had been his first summons to the Sacred Place as a child.

Far Walker raised his arms and communed silently with the spirits until the sun rose higher and the reflected ray disappeared. He lowered his gaze and regarded each in turn.

"The First Peoples lived in harmony with this great land for countless generations. We recognized our part in the Circle of Life that embraces all animate and inanimate things. We revered the spirits, our ancestors, the animals who shared this life, and the Earth that supports us. The land was beautiful and we lived meaningful lives.

"Five hundred years ago new people entered our land. They were despoilers of the Earth and wanton destroyers of life. They spread across our lands killing our people and driving the remnants onto ever-shrinking reservations to live as beggars. We call these despoilers the wasichu, the greedy ones: corporations, politicians, mining companies, lawyers, governments, and so on.

"For more than one hundred years we have wallowed in despair. We lost faith in our Spirits, our ancestors and ourselves. We have lost touch with our past and have no future. Much of our present is poverty, isolation and drink. Where is our hope? Will the First Peoples and their ways go to extinction? Wovoka's Ghost Dance did not help: we nearly danced our tribes to oblivion!

"Eleven years ago in the desert near Tehachapi, a Yakut village befriended a young woman, Brisa, and her child Brandon. He is with us now. In turn, this woman and her child put the Yakuts in touch with the ways of their ancestors – ways such as water dowsing, rapport with animal life, and even with the rhythms of the Earth. For the Yakut shaman, 'Dreams With Manitou,' it was a rebirth of faith. He christened the boy 'Soars With Eagles.' Several of those who knew him, myself included, had transformative visions. It is natural that we regard this young man as a Sacred Person.

"Brandon's mother was kidnapped, and our people helped him escape to the north. It was the will of the Great Spirit that he should escape. Quiet Fox met him and taught him the silence of Wovoka. He disappeared from view at Lake Tahoe. Several years later Quiet Fox discovered him here on the Hoag ranch. We have helped him without interfering with the plan of the Great Spirit. Now he is recovering his identity and actively reentering the greater world with a lifetime mission. The attack on the Hoag ranch shows the power of his enemies whom we identify with the wasichu.

"I have brought you here to seek a vision with this Sacred Person on this special day in this Sacred Place. I shall ask for guidance in ways that we can help Brandon to fulfill his mission in life. This day we seek a vision in a new way. No fasting, no lonely meditation. We are from different clans without common rites. I propose that each group appeal to the Great Spirit in its own way. The rest can join in as seems fitting. We will form a circle, join hands and seek the vision."

Far Walker spoke to the Paiutes from Tehachapi. "I met Brandon in this Sacred Place and through him was granted a vision. Quiet Fox persuaded me to live with the Sioux for a time to protect him. Three of my Sioux brothers sit here: Elk Brother, Dawn Light and Longbow." To the three in buckskins, he said, "The two whom you have not met are Brandon, now called Cody, and his friend Kim."

"Quiet Fox and I shall begin with a prayer," and the Paiute shaman intoned a litany in his own dialect.

"From the depths of our despair--," Quiet Fox responded, "Great Spirit guides us." The litany continued with the others picking up the response.

"From subjugation and oppression--"

"From the prison of our unfaithful hearts--"

The litany continued in hypnotic cadence asking for guidance through the conflict with powerful enemies to achieve a resurgence of cultural identity that would recover the bountiful life of their ancestors.

"Through the depredations of the wasichu--"

"To a renewal of the Circle of Life--"

The three Sioux rose and began a deer-hunting dance. The others rose to form a dance chorus that provided a cadence and background dancing for the three buckskin clad Sioux. They became part of the tale of deer hunting in game-rich land, a reverence for the game and the land, the disappearance of game, and their hopes for return of the lush land. The Paiutes, danced and sang of life conforming to the hard dictates of the desert yet finding rich rewards in this harmony of human life and nature.

Cody stood silently for several moments, seeking rapport. Then they experienced a graphic tale of a cold and barren Earth warmed by the breath of the Great Spirit and blessed with fertility. The animate creations were not separate but composed of the same materials and the same spirit as the Earth. Being connected, what they did to each other and to the Earth they did to themselves. The dance-prayer ended with a plea for enlightenment of the despoilers of the Earth and a return to a bountiful life.

The circle formed, hands clasped. They sat in the morning sun and merged their souls....

Tall grass swayed in waves to the horizon. The cool breeze moderated the heat of the sun. Watercourses traced dark green lines across the plain. The shaman led them toward a region rich in game. A small herd of deer browsed in the distance. Birds flushed from their path. They walked with light hearts, knowing that plentiful food, ready shelter and pleasant times lay ahead. The rhythm of their pace merged with that of the waving grasses and calls of birds to produce a song of nature integrated and healthy again.

Soft clouds drifting on the horizon firmed in outline, thickened and took on many colors. The aimless drifting became a martial cadence that overwhelmed the gentler rhythm of the Earth. The clouds increased in number and grazed the surface. Behind the cloud front the land turned barren, air roiled to dusty brown and the sun grew dim. Disharmony and discord were fueled by thunderbolts, roaring gusts of wind, the crashing of trees and the cries of frightened animals. They walked uncertainly through a silent and barren land. Their pace slowed to the beat of a halting dirge: joy fled. They felt no pulse of life. Dead time.

A pulse fluttered, steadied and set a tentative rhythm. Flattened grasses rose and swayed to that gentle beat. Fallen bodies came erect and walked erratically. A leader emerged who danced, gestured and sang to form the bodies into marching ranks. Their voices rose in a chant, their ranks reshaped to form a circle clasping hands and dancing in a tale of rebirth. Within that circle new life sprang forth, revitalized by this Hoop of Life.

The swelling tramp of storm clouds pressed against the Hoop of Life. Weapons flashed and bodies fell but these were replaced by new life from within the protective Circle. The Circle firmed and expanded as the dark clouds at the interface were transformed by the Dance into defenders of the Circle. The clangor of attack became a dying rattle. Deprived of the bounty within the Circle and having no resources of their own, the destroying clouds starved and faded away. The Hoop of Life expanded. The Earth became beautiful again. The sunlight strengthened. The Hoop of Life became their group clasping hands in the Sacred Place.

Mount Shasta at Last

Les Harlan lifted off the twin engine Beechcraft from the Reno airport and took a northwest course to Mount Shasta for the environmental conclave. Cody, Kim and Elaine sat at windows to view the forest-covered Cascade Range on their 170-mile flight. It reminded Cody of his hike north as a boy through the Sierra Nevada Range from Tehachapi to Lake Tahoe. He never reached his destination, Mount Shasta. Now, the rugged country with early snow crowning the peaks told him how difficult the rest of that journey would have been.

Kim tapped his shoulder and pointed off to the left to a massive snow covered crater. "Mount Lassen volcano!" Harlan banked the plane left and approached closer to give them a better view of this crustal souvenir of a geologic cataclysm. After passing the crater they turned their attention straight ahead where Mount Shasta's eternal mantle of white reflected the late morning sun. The serenity of this mountain mirrored the persistent forces of continental plate compression that had gradually raised the peak skyward.

The Beechcraft made a feather light landing and taxied directly to the public hangar. A Lincoln immediately arrived beside them. One of Harlan's men, introduced as Arnie, transferred their baggage to the trunk. Les took the front passenger seat and the others occupied the rear. When they drove off, a glass partition rose between the two compartments so that Harlan could question his advance man privately.

Cody sat up tall and read the driver's lips in the rearview mirror.

"Our two houses are side by side two blocks from the exit. I'll stay with you to take care of things. We have nine men and three cars at the other house. We've all been scouting out the area and sizing up the ecology freaks."

"Anybody of interest?"

"Just the usual crowd: those two spotted owl fanatics who wear horn-rimmed glasses; Lenny, the tree hugger; that big fish man from the hatchery; the meeting organizer, Francine; a couple of Greenpeace guys; several 'Save the Whale' shirts; and a number of the local marijuana growers."

"The antis?"

"A group of loggers were standing near the hall; Jack, the fishermen's rep was with them; the Japanese rep, Hideoka, was talking to Skorsvold from the Scandinavian fisheries; Harper, the oil tanker man was in the Cascades Lounge; and several people from International Trade Fairs were at a table there. Nobody out of the ordinary."

"Odd balls?"

"Naturally. Boomer was having a drink with that other Bigfoot hunter, Kravitz. Stavich, the guy who puts spikes in trees to break saw blades was haranguing some teenagers outside the Motorlodge. Klasdorf, the mad bomber, was strolling around estimating the charge needed to take out each building. Carver and six of his Swatters were marching in a column of ducks and trying to be inconspicuous. A bunch of "I AM" people in blue serge and wing tips looked like Mormons lost in LaLa Land. The ordinary people had more nose rings and earrings than noses and ears. In some places it looked like Hollywood North."

"What do you mean, 'ordinary people'?"

"Well, yeah. I saw some Indians in Levi's. There was a band of tourists with kids in Mount Shasta T-shirts. Six totally average people were having lunch at a vegetarian restaurant. Everybody else there looked skinny and hyper."

"Describe these totally average people!"

"That's it! Totally average. Mid-height. Medium build. Dark brown hair. Brown eyes. Medium noses. Good teeth. Tan skin."

"Rava?"

"Yeah. I see what you mean. She could have sat with those people. Except that they weren't talking much. Just average people out for lunch. – Here we are, Les. The other house is there on the left. We set up an intercom. Public phone is just one digit higher than yours."

The 'Bed and Breakfast' sign before the two-story shingled house declared, 'No Vacancy.' Bright splashes of color livened the garden and flowerpots. Clean windows, fresh paint and starched lace curtains showed the pride and care of the owners. Without a doubt, 'cozy' and 'traditional' would describe the interior.

Arnie let them in to a large parlor done in rose patterned chintz. A spinet piano graced the corner. A small office area was on the right and stairs between led to the second floor. The women walked down the hall, which had a master bedroom, sitting room and bath on the right. A small bedroom was on the left. Beyond it were the kitchen and a large dining room at the rear. A window wall gave diners a full view of the flower garden. The house provided food for the soul as well as bed and breakfast for the body.

"You folks will be upstairs," Arnie informed the young people. "Master suite is in front. Two bedrooms with connecting bath in the rear."

The women opted for the rear bedrooms. Cody brought his pack to the suite.

When they returned downstairs, Les and Arnie were talking in quiet tones in the office. Les suggested affably to his guests, "Why don't you folks see the town? You can take the car if you want but it's only a few blocks to the downtown area. You'll see more of it walking. Arnie and I have some business to go over."

Glad to be free, the three young people set off at a good pace to explore this little town at the center of so much physical beauty and psychic mystery. The stately fir-clad and snow-capped Mount Shasta, a dozen miles to the northeast, dominated aesthetically and emotionally. Pristine wilderness called up a primitive urge to be one with Nature. Anything good is possible under such a spell. That spell had worked its magic on the builders of the town. A sense of cohesiveness, warmth and friendliness emanated from every aspect. The houses showed individuality in design but a community of expression. The streets themselves fit the lay of the land and asked to be used as much for the charm of the journey as the lure of the destination. Along the way greenery and flowers graced the yards, porches and windows with their colors and fragrances. But this was no sterile model town. Residents and passersby exchanged smiles and friendly greetings with them. Interest in a garden brought an invitation to stop and smell the flowers. Cody felt the harmony along these streets more than in any other town he had visited.

Downtown, the ambiance changed. The commercial center displayed the usual T-shirts, souvenirs, fast foods, doughnuts, clothing, liquor and sightseeing folders. Gas stations and minimarts filled out the scene of Everytown USA. The serene and steady pulse of Mount Shasta fluttered and nearly failed here.

Various types of people walked the streets, the people Arnie had described to Les in the car. These were people exploiting Mount Shasta rather than living in harmony with it. These included physical exploiters of forests, streams and mountains for mines, drug farms, and tourist attractions; spiritual exploiters with cults based on lost races, subterranean cities, visitors from space, and intersecting ley lines of psychic force; and anthropological exploiters with tales of Bigfoot hunting expeditions, and plaster casts of over sized footprints. Among these larger than life caricatures only the "ordinary" citizens stood out as they pursued their mundane errands supporting the daily life of the town. Where else would postmen and plumbers, electricians and window washers appear as interlopers in an urban scene?

The sidewalk became impassable. Everyone they passed handed them a flyer. Tables with petitions lined the walls: "Save the Whales," "Save the Forests," "Save the Spotted Owl," "Protect the Wilderness." These activists rubbed shoulders with others proclaiming, "Save Our Jobs," "People Before Animals," and "Manage Our Resources."

"I think we're at the Conference Center," laughed Cody. "Every group concerned about ecology must be represented in this block. What can the speakers say that isn't printed on these posters?" Single file, they threaded their way to the meeting hall. The list of papers and seminars was posted on a board. Beneath it printed schedules filled a tray.

They continued past the hall and on toward the beckoning Mount Shasta. As the clamor of the marketplace and meeting hall diminished, the sense of harmony and age old mystery returned. The mountain seemed clearer against the sky. Flowered gardens appeared. People became open and ready to stop their chores to chat. Beyond the moneychangers, the temple honored God's natural creation.

Cody sensed the emanations of people like his mother and Rava! His mother had directed him to this section of town when he had fled Tehachapi a dozen years ago. He turned left at the corner and walked more quickly as the sensations became stronger.

"A penny for your thoughts!" Kim's offer snapped him back to the presence of his companions. He smiled sheepishly. "Hunger. I saw the restaurant up the hill and thought we could scout up a good meal."

The restaurant occupied the ground floor of a two-story house. Walls of three rooms had been partially removed to provide a connected eating area. The blackboard listed only vegetarian fare. A smiling waitress appeared from the kitchen. Ordinary?... yet Cody knew that these people were like him. He decided to reveal himself. The excitement of proximity to his goal overcame his innate caution. Kim and Elaine perused their menus. Cody addressed the waitress vocally and with body language. "What are the specials for today?"

The woman remained calm outwardly but he could feel her startled reaction. "Who are you?" she thought, while reciting the menu, "Napa cabbage, leeks, brown mushrooms, pine nuts, taboose nuts, grass seeds, and rosemary. Dressing of olive oil, apple vinegar and herbs. Dessert is mixed seasonal berries."

"Sounds good. I'll have the special."

"Ladies?"

"I'd like the avocado salad, please," responded Elaine.

"The Caesar for me, please. And herb tea," said Kim.

"What is your name?" inquired Elaine.

"Hanna."

"I'm Elaine. This is Kim and he is Cody. We love the coziness of your restaurant." The waitress stiffened at Elaine's name.

"Thank you," she answered and walked back to the kitchen. Two other diners glanced at Cody's table, then rose and left.

The women praised their salads. Cody's meal was an adventure to him. Some ingredients he knew well, some he had tried with his Paiute friends, and others smelled vaguely of forest, marsh and grassland. Their chef obviously did not limit himself to the local market. Cody settled the check with Hanna.

"There is a coffee house on the highway a quarter mile north of the railroad tracks. It has disk jockey dancing in the evening. It's called Du-Gi's. You might find it interesting." She disappeared into the kitchen before he could inquire further.

The coffee house was on the east side of the highway on a large lot. Trees in front and a garden decorated with topiary almost hid the two-story building. No signs or lights identified it as a club. Not a sound emanated from it. "Are you sure this is the right place, Cody?" Elaine peered at the dimly lit house and noted the absence of a parking lot or cars parked on the street.

Cody's excitement leaped. He discerned hedges trimmed to the likeness of animals. His play table as a boy in the cave garden came to his mind's eye. It had a grizzly, a dire wolf, an eagle, a saber-toothed smilodon, and a mastodon. A grizzly stood by the gate. Other shapes loomed in the shadows. He jumped from the car and ran into the garden. Just like the miniatures he and his mother had grown and trimmed. The howling dire wolf was silhouetted against the autumn moon. Beyond it, an eagle with wings half extended appeared ready to leap into flight. The hulking mass behind it must be a mastodon. Crouched at its flank, poised to spring, was the fearsome smilodon. His mother's directions for sanctuary in Mount Shasta had been clear. "Look for a flower garden along the highway on the northeast edge of town. It will have your topiary play animals grown on a larger scale. Friends will watch over you until I come."

Elaine called. "Come out, Cody. There's no club here. It's just somebody's home. Let's find a lounge downtown."

Kim touched his arm. "What are those things, Cody?"

"Extinct and endangered animals," he answered, indicating them in turn. "Bear, wolf, eagle, mastodon, saber toothed tiger.

"Why don't we come back in daylight? Trespassing in the dark might be dangerous."

He laughed at that. "No fear, Kim. This is the right place."

"Elaine!" he called. "Come on in. This is the club." He strode confidently up on the porch and rang the bell. The door opened immediately. It was Hanna. "Good evening, Cody. We hoped you'd come." She greeted the two women. "Kim. Elaine. I'm glad you could make it. You'll find it a friendly place."

They walked the length of the hall to see only an ordinary residence with dim lighting. Hanna opened a door at the end and descended a lighted staircase. Faint music could be heard. They followed her down. The lower door opened and the music swelled. They entered a full basement that had been decorated as a coffee house. A dozen tables surrounded a dance floor. Most held two to four people who were all looking with intense interest at the newcomers, particularly at Cody. The DJ turned off the sound system when he saw them.

Cody could feel the emanations in this room. Startled, he realized it was an entire room filled with people like himself, people with his style of expressiveness, and maybe with his sense of fun.

Hanna introduced them to the crowd although it obviously was unnecessary. "Everybody!" she called. "Our guests are Cody, Kim and Elaine. You can introduce yourselves when you ask for a dance."

She seated them at a table next to the dance floor and explained the club rules for sociability night. Anyone could request a song from the DJ but must wait his turn for a second request. Anybody, man or woman, can be asked to dance. No hard feelings for a refusal. One dance per invitation. Wait your turn for a repeat invitation to dance. No exclusive couples. Her parting admonition was, "You're on your own!"

A slow disco beat began and couples moved to the floor. There were no inept dancers. The newcomers watched for a few moments and decided this could be fun.

Before Cody could ask one of his escorts, a voice from his side asked him, "Care to dance with me, Cody? I'm Elda." He wondered about the expectations of the women with him but saw that both were being asked already. The sociability rule seemed to be working. He rose and followed Elda to the floor. Everyone put them at their ease and gradually exercised their dancing capabilities. The beat grew faster and more intricate, the dancing more athletic and improvisational. Elaine had a ball. Her training and discipline plus her newly regained self expression made her a marvel to these club members who had not known what to expect from their guests. Prospective partners waited their turns with her, eager to learn from her, to demonstrate their own capabilities, and to experience the thrill of dancing with a talented new partner. Elaine, in turn, found a roomful of partners as adept as Cody but each with an individual style. It was a dancer's dream.

Taking a break at last, she asked the DJ to show her his music list. It included all types of music – disco, pop, big band, western, folk and classical. Mischievously, she selected one number of each type and pled to have them played as a set. It turned into more fun than she had anticipated. She reached into her repertoire for line dancing, clog dancing, round dancing, square dancing, ballroom dancing and folk dancing. The room came alive to her challenge. They emulated her steps with zest. When the Polovtsian Dances played, Elaine improvised on Cossack acrobatic dance steps, kicks and leaps. A dozen others were on the floor trying to watch and imitate her at the same time. Inevitably, they collapsed into a kicking, laughing pile on the floor. The DJ called an intermission and they all pushed the tables together to form a single group. The ice was not just broken but melted.

Coffee and cakes kept them going until after midnight. Dancing, laughing and exchanging dance steps brought them together in camaraderie. The evening ended with hugs and kisses, laughter and admiration – and promises to do it again. Elaine eased the car down the street, unlike her usual jackrabbit maneuvers.

"You fit right in here Cody. These people dance like you. They know what I'll do before I do it. They even look like you and act like you. I saw you dancing – you looked like a lifetime member of their club. Are you sure you don't have relations up here?"

"None that I know of, but they do seem like my kind of folks."

He realized what she meant about family resemblance. All the club members looked average. They looked the same "average" without diversity in height, eye coloring, hair, facial features and skin tone. They were just all too close to some mainstream average. In this town at this convention time they stood out from the conventioneers because they were just average. Was this what Les Harlan had been asking Arnie? Were these people other than chance neighbors in this end of town? Were they closer to his mother – and to him – than mere hometown friends... were they his *tribe*?

The next morning the crowd outside the meeting hall presented a chaotic sight. Signs waved at all angles. Banners were strung and posted wherever space existed. Orators appealed, protagonists sang and chanted, raucous groups shouted and pushed. The random turbulence confined itself to discrete groups rallied around their foci – usually a banner espousing a particular ecological viewpoint. A slowly advancing line of admission ticket holders threaded through the clumps. They argued with antagonists, cheered their supporters and generally enjoyed their privileged status as participants in the conference.

A commotion on the far side arose as Harlan's men pulled the international corporate representatives through the crowd. Like Moses parting the waters of the Red Sea, an immense man in a black suit strode menacingly through the crowd, which parted to permit two Corniches to drive up to the entrance. Two other men in black suits drove the cars away. The sheriff's officers were ineffectual. They pushed through the crowd shouting for order and dispersal. The throng allowed them enough room for shallow breathing.

Elaine pulled Kim in behind the Corniches and with Cody behind they progressed straight to the entrance. A flash of tickets and they entered to seek their seats. Harlan beckoned them to the right rear corner where they had a panoramic view of the stage and hall. Two of his men leaned nonchalantly against the wall flanking an emergency exit beside their section. The meeting assumed the worst features of a town hall brouhaha and an interactive in-depth television political program. Each interest bloc occupied its contiguous set of seats and emoted in unison to every prepared paper, audience comment and question. Fundamental and irreconcilable differences in perspective prevented reasonable discussion of the issues and stifled an appropriate value system for weighing proposed solutions:

Should humans strive to preserve the natural pristine state of large areas of the Earth?

Or, should we exploit to the fullest all of the resources of the Earth with minimal regard for environmental concerns?

Should wildlife and vegetation be protected against human exploitation and pollution?

Or, was protection of non-human species irrelevant?

Was the existence of human life intertwined with the continued existence of a natural balance of species?

Or, were other species of non-economic benefit and therefore irrelevant to the human species?

Cody followed the thread of each argument as it twisted sinuously through the perspectives of the interest groups. Forests would disappear in 20 years to the deterioration of the global environment. Logging jobs were disappearing today to the harm of logging families. Fishing restrictions were putting fishermen and their boats permanently on the beach. Drift nets and purse seines were putting most species of fish and sea mammals on the endangered list. Corals were bleaching out, losing their essential symbiotic algae as the seawater changes became intolerable. Industrial pollution was making large areas of the Earth uninhabitable for humans, let alone for wildlife. Anti-pollution laws were throwing millions of workers on unemployment lines in many countries and exporting jobs and pollution to poorer countries less able to cope. Human encroachment had destroyed animal habitat and threatened extinction of many species. Human rights came before 'animal rights' postulated by urban do-gooders.

The premises were simple. The emotions, confrontations and outright violence they engendered make compromise difficult. Climatological, ecological and environmental perspectives are long term, global in scope and utopian in philosophy. Jobs, income, food and land are immediate and local pressures involving the personal welfare of individuals and families. Their conflicting agendas defy reconciliation.

Charges were hurled of tree spiking that endangered loggers, cutting of fish nets, booby trapping wilderness trails, and dynamiting facilities. Counter charges included poaching, illegal and legal clear-cutting on the lands of our heritage, trespassing on preserves, and indiscriminate pollution.

The moderator tried to maintain an air of rational discussion among the speakers and panelists. The undercurrent of irrational violence in the audience reduced the prepared agenda to meaningless posturing. What was the purpose of the meeting? There were no solutions coming out of this event. Cody ignored the droning speakers and the ranting of the audience. He let his eyes and mind wander the hall.

Les Harlan and his men had the participants under intense scrutiny. Cody detected the occasional clicks of concealed cameras that were adding picture identification to the dossier of information being scribbled on palm size computers or cell phones. Harlan himself appeared detached and scanned for something not evident – probably subtle links to a *sub rosa* group of activists. Cody searched the hall for Rava or any of the dance club members. To him they were conspicuously absent. Were these Harlan's real targets?

The international corporate representatives looked like their caricatures. They sat at front center in a compact block, their perimeter defined by stern young men who observed the audience rather than the platform. The group was uniformly clothed in conservative suits, white shirts and geometrically patterned dark-hued ties. They were attentive to all the speakers and took copious notes. Public relations, Cody surmised. The overdressed, bejeweled, casual wear coterie he characterized to himself as the entertainment crowd. One faction was composed of obvious show business people who emoted over every threat to the pristine environment and biodiversity. The other faction was even more outlandishly dressed and bejeweled. Their bodyguards were bigger and more threatening in appearance that any others. These must be the drug lords concerned about their farms on private and public lands.

Next to the lords, a boisterous group of roughly clad people who supported the inviolate nature of public lands turned out to be marijuana growers who wanted to maintain their isolation to escape surveillance by drug enforcement agencies. Other groups included the vociferous loggers in Pendletons and fishermen in heavy knitted sweaters. An eclectic group of pedants and minor government functionaries kept interjecting statistics on every aspect of ecology – fish populations, habitat acreage per wildlife unit, annual tree growth, reforestation growth, carbon dioxide emissions and absorption, and ecotourism. Several reporters doodled on their pads.

Boredom overcame Cody. There could never be a common ground for this motley assemblage because their perspectives were strictly human. They had no empathy with Nature. Making an excuse to leave, he leaned over to Arnie. "Where are the rest rooms?"

Arnie smirked. "Rest rooms? You got to be kidding. There's one toilet with ten women queued outside. Go down the street to a bar. That way – out the side door." He made a head movement to direct one of his men to follow. The crowd had increased in density and vocal volume. Cody threaded his way as unobtrusively as possible. People jostled him, harangued him and confronted him.

"The Earth belongs to us. Right?"

"Sign up to rescind the fisheries agreement."

"Hey, guy! You got any change?"

"You a damn government observer?"

A hand grasped his elbow. He tried to shake loose but it was an iron grip. He glanced at his captor to see a slim dark-haired girl, Elva from the dance club. "This way Cody." She led him between two buildings, through a back yard and a gate to the next street. As they walked she told him, "This meeting has become a big enough distraction that we could get your mother free of surveillance. Come to the club at seven o'clock tonight. She'll be there." Pointing across the street to a market, she added with a smile, "They have a rest room. No line." She stepped back through the gate and disappeared before he could question her. He stood irresolutely at the gate, shrugged and crossed to the market. His excitement grew. Eight more hours and he would see his mother!

Cody and Kim walked at a carefully nonchalant pace down Alma Street toward Mount Shasta Boulevard. As he expected, one of Harlan's agents came out of the house next door and followed them. They turned left on the boulevard. It was now 6:25 pm and dark. He estimated that the club was two miles away. That was a fast thirty-minute walk. He had to shake the tail quickly.

He steered Kim into the sporting goods store. "I'm going to meet my mother at the club, Kim, and I don't want to be followed. Please, go into the ladies' room, wait several minutes, then come out and browse for a while. If I come back, I'll meet you at the Bavarian Restaurant on Chestnut Street in an hour and a half.

Without a question, she tapped his shoulder, pointed to the rest rooms, and left his side. Cody sauntered to the ski shop, picked up a pair of pants, and went into the fitting room. Dropping the pants on the service counter, he continued through the employee's door and out the back. A twelve-foot fence enclosed the rear loading area. Without a pause he took three running paces and leaped to grasp the top of the wall. He pulled himself up effortlessly and vaulted over. Moving quickly through the alley to Chestnut Street, he cut over to Castle Street and headed northeast. Where Castle Street intersects Alma Street, he glanced warily back toward their rented houses. Two cars were pulling away headed downtown.

He crossed Alma Street and continued northeast. He sensed no one following and it was only a mile to the club so he slackened his pace. Pursuit should center on the downtown area for a while. Past the McCloud River Railroad tracks the road became the Everitt Memorial Highway. A quarter mile ahead he could see the garden entrance to the club. His pace quickened. Brisa was only minutes away!

Cody paused at the gate. He was a child again, standing at his play table in the cave. In front of him were the topiary animals he had fashioned with care from the ancestral memories his mother had recalled with him. Nearest were the grizzly, dire wolf and eagle. For his ancestors these were the common fauna. Further back, shadows conspired to give a half finished appearance to the mastodon and long-fanged smilodon. Across the table Brisa was smiling encouragement as he contemplated the trimming and wiring necessary to bring these beasts to life in his garden.

Brisa extended her arms to him – only it wasn't across the play table of his dreams. She was real. She was here on the clubhouse steps. Cody ran to her arms and they embraced. Their voices interlaced in a maternal counterpoint.

"Mama! Mama!"

"Brandon! Oh, my darling Brandon!" Over and over...he could feel the hunger in Brisa to hold him, to express her love, to know all about his life since that day he had fled to the mountains. Brandon opened his memories to her and felt the awareness flood through her – the Pacific Crest Trail; the pursuit; the deluge that had washed him onto Marly's van; his wonderful adolescence at the Hoag ranch; his gradual recovery of his memory and his search for her. Her joy expanded at his rich life. Her sorrow deepened that she had not been a part of those formative years.

She stood back and regarded him, drinking in every detail. Several inches taller than she, medium build, lithe and smooth muscled, dark hair, and regular features reflecting her looks. Brandon, in turn, saw quick glimpses of her life at Mount Shasta. She lived among people like herself, outwardly so much alike but differing in their sensitivity to each other and to the natural world. Brisa wanted to reveal her people to the world of *Homo sapiens* and cooperate in maintaining an ecological balance and sensitivity that would serve all species. Most of her people wanted to remain unknown, existing in small groups on the fringe of human society. They were hoping that human global despoliation and pollution would not destroy all species together. They hoped that they were not dancing toward extinction themselves, ending in a whimpering expiration or a mushroom cloud of radioactivity.

Brisa explained, "The only way we can preserve our world and our people is to come out, to reveal who and what we are. We must convince everyone that the Earth, as we know it, will die if we do not live in harmony with Nature. You must help to galvanize our people, to inform them and those who are hybrids like yourself, as well as those who have smaller sets of Neanderthal genes. We all belong to the sentient beings of this planet and have a responsibility to the global ecosystem. I cannot because those hiding here sense my movements and restrict me."

Cody thought of Wovoka's Silence. "They can't track me, Mama."

She replied. "No. Not when you had amnesia. Now that you have recovered, your bioelectric waves are readily detected."

"But they're not! Quiet Fox taught me a silencing technique. Try to sense my emissions as I go into Wovoka's Silence." Brisa stood watching him with a skeptical expression that gradually evolved into incredulity.

"If I did not see you, I would believe you were not here!"

"Let me teach it to you, Mother. Then you can walk away from here."

They joined hands and entered rapport. The technique was transferred.

"It's beautiful, Brandon, and so simple. Now you can come back to the house with me. We'll get my things and be off. There is much to do. We can become more open. We'll bring the world back from the brink of ecological destruction."

"But Mama, what about my friends here? Quiet Fox, the Hoags... and Kim?" Although a family-oriented person, loyal to her friends as well, her attitude dismissed them, and Cody frowned, unable to understand his mother's single-minded purpose. He stood not knowing what to say or think.

"Cody! Cody! Where are you?" Kim's shout was muffled and urgent as she tried to be heard but not too far. She stood inside the gate, peering through the darkness. Cody stepped onto the path. "Over here, Kim." She ran to him and clutched his arm for emphasis. "Cody. Harlan and Carver are coming. He made Elaine tell him where the club is. He suspects that you are a mole sent by the ecology underground to spy on his operation. He's coming after you as the breakthrough link he's been seeking. You've got to run! – Oh!" Kim jumped as another figure stepped from the shadows.

"I'm Brisa, Brandon's mother."

Kim looked carefully at the woman, seeing the features so like Cody. She glanced at his face expressing tender joy. "I – I'm so happy for you both. This moment became my quest, too."

"I'm glad to meet you, Kim." She embraced her briefly. "But come." She took Cody's hand. "We'll go out through the back gate and head for the logging road up into the mountains. I know Brandon's high regard for you, Kim. And I know that you are attracted to him. You must have realized by now that he cannot be sexually attracted to you. We are a different people, Kim. You know how sensitive Brandon's sense of smell is. Your scent is not like that of our women when we are sexually excited. Nothing you do can change that. You must forget him. Find a mate among your own kind. Pursuing Brandon will bring loneliness and regret. He may be near but he will always be just beyond your reach." Brisa ended with words of sympathy for Kim's misguided love. Yet, the soft words barely cloaked an undertone of stern warning to stay away from her son.

Kim had long ago grasped the concept that Cody loved her but she could not sexually attract him. Those words passed her by with the negligible impact of an advertising jingle. It was the forbidding undertone that caught her attention.

"It's more than body scent, Brisa. You have a deeper antipathy to my love for Cody." She deliberately used his Hoag name. "What is it? What's gnawing at you?"

Brisa was visibly disconcerted by Kim's perception. She stopped by the old outbuilding across the back access road. "You do not understand. You will only hurt him, mislead him. Forget him, Kim."

She turned to Cody. "I have to go back for my things. You and Kim can cut across this field to the logging road. I'll catch up."

She ran lightly up the access road to the north. The two young people watched her disappear in the night. They headed east across the field.

Headlights illuminated them momentarily, swept past, then swept by in the opposite direction. They dropped to the ground. A four wheel drive utility vehicle heading north roared up to the outbuilding, churned through a skidding turn, and drove over to the back of the club. Two men unloaded boxes from the vehicle on to the back porch.

More lights approached from the east along the logging road. Sirens wailed and lights grew brighter from both north and south on the Everitt Memorial Highway. All converged on the club. Behind the official cars came dozens of other people who stopped along the highway and on the rear access road.

Carver's voice blared commands through a bullhorn. "Come out with your hands up! Clear the area! Get back! Surround the building! They're armed and dangerous. Throw down your weapons!" A crowd of civilians was approaching shouting conflicting slogans.

"Due process!"

"Shoot the bastards!"

"Press! I'm press!"

"Charge!"

Headlights illuminated the dark and silent club. Shadowy figures stood behind the lights with weapons raised. The topiary animals in the garden seemed mobile under the moving lights and the dancing shadows. The crowd segments moving closer evidenced conflicting moods of party fever, hostility, bloodthirsty violence, support and confrontation. Some carried sticks and placards on poles that might become weapons. Jostling began as conflicting groups collided. The embroilment spread and swirled toward the club. Part of the SWAT team faced the crowd rather than the target building. The bullhorn commands became imperious.

"Throw out your weapons! You have one minute to clear the building. Come out now!"

The crowd violence grew and impacted the SWAT team. A shot rang out that silenced the commotion.

"Here they come! Through the garden!"

A burst from an automatic weapon scattered leaves from the ominous grizzly. Rocks and sticks flew through the air. The SWAT team grew restive. Another extended burst blew splintered wood from the club front and shattered the windows. Rear facing members fired shots over the crowd. Some spectators hit the dirt. Others turned and ran. Return fire hit a SWAT vehicle. A fusillade hit the club. The truck at the rear roared to life and headed for the access road. Sight of a live enemy galvanized the SWAT team to action. They loaded into their vehicles and crashed through the garden fence in pursuit. The grizzly wrapped one in its strong-limbed embrace. The eagle clung to the hood of another and flapped its wings blindingly across the windshield. The mastodon, smilodon and other shadowy beasts joined the fray. The mobile attackers slowed and halted in the dense foliage of topiary.

A blinding flash illuminated the garden. The situation swirled downwards, crumping into chaos and violence. The sound of a high explosive blast was followed by a startling lift of the club and then its collapse into rubble. The crowd fell flat. Several vehicles overturned. A rain of fragments littered the garden and adjacent highway. The assault collapsed into major confusion. Injured and terrified people screamed while the bullhorn blared in vain. Vehicles sped away, leaving a few caring people to tend the wounded. The commotion died down until the disorganized battlefield emitted only whimpers of the injured and anxious cries for missing companions.

Finding the Way on Mount Shasta

The bright lights, turmoil and gunfire kept Cody (?)... Brandon(?)... and Kim crouched low in the field. They lay behind the outlying building waiting for an opportunity to flee. A rain of debris from the club followed the pressure wave of the demolition charge. Compact fragments whistled past, lighter pieces spun through the air with the uneven thrum of unbalanced helicopter blades. All impacted the ground with unnerving thuds. A whirling board dug into the ground two feet away before its shank angled across them from Cody/Brandon's upper left side to Kim's right thigh. Their pained cries were lost in the reverberation of the explosion. When the initial shock wore off, he gasped, "Kim? Kim? Are you all right?"

She responded weakly. "My thighs hurt but I can feel all the parts. Let me try to move." She tentatively rolled over on her side and pressed herself to a sitting position, gasping at each awkward movement. "Lots of pain but everything works. No blood. I think I can walk." Brandon sat up, and then struggled to his feet. "My left arm seems weak, my ribs hurt and I feel as though I've been thoroughly spanked."

He lifted her to her feet with his right hand. Kim stepped, moaned and stumbled. She gritted her teeth and took several limping steps. "My left thigh hurts like hell but I can walk. Cody, let's go now before they find us."

He supported her at the left forearm and elbow, easing the load on her bad leg. They limped across the field to the logging road. The noise of the battlefield faded behind them as they headed toward Mount Shasta for their rendezvous with Brisa. Kim leaned more and more heavily on his arm as they hurried through the night on the uneven logging road. They had anticipated a ten-mile dash to freedom, reunion with Brisa and a new scope to their adventurous search for his identity. Instead, it had become only painful random motion into an unknown and threatening future. Brisa's hostility augured badly for their continuing relationship. Brandon's reunion with Brisa to work in their 'homeland,' wherever that was, would mean separation from Kim. Brandon had not found his home at Mount Shasta. Rather, he had found his mother's detention place peopled by uncertain friends and undecided enemies. Freedom was blocked by enemies with global reach who controlled money, armed agents and political entities. Loosely allied with their enemies were workers whose economic survival entailed exploitation of diminishing natural resources. If he was to pursue the life mission thrust upon him, then their allies were not likely to help much—just disorganized groups of environmentalists who did not have a common agenda.

They paused for a breather. Brandon, normally indefatigable, was laboring under the exertion.

"Why does your mother want me out of your life? Why does she hate me?"

He was bewildered and sorrowful. "She doesn't hate you, Kim. She doesn't share all her memories with me. There is an area of her memories emanating resentment and fear that is completely blocked to me. It's locked away like my memories during my long amnesia."

"And what about your family origin? Who are your people? Have we completed our quest?"

"I know now that she and her kind are Neanderthals. She calls me a hybrid of Neanderthal and *Homo sapiens.* The details are locked within her region of dread. I have learned no more." Kim put her head on his shoulder in despair. Her arms encircled his waist. She released him quickly and stepped back, concern on her face and in her voice.

"Cody! You're bleeding. Let me see."

He turned his back to the moonlight. She raised his blood soaked Pendleton shirt and T-shirt. A bruise angled across his back. Blood seeped from an open wound under his left shoulder blade. Her fingers traced the injury. He winced when she touched his ribs.

"You should have this treated. It must be painful to walk and have to support me."

"It hurts a lot. But where would we go?"

She removed her sweater and shirt, and then replaced the sweater. Several quick rips gave her a bandage long enough to circle his chest. She pressed her bandana over the seeping wound and tied it in place with knotted strips from her shirt. "Now. Let's rest awhile, and then I'll walk on my own. You can't support my weight in your condition."

They resumed walking at a slower pace. Twice they ducked into the brush to avoid vehicles that carried people loudly discussing the raid. A third vehicle, its occupants quiet, passed by but stopped a short distance ahead.

"We passed one just now. He's a little behind us. I can sense those beasts, I tell you. We've got one now." Brandon recognized Boomer Bomano's voice. Not using the Silence had exposed him to detection by this sensitive Sasquatch hunter. The truck backed slowly. Gun bolts snapped. The hunters meant business.

Brandon and Kim silenced themselves and carefully moved further from the road.

"Stop here!" Bomano played a spotlight over the woods in their direction. "Spread out and head straight in. Try to capture him but shoot anything that tries to escape."

Kim could not walk without making noise in the shadowy brush. She couldn't possibly outrun them. Brandon was weak and sore but knew that they had to make a break. His fingers searched the ground for stones. His first throw from a crouched position rattled against the truck. The hunters swiveled about. "He's at the truck! Get him!"

Taking advantage of the diversion, Brandon rose and rifled a rock at the searchlight. It smashed into darkness. He picked Kim up in his right arm, threw her over his shoulder and ran off through the trees and brush. His low light level vision enabled him to pick his path with relative ease. Behind him, Bomano screamed, "He's running. Get after him!" They couldn't match Brandon's speed in what for them was near total darkness.

"Shoot him! Shoot him!"

The trio fired their dart guns toward the sound of Brandon's flight. They reloaded and fired again at the fading footsteps. Crashing sounds came back to them from the dark forest. Then silence.

"Hot damn!" shrieked Boomer. "We got him! Sounds like a big one, too."

"Get a new bulb in the spotlight."

"Point the truck this way to use the light bar."

"Bring the flashlights. We've got Big Foot now."

Brandon lay unconscious at the base of a ten-foot drop. Kim lay dazed beside him. The hunters beat their way through the brush in the confusing glare of the truck lights. "Fresh trampled brush, Boomer. We're on his trail." Kim lapsed into unconsciousness. She roused as large rough hands lifted her. A strong body odor swept over her olfactory senses. She passed out again.

Kim opened her eyes. It was daylight. Evergreens rose tall about her. Their resinous odor filled the air. She lay on soft lichens and was covered by a heavy blanket. She turned to one side and groaned with the pain in her thighs. "Good morning, Kim. How are you feeling?" A heavy-set dark haired woman about forty years old came into view. She observed the girl with friendly concern. "Where – where's Cody?"

"He's in that tent, sleeping." Kim pushed to one elbow. She saw a small tent with flaps open. Cody lay quietly on bedding on the ground, sleeping on his right side.

"How is he?"

"Mostly bruises and scrapes. Worst is a gash below his left shoulder blade."

"Let me see him," implored Kim.

"Sure, honey. But he's okay."

The older woman helped Kim to her feet and supported her stiff-legged stagger to the tent. Kim brushed Cody's hair back and kissed his cheek. She then lifted the blanket to see his back. Her bandana had been replaced by a poultice of herbs and covered by a strip of birch bark. Her torn shirt held it in place. "What's this?" she snapped.

"I dunno. Some natural remedy they use. Pretty effective."

"Who are 'they'?"

"The mountain guardians. The ones who brought you."

"Boomer—the hunter?"

"Who?"

"Boomer Bomano. The one chasing us."

"Oh. That nut. No. The Old Man. Oo-Mah. Big Foot."

"Big Foot brought us?" She rolled her eyes in disbelief.

"Yeah. Big Foot. That's what we say when something strange happens around here. I woke in the night, looked around and there you were. I figured Oo-Mah wanted me to take care of you."

"What did he look like?"

The woman laughed. "Look like? No one sees Oo-Mah. You just know he's there... sometimes you smell him."

The conversation wasn't satisfying to Kim. "Where are we?"

"On the south slope of Mount Shasta. About a dozen miles northeast of town. My man Brett and I work this farm."

"Farm?" Kim looked around and noticed tilled ground under the trees. Scattered tall thin-leaved plants were still in the ground although harvest time had passed. "Marijuana!"

"Yeah, California's biggest cash crop. We're just little entrepreneurs scraping out a living."

"Who are you? Who told you my name and Cody's?"

"Don't you know? I'm his mother. I'm Marly Hoag." Kim's mouth stayed open, unable to frame a follow-up question. Could this serene, broad faced, heavyset woman be the thin tense girl in the Hoag's pictures? She concentrated. Though distorted by time, weight and attitude, the resemblance was there.

"You're not his mother!"

"Lots of people say I am."

"Brisa is his real mother."

"Who's to say? I saved his life. My mother raised him. Where was Brisa all those years?"

"Why don't you go home to the ranch? Your folks need you. They think you're dead."

"I can't go home," Marly replied with sadness in her voice. "If I did some people who think I screwed them on a drug delivery would come down on the whole place, destroy me, the ranch and my folks. Cody, too, if he was there. Here, I'm safe. My man Brett and my friends protect me. Oo-Mah watches over me. The mountain calms my spirit, soothes my sorrows. It won't let me go."

"Don't you worry about your parents?"

"All the time. If I didn't, I could go home. Could they have a better, more protective child than Cody? Oo-mah brings me visions of the folks and the ranch. Far Walker keeps me informed. He knows that I will continue to protect their sacred place if I inherit the ranch – and so will my granddaughter." Incredulous, Kim exclaimed, "You have a granddaughter?"

"Not yet." Marly wore a mischievous grin.

"You have another child?" Kim saw no signs of one in the camp.

"No."

"You mean daughter. You're pregnant," guessed the girl.

"Not a chance!" laughed Marly. "My child bearing days ended with my Cody."

"Then what makes you think you'll have a granddaughter?"

"Oo-Mah showed me in a dream."

"That's only wishful thinking, Marly. It's a fantasy. There's no Oo-Mah. There will be no granddaughter. Why are we even discussing this?"

The older woman regarded her enigmatically. "Because my granddaughter looked just like you."

Kim, startled, caught the implication. Her shoulders slumped, her face dropped and she gave way to deep gasping sobs. Marly enfolded her in her arms and patted her back. If Kim denied Marly's dream, she denied her own. A German shepherd trotted into the clearing, skirted Kim, and went over to nuzzle Marly. Satisfied that all was well, he walked over to sniff the seated girl and then to inspect Cody. Moments later a tall wiry man in Pendleton shirt, Levi's and boots came out of the trees. He was bald on top with blond hair on the sides, a drooping mustache, and a ponytail down his back. Wire framed glasses softened his appearance. His face and hands were weather-beaten. Brown stained teeth identified him as a smoker. He glanced at Kim and Cody, then inquiringly at Marly.

"A gift from Oo-Mah, Brett. Brisa's son, and mine – Cody. This is Cody's friend, Kim," Marly explained succinctly. A broad grin widened his narrow face. "Delighted to have you," he told her in a resonant cultured voice. "So few friends drop by nowadays." He swung a heavy-laden pack down from his back. "Hope you haven't eaten. I've got rations for the week in my pack." Marly rose to take the pack to a tarpaulin-covered kitchen area behind the tent.

"Quite a bit of excitement in town last night," Brett remarked. "Carver and his SWAT team got a big surprise at the animal gardens when the explosives blew. But then, you were there, I gather."

"Yes. We were there." Kim gave a rueful smile. "Cody went to the club to meet his mother. I went to warn Cody that Harlan's feds was looking for him. We were in the field behind the outbuilding when the raid started. A piece of the building hit us. We were able to walk up the logging road a few miles. Then Boomer caught up with us. We were running through the woods in the dark when we fell into a hole and knocked ourselves out. The next thing I knew we were here."

"I saw Boomer's truck parked on the road. He must still be hunting you."

"Oh, no! Are we safe here?"

Brett smiled. "I'd say so. No one can track Oo-mah. And cutting through this territory could be dangerous even for Boomer. The growers don't like unexpected company."

"The raid is over, then?"

"It's stalled, anyway. The local police, the sheriff, the fire company and some feebs were still poking around the ruins when I left town. A rowdy crowd is drunk and demonstrating."

"Is it safe here, then?"

"For a little while. When Cody wakes, we'll see if he can travel. We can take a fire road to a friend's house and get you out of the area on back roads."

"You're very kind to do all of this for us, Brett."

"Kim! You're family! Marly is Cody's adoptive mother. You're his girl. You're family."

"Breakfast! Come and get it." Marly stood by her stove with pancake turner in hand.

As they passed the small tent, Cody propped himself up on his right elbow and asked in a hoarse voice, "Where are we? Kim? Who's here?"

Marly approached with a plate of pancakes, eggs and sausage. "Feeling better, Cody? Are you hungry?" She examined him with a caring look."

"Marly? Marly! How did you find us?"

She and Kim sat on the tent floor beside him. "You and Kim are my present from Big Foot. How do you feel?" He sat up fully, grimaced when he leaned on his left arm, and then moved it cautiously to test its mobility. "Better than I thought I would be last night." He felt the bandage and poultice with his right hand. "What's this?"

"That's my shirt, Cody," Kim informed him. "And some kind of poultice from Big Foot with a birch bark covering. Eat first, and then we'll look it over. You're not bleeding, you have no fever and you're looking good. It must be working."

Marly proffered plates and utensils. "Eat up. All that running around last night and that wound on your back require a he-man breakfast."

Cody put the plate beside him, took a tentative bite and then dug in. The others brought their plates and sat nearby. Brett expanded on his description of the turmoil after the SWAT raid, describing the angry confrontational groups and the general ignorance about the reasons behind the raid. Their quarry had obviously escaped. The frustration of the SWAT team was unbounded. Angry local authorities and the jeering crowd were goading them to lash out at any plausible target. It was an unstable and volatile situation.

They finished eating and Cody turned his back to the women for an examination of his wound. Marly loosened the shirt bandage and gingerly lifted the poultice.

Kim gasped. "It's healed! There's only a small scab. The skin is all pink and new like a baby's."

"Looks okay to me. Where did all the blood on the bandage come from?" asked Marley.

"He had a long, nasty, bloody gash from a piece of flying debris. I had to wrap it in my bandana and shirt. I don't know how he kept going last night." She turned to Marly. "What's in that poultice? It's a miracle cure."

The older woman shrugged. "Oo-Mah isn't in the prescription business. I've never seen a poultice before. Just heard of them." Gathering that there was no remaining surface damage, Cody rose to his feet with care as the others watched with concern. Brett put his Pendleton jacket over the boy's shoulders. Cody's ribs ached but he moved easily.

He looked beyond his seated audience. His eyes opened wide in amazement. Brisa stood there carrying a large backpack.

"Good morning, everyone. Ready to go, I see, Brandon. We'd better be off. The town is still in an uproar. I'll tell you everything on the way."

"Mother! You're all right! We were injured by debris from the explosion, pursued by Sasquatch hunters, fell over a cliff and were knocked unconscious. Then we awakened here. I've been reunited with Marly! How did you find us?"

"Your Sasquatch friend. I had a true dream that you were safe with Marly this morning. Let me see your injury." Brisa gently lifted the poultice, examined the area with her fingertips and traced his ribs. "The abrasion is healing perfectly. No deep damage, no infection. Your ribs are bruised. They'll be sore for a week. Otherwise, you're in perfect shape to travel." Marly offered a cup of herb tea, which Brisa accepted.

"Where are you going, Brisa?" asked Kim in a controlled voice.

"To Asia. My people have been concerned about the deteriorating environment for years. We have been doing our work quietly through the volunteer environmental groups. That is no longer enough." Her eyes focused on an internal vision. Her voice took on the cadence of a missionary. "Our world is in crisis. We can no longer live on the fringes. We must come forth as a people, generate mass awareness, and negotiate with governments to control exploitation and destruction of our environment. Worldwide species extinctions have occurred several times in the Earth's history. We do not want the dominant primates to be responsible for all of mammalian, bird, reptile, and amphibian extinction. We will not allow it."

"And you, Cody?" Kim asked softly, deliberately using the name that he had borne with the Hoags, the name she knew him by when they had become so close. He had been watching his mother with awe. Here was a woman of fierce determination who had been shown a vision of the world being destroyed and given the mission of saving it. She had a people to rouse to the crusade. She had a world to mend. Obstacles, detention, family separation, legions of opponents and lukewarm supporters meant nothing. Her own burning zeal would overcome. Her own son was her first recruit on this march to save the holy land. The trumpet blare of a triumphal march could be heard in her oration.

Brandon/ Cody turned the fringe of his attention to Kim; a genuine sorrow underlying the glow of mission dawned in his eyes. He embraced her and kissed her tenderly on the forehead, "I have to go, Kim. I have to go. Everything must wait until this battle is won, destruction is halted and the world can be repaired. My mother needs me. And I will find my people. Then I'll come back to you."

Brisa held her arms out to him. "Let's try walking, Brandon. If you're up to it we'll take some supplies and go down to Brett's friend for a car ride to Oregon. We have to start before Harlan's hunters pick up our trail." Brandon took her hand, held himself erect, and they walked down the trail leading across the narrow canyon. Brisa communicated animatedly while Brandon listened with rapt attention. His indoctrination was underway.

Kim bowed her head and tears gathered in her eyes. She clamped her lips, jutted her chin, and raised her eyes to watch them. Brisa was not the only one committed to a long campaign. Marly touched her shoulder in sympathy. "His mother has caught him at a vulnerable time, Kim. You can't compete with Joan of Arc today. But believe my dream. You will be the mother of my granddaughter."

She opened her arms to Kim. "Love me, Kim. Love my folks. Love Cody. With all our faults, all our inadequacies, we are bound together. And I feel that you are the glue!" As Cody disappeared in the canyon, she felt little like glue and instead dissolved in tears in Marly's arms.

The Journey Continues

Two pairs of footsteps, one set large and one small, traversed the barren mountain landscape. Brandon followed in his mother's tracks, following in her footprints for secure footing. His larger tracks covered hers completely. He could see himself following her across the desert thirteen years ago, making a game of fitting his footprints inside the outline of hers. The desert wind had filled their tracks as they cut themselves off from one life and started a new one in their desert cave.

Brandon glanced back and saw that these tracks were also being obliterated by the wind, this time with its mantle of snow. The noise, fire and smoke had long since been muffled and disappeared behind this crystalline curtain. Kim had been left behind. Marley, the Hoags, Quiet Fox, and all his other friends were beyond that impenetrable curtain. Was he fated to live in disconnected segments or was there a unified pattern to his life that would soon be revealed?

He felt the remembered excitement in Brisa now as she strode up the slope, paused to look back at him, then entered a fissure in a rocky wall. This was no blind and perilous flight to freedom. They had reached the first station on her underground railway.

The narrow fissure was deceptive. It snaked back a short distance, then became roofed over and disappeared into the total darkness of a cave. A lighter flickered and then a kerosene lamp flared. Brisa stood by a small shelf alcove, shadows from the lamplight giving her face an ancient appearance of sharply defined contours.

"Welcome to our ancestral home, Brandon." She made an expansive gesture toward a stone hearth, two log benches and a sleeping platform. Wood was stacked against the wall. She rolled a boulder to uncover a storehouse of food and a capacious rucksack.

"I knew that I would escape someday. Eight years of hiking have taught me much about these mountains. And I've prepared supply caches like this. The rest of our journey will be a nature walk." She put tinder and twigs on the hearth, used her lighter, and in a moment had a fire going. Larger sticks augmented the flames. Now the light was sufficient to show a roof vent that drew the smoke upwards. Brisa produced a small pot that she handed to her son.

"Pack this with snow, Brandon. We'll have tea, biscuits, canned fish, nuts, trail mix and dried fruit. It's a victory feast. We're together. We're free. We're going home." She impulsively hugged him. He shared her soaring elation. She stepped back, gripped his shoulders for emphasis and repeated, "We're free."

He returned with the pot of snow to find a growing homey atmosphere. The fire was larger. Warm air, slightly aromatic from the pine fuel, was fast removing the chill from the cave. Radiant heat warmed his face. The food was set out. Hot coals had been raked to one side of the hearth between two parallel rocks that provided a stand for their pot. They sat, sipped their herb tea and ate.

"We have much to discuss, Brandon. You know that you are different from most people. You have met several of your own kind, starting with Rava. On our journey you will meet other groups of our people in Asia, Europe and Africa. They are scattered and isolated, fearful that they may be discovered, attacked and eliminated. Yet, because they do not speak up about the deterioration of the Earth's environment, they will more surely be destroyed. You and I must become the catalysts to bring our people into the open to save both themselves and the world."

She pulled him close and vowed, "Together we shall make a difference. I swear it. We will show them all. You were given to me for this.... Take my hand, Brandon. Relax." They sat quietly in the dark rose glow of the embers. The dim corridors of memory in Brandon's mind were an extension of the shadowy recesses of the cave. The journey through his mind might be as arduous as the journey through the Sierras.

Was this search for identity going to be worth the loss of all those who had nurtured him and grown dear over the past ten years? He trembled at the brink of an abyss that would separate his two lives. He would seek a bridge to some day bring him back....

Dr. Charles Hardy Kelley is a nuclear physicist who worked many years in the aerospace industry in New York and California. His interests in engineering and clean energy led to his concern for the degradation of the global ecology. Born in Brooklyn, New York, he is a veteran of World War II, during which he served in the 10th Mountain Division in Europe, for which he trained in the Ski Patrol in the Colorado Rockies. He is happily transplanted to Nevada where he lives with his wife Audrey and their cats, and writes about the continuing adventures of Brandon/Cody as well as non-fiction treatises on clean energy sources.

CPSIA information can be obtained at www.ICGtesting.com
Printed in the USA
BVOW01s1714111114

374143BV00012B/11/P